A Match for Melissa

Susan Karsten

This is a work of fiction. Names, characters, places, and incidents either are the product of the author's imagination or are used fictitiously, and any resemblance to actual persons living or dead, business establishments, events, or locales, is entirely coincidental.

A Match for Melissa
COPYRIGHT 2017 by Susan Karsten

All rights reserved. No part of this book may be used or reproduced in any manner whatsoever without written permission of the author or Pelican Ventures, LLC except in the case of brief quotations embodied in critical articles or reviews.

eBook editions are licensed for your personal enjoyment only. eBooks may not be re-sold, copied or given to other people. If you would like to share an eBook edition, please purchase an additional copy for each person you share it with.

Contact Information: titleadmin@pelicanbookgroup.com

Scripture quotations, unless otherwise indicated are taken from the King James translation, public domain.

Cover Art by *Nicola Martinez*

Prism is a division of Pelican Ventures, LLC
www.pelicanbookgroup.com PO Box 1738 *Aztec, NM * 87410

The triangle prism logo is a trademark of Pelican Ventures, LLC

Publishing History
Prism Edition, 2017
Paperback Edition ISBN 978-1-943104-91-8
Electronic Edition ISBN 978-1-943104-90-1
Published in the United States of America

Dedication

To my husband, John, who is truly my gift from God.
He has provided the security and support that
allows me to spread my creative wings.

Coming Soon in the Honor's Point series

A Refuge for Rosanna
An Escape for Ellie

1

Stomping her feet on the hard-packed road didn't relieve her frustration. Aggravation fueled her pace, destroying the usual peace found on her morning walks down country roads. Melissa clenched her hand around the letter ordering her return to London. Father and his plans took precedence over her wishes.

She stopped, unfurled the letter, and read the offending passage one more time.

You shall cut short your visit to the country. I have plans for you, plans that will be of much interest to you.

So like Papa to assume she'd fall in line with his schemes. She crumpled the letter and strode on, staring straight ahead. Visiting the vicarage to which her former governess, Miss Cleaver retired, helped restore Melissa's equanimity. The hovering cloud of melancholy brought on by her mother's death lessened each day. Returning to her home in the city did not sit well, as she disliked London with its smoke and the lonely life she lived there. But Papa's command and mention of his plans brought further dread.

Regret about ending her visit lowered her mood, but Melissa took deep breaths and resisted thoughts of departure by concentrating on the cool, fresh, moist air entering her lungs. Spring mud invaded southern England, but the road was good, and Melissa loved her morning walks too much to let a little mire stop her.

She took in her surroundings again, glancing from

the light green forest views on either side of the road and the lane ahead. Avoiding mud became a game of distraction—until an indistinct brown lump came in sight on the edge of the road. Puddles forgotten, she hurried forward to discover a monogrammed leather saddlebag. Ignoring the dirt-spattered bag's condition, she lifted it and peered inside. Empty. She dropped it to the ground.

Scattered nearby, she spied a London *Times* half in a puddle, and an ivory comb in a muddy rut. Chills ran up her arms and tingled down her spine at the evidence of a traveler's misfortune. Surveying the scene, she cast a glance down the banked slope. Her breath caught even as her heart raced.

About twenty feet away in the lowest part of the ditch, she spied a man prone, half-hidden by brush, only inches from a trickle of dirty water from the last of the spring thaw.

Melissa shoved aside the momentary numbness brought on by the dreadful sight. She took a deep breath, hitched her skirts, and clambered down into the ditch. Disregarding the mud, she knelt and stretched out her hand. Her fingers found a pulse on the cool skin of the man's wrist.

She peered at his chest with her face only inches from his body. She detected a slight rise and fall. Thank the Lord the water level had receded. The stranger could have drowned.

The young man's eyes fluttered open. "Where am I?" He groaned, his voice barely a whisper. He passed a hand over his face before letting his arm fall to the ground.

She reared back and staggered to her feet. A shiver of pity ran through her—helplessness did not fit this strapping male. Fear compressed her heart upon viewing the evidence of violence.

"You are in a ditch, outside Russelton. By the look of the grass, someone dragged you here." She pointed to some lines in the wet grass.

"Beautiful," he gasped.

"I beg your pardon?"

A slight smile graced his bruised face. "You. Beautiful."

"Sir, it appears you've been beaten, robbed, and left for dead." She squared her shoulders in wounded propriety. "This is not the time for Spanish coin."

Her heart skipped a beat. Even muddy and injured, he exuded raw masculinity. Lack of a proper introduction didn't stop the immediate attraction that drew her to him.

She was about to say more, but his eyes closed, and he groaned and fell unconscious. What to do? It was impossible to carry the man, but he required medical attention. A flutter of fear roosted in her chest, but she fought it down.

Her long habit of self-control came to the fore, and her chin rose in resolve. Melissa gathered the skirt of her brown walking dress, clutched it in one hand, and bunched it well above the ankles and the top of her half boots. Unmaidenly, yes, but with no one present to cause a scandal it mattered not. With the other arm extended for balance, she scrambled up the steep bank and ran to the vicarage for aid.

Nearing the village outskirts, she summoned up energy from her reserves and sprinted the remaining distance.

"Mr. Cleaver!" She gasped as she threw open the front door of the vicarage. "There's been an accident!

Mr. Cleaver!"

"Whatever is it, Melissa?" He emerged from a door down the hall, wrinkles etched in his forehead.

"Come with me right away. I found a man unconscious in a ditch. About a half mile away." She bent over, hands on knees, to catch her breath.

"What? Say that again? Calm down, Melissa."

"There's no time to waste. Hurry." She turned and raced out the door. "Come on."

"I'll get the wagon. Bert and Toby went to town for supplies, but I can manage. Please go to the parlor and summon Priscilla." He put on his hat and dashed past Melissa toward the small stable behind the house.

She pivoted and hurried down the hall. "Miss Cleaver!"

The auburn-haired, kindly woman emerged from the kitchen. "What is the commotion, dear?"

"I found a man unconscious by the road. Your brother's getting a wagon. We must hurry."

The older woman snatched up her shawl and bonnet on her way past the hall tree and emerged to wait on the steps. Mere moments passed before the horse and wagon appeared. It stopped only long enough to allow the women to clamber up next to Mr. Jeremiah Cleaver onto the seat.

Melissa motioned with her hand. "That way."

The wagon jolted violently against the ruts, and the women hung on with two hands. Melissa's bonnet fell back, held on only with the ties. Her hair slipped from its pins and annoying strands blew across her face.

Nothing mattered but getting back to the man.

Melissa directed him to stop. "There," she pointed, "there he is."

A Match for Melissa

The minister jumped from the wagon. He raised his hands to assist Melissa and his sister to the ground. Mr. Cleaver yanked off his black tailed coat, threw it onto the wagon's bench and rolled up his shirtsleeves. With long, leaping steps, he descended into the ditch.

Melissa eased her way down for a second time and stooped to check the man's pulse again.

She got another clear view of him. Blood matted his hair on one side. Though he was muddy, bruised, and bloody, his firm jaw, chiseled nose, and thick eyelashes aroused Melissa's interest. Who could he be?

Miss Cleaver called from the edge of the ditch. "I'll gather his things."

"Nothing appears to be broken. No limbs awry or askew."

Mr. Cleaver breathed heavily as he half-lifted, half-dragged the large, listless burden up the bank. He reached the roadside, gently laying down the still-insensible victim. He removed the side boards from two slots in the wagon bed before issuing the next instructions. "You two ladies, help me lift him on the count of three. He's a big fellow." Mr. Cleaver positioned one hand under each arm. "One, two, three!"

Melissa picked up his feet, ignoring the boots pressing into her midsection. Miss Cleaver lifted at the waist. The ill-treated man did not make a sound during the transfer, nor did he wake.

Melissa climbed into the wagon bed and settled next to him. She covered him with a blanket taken from a trunk under the seat. An unfamiliar knot of responsibility sat in her stomach like a worrisome weight. Her breath caught with worry, and a well of deep sympathy bubbled inside. As she gazed at him, she made mental notes as to how she would take care of the victim.

"So you'll ride back there, with him?" Mr. Cleaver's voice carried concern.

"Yes. I'll be fine." Melissa kept a hand on the blanket-covered mound as if to provide a steadying comfort. Cold, shaky, and a bit queasy, she only wanted to get back to the vicarage. The possibility the attackers might still be around traveled across her mind like clouds passing the sun. She constantly scanned the woods along the road. The belated thought of potential danger caused her heartbeat to quicken.

"Jeremiah?" Miss Cleaver's voice rose above the clip-clop of the horse's hooves as she spoke to her brother. "What do you think happened? I'm guessing robbers or highwaymen left him for dead. Nothing much to identify him among the items I gathered. Only this monogrammed bag. The letter 'M' with a superimposed 'R'. Who has those initials?"

The deep rumble of Mr. Cleaver's words came next. "I hate to speculate, sister. Whoever he may be, we must take him in and provide for his needs. Acts of mercy are always to be done whenever opportunities arise. Examine the things in his traveling bag again. Perhaps there's another clue."

"Yes, indeed, that's the thing to do." Priscilla went through the bag again. "Paltry leavings, with no further information to glean. The monogram on the bag is the sole clue." Finished perusing the contents, she let it drop to the wagon seat.

Melissa kept up a stream of inward petitions that he'd live. She studied his pale, handsome face. Her fingers took on a life of their own—stroking to smooth a strand of hair off his forehead. With the Lord's help, she'd be a part of his care. When he recovered, she'd like to meet this man.

2

Miss Cleaver bustled into the vicarage with Melissa in her wake, aiming for the kitchen at the back of the house. "Betsy, boil some water, please. There's been an accident."

The rotund cook went about the task. "What be wrong, Miss Cleaver?"

"We found a man who's been beaten. More than that, we don't know." Miss Cleaver strapped on a large apron and opened the linen closet. She stuck her head in, shuffled around a moment, and emerged with a small stack of towels. "Melissa, help me make these linen towels into bandages."

Melissa wanted to sit with the unconscious victim, but he had yet to be carried inside. Lightheaded and a touch dizzy, but determined to help, she sat at the kitchen table and tore a few linens into strips, hands shaking with the effort. She rolled several strips before her head sank to rest on her arms, eyes closed. "Oh my. I'm not well." Hot followed cold, a wave of queasiness rose and fell with the slightest movement of her head.

"Keep your head down, dear." Miss Cleaver patted Melissa's shoulder.

Shuffling footsteps sounded in the hall. Mr. Cleaver had summoned Toby to assist him as the groom had returned from his errand in town.

"Easy, there. I'd not like him jostled or injured further. Careful now. Hold tight." Mr. Cleaver's voice faded as it climbed, yet Melissa caught a disturbing snippet. "We'll need to keep a sharp eye. Appears like a robbery. His horse will be running loose if it wasn't stolen."

"I'll carry these bandages up. Melissa, stay here and drink some tea, please." Miss Cleaver scooped up the rolled cloth strips. "When your spirits are more niffy-naffy, you'll want to change clothes."

Melissa opened an eye as Miss Cleaver left the room. With effort, she raised her head and lifted the cup, sipping the restorative, fragrant brew. Glancing down, she rued the condition of her dress and gave it an ineffectual swipe of the hand.

She stood when Miss Cleaver returned from delivering the bandages. "Tea did wonders. I am much better. May I help?"

"Let's get you changed into a clean dress, and go to the parlor to wait for the doctor." Melissa appreciated the woman's comforting arm around the waist as Miss Cleaver guided her up the stairs to change clothes.

"I'm fine now. It was only a delayed reaction to the shock." Melissa made her way to an oval wall mirror to tidy herself. Wind-blown tendrils escaped her chignon, and she finger-combed and tucked the wayward tresses into a semblance of order. Staring into the mirror, she tried to read her future, but no prophecy or clue showed there. Melissa turned away from the glass.

Docile, and soon clad in a clean dress, she addressed her fears to Miss Cleaver. "I'm grateful for the assistance, as my fingers are nerveless. Do you think he'll live?"

"Lord only knows, dear. He's beaten fairly bad."

Melissa whispered, "Lord, don't let him die this way." No one should be assaulted and left for dead. For a strong, handsome young man to be struck down was worse, somehow.

"Amen. It is frightening to witness a stalwart male taken down like that." Miss Cleaver cleaned her glasses and perched them on her nose. "I'll bring the linen strips to the parlor. You'll be more comfortable there."

Once settled in the parlor, Melissa rolled a few strips with clumsy hands and sat, rocking idly. Uncertainty as to the extent of the man's injuries left a weight of anxiety, but another cup of hot tea dispelled the remaining results of her delayed shock. "Such terrible violence—I hope he escapes permanent injury."

Mr. Cleaver entered the room after a short time, having changed out of his muddy clothes and neatened his graying auburn hair.

"How fares the patient?" Miss Cleaver leaned forward, folded hands resting on a small pile of bandage rolls.

"Got him settled. After the doctor visits him, we'll learn more." He opened his Bible, laid it on his lap, and sat pensive.

Dr. Swithins and his assistant Mr. Doone arrived within the hour. The doctor's rosy cheeks and plush, white beard didn't obscure his intense demeanor. "Where's the injured man? Any idea what happened?"

Melissa appreciated the doctor's urgency, and Mr. Cleaver's immediate rising from the chair brought even more relief to the tension of waiting. "I'll lead you to the patient."

The two medical men followed Mr. Cleaver out to

A Match for Melissa

be led to the sickroom.

"Don't be shocked by the pronounced unhealthy mien of the assistant, Mr. Doone." Miss Cleaver patted Melissa's hand. "He's been like that his whole life."

Reassured, Melissa relaxed, hands unclenching. "The man is quite a contrast to the robust physician."

"Appearances can be deceiving. For example, Melissa, few would guess at the brilliance of your mind, based on your loveliness."

She gave a dismissive wave. "Don't flatter me. In London, one has to be so careful of quacks. They're everywhere with their false remedies and dangerous treatments. What's our guarantee Swithins is a good doctor?"

Mr. Cleaver returned, catching the tail end of the conversation. "Don't worry. He studied in Edinburgh and keeps apprised of the many new developments in medicine." Mr. Cleaver raked a hand through his hair, sat near the women, and reached for his Bible again.

"Does the doctor wash his hands? I recently read that unclean hands are a source of many ills." Melissa shuddered, revolted at the thought of dirty fingers probing wounds and spreading disease instead of curing it. "Who'd have expected doctors with healing hands to be carriers of illness?"

Mr. Cleaver's kindly grin reassured her. "I personally observed him cleanse his hands. Don't fret, Melissa."

~*~

Before the clock stroked a new hour, the doctor entered the front parlor. "I've given him a full examination. Doone is putting him into a nightshirt.

Good thing you moved him as little as possible."

"What is the diagnosis?" Mr. Cleaver rose to his feet.

The doctor stroked his beard. "Classic case. I've treated many like it. Ankle. Yes, a severe sprain to the ankle, bruised ribs, and a large lump on the head."

A sprained ankle, bruises, and a bump? That didn't sound so bad. Perhaps her concerns were unfounded. "Has he awakened? Said anything?"

"No, Miss. He remained unconscious for the entire examination."

"Can you tell what happened to him?"

He smoothed each eyebrow before responding. "If I were to guess, I'd say he charged his assailant, stepped into a pothole, stumbled and was struck from behind by an accomplice, perhaps? Dragged him into the ditch. No honor among thieves."

Was the man an amateur detective as well as a doctor? Melissa found his scenario too pat. Was he a seer? Not that it mattered. "But how can you be certain?"

"Young lady, merely a guess, as you asked me for a conjecture as to what befell him. I only put together a rough scenario based on the few signs available."

"Oh, of course, I'm sorry. I'm simply so worried. He's special, to me, since I found him." She clamped her lips shut against such babbling, not wanting to reveal her heart any further. She glanced at Mr. Cleaver, eyebrows raised and questioning, pleading for distraction from her foolishness.

Mr. Cleaver passed a hand over his brow. "Thieves in the district represent a concern."

Dr. Swithins slurped his tea and checked the clasp on his leather medicine satchel. "Either way, with this type of head injury, combined with his ankle, I prescribe bed rest for two weeks and willow bark for pain."

"What about his wounds?" Deferential, Miss Cleaver held her pencil above a tablet, ready to take notes.

Smiling with approval, the doctor gave instructions. "The wound on his head is superficial, but the blow was heavy. Change the dressing in the morning and keep the room dark and quiet. If he avoids fever, he'll be well. The patient seems quite healthy and strong. I expect him to regain full consciousness soon. I shall return to check on him tomorrow." He peered over his spectacles at Mr. Cleaver. "You've alerted the magistrate?"

"Yes, I've sent Toby to the village. I hope the trail hasn't grown cold. It's essential for thieves to be brought to justice. Praise the Lord we found him, and he wasn't killed, whoever he is."

Mr. Doone stuck his head in the door. "All's set with the patient. I tucked him in and he's sleeping restfully. Shall we go, Doctor? To take care of the squire's servant?"

"Ah, yes. Off to another case. I'll be back tomorrow. Follow my instructions."

"We will." Melissa smiled. She hoped the Cleavers would allow her to help. To do something besides rolling linen strips into bandages.

Strong desire flooded her heart. Desire to care for the man as he recovered. She wanted to tend to him until he was completely healed. Her planned departure couldn't come at a worse time.

3

Lord Mark Russell opened his eyes. His head throbbed with a pain reminiscent of his hangovers before he gave up drinking. *Where am I?* He glanced around the room, and then down at his bandaged lower leg. The light hurt, and he dropped back on a soft, scented pillow, flinging his arm across his field of vision. Peeking under his arm, he spied a tall woman bustling into the room, wearing a blue and white striped dress, her ample form covered by a large apron.

She smiled, her cheeks rounded and flushed. "You're awake."

"Water," he croaked out on a gasp of effort. His lids clamped shut briefly before he forced them open again. The sounds of water pouring and footfalls scuttling toward him made his sore head pound. She lifted his head, and then held the cup tilted to his lips. Water never tasted as sweet.

A few sips later she pulled the cup away and dabbed his chin with a soft cloth. "There. That's enough for the moment. You've been terribly injured, but besides a fever, little permanent damage is expected. Your color is better, and the swelling is down."

"Where am I?" Mark whispered. The effort drained him. That wouldn't do.

"You are in my brother's vicarage on the outskirts

A Match for Melissa

of Russelton. I'm Miss Cleaver, housekeeper to my brother, Mr. Cleaver, Russelton's minister. We brought you here after my young guest found you in a ditch in a bad way."

Mark made a gesture toward the cup and raised his hand in a pantomime of drinking. She moved close to the bedside and complied.

He relished a second sip. "How long have I been here?"

"Since yesterday. It is Wednesday. The doctor will return to check on your injuries. You rest, now, and soon, I will bring you some broth." She clasped her hands at her waist. "By the way, who are you, young man?"

"I'm Lord Russell." It was odd to be called by a title that once belonged to his elder brother. Grief lanced him anew.

"Oh my. Do tell. You're the new heir? The entire town's yammering on the topic. Fancy that." She brought both hands up to her cheeks. Her fingers moved to press her chin, and her eyes widened "The whole neighborhood's been speculating up a storm about your impending return to take up the reins of the family estate."

"Yes, I am he. Glad to give folks something to talk about." He closed his eyes and subsided into silence.

"What a sad state of affairs that you, of all people, ended up in a ditch. Robbery's a black mark on the community. That one such as you would be struck down in broad daylight is a scandal. I'll return in a while with that broth, and you can tell me what happened."

She patted his shoulder, moved towards the door, stopped short, and turned, "May the Lord be praised

Miss Southwood found you. You being unconscious out in the damp could have led to pneumonia or worse. In His providence, all things do work together."

~*~

Whatever had Miss Cleaver meant, 'the Lord be praised'? Why? For being discarded into a ditch? Providence? He was headed to Russel Manor to do the right thing, only to be set upon and left for dead. Who was Miss Southwood? Apparently, the person who found him. He had no clear recollection of her.

He needed to get home—enough of this sickbed.

Lying back, marshaling his energy, he mulled over Miss Cleaver's words. She expected him to explain what happened. That would be impossible. Even forcing his mind to attempt recall brought no memory of the incident. Everything beyond leaving the inn Tuesday morning for the last leg of his journey remained blank.

A mere two weeks since he received a summons to a meeting with his family's solicitors. He came away from the brief conference informed of a great change in his worldly status. Due to the death of his brother in a carriage accident, Mark now held the position of head of the Russell family and the title that went along with a fine manor and estate outside of Russelton.

Upon hearing the news, disbelief hit. His brother James had been healthy and strong, both physically and morally. How could he be gone? Mark's gut churned even thinking about it.

The need to prove himself worthy enough to take his brother's place weighed him down. He'd never accomplished much in his life, and suddenly, many people depended on him and expected him to be competent with his duties. Landing in a ditch was a mere detour. He needed to get to Russell Manor.

He closed his eyes and sank deeper into the pillow, turning his face to the wall. Perhaps that's what he deserved. Being left for dead in the mud. Foreboding clenched his chest, and anxiety squeezed until he could barely breathe. Was it possible to step into his brother's shoes when he'd failed to manage his simple, selfish responsibilities well? Regardless, he needed to make the attempt.

~*~

Melissa's fitful sleep alternated between nightmares and repetitive thoughts about the tumultuous events of the day. But morning dawned, and her eyes flew open. She threw back the covers. Motivated by the idea of seeing the patient, she rushed into her clothes, swept a comb through her hair, and jammed her feet into shoes.

Rounding the corner to the dining room, she almost crashed into Miss Cleaver.

Melissa grabbed her former governess by the arms to steady her. "Well, how is he? Any news?"

Miss Cleaver's face bore resemblance to a cat in the cream pot. "You'll not credit this—when I tell you."

Melissa let go of Miss Cleaver and went into the dining room before rounding on her. "Tell me what? I want to hear everything."

Miss Cleaver closed the door before responding. "Everything? Let me think. He woke up, praise God. Or should I say he opened his eyes after coming to?"

Melissa bounced on her toes in her eagerness.

"Whatever he did—asleep, awake—what happened then?"

"He requested water. My, his voice was raspy. The poor man had no idea where he was. I told him."

"And?"

Miss Cleaver's tone held a teasing twist. "I inquired as to his name."

"I am curious. Please tell me."

"This is the biggest surprise of all, Melissa." She clasped her hands under her chin. "He's none other than the new lord of the manor. Lord Russell!"

"Of Russell Manor? He's the heir." She breathed the words, quieted by wonderment. Melissa's hand flew to her brow. "How scandalous. Attacked returning to his estate."

"I agree it's a terribly shocking event. But enough of that. Now I must get him some broth. I'm on my way to the kitchen."

Cheeks warm, Melissa asked, "May I check on him? Determine if he's comfortable?"

"I suppose that would be acceptable, but leave the door open."

"I will most certainly do so. I shall observe all rules of propriety." Relieved at the assent, Melissa selected a piece of toast from the buffet and left the room.

~*~

A slight shuffle of tiptoeing feet intruded upon his thoughts. Miss Cleaver back with broth? That was too quick. He'd rather be alone.

A whisper sounded. "My lord? Are you awake?"

The voice was kind. "Yes."

She laid her hand on his shoulder in a gentle, comforting pat.

Mark opened his eyes and turned away from the wall, toward the room. Who was this lovely creature?

"How do you do, Lord Russell?" She curtsied. "I'm Miss Southwood—the one who found you. Yesterday. In the ditch."

"Pleased to meet you. You'll need to excuse me for not rising. I'm not—"

She waved him off. "Think nothing of it. I'm here to help take care of you. How are you?" She wrung her hands.

"How am I?" He paused to consider. "My head and ankle have seen better days. It's nothing, though."

She moved toward the door. "I can go get willow bark tea for the pain."

Her pleasant voice didn't grate on his ears. But urgent goals nagged at his peace. "No, stay. Tea can wait. Has anyone found my horse? Estate matters await my attention."

He struggled to rise, but fatigue left him weak as a kitten. His head throbbed, and he collapsed on the pillow with a groan.

Melissa drew near and touched his shoulder again, fingers light and soothing. "No news about anyone finding a horse, but perhaps Miss Cleaver will have word. She'll soon be bringing broth."

His attempt to smile in response achieved only a weak quirk of the lips. He tried hard to inject nonchalance and courage into his response. "I can't remember what happened on the road." He averted his face again, anxiety lancing through him.

"I'll get a cool cloth for your brow."

She disrupted his brooding, and at the sound of

her sweet voice, courage strengthened within him.

Her slender figure moved to the water pitcher, and with delicacy, she moistened a folded linen towel. Returning, she wiped his face, refolded the towel, and laid it on his forehead. "There, now. No worrying about the estate for a time."

"I need to be at Russell Manor to manage things. I cannot stay any longer."

"Be that as it may, you must wait for the doctor, and the broth."

"That's reasonable but not much beyond that." The only benefit to lingering was this charming lass. Oh, to have met her in other circumstances. Her loveliness stirred his senses, and her kindness warmed his heart.

"As for remembering the attack, God may have a reason for your forgetfulness. Maybe the truth would add to your suffering."

Mark recoiled at her words, not liking the sound of the word *suffering*. He let it pass, however, because quibbling with her gained him naught.

"Doctor Swithins has recommended bed rest, sir, for up to two weeks if necessary. The Cleavers will send a message to Russell Manor as to your whereabouts, but you are not to be moved. Estate matters shall wait."

"Preposterous. That is not going to happen. I vow to be up and gone, today."

Miss Cleaver returned. "Here's the broth I promised. Hot and full of restorative qualities." She set the tray down on the bedside table and wiped her hands down her apron's skirt.

Melissa arched her brows. "Miss Cleaver, Lord Russell can't help being worried about his horse—any news?"

"Word just arrived that a fine animal appeared without a rider near the village green. One of the grooms at the manor recognized the stallion as one your brother took up to town last year."

"James brought it to me as a birthday present. He liked any excuse to buy a horse." Mark flung his forearm over his eyes, not wanting these ladies to see his grief. "That news eases one concern."

"Miss Cleaver? Could you arrange a cup of willow bark tea? And, may I feed the patient?"

"Yes. I'll send up tea, and I suppose it would be fine for you to spoon feed him." The older woman bustled around tucking and clucking, and then departed after checking the position of the doorstop. "I'll be back to check on his progress after a while."

The young beauty moved a chair next to the bed and sat down. "Are you ready for your broth, Lord Russell?"

"I am." Any effort to talk hurt his ribs and sapped his strength, what little he possessed. He lapsed into silence.

"My lord?" Melissa murmured, indicating the spoonful of broth.

Mark complied, and she brought the spoon to his mouth. While feeding him, she kept up a stream of quiet conversation. "You have a severe sprain, bruised ribs, and a head injury. You cannot walk or be moved for some time. Stillness and a dark room will help your head heal. Can you tell me anything about what happened to you? What's the last thing you remember?"

"Leaving the inn." He waved away the next spoonful of broth and closed his eyes while she dabbed his lips with a napkin. He noted she relished her role as nurse. There were worse things than being taken care of by a pretty girl, but the estate needed him more. No time for any indulgence of weakness. He'd wasted too much of his life on idle pleasures.

With a rattle of china, Miss Cleaver re-entered the sick room with a tea tray. His eyes flew open.

"Miss Southwood, please go to the kitchen now, dear. There are bandages to be rolled."

"Good-bye, Lord Russell."

"I must thank you for finding me and going for help. Without you, I may have caught the fever or even died."

"You're welcome, my lord. I'll return to care for you again later." The young lady meekly left the room without a backward glance.

"Good-bye." He spoke to her retreating back, wanting to say more. The moment passed, and he turned to Miss Cleaver. "You and Miss Southwood are so caring."

"Miss Southwood's a dear young lady." The woman covered her lips as if to forestall more she would say.

"Yes, she's quite astute." Mark closed his eyes for a moment. How odd to meet a lovely girl now when he was flat on his back. Normally, he'd be very interested. He hoped to see her again. His first priority, however, was to get to the manor.

4

"How did the broth sit with you?" The older woman asked.

"Fine, I don't have much appetite, though." Mark reached up and touched his head. Her voice wasn't as soothing as Miss Southwood's.

Miss Cleaver came over and propped him up on a stack of pillows. The movements made him wince, but he'd experienced worse pain in his life.

"Drink this willow bark tea, please. If that doesn't help with your soreness, I can offer you some laudanum. I'd rather avoid that, with its unpleasant side effects. I've found prayer to be an excellent antidote for one's ills. May I pray for you?"

He downed the medicinal tea before speaking words to put her off. "I'm tired." He clattered the empty tea cup into the saucer, and she took it out of his hands.

She removed the extra pillows and set them aside. "I'll do all the praying. You rest."

Mark looked over at Miss Cleaver, noticing her eyes downcast, giving him privacy. A lump formed in his throat. To be prayed for sounded appealing, considering his state, but unworthiness and embarrassment crashed over him in waves. Where did this excess emotion come from? He opened his mouth and words emerged, almost of their own accord. "Please pray. By all accounts, I need it."

He turned his face away and clasped his hands over his chest.

"All right." Miss Cleaver paused before speaking in a soft voice. "Dear Lord, this gentleman's in a bad state. Please heal his injuries and set him on a straight path. We thank Thee for the deliverance provided to him. We give Thee all the praise. Amen." She cleared her throat and patted his shoulder. "There, now."

"I don't feel anything." He didn't like the sense of helplessness.

"Emotions are unreliable. We can find peace only when we look to the Father."

Willing or not, calm washed over him in the wake of the prayer. Exhaustion warred with the urge to get on home.

But before he left, he wanted to ask the older woman a question or two. "One slight memory of the attack is coming to me. In the ditch, there seemed to be—now don't laugh—an angel by my side. It's foggy, but a gentle, loving presence. Do you suppose that was my guardian angel?"

"That was Miss Melissa Southwood, the one who found you."

"The girl who spooned broth into me?"

"Don't you remember anything?" She smirked, revealing a fleeting dimple.

"Only an angel."

"That was her. You rest now, Lord Russell." She rustled the thin pages of a book and cleared her throat. "I'll be reading God's Word."

"The Lord is my Shepherd, I shall not want. He maketh me to lie down in green pastures, He leadeth me beside quiet waters, He restoreth my soul. He leadeth me in paths of righteousness for His name's sake. Yea, though I walk through the valley of the shadow of death, I shall fear no evil, for Thou art with me, Thy rod and Thy staff, they comfort me. Thou preparest a table before me in the presence of mine enemies: thou anointest my head with oil; my cup runneth over. Surely goodness and mercy shall follow me all the days of my life: and I will dwell in the house of the Lord forever."

The refreshing words comforted Mark, and he fought off sleep. The last thing he remembered was someone tucking the blankets around him.

~*~

Melissa attempted nonchalance. "How does he fare?"

"As well as can be expected. That knock on the head must be painful." Miss Cleaver untangled embroidery threads. "He's asleep now, and that will help."

Melissa's hand lay across the open book in her lap as she stared at the fire. They'd lit a small blaze in the grate to fight off the late afternoon chill. "What is your opinion of him?"

"Well...I'm barely acquainted with the man. Let me think." Her old governess snipped a thread at an angle to create a point for easier threading. "He's young and strong. Appears to own a good mind."

Melissa waited and turned her gaze on her dear friend, whose lips had gone tightly shut. "Is there more? Something you're not saying?"

"No, no. It's simply that the poor man is at low ebb as far as his morale, or perhaps spiritually, and I don't believe I should discuss the particulars of that behind his back."

"True. I'd appreciate discretion if I were in his position. But you do find him splendid, don't you?"

"Splendid? Now there's a word. I won't say no, but I must say he's a fine young man."

Melissa stared into the fire again. Lord Russell's presence at the vicarage caused a level of interest within her that she'd never experienced before. Her thoughts kept flying to him. How was he sleeping? Was he in terrible pain? Hungry? Lonely? She didn't understand why, but an inner pull that wouldn't go away nagged at her, making her want to be with him. To care for him until he was well—and beyond.

Melissa took her eyes off the flames to glance at her friend.

Miss Cleaver hummed before speaking without looking up from her stitchery. "My brother's at Squire Hannon's. The cook there had her bad foot operated on, and Jeremiah's paying a pastoral call."

"Surgery? Dr. Swithins, correct? I hope he had clean hands. Not that I perceived anything to the contrary. It's just that I've read what a scourge that can be. Healers spreading illness." Melissa clucked her disapproval and made a hand-washing gesture.

"I agree. Sanitation is improving, though—not one woman in the village has died from childbed fever in several years."

"May I take supper to our patient later? When it's time."

"Yes. The sight of you ought to perk him up. An old biddy like me might send him into a decline." She laughed in her usual self-deprecating fashion.

"Now stop that. You're a darling, Prissy." Melissa closed the book, set it aside, and rose from her chair by the fire. She brushed down the front of her gown, smoothing out the creases from sitting. She walked over to the window, peering first left, and then right, and then down the driveway. "It's certainly quiet here today. Excellent for Lord Russell."

"Hard to believe the district hosted robbers a few, short days ago." Miss Cleaver tied off a knot with vigor as if she were tying up a robber. "Supper's too far off. One of us should check on him soon. He might be hungry. I wonder when Dr. Swithins will get here. He did say he'd visit the patient today."

Miss Cleaver made to rise, but Melissa held out a staying hand. "I'll go. I'd like to check on the patient. You rest because you will possibly need to sit with him all night. And I couldn't do that, now could I? Not proper. So I'll take a turn at this time."

She departed with a resolute nod since Miss Cleaver made no objections. She enjoyed her visits here—such an unfettered life compared to that in London. In London, she'd never be allowed to play nurse to an injured nobleman.

Melissa slipped into the small sickroom at the second story rear of the house. A glance told her the patient slept, but she tiptoed over and stood by the bed. Her gaze roamed over him, checking that he was covered, warm and still.

Silly, you've checked on him, now go. But she stayed near, hands clasped at her waist. *Lord, please be with this man, heal him, and return him to good health. Amen.*

She reached out, and then drew her hand back. If she touched him, he might wake. He needed the curative of sleep. The green-painted wooden chair didn't weigh too much, so moving it into position made little noise. She sat next to the bed, hands folded, hoping that was what a real nurse did in a case like this. She settled herself and tried for placidity. Posture erect, clasped hands, eyes demurely focused on the carved footboard. The whorls of design only held her attention for a minute before her gaze drifted to the man's face again.

A straight nose, strong jaw, dark lashes splayed—quite entrancing. A trance, yes, that's it. He'd put a spell on her—one of attraction. *No, don't be preposterous. The poor man's done no such thing.*

Lord Russell's eyelids fluttered. Sitting there quietly with him suited her well, but the thought of his eyes opening caused a flicker of excitement to shoot through her.

Melissa looked inward, questioning her sudden interest. Never before had a man awoken even a glimmer of attraction within her heart. This one, however, having not done a thing to draw her, captured her fascination.

The sea-blue eyes opened, and he turned toward her, gaze widening as though in surprise. His hand lifted to tug the covers over his chest. He rasped out the word, "Water."

"Ah yes. Let me get that straightaway." Melissa scampered across the small room to the washstand where a glass water pitcher sat ready in anticipation. Shaky hands caused a few clinks, but she was soon back at the bedside.

She must reposition him, or the water would end up bathing his face and neck. She set the drink on the bedside table and shoved her cuffs out of the way. Wringing her hands, she edged closer until her legs met the side of the mattress.

Heart in her throat, she slipped a hand under his warm, muscular neck and lifted. She tugged the pillow down lower and placed a second pillow under his head before laying him down. She hoped this would be enough of an angle for him to drink. He gave her a smile.

As she provided this tender service, the rosy-cheeked doctor blustered into the room.

"Oh ho. You've got yourself a nurse."

The doctor's jesting tone hit a nerve. "I'm serving water to the patient. His throat is parched."

Turning her back to the doctor, she resumed her efforts with Lord Russell. "Can you manage a sip or two?"

Several healthy swallows later, he lifted his hand to make a faint slicing motion, and she withdrew the glass.

She bustled over to the washstand to deposit the glass, and then diverted to the window while the doctor took the patient's pulse. It crossed her mind that the doctor hadn't much to offer for these injuries. Tender care alone would speed the healing.

As if he read her mind, the doctor stated, "It is my opinion the patient needs nothing more than rest, willow bark tea for his pain, and the good people of this house to keep an eye on him." He rested his fingers on Lord Russell's shoulder. "Simply endure and you'll recover."

The doctor bustled out, and Melissa didn't mind one bit. She preferred being here, taking care of Lord Russell, alone. With the door propped open, propriety was well-served. This was a work of mercy as well as necessity, after all.

Light snoring came from the bed. Her fingers crept

over and touched his arm. The layers of sheets and blankets muted the unmistakable zing that coursed through her fingers and all the way to her heart. She left her hand there, making sure to put no pressure on Lord Russell.

Minutes passed at a crawl, but she liked that. The slower time went by, the further off her departure to London. But no, best not to think of that, rather about this poor man, beaten and left for dead. Lord Russell was much more interesting to ponder. And so handsome, too. Questions she'd like to ask formed. How old was he? Had he been happy to inherit an estate?

Would he be pleasant, arrogant, or foppish? So odd to meet someone who was incapacitated. All that was certain was that he was young, yet older than her, and was going home to become Lord of Russell Manor.

Movement from the bed caught Melissa's attention. A bit of writhing alerted her that he might be waking. She leaned over, taking a good long look. His eyes opened—while she hovered eight inches from his face.

She gasped and reared back. "Pardon me, sir." She plopped into the chair, chagrinned.

He cleared his throat and, voice dreamy with sleep, made a request. "Tea?"

"Oh, yes, right here. Willow bark tea." She plumped and propped the pillows, nurse-like, and turned to serve the tea, first cupping the pot with her hands. "Ah, good. The pot's still warm."

"I'll try a sip or two. But that will be enough. Thank you." The hushed tones of his voice lent an intimate flavor to the words.

Positioning the cup, she let him drink his fill,

withdrawing it when empty, dabbing his lips with a linen cloth.

He reached over in an arc, palm up. Tentative, she laid her fingers on his. He closed his hand around hers and let his arm drop to the bed.

Holding hands. Why had he reached for her? Was this a normal part of nursing care? It could be, for to hold a patient's hand seemed to be within the realm of possible normalcy. But she wasn't sure.

The intimacy of the moment choked her up. Having been so lacking in companionship the last year, physical contact comforted a part of her she hardly remembered existed.

Not simply any someone, either. A shivery thrill ran up her spine, and she sat straighter, trying to rid herself of such errant thoughts and emotions. Inappropriate longings for her patient warred with demure self-scolding. What would it be like for those strong arms to come around her? *I must stop this madness.*

He released her hand. "You're an excellent nurse." He reached up and gingerly touched his forehead, all the while gazing at her from beneath heavy lids and a thick sweep of bronze eyelashes.

To her surprise, he flung back the covers from his upper body and sat up. Flustered, she leapt to her feet and took a step back.

"Do you reside in Russelton, Miss Southwood?"

His smile held a hint of flirtation if she wasn't mistaken. She whisked her hands behind her back to hide their sudden shaking. His low voice trickled through her confusion. She must answer his simple question. "Honored to make your acquaintance, and no, I don't live here. I'm a guest—from London."

Highly irregular, but Melissa strove to say all the proper things. Difficult to do in such a setting.

She brought the cup to his lips again, and he took a sip, and then pushed it away.

"You've had enough?"

"Yes. So, kind. I lived in London, too."

"Could you eat some food? I can have the cook put together a light supper."

"That sounds excellent."

"I shall get you a tray."

"Very well."

He appeared to be a man of few words, but injuries could account for that. Agitated by his nearness, she glanced over her shoulder on her way out of the room.

Reaching the kitchen via the back stairs, she quickly assembled what she thought would be an appropriate meal for an invalid. Thinly sliced bread, a small bowl of plum sauce, and broth from a pan kept hot on the stove. Bustling, she re-entered the sickroom in less than a quarter-hour.

"Here is your food."

"I'll hold the tray on my lap, if you please." In her absence, he'd propped his pillows against the headboard and sat up against them.

She handed over the meal and pivoted away, scuttling over to the window. The man's nearness undid her usual calm propriety. Nothing in her previous experience prepared her for the presence of this man, nor for the sensations he aroused within her.

5

"How do you like your bread? Or the fruit sauce? What's wrong? Are you suffering?" The words came tumbling out.

Mark kept his tone measured and pleasant. "The food you brought is delicious. I am not in pain."

The young lady's eyes flew wide, and her hand covered her lips. He hated having alarmed her. Bad enough she had to see him thus. Helplessness didn't suit him. His main purpose was to get home. How ironic, that when he finally resolved to walk the straight and narrow, he'd been struck down.

"Is there anything else I can do for you?"

"No, just call a manservant."

"Certainly, my lord."

The little lady slipped out of the room. He missed her already, but he needed to get home.

A servant clad in workman's garb arrived a few minutes later and stood just inside the door, turning his cap in his hands. "May I help you, milord? The young lady said you were asking for me?"

"Yes. What's your name, fellow?"

"Toby. I work in the stables and as a handyman for the minister. At yer service."

"Be a good lad, Toby, and bring me my clothes—there, hanging on that hook. Yes, those. See if you can locate my boots."

While the servant searched for the boots, Mark

dressed. When he got to the neckcloth, he shook his head at the crumpled mess that once was a gleaming, starched fashionable cravat and shoved it into his jacket pocket.

Toby returned with the boots. "Found 'em in the hall."

"Very good. That's all for now, thank you."

Alone again, he forced his feet into the snug boots. The sore ankle protested, but happy to be dressed and resolved to get to Russell Manor, he bid a mental *adieu* to the sickroom and headed downstairs to bid farewell to his hosts.

~*~

In the cozy parlor below, Melissa started at the sound of booted feet coming down the front stairs. "What's that?"

The appearance of a bedraggled Lord Russell answered her question as he limped through the door and stopped a few paces inside the room.

"I don't recall Dr. Swithins suggesting you come downstairs."

"Pardon my dishevelment, Mr. Cleaver, Miss Cleaver, Miss Southwood. It's past time I get to Russell Manor. My injuries are not major, and I simply need healing, which I can do there, without inconveniencing your entire household."

Since the Cleavers sat silent and dumbstruck, Melissa seized the moment. "That's all very well, but the doctor said—"

"Yes, he did say something such as to imply all I needed was rest. Dear friends, may I call you friends? I must get to the manor and tend to my responsibilities."

A Match for Melissa

Mr. Cleaver found his voice. "Indeed we are friends. It's been an honor to have you under our roof and now that we are neighbors, hope to see you hither and yon for many years to come."

"I am eternally grateful for all you've done," Lord Russell said, his glance touching them all. He clasped the minister's hand in a strong grasp. "Though I am up on my feet, I'll need another way home—not sure I'm up to a walk of that length."

"Ah yes, I'll prepare to drive you home. Happy to be of service." Mr. Cleaver departed.

A flicker of loss cascaded through Melissa's chest. Would the man, her patient a few minutes ago, leave with mere commonplace farewells? After what she believed to be a special connection? *Foolish, silly girl!*

He moved to bow over Miss Cleaver's hand. He murmured more words of appreciation before turning to Melissa. "Miss Southwood." His gaze direct, he went on, "To you, I offer my sincere gratitude for your tender care. I swear it was your sweet succor that brought me to my senses and gave me the strength to do what I must." With this bit of flattery, he swept up her hand and placed a kiss a mere hairsbreadth from her skin.

She withdrew after an acceptable time passed. Though wanting to cherish the feel of his touch, she needed to act as though she accepted his parting with maidenly submissive equanimity.

"You're welcome. I'm glad you are stronger than the doctor thought." *I sound insipid. He'll never want to see me again.* As if seeing her once more mattered to this lord. It had been hard to witness a strong, virile man like him down, even though he'd been attacked and had every reason to lie low. So her time of playing nursemaid came to an end. She'd still possess sweet memories.

Lord Russell nodded toward them, pivoted, and left the room

"Now, that was a surprise." Melissa shoved aside the curtain and watched him until he disappeared around the corner of the vicarage.

"I agree. A shock." Miss Cleaver collapsed onto the settee with a flounce of her skirts. "I hope he doesn't experience a terrible setback. So like a man."

Worry lanced through Melissa. "Is there anything more we should do?"

"We need to keep him in our prayers. Rising from a sickbed before one is pronounced well is not preferential to one's health." Miss Cleaver wagged her head. "We can't gauge the real state of his recovery."

Miss Cleaver's declaration didn't ease Melissa's mind. "I wanted to do something tangible for the poor man."

Miss Cleaver gave her an assessing stare.

"What? Isn't wanting to help normal?"

"Oh yes, very much, dear Melissa. But he's gone, now. We should take tea. Perhaps that will settle our spirits."

Melissa let the curtain fall and returned to the settee. "Yes, yes. That's right, tea. I was expecting to take him some tea, but I'll get a tray for us instead."

As she gathered the tea things, she steadied herself with a few deep breaths and closed her eyes. With hands clenched on the tray handles, she sent up a petition, the only one she could think of with her thoughts whirling—*Jesus, help me. Help him.*

Melissa regained a measure of peace by the time she reached the parlor again. She poured tea for Miss

Cleaver and spoke. "Upon reflection, I admit though Lord Russell's color tended to the pale side, he didn't appear to be in true agony. Let us hope his departure won't cause a setback."

"I agree. Worry does no good. We can only pray." Miss Cleaver's voice rang with finality and approval.

Melissa lifted another silent petition for help as she held a warm teacup between both hands.

Sitting in companionable silence with Priscilla, Melissa allowed herself to daydream about the unusual experience of being alone with a man. A young, handsome, albeit bedridden, one. The lack of rigidity here at the vicarage was a treat compared to the stiff social mores of London. How generous of Miss Cleaver to allow Melissa the small freedom of nursing Lord Russell. After all, he certainly hadn't tainted her reputation, either when unconscious or awake and flat on his back. She recalled the moment he opened his eyes, while she tended him at the bedside. Shaking herself when this waking dream went on too long, she said farewell to the man of her dreams. *Good-bye. You could have been my hero.*

Miss Cleaver broke the silence "Remind me to talk to my brother about hiring a housemaid. I'm beginning to be acquainted with the stairs all too well. What made him think we needed only a cook, groom, gardener, and a day girl coming in from the village?" She threw her hands up in mock despair and departed.

Melissa's thoughts kept her silent. Tending Lord Russell proved more delightful than one would expect, giving her a sense of worth. She'd basked in it, but it was over.

6

The next day dawned bright. Melissa needed the sun to overtake her *ennui*. Thoughts of Lord Russell crashed in before she even left her bed. *Bless and keep Lord Russell. Please continue to heal him and guide him, amen.* The gloom lifted for the time, but she dreaded the day. And her departure on the morrow.

The invigoration of taking care of the injured nobleman, even when he slept, enjoying his nearness, sitting ready if he needed help, gave life momentary purpose. But with that vigor gone, her motivation lagged.

Sun lanced into her plush bedroom, and she forced herself to throw off the silken bed coverings. She swung her feet to the floor.

After washing her face, she donned her most serviceable dress, one of the few that didn't require a maid's assistance. It slipped over her head and tied under the bust to draw in the fullness. A swift run of a comb through her hair, and twist, twist, pin—ready to face the day. What would it bring?

Breakfast waited, served from a buffet in the dining room. Covered dishes held eggs, ham, toast, jam, and coffee. She made her selections and joined her host at the table. Hidden behind a newspaper, he didn't show any sign of noticing her presence.

"Good morning," she sang out. "Where's Priscilla?"

A Match for Melissa

"What? Oh, it's you. Good morning, Melissa." Mr. Cleaver lowered the paper and lifted his coffee cup. "She's gone to the village to replenish some stores."

"I imagine she'll return soon?" Melissa savored the fresh coffee. It made any breakfast taste even better. "The coffee here is superb. I must ask Miss Cleaver for the instructions." She nibbled at the toast while Mr. Cleaver disappeared behind the paper.

"Mmph. Soon."

"I think I'll go back to my room." She pushed back her chair and made to rise.

"Just a moment, dear. I'd like a word with you."

At the minister's command, she plunked back into her chair, deflated.

He lowered the paper, and with a sigh, folded it. "Ahem. You are here under my care, and I don't like it that you've not gotten one dab of fresh air since two days ago. We appreciate your service to the injured, but Miss Cleaver and I must consider your welfare as well. Sending you back to London in a peaked state would not be acceptable."

"I feel fine." Melissa sat up straight and tried to exude excellent health. She hated the thought of being hemmed and cosseted here in the country, too. But perhaps Mr. Cleaver wondered about her interest in Lord Russell. Did fear underlay his worries?

"Good to hear. I'd like you to take a turn or two in the garden this morning after breakfast."

"It will be my delight to comply." She didn't want to spare a minute thinking about returning home, but she had this last day to spend in the country with her good friends, the Cleavers. "When I came to visit, I never imagined I'd learn to be a sickroom maid," she said with a laugh and lifted spirits.

From behind the paper, Mr. Cleaver spoke. "Perhaps you'd like to go on a call with me this afternoon?" He raised the paper again and rattled it.

"To a sick parishioner? Since I am now so experienced in caregiving?"

"Not exactly. I was thinking to call on Lord Russell, to ease my mind."

Melissa reached over and pushed down the newspaper. "Yes, yes, yes. I'd love to pay that visit with you. One o'clock?"

"One will be fine." He rattled the paper back into position.

"I'll go out and stroll in the garden now." At least at the vicarage she could set a toe outside without a chaperone—whether maid or companion. In London, she dared not take a walk alone. She hurried to drink the rest of her coffee, retrieved her shawl and bonnet from the hall, and exited the front door while tying the strings under her chin.

A deep mouthful of fresh country air woke Melissa all the way. She breathed in the early spring as she moved toward the garden paths behind the house. Earthy scents hinted at the glories to come. The smell of rain so prominent in the air, she held up a palm to test for raindrops. Precipitation would make the morning drag, and her heart clamored to get over to Russell Manor to check on Lord Russell. Since she had to wait until one o'clock, she puttered around to the back of the house and glanced up at the window of the room in which he'd lain. How was he today? Better? She hoped Miss Cleaver purchased plenty of medicines. She could take some along in case he needed them.

She'd pick daffodils later. They'd be cheery for

Lord Russell. Half-reluctant, half-enjoying the moist morning air, Melissa entered the path. In the shape of a cloverleaf, the vicarage garden paths offered a route that looped around three beds and boasted a fountain and bench in the center.

Meticulously set paving stones made the way smooth, and Melissa meandered to the third loop before the first rumble of distant thunder. She loved storms but not getting caught out in them. She grabbed up her skirt and ran to the kitchen door, reached in, and took a pair of shears off a hook nearby. "Betsy, I'm borrowing these shears. I'll be right back."

She scampered over to the yellow blooms and lanced off half a dozen before fat raindrops began to fall. These would do. A dash to the kitchen door prevented a full soaking, and she entered and stripped off her damp bonnet and shawl.

"Where might I find a vase?" She held up the small floral offering, a handful of daffodils.

"I've got something under here." Betsy squatted down and rummaged in a lower cupboard, emerging with a dented pewter cup. "Will this do?"

"That's perfect. Exactly the size." Melissa filled the impromptu vase from a water jug and placed the flowers within. "I love the sound of rain. Don't you?"

"The sound's fine, but the mud, no." Betsy turned away and went back to her baking, Thursday being the day she made a dozen loaves of bread to last the week through.

Heart skittering in anticipation, Melissa arranged the blooms. She carried them to the study to pass the time until the visit and arrived at the door only to hear the end of a conversation.

"I told him to rest. No getting up unless absolutely

necessary. Moving to Russell Manor was not my prescription. Instructed him to stay in a dim, quiet room. That's what'll fix him. The nasty cudgeling he took could have severe consequences to his mental abilities if he doesn't follow my orders." The doctor's voice carried well.

A second voice mumbled an assent.

Dr. Swithins emerged from the study, almost colliding with Melissa. With a curt nod, he departed.

Overhearing the doctor's dire warnings caused her a pang. She hoped the doctor was wrong about Lord Russell. She missed her patient. Who'd have thought tending a sick person would be so rewarding? She did hope he'd recover—soon.

7

In the dimly-lit library at Russell Manor, Mark scowled at the account books open on the massive desk in front of him. He shoved them away, avoiding the tray of lunch he'd ordered and ignored. Concentration eluded him. However anxious to take his place as master of the estate, he chafed at the restrictions enforced by his recovery. Languor hung over him like a heavy cape, with only moments of improved strength and vigor breaking through. Such responsibility as he'd not been trained for also weighed him down. His brother James, a superlative landowner, left big shoes to fill.

Forearm over his eyes, he allowed a daydream of her again. *Miss Southwood.* He missed her gentle touch and sweet spirit. Her presence once brought a balm to his wounds, but thoughts of her were all he had for comfort now. She was an angel—a darling angel. Regret laced his memories of her tender mercies.

Physical symptoms lessened even after one day home at the manor. He gave his foot a tentative wiggle. The pain in his ankle throbbed less. He took a few deep breaths and ran fingertips over the bump on his head. *Ouch.* Better, but tender.

The drive to be more active, to take the full reins of the estate, itched like a burr under a saddle. Why had the attack happened? Possessing a tenuous new lease on life, and on his way home, and then cast down to the depths of pain, despair, and loss.

He tussled a while longer with the mental quandary of 'why?' and then vowed to recover his health. No criminal act would rob him of his heritage. He smacked his fist on the desk, pulled the account books toward himself, and gathered his remaining scraps of determination.

Victorious, he gave the accounts his full attention for almost an hour, when Crabtree, the butler, stuck his head into the room. "Visitors, Lord Russell."

"Well, my good man, who is it?"

First glancing over his shoulder, Crabtree answered. "It's the vicar and a young lady. Didn't catch her name."

Mark's heart leapt. *The ministering angel from the vicarage?* "Put them in the drawing room. I'll join them soon. Have tea brought in."

Crabtree closed the door. Mark leaned back in his chair, steepled fingers under his chin, his attention once again drawn to the portrait of his brother hung above the fireplace. The commanding gaze even now humbled Mark. His brother had been such a champion. Whatever he'd set his hand to, he'd excelled. Boxing, fencing, investing, marrying well, raising a family, managing the estate, doubling its acreage. And on and on. Mark stiffened his spine and gave himself a lecture. No dabbling with the hearts of young ladies—raising their expectations. A titled man now, he needed to proceed with caution and steel himself from developing a tendre for little Miss Southwood from the vicarage.

Rising, he winced, but less than the day before. He yanked down his waistcoat, smoothed his lapels, and raked fingers through his coarse curls. As if these motions could order his heart.

He entered the drawing room full of half-forced bonhomie. "Welcome, Mr. Cleaver, Miss Southwood. I've ordered tea." His heart chimed at the sight of her loveliness. She wore a ruffled white dress which suited the innocent maiden well.

"Thank you for agreeing to our visit. Such an impromptu call imposing on a newly-arrived neighbor…" Nerves tinged the pastor's words.

"Not an imposition. Nothing of the kind. You brought my sorry self back from death's door. You are always welcome here, Mr. Cleaver." He patted the man's shoulder and gestured toward a cluster of comfortable armchairs. He stepped aside and waved Miss Southwood to precede him. "Let us sit."

"How are you today?" The minister opened the conversation.

Mark didn't want to be fussed over anymore, no matter the level of pain and exhaustion.

"Never better." He lied and closed his eyes fleetingly, assessing the truth of this statement. When he opened them, he caught her glance before she looked away. Good. She mustn't be encouraged by errant favors. Meeting her was the merest happenstance, regardless of how much affection for her warmed him. The manor needed his full attention.

"Welcome to my home. I'm pleased by your visit and to thus return a small measure of your hospitality."

"Our pleasure. I can now boast we were the first to claim the honor of entertaining you under our roof."

"Dubious honor." Mark smiled, enjoying the minister's light humor. "Must say, not the arrival I imagined either, to land flat on my back in one of the vicinity's wetter ditches."

"Indeed, quite an out-of-ordinary advent." Her musical, feminine voice soothed him, but he mustn't focus on such distractions.

"You gave us quite a start when you departed so soon." Mr. Cleaver's eyebrows shot up.

"I couldn't delay taking up the reins of Russell Manor. I am sorry if I offended you."

"Don't mention it. We understand. It was a shock, as we expected a long, slow, recovery."

"Yes. Well, it's in the blood. Russells are hard to keep down." Perhaps now they could speak of something other than the troubles of the lord of the manor.

"Are you healed?" Melissa's fingers flew to her lips as if she regretted her words.

"A few pangs. I won't deny several more days in bed would have been a pleasure. However, duties called. I've inspected the stables and plan to tour the farms later today." As much as he enjoyed her company, he needed to run an estate.

"Miss Cleaver and I will pray for your return to good health." Prim, she made this statement while staring down at her folded gloved hands in her muslin-gowned lap.

That's when he noticed she was holding a container of daffodils. Her cheeks turned a delightful shade of pink as she held them out toward him. "These are for you. It's traditional to bring flowers to the sick."

"Thank you very much. Charming." He took the blooms and set them on the table. *Where is that tea?* Acting the lord was annoying, and the sooner the beverage cart was rolled in and the tea consumed, the better. Perhaps then he could get this darling girl and her daffodils off his mind. How singular…receiving flowers from a young lady. Life in the country must loosen the rules.

Tea arrived, and the visit wore on with Mr. Cleaver nattering.

"As I was saying, the church will welcome your presence in the Russell family pew."

"Yes, I'm sure…when I can attend." His guests' crestfallen expressions would be funny if guilt hadn't blindsided him. He'd never yet understood the appeal of attending worship services, and it wouldn't do to raise false hopes. Making occasional appearances at the local church may be part of the duties as lord of the manor and leading citizen of the district, but could be limited.

When twenty minutes elapsed, the chatty minister rose, signaling an end to his call. "Again, we're happy with the evidence of your recovery. The district will be the better for your presence."

"Thank you for that welcome and for rescuing me. Let's hope that's the end of crime hereabouts for the nonce." He turned to Melissa and bowed over her hand. As he stood erect again, he allowed his eyes to enjoy her demure form, her alabaster neck, and her lovely face.

"Lord Russell, I am glad you are mending. My mind shall rest easy on that point as I journey to London."

"Thank you again for the flowers—for everything, Miss Southwood." Her pale face held a guarded quality—so different from the tender expressions she wore as she took care of him. Perhaps he'd gone too far at depressing any attentions from her in the future. He bowed. "Good-bye, fair heroine. May London treat you well."

~*~

Melissa prepared for the scheduled trip home. Her bag packed, she waited for a female servant. Such a bother to need help to fasten the back of one's gown. At least panniers were no longer in style. While waiting, she mused over Lord Russell's odd demeanor yesterday afternoon during the call. One moment he appeared to be all admiration, the next, neutral and distant. At least he wouldn't cut up her peace in London.

Arrangements were in place for her to be picked up by her father's coach today. What Papa wanted, he got. But on the heels of two exciting days with her patient, fantasies taunted her. Fantasies in which Lord Russell stayed abed and she continued to assist with tending the handsome and fascinating victim.

Papa harbored mysterious plans for this spring and hinted at marrying her off. How he planned to achieve that was a mystery. He had a reputation as an effective businessman, but surely matchmaking remained beyond him. Perhaps he'd only planned a trip to Cornwall to visit the relatives. She might be anxious for nothing.

Still, she didn't want to leave for London today, whatever the reason. She loved her former governess Priscilla, now housekeeper at her brother's vicarage. And the country provided Melissa much more freedom. Never in London would her wealthy merchant father allow her to step out of the house alone. In idyllic rural Russelton, however, a simple stroll could be taken without being hemmed about with maids, grooms, or chaperones.

Even more than ruing parting from her place of freedom, she found that Lord Russell drew her thoughts like a magnet. If she were honest, what young woman would want to leave now when a fascinating gentleman appeared on the quiet scene of country life?

Betsy bustled in, wiping work-worn hands on her apron. "Came as soon as able, miss."

Melissa turned her back toward the woman. "Thank you for breaking away from your duties. I can't reach the fastenings myself." Betsy had the dress hooked in no time.

The crunch of gravel outside the vicarage indicated the arrival of her father's carriage, right on schedule. She peeked out the window to verify her fears. Yes, there sat the glossy black Southwood family coach. The retinue sent to retrieve her included a coachman, a groom serving as outrider, and her lady's maid, Tessie. It would be good to have Tessie around again, even though she'd gotten by without her. However regretful to leave, such careful planning must stand, not thrown over merely for her whims.

She rapped on the windowpane and waved at Tessie before snatching her cloak and descending to the parlor where she found her former governess, Miss Cleaver. After such an unusual ending to an initially placid, bucolic visit, as well as not knowing what awaited Melissa in London, farewells carried more weight and portent.

She linked arms with her friend, and they stood side by side, facing the window, observing the groom stowing Melissa's bags. "Priscilla, going home now doesn't suit me."

"Now, now, dear. You can visit again, Lord

willing." She touched Melissa's cheek with a caress.

"Don't. You'll make me cry. Leaving when something so out of the ordinary has happened doesn't seem right. But Lord Russell is back on his feet, and only his return to health matters."

"Indeed. Finding him as you did was dramatic." Miss Cleaver sighed and moved away from the window. "I must bid you farewell now."

Melissa followed Miss Cleaver out to the driveway. Near the open coach door, Melissa stood hand-in-hand with her friend for a bit of last-minute conversation. "Please write soon, Priscilla." The main news she wanted was of the patient, but she didn't voice her desire.

Miss Cleaver gave Melissa's hand a squeeze. "Yes, I will, dear. Have I ever told you wearing brown does wonders to your eyes?"

"You have, once or twice." The transparent attempt at distraction made her smile, but only for a moment. "I'd rather be staying."

"I hope you are healthy enough to travel. Did the tisane I prepared for you completely relieve your symptoms? You suffered no recurrences, correct? After your initial state of shock after the rescue?"

"The tisane helped quite adequately. That little spell of lightheadedness is long over, but my concern for the unfortunate Lord Russell continues to weigh on my heart. When we visited him yesterday, something told me he was in considerable pain, even though he did not mention it." Melissa held a gloved hand flat against her chest where warm compassion insisted on throbbing for him. "Such a pity the attack happened in this normally-peaceful district. I'm relieved Papa sent the armed outrider."

A Match for Melissa

Melissa hugged Miss Cleaver, kissed her on both cheeks, and waved her handkerchief until a curve in the road put her out of sight. With her eyes closed, Melissa rested on the squabs. Absently, she twirled one long golden curl, pulled it, and let it spring back. Headed home to London to face her father's machinations did nothing to dispel thoughts of the man recuperating alone on his lavish estate. Though she was curious about her father's plans, Lord Russell's image kept intruding in her mind's eye, and her disobedient heart ached.

8

"Sir?"

The sound intruded on his sleep. Lifting his head from where it fell over the account books late last night, Mark opened his eyes to the sight of the butler approaching, a quizzical frown on his face.

"Ah. You are awake. A visitor awaits in the morning room. Shall I send her away?"

"Who is it?" Mark massaged the back of his neck, gaze landing on an empty brandy decanter. Memories of wallowing in an agony of confusion wove through his painful head.

"It's Miss Cleaver. She has something for you. In a basket."

"I'll need ten minutes, but bring some coffee to my rooms first."

"Yes, sir. Of course. I'll get coffee to your rooms shortly."

Mark ran light-footed up the stairs and dashed to his room. A servant had been in, because clean linens were laid across his dressing chair. Mark splashed his face with cold water from a pitcher and stripped off his wrinkled clothes from yesterday. Crabtree entered with a steaming silver coffeepot and poured a cup of black coffee.

"Crabtree, can you help a moment with this cravat? Can't seem to manage the knot today." He held out the strip of linen and took that chance to down an entire cup of the black rejuvenating brew before subjecting his neck to Crabtree's ministrations.

Scampering down the stairs, tiredness forgotten, and with an elegant knot in his tie, he entered the morning room to meet his guest. Miss Cleaver was seated near a window, holding a basket on her lap, using two hands to grip it.

"Good morning, Miss Cleaver. To what do I owe the pleasure of your call?"

"Heavens, I hope I didn't disturb you, but I wanted to bring you some restoratives." She rummaged in the basket and drew out a jar. "Calf's foot jelly—for healing." She replaced the wide jar, and then withdrew another item, a crock. "Broth. Nothing like broth to speed a return to high good health." After repositioning the crock, she withdrew a packet. "Dried powder of willow bark—for any lingering pains."

"I'm grateful, ma'am. So thoughtful of you." He smiled. "Might I ask if Miss Southwood will be at home later?"

"Miss Southwood departed for London earlier this morning. Her father sent a coach as arranged."

A stab of loss and loneliness crashed in the region of his heart. Not trusting himself to speak, he simply gave a barely-audible, involuntary groan.

Miss Cleaver fussed with the basket. "She's a lovely person, and we will all miss her."

He gathered his wits and popped out the first thing that entered his mind. "Weren't you speaking to me about green pastures whilst I tarried at the vicarage?"

"That was Wednesday night you must be recalling. I read the twenty-third Psalm to you. I always share the passage with sick or injured folk. It offers a balm to all men. Was it that for you?"

"I suppose, in as much as the valley of the shadow of death can be. It pertained somewhat to my situation."

Uncertainty flickered as he thought over the Psalm again. He had no right to take comfort from such goodness because of the way he lived. His life would not please God.

When flat on his back, despair bore down on him. Now that he was home, another type of flatness descended on his spirits. It stung to admit even to himself how low he'd fallen. Halted from a descending spiral, he hit bottom with a sickening thump, landing at what appeared to be a fork in the path. "My morale is low."

"That can happen after an illness, however brief."

"A new opportunity has been laid before me. Changes to be made. When I inherited the title and the estate, I received the beginning of a new life. It seems more is necessary." He sensed something lurked beyond his grasp—an elusive truth, perhaps.

"One thing is true—there's no proper happiness to be found without a life of faith." Her face was as calm as if they were discussing the price of wheat.

She reminded him of his Aunt Lucy. That relaxed his guard, allowing vulnerability to worm its way out. The next words out of his mouth surprised even him. "Miss Cleaver, I intend to firmly resolve to live right as I take up the serious matters of life."

"That's admirable, but with all due respect, my lord, lacking the help of our Maker, none of us can do anything good. Any attempt to reform ourselves without His grace and mercy shall fail. No matter the strong resolve one may vow to live aright, one must submit to the Almighty and cast oneself upon His care." Miss Cleaver leaned forward in her chair with her eyes intent and a smile on her face—again, as if she were discussing crops.

"If I put in a great effort...you are saying even that won't be enough? Won't bring me peace?"

Miss Cleaver paused, took a breath, and Mark sensed an imminent sermon. "In the same Psalm was the line, 'Yea though I walk through the Valley of the Shadow of Death, I shall fear no evil. For Thou art with me...' God is with him. That's the difference. This does remind me of your mishap. This is an example of the Word applying to one's lives. Scripture is like a double-edged sword."

"But I'll do my best."

"I'm sure you will." Her sincere tone dragged Mark's mind back to his insecurities about living up to his brother.

"You've resolved to live better. But remember, not one of us can reform without God's grace and mercy."

Mark's gut clenched since he never expected to take part in a conversation of this depth. Now he'd be in for a lecture. *Do I really want this? I'm so tired.*

Crabtree stuck his head through the open door. "Sir, there's an emergency in the lower field. The steward needs you."

Mark stood, and bowed over Miss Cleaver's hand. "Thank you for the basket. And for the visit. Please, excuse me." He left the room with a sense of escaping her net.

~*~

Later that day, Miss Cleaver recounted the visit to

her brother. "The moment I was ministering to Lord Russell's spiritual need, he left to take care of an emergency."

"All is yet well, Priscilla." Mr. Cleaver tried to temper his sister's disappointment. "He needs time to digest your words. He'll be here many years to come, Lord willing. I am sure God will give another opportunity to share the Gospel with him."

"You're right. That man has a need for truth."

"I agree," said the minister. "He requires God's wondrous grace."

Betsy spoke from the doorway and held out a stiff vellum envelope. "Excuse me, Mr. Cleaver, Miss Cleaver, but a messenger from the manor delivered this."

Miss Cleaver rose with alacrity and took the message from the servant. "That will be all, Betsy." The door closed with a click.

"What do you suppose that is?" Mr. Cleaver stretched his feet out toward the fire and put his hands behind his head, leaning back.

She moved to a desk in the corner, slit the envelope, and withdrew its contents. After a moment's perusal, she answered. "It's an invitation to dinner at Russell Manor tomorrow night. How kind of Lord Russell. I shall send our acceptance immediately." She sat at the desk and pulled together writing tools: pen, bottle of ink, blotter, and a sheet of foolscap. She scribbled for a minute or two, sanded the letter, and folded it.

"It shall be a pleasant evening out. I'm glad we are on such a friendly footing with the new lord of the manor. His brother was very pleasant but kept busy with his family. I do believe Lord Russell might be

A Match for Melissa

lonely."

"Perhaps. We can say for sure that he is hospitable. Kind, too, when I called on him yesterday with Melissa."

"I enjoyed being a part of his rescue and recovery," Priscilla added. "That over and Melissa gone, it's terribly quiet here with only you for company."

Mr. Cleaver smiled at this remark but said only, "Indeed."

"I shall read to you for a while." She did, until snores told her he was asleep, and she quietly closed her book.

~*~

The next evening arrived, and by seven, the Cleavers and Dr. Swithins, the only other guest, were seated comfortably in the elaborate drawing room on the west side of Russell Manor.

"I've invited you, Miss and Mr. Cleaver, Dr. Swithins, to dinner to show my gratitude, in a small way, for all you did for me in my hour of need," Mark spoke from his position near the fireplace.

"You are quite welcome. Isn't that right, Mr. Cleaver?" Miss Cleaver glowed with pleasure, a sparkling crystal glass of cordial in her hand.

"Yes. We are very happy and blessed to have been of service. I don't even care to think of what might have happened if Melissa hadn't found you. Why, you were inches from being under water." Mr. Cleaver loosely clenched his fist and waved it vaguely in the direction of the road.

Not caring to dwell on might-have-beens, Mark

landed on a somewhat lighter topic. "Too bad Miss Southwood has returned to London. Otherwise, she'd be here tonight as well."

Dr. Swithins and Mr. Cleaver began a debate on probability versus providence. That gave Mark the chance he wanted to speak to Miss Cleaver. "I hope you didn't think me foolish yesterday with all my talk of matters of faith."

"Oh, la! Hardly that. I assure you that your conversation was perfectly in order. Can't say when I've discussed topics of such importance with a young man, if ever. I enjoyed every minute of it. We can't chatter on nonsense forever—occasionally we must discuss the essential things of existence."

"You spent many years as a governess in the Southwood home, correct?"

"Indeed, yes. The best times of my life. Caring for such a dear girl as Melissa Southwood. Oh, yes."

"Can you tell me some stories of those times in London?" Mark wanted to learn more about her. Only a few feet away, the other men were intently hashing out matters of great import, but he didn't have the stomach for serious talk right now. The lighter side of life would relieve his angst, if only for the time.

"Let me think." She retrieved her reticule and rummaged for a handkerchief before speaking. Letting out a sigh, she began to reminisce. "I remember when Miss Southwood got the idea in her head to learn everything about how to run a fine home. The Southwood mansion consists of upwards of thirty rooms, making it quite a task she set herself."

"Large for a London house."

"Yes, and so, during the course of an 'apprenticeship' with the housekeeper, she found a sad lack in the furnishings of the servants' quarters. Miss Southwood was told it had always been that way." Miss Cleaver chuckled at the memory. "She approached her father. A week later, three wagons full of sturdy furniture arrived to replace the shabby furnishings. What a darling! She selected it all herself and even ordered a new sewing rocker for my room." She dabbed her eyes with the square of linen.

The poor woman seemed bereft. "Miss Southwood sounds like a fine young lady."

"Oh, yes. The finest."

"She took care of me at the vicarage, but I didn't really learn much about her." He delighted in the memory of the sweet young lady's presence. Was it wrong to want to escape the pressures of his new responsibilities by hearing about Miss Southwood? He listened and painted a mental picture.

"Oh, what can I add? She's a paragon of character and maidenly virtue. Miss Southwood is also quite talented in drawing, languages, embroidery, and home management. She has an eye for style and fashion, too. Her taste is exquisitely subtle and feminine." Miss Cleaver trailed off, lost in thought.

"What color are her eyes?" He'd seen her but wanted to hear about her, especially since she was now gone. No chance of simply running across her in the neighborhood.

Too bad she'd had to depart.

"Pretty brown velvety eyes. It's hard to describe why, but they remind me of a pansy flower. Do you remember her eyes?"

"Yes, but you're painting a lovely picture with words." Mark savored the mental vision of Melissa. Poor Miss Cleaver must think him an odd duck. Better stop with the questions.

~*~

Miss Cleaver fell silent, musing about the attraction between the two young people. She glanced over at Lord Russell. He'd joined the men and was drawn into their conversation, which had moved on to the topic of hunting. She hoped he wasn't bored with all her talk.

She took this moment to send up a thought to God to forgive her for pride in Melissa's accomplishments and beauty. Her thoughts flew to that young lady, now without Miss Cleaver's companionship and in need of God's protection. The poor girl's hands were full dealing with such a father.

9

Mr. Southwood's secretary brought Melissa instructions to appear in the study at three. This formal summons was unprecedented. With an hour to wait, she sat and hummed to herself in the drawing room in her family's London home, luxurious compared to the vicarage. The unusual ending to her visit in the country had been set aside. Pining for those uncomplicated days must end, or she'd never be content. Meeting Lord Russell was a fluke and was in the past, not to be mentioned here in London. Heavens! If Papa became aware of how free her life was on those country visits, he might forbid them.

A persistent sneaking suspicion crept in that her father would try to arrange a marriage. What else could the meeting be about? He rarely met with her alone.

She called to mind her favorite verse and quoted it, speaking the words softly to herself. "Delight yourself in the LORD and he will give you the desires of your heart." She soon fell into silent prayer. *Lord, thank You for Your promise to give me the desires of my heart—to be a wife and mother. Please help me delight in You while I wait for the man of Your choosing.*

Humming, Melissa twirled a curl near her cheek as she pondered her future. Marriage. She forced down the pulse that throbbed when Lord Russell came to mind. Matrimony was her only realistic choice, and she wasn't opposed. In fact, she would love to be a wife. God would sustain her, come what may. If it were a man even half as attractive as Lord Russell, she'd need to be satisfied.

A mere month shy of nineteen, the social order's label of spinster would soon descend on her shoulders. How unfair. If a man put off thoughts of marriage until he reached thirty or more, no one blinked an eye.

She'd had no coming-out ball or presentation at court as the daughter of a merchant. Her father's low birth, despite his great wealth, excluded her from participation in the *haute ton's* marriage mart.

Her unique position posed a dilemma. Brought up to be a lady, yet barred from high society. How did anyone expect her to make a desirable union with an appropriate man?

With God's help, she must marry a believer, however, and her determination not to stray from that precept might not please Papa. The manner in which he'd raged at God after Mama died left her in the dark on his current beliefs. When she reaffirmed her convictions regarding marriage to Papa, his faith crisis could cause ructions. Though under the authority of her father, she must hold fast to her ideal of marrying a man of God. A kind, honorable man.

Antsy, it was hard to be still. She stood, smoothed the skirt of her white, high-waisted gown, and paced from one end of the sizeable room to the other. Her patience was tried, waiting to find out what decree her father would be handing down this time.

What else could it be? Not a trip—he never left the business. Her father's loss of faith lessened her hopes of marital bliss. Without faith, what would be his guide in the selection of a husband? She knew enough of him to guess aristocratic lineage would be the foremost criterion. He was obsessed with gaining a title. Could he be counted on to choose a man of good character?

She absently stroked the soft green velvet sash of her dress and remembered.

Soon after her eighteenth birthday, life changed. Her mother's death at only eight and thirty years shocked everyone. One day, happiness and laughter over a joke at the family supper table, and the very next day saw the onset of a mysterious illness which quickly worsened and claimed her mother's life. She understood Papa's pain.

Melissa wiped a stray tear from her cheek with the back of her hand—not much longer until she discovered her fate, but the minutes crawled.

In her circumscribed life, she'd met not one potential mate. Not one. If only there'd been an opportunity, love's potential may have flowered and taken its natural course. But her father would not wait or waver. When he planned, he succeeded.

Might he not yet allow her to find, or be found by a prospective suitor on her own? But she must admit she knew not where. She'd met Lord Russell under such odd circumstances. Besides, that almost-opportunity lay in the past. With him busy establishing himself in a new life at his estate and her called home to London, the chance of encountering him again was negligible. Even if he came to town, she'd never cross his path.

It seemed near impossible to meet anyone suitable to both her and her father. The clock struck three, and she stopped to primp in the mirror for the important appointment. Her dress of frothy white muslin, sprigged with green, featured a band under the bust with apple-green velvet ribbon—one delicious concoction out of a wardrobe full of gorgeous dresses. After a last critical glance in the mirror, she lifted her chin in resolve and marched to the door.

Muted chimes sounded from the hall clock as she slipped into Papa's study and approached his desk with a respectful smile. In no position of power, her best strategy was to try to avoid being forced into anything regrettable.

"Papa, before we begin, may I touch on two matters of importance to me?"

He pulled out his watch, flicked it open, and answered, "Yes, daughter. What matters?" He came around the ornate desk and laid his hands on her shoulders. "My, oh my, you do remind me of your mother. You're so grown up now." He kissed her forehead, and then steered her to a large armchair.

She sat, and before courage failed, she blurted her first request. "I'd like to hire a companion."

His answer held great influence on the course of her life. Her father fiddled with a pen, eyes down, as if he were hiding their expression from her. The glossy surface of the desk between them stretched like an impassable gulf.

"Papa? I assume you would be amenable to me hiring someone?"

He sighed, as if returning from faraway thoughts. He tented his fingers. "Yes, you may contact the agency tomorrow. I approve of you hiring a companion. You'll need a chaperone while courting."

"Courting? Courted by whom?" Though she suspected such, the words caught her by surprise. "Wait, don't answer. This touches on my second point. I'd like a say on the type of man I believe best for me."

With a wry chuckle and quite cheerfully, Papa reached into the top drawer and took out one sheet of paper which he held up. His shrewd brown gaze met hers over it. "Quaint that you and I both require certain qualities for your suitor, my dear."

Her stomach clenched. She formed the words she'd rehearsed, and rushed into the main thrust of her request. "My highest priority is to marry a believer." Nerves clamped her mouth shut, and she scuttled the entire remainder of the lengthy preamble prepared during her brooding.

A scowl formed on his face. "Daughter, faith is not high at all on my priority list. My top standard for a suitable husband lays in his aristocrat lineage. I want you to become a titled lady. Your refinement lacks nothing other than a title, and I aim to obtain one for you before the year is out."

"Papa, I don't possess any way to gain entrance into the world of the *haute ton*. No avenue even exists for me, as a merchant's daughter, to meet a titled suitor, no matter how long you've dreamt this for me." She regretted the sting of her words. Outrage wouldn't do her case any good.

"This piece of paper tells a different story." He brandished the sheet, waving it at her. "Through confidential channels, an aristocrat who is amenable to wed someone of our status has been identified."

Her father stared across the desk at her. The leashed power of his personality made her quake. She clenched her fists in her lap. "Channels? What? Am I to be dealt out to a man I've never met?"

"No, no. You will, of course, meet the chosen candidate. The first one I deem worthy is Lord Peter Winstead, a marquis. Additional research is to be performed before you are introduced." He leaned back in his chair.

"I shudder to think what you've done to locate this man. I'd rather not find a husband through research."

"Since, as you say, you possess no better alternative to obtain a husband, therefore, no choice, I shall do right by you. Don't worry, Missy."

Wounded by her father's insensitive plan, it took all she the strength could muster not to cry as she'd done in her younger years. She needed every ounce of self-control to respond to her father. Speaking with a soft, measured voice, she tried a humble approach. "Papa, I hope you are sure. For to me it sounds havey-cavey. Not at all *tonnish*."

Could fear of societal scorn shake his certainty? Let her remark hit home.

"Been told firsthand that such arrangements are often done among the *haute ton*, and you needn't worry. I picked a fine young man." He placed the paper on the desk and lined up the edges with precision.

Not only did her father's enthusiasm for his plan not wane, he exuded a hearty, confident ambition, and purpose. He refused to bend to her basic opposition to his plot. To reach his goal of joining the aristocracy via her marriage, he'd let nothing stand in his way.

Her father's determination and her convictions stood in conflict with a probable clash on the horizon. In the shadow of the slim likelihood of getting her way, her other problems paled.

She rose, her clenched hands hidden in the folds of her skirt. "Is that all for now, Papa? I'm late for a dress fitting."

"By all means, you may go now, dear. Make sure

to select some elegant new styles to impress your future husband."

Returning to her suite, it hit her. God's plan required her to obey her father, except unto sin, and honor him. She should not—could not—reject the scheme. At least courting might lift some of the boredom of the endless, quiet days she'd faced since Miss Cleaver's dismissal. And Papa approved the hiring of a companion.

She penned a quick note to the hiring agency. The sooner she began the interviews, the sooner relief from lonely tedium. Lord willing, she would find a woman to provide true companionship.

Fingers pressing her brow, she tried to rub out the knowledge of her father's strategy. But her thoughts flew on ahead, wildly ranging from acceptance to fantasy.

If only the man her father put forward were a believer. She must make peace with the baldly calculated nature of her father's plan.

Her habitual optimism took flight, and she imagined scenarios of how learning whether the candidate would suit. Perhaps she'd catch a glimpse of the man praying, or he'd discuss a sermon, or ask her for her favorite verse.

A muffled knock intruded on her reverie. Expecting the seamstress, she rose from her tufted satin chair to respond. "*Entre!*"

The popular modiste, Madame Olivier, sailed through the door and set down her workbasket. Of indeterminate age, she wore all black with eyes and hair to match. Full of vitality, her vivid personality belied the color. Her eyes snapped and sparkled.

She creaked down into a curtsey. "*Bonjour,*

Mademoiselle Southwood!" Her exuberant voice bordered on a chortle.

Melissa held out one hand. *"Bonjour,* Madame Olivier."

Madame Olivier took the fingers and gave a tentative squeeze combined with the smallest shake.

Another knock on the door, and three footmen entered. They deposited at least thirty bolts of fabric on a large table in the sizeable private sitting room next to her bedroom.

"Enchanté! We shall select fabric here, *non*? And do the fittings here in your suite as well, if that's acceptable?" The modiste stopped speaking and riffled through the bolts waiting for Melissa's assent.

"That is the plan. The sewing, however, will be done at your *salon* as usual." Melissa moved to the table and fingered the edge of a bolt of green silk.

"Have you zee sketches this time?"

"I do, Madame Olivier. We will refer to them later."

The modiste clapped her gloved hands. *"Bon.* Your designs rival zee best."

"I've decided I'll need morning and afternoon dresses, four evening gowns, and a ball gown." Melissa ran her fingers down the stack of fabrics.

"Oui, oui. Merci, Mademoiselle Southwood." The seamstress rubbed one hand over the other, pleased at the large order to come.

Many of the best French modistes were plain Englishwomen. These harmless imposters put on French airs to gain cachet. Though Melissa possessed superior schoolroom French, far be it from her to snicker at Madame Olivier's efforts. The woman's talent and business acumen caused her rise to the pinnacle of London's dressmakers. Pretend-French or not, she was superior.

At the table, Madame Olivier helped Melissa narrow the choices, often referring to Melissa's sketchbook or to pictures in *La Belle Assemblee* to develop ideas. Adding touches to the latest styles, she enjoyed the process.

"Let's begin with the ball gown. Creamy white crepe suits me. Bodice and sleeves of matched satin. A train, I think, not too long, and laurel leaves embroidered down the front of the skirt."

"*Oui, oui.*" Madame Olivier concentrated to keep up with the flow of instructions.

"Embroidery silk the same color as the cloth, but entwined with a bit of gold thread and touched with seed pearls."

"Yes, *tres bien.*"

Melissa pointed to an illustration. "One last thing. Do a square neckline like this but two inches higher." She made this point clear, since in the past she'd battled Madame Olivier, who thought it wise for a woman to display her wares.

Vanquished, the woman merely nodded her assent.

In addition to the creamy white ball gown, she also selected fabrics for evening gowns. One of palest pink taffeta trimmed with satin rosebuds, one of white silk sprigged with green and accented with black velvet ribbon and white Van Dyke lace, another of ivory muslin figured with gold, and an exquisite gown of pale blue with a white lace overskirt.

She loved deciding the details for each gown. Her hobby of sketching and designing frocks gave her mental escape from her father's machinations. She chose a crisp neck ruff called a Betsie to add to one ensemble. For others, she selected stoles, capes, shawls, pelisses, spencer jackets, or fichus. Swatches of each chosen fabric were set aside to match against fans, slippers and reticules to be purchased later at shops in London's warehouse district.

"I love zee suggestions, Mademoiselle Southwood. The dresses will be *c'est belle.*"

Pleased that Madame not only accepted her participation but respected her ideas, she returned a compliment. "Your gowns are always superb and so appropriate. No other modiste approaches your skill with fitting or your flair with style."

Throughout the enjoyable morning, a thread of worry lurked at the back of Melissa's mind. What if Papa's plan became a public embarrassment? As to the timing, she must insist on two months to decide. Also, what if her father rushed in with a second-choice man if she refused the first? So many things to go wrong. She didn't care about the season, but the aristocrats fled to the countryside and absented themselves from London as soon as the season ended. What dregs would be left?

Selecting a large number of dresses required several appointments spread over a week. By the time she was done, she'd ordered twenty ensembles, including the evening gowns and ball gown.

~*~

At the end of the week, Melissa requested the preparation of a food parcel for the seamstress. The kitchen servants filled it with sausages, pies, cheese, and other nutritious comestibles for the woman to take back to the workroom.

As Madame Olivier departed, Melissa herself handed over the basket. "A *petite* something for the salon seamstresses."

"*Merci*, Mademoiselle Southwood. I shall have all the *ensembles* to you within zee month." Madame Olivier promised. Footmen carried out the bolts of fabric, but the modiste carried the basket herself, face wreathed in smiles as she bid Melissa adieu.

As much as Melissa enjoyed choosing fabrics and trim and adding to her wardrobe, a swell of relief at the selection process's completion swept over her. Enough time still would be spent in fittings—those weren't as enjoyable. Though fashion would always be one of her favorite hobbies, charity and service met her yearning for true meaning. So she turned her thoughts to the future days she'd have time to get to her charity work, of helping feed the hungry.

How long would it take for her father's plans to progress? Even though his outlandish approach offended her own sensibilities and spirit, he always kept her best interests at heart. He possessed a knack of receiving what God gave and turning it to a profit as well. No choice but to trust Papa and still hope in God.

After dinner on a tray, and reading, she closed her eyes on another day. She thanked God for upholding her even in this uncertainty about the man who would soon court her. After saying 'amen,' the image of Lord Russell entered her mind. Their few short hours together often danced through her dreams. She'd love the opportunity to see him again if the chance ever arose.

10

Time flew by for Mark during another week of learning to manage the estate. Speeding hours didn't stop the hourly lowering of his mood. A rap came on the study door.

Crabtree stuck his head through the crack, interrupting Mark's glazed-over scrutiny of the tally of grain sacks delivered by the carter. "Sir, Mr. Cleaver's calling."

"Send him in here, please, and bring some tea."

Mr. Cleaver entered the room, and his booming voice came as a shock after the excess of quiet. "How do you fare this fine Saturday, Lord Russell?"

"Enjoying my new life." Mark closed the account books and came around the desk to shake hands. He sat on one of a pair of armchairs and faced the minister who'd sat in the other.

"I perceive you're back to a full measure of health, praise the Lord."

Mark's hands clenched involuntarily. "I am well."

As Mr. Cleaver chatted about neighborhood news, Mark relaxed, deciding no hidden agenda was in play. The minister's next words, however, shot that idea out of the water.

"Are you familiar with God's Word?"

"Only enough to pass my exams. That was like being force-fed medicine."

"How sad. So many scriptures give us direct

inspiration." Mr. Cleaver held up a finger for emphasis. "And are able to change our lives. In fact, there's an important passage from the Bible I'd like to share with you today."

Mark sat back and gripped the arms of the chair. "I'm all ears. After all you've done for me, the least I can do is listen."

Mr. Cleaver cleared his throat. "That if thou shalt confess with thy mouth the Lord Jesus, and shalt believe in thine heart that God hath raised him from the dead, thou shalt be saved. For with the heart man believeth unto righteousness; and with the mouth confession is made unto salvation. For the scripture saith, Whosoever believeth on him shall not be ashamed."

"Unashamed." Mark murmured the words to himself. Incidents from the recent past flashed into his mind. His wild London life wasn't suitable to bring out into the light of day. Alcohol, cheap women, buying on credit, and living in a set of rooms well-known as a place of lewd revelry didn't reflect well on his character.

"Where is that found in the Bible?"

"In the book of Romans, written by the Apostle Paul."

"Do I really need this? After all, what do God's words mean in my life?"

"God's Word is always useful, and it is the Truth. All I ask is that you think about it."

He assented with reluctance. What would it be like to rid himself of the shame that clung to him after the way he lived in London? How else could he aspire to filling his dead brother's honorable shoes? Unwanted emotions plagued him of late. He contained, with difficulty, more sentiments now welling. "That isn't for the likes of me." He lowered his eyes. His chin quivered, and he swept his hand over his jaw to conceal his weakness.

The minister pushed on, unrelenting. "I beg to differ. God's kindness is for all who have been given the gift of faith. God's Word says, 'For by grace are ye saved through faith, and that not of yourselves, it is the gift of God, not of works lest any man should boast.' Lord Russell, all have sinned and fall short of the glory of God. Everyone. If we confess our sins, God is faithful and just to forgive us our sins and cleanse us from all unrighteousness."

"From the Bible, too? Or your personal philosophies?" Mark suspected the answer but perversely insisted on asking.

"Straight from the Word of God, and not merely from my lips. The way to be saved is to repent, to turn away from one's sins and believe in Christ alone as your Savior from sin through His death on the cross." The sound of deep conviction gave the minister's words *gravitas*.

Oh, how sweet would be peace with God, but he found it hard to accept the offered grace. He blurted out the thought that hampered him. "I could never be that good, Mr. Cleaver."

"It is not us who are good, sir. The Bible says that left to ourselves, no one is righteous, no one."

Mark protested. "Then why try?"

"Once we repent and believe, though, we can change with God's help. He helps us to do any bit of good, and as we go on in life, He makes us over into a new person."

"Even me?"

"Yes, you. In other words, only with His aid," the minister pointed upwards with his index finger, "do we get better from the sin-sick, sorry state of spiritual death we are in without him. So, don't let your sinful condition stop you from trusting God." Mr. Cleaver sat back and crossed his legs, as calm as if he were discussing the weather.

"Plenty to think on." Mark crossed his arms across his chest and closed his eyes.

"I shall pray for you now. Try to follow along with me." Mr. Cleaver leaned forward, folded his hands, and bowed his head. "Dear Lord, please accept this man's sorrow over his sins. Please take him as one of Your own and cleanse him from his transgressions. Give him the gift of faith. Change his heart and transfer him from darkness to the light. And bless all Lord Russell's days so he can live to serve You out of gratitude."

"Amen." Mark stood and stepped to a nearby wall mirror. For the first time in too long, he could look himself in the eye. The shame of his former life slipped away and the weight of self-doubt fell off his shoulders. With God's help, maybe he'd do his title justice, and find peace in the process. "We'll have to see what God does with someone like me."

11

The day to interview the candidates for companion arrived. The choice was to be Melissa's own. With this courtship scheme of her father's hanging over her, she needed a confidant. Occupied with grief for her mother, the full impact of her solitude hadn't hit her right away. But now, even though busy, loneliness rose up against her.

The agency lined up five candidates to be interviewed this morning. The first interviewee waited in the hall. Melissa rang the bell. This pre-arranged signal brought the butler to the sitting room door. "Miss Dickson," he intoned.

A woman dressed all in dreary grey and black glided into the room on silent feet. Melissa bade her to sit and offered tea. Drinking tea together was meant to warm up the interaction and give Melissa a sense of each candidate's personality.

Miss Dickson trembled as she accepted the tea, and she proceeded to clutch it on her lap with two hands during the entire interview.

In an attempt to set the woman at ease, Melissa took a sip and chattered of nonessentials for a few minutes before she asked her first question. "Miss Dickson," she glanced down at her notes to make sure of the name, "tell me about your faith."

The woman's wispy eyebrows flew up, and she rushed to answer. "I believe in faith. I go to services as a rule. Every Sunday as a lifelong habit—if I can. It's my tradition."

"Faith is a blessing, Miss Dickson, would you say?" Melissa set down her cup.

"My traditions comfort me." The woman trailed off.

Melissa waited for more, making an encouraging expression. With nothing more forthcoming from dreary Miss Dickson, Melissa decided to move on to the next candidate. One requirement for the companion was that she be a sincere believer.

The next candidate wore a brown dress with a shabby brown pelisse. The butler announced this one as, "Mrs. Croft."

After she served the woman a cup of tea, she began to question. "Mrs. Croft, tell me about your previous experience." Melissa glanced at her notes, which told her the woman was a widow.

The shabby vertical feather on the woman's hat quivered as she spoke. "Aye. My last situation was with the first Mrs. Croft. She died and Mr. Croft, he took a fancy to marry me. Now he's dead and I's at loose ends."

The way the woman presented herself didn't sit well with Melissa, so she only asked a few more courtesy questions. Would the next candidate wear all green?

The next two candidates proved uninspired, too. These two were garbed in a mix of colors, unlike the first two. But with one a flibbertigibbet a mere two years older than Melissa, and the other so ancient as to be hard of hearing, missing most of Melissa's questions, neither fit the position.

Patience and hope were now in short supply, the

morning having turned into an unexpected trial. She rang the bell for the last candidate of the day.

"Miss Dean." The butler ushered in a spry middle-aged woman. She wore a cloak of good fabric dating from the last century. Her tentative smile held a friendly reserve Melissa liked.

She served the requisite tea before the questions and answers commenced. "Do you go to church?" She started right out with an attempt to discern Miss Dean's faith.

"Oh yes." Miss Dean's eyes lit up. "I love going to God's house. My life would be dross without him." She lifted two fingers to her lips and shot a worried glance at Melissa.

"Wonderful. Tell me more about yourself, Miss Dean. Do you enjoy needlework?" Melissa smiled encouragement to the best candidate of the morning.

"Oh my. Yes. I'm an inveterate knitter. I also make lace and embroider." The woman visibly relaxed and gave an abbreviated history of her life with her minister father who'd recently passed away. "And that brings me to now. I am alone in the world and thought a position as companion to a young lady suitable to my abilities."

The two launched into an enjoyable discussion in which Melissa learned all she needed about Miss Sarah Dean.

"I shall contact the agency immediately. You're hired." Her protracted solitude caused by her father's angry dismissal of Miss Cleaver was over. At his lowest ebb, he'd lashed out bitter words at the governess, chastising her for her steadfast faith. Melissa breathed a sigh of relief. Miss Dean accepted the position and agreed to move in that afternoon.

A Match for Melissa

Interviews over and companion hired, Melissa's worry bloomed anew about her father's scheme. Her fears mounted by the hour. The day was coming, however, when she was certain he would force the next phase of his plans.

12

Melissa's expert management of the Southwood household continued. She also partook of typical feminine pursuits. But not content to fritter away her whole life with fashion, embroidery, sketching, watercolor painting, and poetry, she took an active interest in charity work and read the Bible and other literature. Even with all this, however, she was not fulfilled. Her life consisted of an endless stretch of days.

At least Papa shared his plans of what was to come—giving fair warning. She must be grateful for small favors. As she sat alone in the private sitting room off her bedroom, she tried to convince herself of the plausibility of her father's plan to find an acceptable or even admirable man to put forward as a match.

Reality's touch was sometimes harsh and full of unexpected difficulties and obstacles. What if no natural affection flourished between her and the aristocrat her father planned to proffer? Would the man share her depth of faith? Questions circled in her mind until she decided she mustn't belabor the dilemma. Worry didn't profit.

A tap came upon her door. The upper housemaid handed her a note which contained a request for her to attend her father in his study in five minutes. Nervous, Melissa checked her appearance in the mirror. She scolded her shaking knees, straightened her shoulders, took several deep breaths, and descended the stairs to meet with her father.

She entered the massive oak-laden library and immediately observed her father's normally cheery countenance wore a guarded mask. She wondered at the reason.

She stood before him, hands clasped on one hip. "Papa, here I am. Is there news of your scheme—I mean plan—to find me a husband?"

"Dear girl, must you be so direct? The nobility requires more discretion in their females. When I deem it, you will learn all." Mr. Homer Southwood hated to lose control of any meeting.

He tugged at his collar and ran a finger around the offensive neckpiece. "My valet can't tie a simple knot."

This avoidance maneuver did not deter Melissa.

She flung out a hand in entreaty. "Papa, please relieve my suspense. Have you decided on the man or not?"

"The answer is yes, Melissa. The investigation of your suitor is complete. His name is Lord Peter Winstead. Sources brought to my attention his amenability to marry, outside the ton if necessary, to restore his fortunes, diminished by unavoidable family circumstances which were no fault of his own. His estate is called Honor's Point and is reputed to be a garden spot of beauty. Thus, I asked you to attend me here, daughter. He is to call on us this afternoon at four o'clock."

"On *us*?" Melissa inquired as she sank into an armchair across from the desk.

"Yes. First, he will appear before me here in my library. In fact, I myself shall interview Lord Winstead to confirm his suitability, followed by him either crossing the hall to meet you or being sent out the front door."

Nervous, yet somewhat reassured by this statement, she smoothed her hair with the tips of her fingers. She hoped her father didn't allow his blind ambition to rule him to the extent that he would abandon proper discretion even further.

Melissa chose an attitude of suspended opinion until she got a gander of the man and an opportunity to evaluate him. Her father's ambition blinded him to other, softer considerations. She kneaded her temples.

The thought of being married for her family's fortune didn't appeal even though in this day and age it occurred quite often in the upper reaches of society. Fortunes, property, and titles were joined thus, and not a lot different from a business deal in many instances. Love and respect for one's spouse didn't form the basis of the average upper-class marriage.

"Tell me what you learned, please, Papa. I am curious about a man who would, in essence, sell himself." Melissa leaned back in the comfortable armchair.

Mr. Southwood didn't answer immediately but swiveled in his chair to gaze out the window onto the attractive, small side yard—thirty feet wide or so—generous by London townhouse standards.

Melissa supposed he was weighing how much to reveal to her and what matters to leave unsaid. She knew him well and could read him like a book.

While her father's gaze was off her, Melissa closed her eyes. *God, I put this whole situation into your hands. Please help me respond to this trial reflecting Christ's love.*

When her father started speaking, she sat up

straighter so as not to miss a word.

"He's not got a lot of blots on his copybook, unlike some of the other ne'er-do-wells I crossed off the list. Simply needs to marry well since his sire died. His father mortgaged the family estates to the hilt, and at the same time, ran the estate itself down to a nub. Several years of excellent management should bring the estate, Honor's Point, back into good heart. Lord Winstead appears, to all accounts, to be upstanding enough, besides residing in dun territory."

"What about age, Papa? Also, 'upstanding enough' does not reassure me. You do recall my hope is to marry a man of faith, which I don't consider too much to ask."

"By upstanding, I mean all evidence shows him to be moral and upright. He attends worship services on occasion, doesn't drink, gamble, or dally with the demi-monde. And he's in his late twenties.

"Well, I am grateful you found someone who seems to be a possibility. For now, I shall retire to my rooms." Melissa's stood. She had no peace about this, and wouldn't until she met for herself the kind of man her father put forward.

Before she turned to leave, she indicated her cooperation. "Later this afternoon, I'll appear at the proper time and place, as you deemed, and await you and Lord Peter Winstead." Courage infused her now, but would her spirit be sustained?

At ten minutes to four, she sat in the drawing room with Miss Dean, waiting for the momentous introduction. Pluck and nerve were in short supply, but her training stood her in good stead. *No one should have to go through this.*

Miss Dean's pleasant face wore an expression of

both sympathy and encouragement. The companion reached across and patted Melissa's hand. "My, your hands are cold. Shall I fetch your gloves?"

Before she could respond, the butler opened the door and admitted Melissa's father. He swept into the room, waved his arm in a grand and cheery gesture which indicated his guest should now enter. "M'dear, this is Lord Peter Winstead, come to meet you."

A pair of sparkly blue eyes found Melissa's before the gentleman moved forward to take her hand. He bowed over it and lifted it, placing upon it the lightest of air kisses.

Melissa snatched her hand away but recovered her composure and smiled up through her lashes. She took in as much of his debonair appearance as possible while avoiding outright staring at his attractive, masculine face and form.

Tall, with curly black hair cut in the latest windswept style and dark blue eyes, he was a sight to enjoy.

"How do you do, Miss Southwood?"

"Fine, sir," she answered as heat suffused her cheeks. *I must look like a radish*.

"Now you young folks become acquainted. I'll be back in twenty minutes to see you out, Lord Winstead."

The twenty-minute limit showed Papa still intended to be her protector. He would not allow improper access to his daughter even for a titled suitor. Her father left the room, humming.

Miss Dean scampered over to a seat in a corner on the far side of the room and raised her knitting from her lap. Her eyes on her work, the needles soon clacked.

"This is dashed awkward, Miss Southwood," he began, in a soft voice. "I hope you aren't completely averse to my suit? For I am not here on a whim."

"Do sit down." She indicated a nearby chair, suddenly nervous. "Not on a whim, you say?" The babbling seemed to have no effect on him.

"Not a whim at all. I'd like to court you with hopes of matrimonial alliance."

My heart is fluttering. Not a bad sensation. This was a challenge. Was it possible to retain her serenity and peace while being courted by this attractive suitor?

~*~

Relief coursed through Lord Peter Winstead's body when he first spied Miss Southwood as he entered the room. Any qualms were put to rest after a sight of her. *It will be a pleasure courting this dazzler. It could have been much worse.*

Winstead, pressured since he hadn't much time, reminded himself that faint heart wouldn't capture a fair lady. To meet his deadlines, the courtship must begin immediately. No mistakes. *Please, let her like me.* He hoped there was someone up there listening, but he wasn't so sure.

Mr. Southwood explained to him in their meeting that his daughter had some say in the choice of husband. After a two-month courtship elapsed, if she didn't find Winstead acceptable and had a good reason for a rejection, Mr. Southwood would move on to other candidates.

It was up to Peter. *I have to win her. If she takes me, I promise to treat her well.* Again, he hoped someone heard his pleas for help.

She wore a frothy white day dress, with a pink sash and pink silk shawl, which set off her creamy, porcelain complexion. As for her hair, the glistening golden mass lay restrained at the back of her neck in a sleek chignon, but wavy strands framed her classically pretty face. A refreshing trace of minty fragrance wafted from her direction. *She's lovely.*

"Would you honor me by taking a drive with me tomorrow? Is half past three acceptable?" He angled himself toward her and leaned forward, full of smiling entreaty. She'd probably like him to be humble.

His good fortune swept over him and landed in his throat as a lump. A beauty with a healthy settlement—large enough to bail him out of all his financial woes and save Honor's Point—the place he loved more than anything in the world.

She twisted a fan between her fingers. "Indeed, sir, a drive sounds delightful. Yes, I shall like above all things to go on a carriage ride tomorrow."

She exhaled as if she'd been holding her breath. The line on her forehead dissolved and her shoulders relaxed. She must be relieved as well. As well she ought. She should be happy with the attractive picture he presented. He had no doubt about his appeal to females. Several aristocratic heiresses dropped their handkerchiefs for him, but their fathers proved disagreeable.

Inconsequential chatter ensued. When Mr. Southwood returned, he gave permission for the drive and Lord Winstead bowed over his intended's hand, deposited another airy kiss, and departed.

He strolled away, a spring in his steps. Her fair face and form were a bonus not to be dismissed lightly. Her money would scatter the duns and save his beloved estate. Freedom from want was near.

13

The next day's drive through Hyde Park at the fashionable hour went off without a hitch. The open carriage did not require Melissa to be chaperoned, which allowed the courting couple to ride alone. Winstead enjoyed Melissa's company, and the eyes of the ton were upon them. He'd been snubbed here and there over the years he'd been on the town, when young ladies and their parents learned of his financial predicament. Now society's tabbies ogled him in the park with a beauty at his side, and until they discovered her identity, speculation would flow.

They wouldn't miss the fact that he drove out with a young lady for the first time since the possible loss of his estate somehow became the subject of public gossip. Rumors would soon mount up like a pile of trash. He'd keep her away from them, so they couldn't spoil his chances with their vitriol.

Later, at the club, he was confronted by two acquaintances.

The first one, a homely dandy in high collars and a mustard-colored vest, chortled a request. "Winstead, give me the straight story. I want to place a bet."

The other man, mature but wearing tight pantaloons, piped up. "There are fine odds about whether you'll step into parson's mousetrap with the Southwood chit."

Surprised his lady friend's name was already

public, Peter raised his eyebrows in feigned nonchalance but clenched his fists behind his back to put a rein on his temper. "It fascinates me that some don't pursue more worthwhile things."

He did not savor being the subject of any gossip, but he'd remain civil. The less said, the better. "I can only hope to win her favor and her heart." He pasted a smile on his face and brushed past the men, heading for the door. Why must these buffoons mix into his affairs?

Before he made his exit, another 'friend' stopped him. "Say, you've finally found a young lady willing to ignore your sad lack of funds? Leg-shackled to a merchant's daughter. Never thought I'd see the day." The man, not even a close associate, snorted a laugh, which held the clear tone of insult.

"So you say. Good day." Winstead steeled himself not to answer this rude sally with violence, moved past the offensive man, collected his hat and cane from a footman, and then departed the club, sorry he'd even gone there.

To shield Miss Southwood from wicked tongues, as well as to protect his own suit, he avoided any future interactions with the *bon ton*. On subsequent carriage drives with her, he eschewed the fashionable hour and kept up a fast enough clip to avoid any stops to chat with nosy acquaintances.

She was a sweet girl. No angling for operas, plays, or parties. He escorted his intended instead on excursions to the Tower, to Astley's Circus, and several times to the famous Gunter's for ices. On most other days, he took her driving. A nod, a smile, and a lift of a hand or hat served to deflect the curiosity of the meddlesome tabbies of the ton.

~*~

He invited the Southwoods to visit Honor's Point, his ancestral home. The ambitious two-day journey might tax his resources, but he counted on the estate's renowned beauty to help win the young lady's assent. The Southwoods and Miss Dean rode in the family's traveling carriage with Peter on horseback alongside. As they neared the estate, his heart beat faster, the old familiar spell again cast over him as the group traveled roads which ascended through dense woods before emerging on the elm-lined drive to Honor's Point. The massive trees formed an arch overhead and framed the first view of his beloved hilltop manor. Pride welled as he imagined the good impression made by the house's balanced façade of mellow stone and twin, arched exterior stairs leading to a massive front door.

Several nights into the visit, he found himself alone on the terrace with Miss Southwood at twilight. The group wandered out through a set of French doors, and Mr. Southwood and Miss Dean stood about twenty-five feet away. Miss Dean's eagle eyes were on him, but he would bet a Yellowboy neither could hear him.

"Do you see why I love this place?" Peter asked quietly and seized the moment to grasp and loosely hold Miss Southwood's hand.

She didn't pull away, and her answer gave him hope. "It is the finest property I've ever had the privilege of visiting. I plan to take my paints and easel out tomorrow."

"You paint?" He put as much interested rapture into his voice as he thought he could get away with.

A Match for Melissa

He'd watch her paint for hours if it would make her want to marry him.

"I dabble. To capture this exquisite place on canvas shall be an enjoyable challenge for my paltry skills."

"Since you like the place, can you envision yourself as its mistress?" Peter stroked her hand with his thumb as he spoke and stared into her eyes.

She withdrew her hand from his. She intertwined her own fingers and began to wring them. "Liking it here doesn't equal wanting to be its mistress. I don't dislike the idea, but for now, I shall hold the possibilities in abeyance, if you don't mind."

Struggling to keep his face calm, Peter responded with all the lightness he could muster. "And I'll hold the possibilities close to my heart." He placed his lightly-clenched fist against his breast and gave her a rueful smile. Taking her elbow, he guided her indoors, chatting about the features of the house.

The trip bore ambiguous results. Back in London after the visit, Peter didn't try to deceive himself or her. True love had not been found. He liked Miss Southwood, didn't object to her person, and indeed, he admired her the more he learned about her throughout his determined courtship. Yet, he cared for her as he would for a sister. He'd always expected to conceive a grand passion for a marriageable miss before pursuing matrimony. In his heart, he admitted the ineffable missing piece of his relationship with Melissa was the spark romantic love gives a courting couple. *But I'll give that up to save Honor's Point. And I will be good to her.*

Since his financial needs were no secret to her, putting on the pretense of love was beneath him, and he'd not sink to pretending. He refused to play his hand as if he loved her and didn't think she'd believe it anyway. No, she'd been aware from the start he was at low financial tide, and she accepted the courtship because her father had ambitions for her to marry a title. For a father to select a spouse for his child was common enough in high society.

~*~

Though lonely and quiet, Mark's days went well in the weeks after his watershed experience with Mr. Cleaver. The manor ran without many problems because James, the prior Lord Russell, had been a fine landowner and left matters in good order. Mark didn't have to sort out James's family affairs, either. His widow liked Russell Manor well enough while her husband lived, of course, but she'd always been attached to her childhood home. Soon after James's passing, Lady Russell removed with her three daughters, eager to rejoin her aged parents at their family home. She desired to live her widowhood with reduced responsibilities and made an amicable departure prior to his arrival in Russelton.

No dishonest steward, no thieving housekeeper, or devious butler complicated his new routine. In fact, most of the staff belonged to Reverend Cleaver's flock—sincere, kind people. The whole estate, inside and out, held an atmosphere and tone of pleasant harmony—a balm to Mark's newly-healed soul and spirit.

Ensconced in a sumptuous tufted leather armchair, he ruminated over the change in his circumstances. The hush of the manor's richly-appointed library suited deep thinking, and he absently jiggled a fob on his watch chain. Since he'd recovered from the attack, his new, sober, and happily virtuous life fit him well. He now understood how God used the attack to get his attention and bring him to a place of spiritual need—a place where he would listen. Gratefulness overwhelmed him.

Entrenched as the new lord of the manor at Russell House, he had to stop and shake himself. The good life he now possessed provided a strong contrast to how he lived little more than one month ago. He fought back guilt about how his blessings came upon the tail of the death of his elder brother.

He reminded himself that an accident took his brother's life, and not him.

At the library's French doors, he pushed the velvet curtain aside. His gaze fell upon the beautiful lawn stretching out toward a lake. The vivid greens of spring beckoned him, and he stepped through the doors out onto the terrace.

A few dozen long strides took him to the lawn, and he walked to a nearby clump of trees. Under them, placed to catch the afternoon shade, stood a stone bench with a choice of views. Its placement took in the beautiful lake or the impressive manor.

He flicked out the tails of his coat, and then plunked down, facing the house. The warm, mellow stone mansion glowed in the sunlight. Sparkly panes winked, and the brick facing trim around the many windows lent a jaunty air to its façade.

For all its charm and roominess, it was a lonesome place.

It needed a family.

He shot up off the bench and paced. *Where did that thought come from?*

The future of marriage, wife, children, and a family of his own never burst upon his consciousness in the past. Yearnings for domesticity took him aback. His bright new life was unsullied by his former immorality, committed to the straight and narrow. But, out of nowhere it occurred to him no obstacle prevented him from setting up his nursery. He'd need an heir, so why not think about finding a bride?

Elbows on knees, he stroked his chin, deep in thought. His responsibility to the estate required him to provide an heir, and as soon as possible. If he took part in the London season and searched about for a wife, the timing might work. He calculated he would be out of mourning and able to be married two months after the end of the season. The urgency for an heir excused the lack of a lengthier mourning.

A nearby statue of a cherub appeared to rise out of a sea of rosebushes. A flash of memory intruded. He pleasantly remembered how she bent over him, touching his shoulder, and gave him water. She was a pure and kind young woman. The sweet recollection reminded him of how much she'd seemed like a ministering angel. Could one fall in love with such a paragon? One met while half-conscious and in a fog of pain?

He snapped back to practical details. The proprieties of mourning of course. With his changed life, travel and disruption didn't appeal to him. But urgent anxiety nagged him. An anxiety that pulsed as though, if he didn't get there soon—he might miss something—or someone important.

London. I must go to London.

14

"Crabtree!" Mark called as he broke into a trot. He entered the same way he'd come out and hurried past his desk, out into the hall where the butler dozed on a padded seat near the front door.

"Crabtree, see me in the library post haste."

He turned back and re-entered the library. He stood behind the desk, waiting for Crabtree to shuffle in. The hushed, yet expectant atmosphere of this room inspired him to action. He shuffled through the stack of mail, attention arrested by an envelope with the address in feminine, loopy script. He opened it and read.

"... and so, nephew, I implore you to visit me this spring. I will prepare a room for you and keep all your favorite foods on hand. I await your answer. Love, Aunt Lucy"

A visit to his aunt was the answer. He'd accept his aunt's invitation. His favorite relative, she was a socialite widow who resided in London. The middle-aged widow's full *entrée* to the ton world abetted his plans. He'd be included in her invitations, and she'd facilitate introductions, since Mark, in the past, always avoided the circles in which marriageable young ladies moved.

He set down the letter and tapped his foot in impatience. Now that he'd decided on a course of action, he was eager to commence. Spring and early summer in London provided the setting for the marriage mart. This year's season was already in full swing, and he didn't want to wait to find a wife. He'd take assertive measures amidst the London season, and at least attempt to solve his loneliness and need for an heir.

Mark was glad the social functions of upper crust society revolved solely around the business of matching young ladies and gentlemen, now that he was on the hunt for a wife. Properties and bloodlines were allied, and the occasional love match occurred as well.

A creak from a floorboard broke into his musings. "Crabtree, pack for the season in London. I will leave in two days, assuming you can get the bags packed in time?"

"Yes, m'lord. What are your requirements as for vehicle?"

"My best traveling carriage."

Crabtree bowed and left the library, rushing off to begin the master's travel preparations.

He wrote his aunt in London. Next, he sent for the steward. Mark gave instructions for several current projects and for the estimated duration of his absence.

The meeting with the steward complete, Mark knew what to do next.

He bowed his head, folded his hands, and bent over the oak desk to lay his concerns before God. Mr. Cleaver impressed upon him how the Christian life involved calling upon God's wisdom for one's life decisions.

"Father in Heaven, thank You for my new life. I don't deserve any of this, but please bless my wife-seeking. I implore You to guide me to the right young lady. And, Lord, please give me safe travel this time. I even thank You for my last trip when I was attacked and robbed, because I now believe that all things do work together for good. Amen."

Ready to move forward with his life, peace settled over him leaving him refreshed. For two days, he visited tenants and checked on a few projects on the estate.

Mark departed the manor after luncheon on the second day and joined the coachman on the seat, eager to take the reins for the first leg of the journey. He'd drive part of the sixty-mile distance to London.

But first, a stop at the vicarage to say good-bye.

Mr. Cleaver emerged from the front door as the carriage pulled to a stop in front of the dwelling.

Mark hopped down and grabbed Mr. Cleaver's hand for a good, firm shake. The men shared spiritual kinship, but even that didn't permit any but stoic and masculine farewells.

"I am, ahem, eternally grateful for all you've done." Mark's sincerity laced every word. He schooled his features to fight back emotion. "I shall depend on your prayers and call on your advice if any spiritual matters arise. For now, I bid you farewell." He mounted the bench and drove toward his future.

The rhythm of the horses soothed him, and he mulled over the qualities he desired in a wife. First, she must share his faith in God. Several additional traits rose up in his mind as he covered the miles and daydreamed about his future bride, whoever she may be. He'd want her to have good character, beauty, personality, and health.

He'd come across an extraordinary verse that very morning, "If any of you lacks wisdom, he should ask of

God, Who gives generously to all." He repeated it to himself now and let the promise sink into his being. He wanted wisdom more than anything.

He planned to use discretion in the choice of a wife when he arrived in London. Even though he'd been a believer for a short time, he already grasped how specifics sometimes had to be left in God's hands. A vision of the angelic blonde from the vicarage entered his mind. Would that he'd find someone like her, or even the angel herself. If only that were possible.

~*~

"Lord Russell. What a pleasant surprise." His widowed aunt sat near the fireplace in her comfortable sitting room.

Mark crossed the room in a few long strides. "Dear Aunt." Happy to see his favorite relative, he bowed over her hand. He straightened up and pulled her into a gentle embrace. "Now give me a proper hug."

Aunt Lucy gave him a playful smack on the arm with her fan. "Let me go, you young pup!" The lighthearted interaction reminded him why he loved her.

"Do be seated." He settled into an armchair covered in yellow striped silk. "So glad you're here as the time of your arrival was anybody's guess." She raised her brows in mock reproach. "Will you bide here at my house as invited?"

"I decided to stay at the club, but I shall be in your pocket." He reassured her of his intentions to spend time with her.

An assessing expression covered his aunt's face.

She looked him up and down as if she sensed a difference. She, however, hadn't changed. Around her mid-forties, she was still an attractive woman bedecked with a kindhearted air.

She gave him another tap with her fan. "Dear boy, you staying at your club's quite all right. Now catch me up with all that's transpired since you inherited the title and headed home to Russelton."

"Certainly. You're in for a tale." Mark regaled her with an account of the attack on the road outside Russelton.

"My boy!" Her soft voice rose to a squawk and she clutched her chest. "Were you targeted? How scandalous for a robbery to occur on your ancestral doorstep, so to speak."

"It appeared to be a random attack. The magistrate is on high alert and has swept the area several times, vigilant for strangers. He's come up empty thus far. I hope they catch the scoundrels before anyone else has to suffer what I did."

He brought her up to date with his move to the manor and assuming the title. "It's all well and good to inherit a fine estate, but dash it all, it's a sore spot with me that my brother had to die for me to gain this blessing. There's more to tell, however, about what transpired after my descent into the ditch."

"More than gaining a title and being robbed? I must have some more tea. Would you care for a cup?" Aunt Lucy poured a cup of hot tea for him from the pot at hand, before topping off her own cup. She held his cup out toward him. "There. Go on."

Mark took a sip of the fragrant lemon spice tea and gathered his thoughts. "Aunt, I wouldn't be honest if I didn't include the fact I have been renewed not only in health but also in my faith."

Her cup clattered into its saucer. "Your faith?"

"Why so baffled and surprised?" He carefully set down his own cup. "After the attack, I began to understand I needed a change in my life. And God worked faith in my heart. He changed me. Prior to that, I lived my life on a direct path to destruction and in a state of spiritual death." Pausing, he gave her a chance to take it in. He hoped she understood. Not ashamed of his beliefs, that didn't mean he was used to conversing about them.

"I approve with my whole heart." Aunt Lucy tapped her fingers in the region of her heart and arched her brows. "You do seem much happier. I must admit I am quite pleasantly taken by surprise."

She took another sip of tea and fell silent. Relieved with her favorable response, Mark wondered what more she would say about his revelations. He waited for her next words.

"My boy, I am glad for you. Many of your scrapes reached my ears. Yes, numerous were the tales that came my way." She raised her brows again and gave him a rueful smile. "If faith in God can help you to lead a happy and upright life, I'm pleased for you. You won't find any criticism from this quarter."

"Thank you, Aunt Lucy. You are one of the few I've told."

"Perhaps I shall dust off my own beliefs. I'll admit to being caught up in London life these past years and not paid the proper amount of attention to faith matters that used to interest me."

"Aunt, I have an idea. Starting this Sunday, I will call for you in my carriage and take you along with me to church. And barring other plans, we can lunch together and discuss the sermon."

She agreed to the plan, and since she'd been such a sympathetic ear thus far, he decided to wade into a discussion of his marital inclinations. He had to tell someone, and Aunt Lucy was a good listener.

"I hied up to London because of my need to find a wife. Not any milk and water miss will do. I want a like-minded bride who shares my faith. Are you aware of any suitable young ladies?"

"Funny, I heard a curious tale the other day. But, I only give half an ear to servant's gossip. Let me think." Aunt Lucy paused and cast her eyes up to the ceiling as if the information were written there. "Seems some merchant, can't rightly recollect the name, but he's one of those who rival Golden Ball, has a daughter he's trying to puff off to a title. Something rings a bell in my memory that her family did a lot of churchgoing before the mother died suddenly a while back. She may be of like mind to you. What about her? You are titled now, and it sounds like you might fit the bill."

"Aunt, I hardly want to be wed for my title, and I don't need this man's money, whoever he is. Besides, you don't even have her name."

"Yes, of course. Silly of me to mention that tattered little piece of gossip. Take your pick of one of the young ladies in this year's crop of debutantes. If I get word of any girl with a religious bent, I shall report to you immediately."

"Your optimism is kind, Aunt, but I am not a great catch. I'll do what I can."

Mark departed his aunt's company after another hug and a promise to call soon. He headed back to his club, eager for some rest—not for the cards, innuendo, and drink, which he would have pursued in the not-so-distant past. The desire and craving for alcohol's effects were removed. A dissipated life held no attraction anymore, and he possessed freedom as never before.

He entered the comfortable men's domain of the first-floor lounge at the club. He nodded to the footman who held out a newspaper to him. He took the paper over to an armchair and sat. The afternoon sun from the window behind his chair provided adequate natural light to read by.

At first, he was the only one in the lounge. Then two other members entered and began an innocent-sounding conversation after they flopped down several chairs over from where he was obscured by the open newspaper.

"I say—any news about Winstead? Is he out of dun territory yet?" one voice queried.

"There's been no announcement yet. I'd say the Southwood fortune is not as easy pickings as many thought. The betting lists are mounting."

"What ho, gents? Are you bringing matrimonial tittle-tattle into these hallowed halls?" Mark lowered his newspaper to join the conversation. *Southwood's the last name of my angelic young lady rescuer.* After meeting Miss Southwood at the vicarage, Miss Cleaver told him so much more—enough to fix the name in his mind. Mark gave a chummy smile and approached the two men who were distant relatives and long-time acquaintances.

Lord Denis Ambruster and Sir Giles Walsh greeted Mark.

"So, you're back in London, Lord Russell. Surprised you're back so soon after you departed to ascend to your title." Fond of stating the obvious, Armbruster stroked his mustache.

These two older men were inveterate gossips, and Mark hoped they were reliable sources.

The three men reseated themselves in closer proximity to each other. Mark proceeded to feed them some pieces of news, mainly estate talk. After a suitable amount of time passed this way, he worked the conversation back around to what he had heard. To hear the Southwood name here filled him with curiosity.

"Do I hear Winstead is hovering about a young lady?" Mark vaguely recalled the man's name, but his true interest lay only in what they had to say about the young lady. Asking the two gossipy gentlemen didn't raise eyebrows. After all, a prime piece of tittle-tattle ran a fast course, and they all traveled in the same circles. Mark sat back to listen to whatever they'd share.

"Harrumph. Yes, he has seemingly landed on his feet in the honeypot. He's the odds-on favorite to marry the Southwood fortune...er, I mean daughter."

"Really, Giles? When is the happy day?"

"Can't say an announcement has come out to that effect. But all word is that he is close to coming to the point. He must repair his fences, because his sire, rest his soul, ran the family fortunes down to nothing, and none of the current debutantes, or more likely their fathers, will drop the handkerchief for him. His looks and title might have done it for him another year, but this season's crop of young ladies did not produce the needed blunt for him."

Sir Giles Walsh stopped speaking and rummaged in his pockets. He produced a pipe and began to prepare a bowl.

Lord Armbruster continued the tale in a deep,

carrying voice. "After the first two balls, Winstead saw how the wind was blowing. Not a chit leaning his direction. So when word got out about the merchant who sought to marry his daughter into the aristocracy..." Armbruster waggled his eyebrows.

Enough. He hated for Miss Southwood to be the subject of gossip.

"I'm late for an appointment. Must run. But good to see you again." Mark rose, bowed, and then departed the club.

He needed to think. As he walked away, he thought over the gossip and compared it to what his aunt told him. The story revolved around his lovely rescuer, the young lady who found him in the ditch and ran for help. One and the same Miss Southwood. The very one who'd briefly nursed him and about whom Miss Cleaver told delightful stories which served to pique his interest.

His mind cast back to those golden hours at the vicarage. He remembered pleasurably the pretty girl hovering over him as he went in and out of consciousness. He whispered the name of the vision of loveliness he daydreamed of on his sickbed at the vicarage and ever since. "Melissa." The name held such refreshment.

Surely the gossip of her father seeking an aristocrat to marry her qualified as something to investigate. No coincidence in hearing of this specific and promising-sounding wife prospect twice. First from his aunt, and then also at the club.

Neither the fortune nor even the great beauty enticed Mark as much as the fine character and purity woven into Miss Cleaver's stories. Miss Southwood sounded like a young woman with a passion for the faith matching his—the sort of wife he wanted now he recognized the need for a helpmeet.

As head of an estate with dozens of livelihoods dependent on him, he needed a wife. Since he'd been converted, he read the Bible every day. By the time he'd reached the second chapter of Genesis, he'd come across a passage which explained how God gave Adam a helper. *Yes, a 'suitable helper.' That's what I need.*

His rapid thoughts coalesced into a plan of action.

15

Mark rapped on the door, using the heavy knocker on the thick oak portal of the Southwood's townhouse. He straightened his cravat one last time, and then handed his visiting card to the starchy butler who answered. After an examination of the card, the butler adjusted his facial expression from one of simmering suspicion to one which exuded the unlikely combination of haughty pride and meekness.

"Right this way, m'lord." The butler took Mark's hat, gloves, and cane. Then he inclined his head, indicating he should sit. He moved down the hall at a measured pace, rapped on a distant door, and entered.

Soon, the butler returned and ushered Mark into the ornate library that doubled as Mr. Southwood's at-home office. Well-polished oak, gleaming brass, and spotless leaded-glass windows established a wealthy glow to the room.

The two men faced each other, and Mark got the impression his measure was being taken. Southwood might or might not have any idea of why he was here. Oh, well, Mark had naught to hide.

After a handshake, they sat, and Southwood leaned back in his chair behind his massive desk, and Mark perched on a chair on the other side of the wide desktop. Southwood folded his hands across his ample front.

Mark didn't expect Southwood to be gentle with

him—there was no need. Mark supposed he was only one of quite a few candidates for both the daughter and the accompanying fortune. Society's buzz said Southwood was confident that Winstead would succeed in his courtship.

Mark thought the man pleasant enough, but better not to underestimate such an expert businessman. A sense of supplication swept over him, and he found he didn't mind humility in this case since the goal was sweet.

"Let's cut to the chase, Lord Russell. Why are you here?" The man smiled and leaned forward. Mark understood himself to be in the presence of a busy man. "I'm sparing you a few minutes between appointments. Perhaps your call will be a moment's relief from my life of monotonous business doings, which grind on day after day and pile up more and more gold in my accounts."

"I'll be happy to get right down to matters, Mr. Southwood." Mark steeled himself against the embarrassment wriggling up from the soles of his feet. "Word has come my way, since I arrived in town yesterday, that you are arranging a titled match for your daughter. I would like to be considered."

"I suspected this to be your reason for the call." With a firm, but kind tone, he put down Mark's hopes. "Gratified, I'm sure, Russell. But my business sense didn't fail me in this endeavor. The nobleman chosen for the opportunity to court my daughter has proved to be a prime goer with an announcement for the papers soon. So, you are approximately," Southwood paused, making a show of referring to a calendar, "two months late. I will keep your name on file. We have nothing more to say to each other."

Rising, and then bowing in silence, Mark turned and left the room ready to grab his things and get out. *That was embarrassing. And abrupt.*

The snooty butler? Nowhere. He hurried down the hall, anxious to retrieve his hat, cane, and gloves, and be gone. Disappointment and frustration welled within, and he would take a brisk walk to shake off the hopes so ruthlessly dashed. But movement caught his eye through an open door on his right. It was a woman, sitting near a window.

Light poured in the window and outlined the breathtaking sight—an exquisite young lady. As though drawn by an invisible cord, he stood in the doorway. According to the strictures of noble etiquette, he shouldn't enter the room, but he could stand here a moment, with propriety served by the open door.

Miss Southwood. Glorious, slim neck held in a beautiful posture, her classic profile angled down over her embroidery piece. The light coming in the window backlit her face.

The noble, perfect nose, the brow that spoke without words of the intelligence within, and the crown of glinty gold hair made his hands itch to touch it. All these components rivaled each other for prominence, and he reveled in the presence of a beauty of historical proportions.

~*~

Melissa started and dropped her needlework. She scrabbled for it and clutched it in a clump to her chest. She stared back at the masculine creature standing just inside the doorway.

The man's fine looks were striking, yet familiar.

A Match for Melissa

But it was more the suddenness of a youngish man appearing before her that stunned her. His presence made her heart beat faster, and all he did was stand there.

With Lord Winstead a foregone conclusion, thus it came as a complete surprise to her she would encounter another young man, especially one who looked familiar. The strong shafts of sunlight glared, blotting out detail.

"Who...are you?" She stammered a bit, lacking her usual composure. And why was he here? She wanted to ask but held her tongue.

The man in the doorway stood over six feet tall and looked muscular. The white inexpressibles he wore hugged his thighs until disappearing into his shining Hessian boots. His subdued black tailcoat, snowy shirt, and cravat were immaculate.

As he took several steps into the room, she could see him clearly now. It was Lord Russell. His sea-blue eyes, high-planed cheekbones and lightly-tanned skin were a pleasure to behold. Crowned by a head of light brown sun-kissed wavy hair that obeyed the dictates of fashion as if it fell obediently on its own into the stylish mode of the times. She wanted to drink in the sight of him all day.

"Miss Southwood, don't be afraid. I came here to meet with your father on, ahem, a business matter and passed the door. I spotted you and had to take this chance to pay my compliments."

~*~

Mark made his bow from about six feet away from the young lady. She would have no way to make sense of how and why he had appeared in her drawing room. He didn't want to scare her.

The palpable sweetness of her presence floored him. This was the girl of his dreams. He could see that now. During his recuperation at the vicarage, she'd tended him while he slipped in and out of consciousness. He daydreamed about this young lady. Miss Cleaver told stories about this particular girl. At the time, he'd no idea she was the daughter of a wealthy merchant, nor that her father was after an aristocratic suitor—if only he'd been aware sooner.

Mark scrambled to improvise conversation and hoped she wasn't about to send him on his way. "Do you remember me? I'm Lord Russell, the unfortunate victim you found in the ditch near Russelton."

"Of course, I remember you." Demure, she neatened her knitting. "Don't you remember me calling on you with Mr. Cleaver?"

"How could I forget? Daffodils, I believe. Isn't it amazing, your Miss Cleaver and I residing in the same burg?" *Am I babbling?* "I am referring to the proximity of my estate to Miss Cleaver's retirement haven at her brother's vicarage."

"Yes, quite amazing. I certainly did recognize you, sir, just not immediately—the sun was glaring. Please meet my companion, Miss Dean." Miss Southwood indicated, with a graceful gesture, the pale older woman who sat tatting, hitherto unseen, in a deep wing chair near the fireplace. He nodded and perched on the chair next to Miss Southwood.

He clung to each moment in her presence, the threat of dismissal hanging over him like a guillotine. Even though Mr. Southwood consigned him to the curb, he didn't want Miss Southwood to send him away.

"You mustn't stay long, but please do tell me, how are the Cleavers?"

His mind was rattled from nearness to Miss Southwood. He managed an answer, "When I left them, they were both in fine fettle. They're good people. Not everyone would have taken on the burden of nursing me back to health. On top of all that, they shared the gospel with me."

Her fingertips flew up to her cheeks. "How wonderful! They are precious friends."

Mutual faith gave Mark's surprise visit a much friendlier base than if he'd only the Russelton connection and the mutual acquaintance to build on.

The clatter of dropped needles broke the moment. Agitated, Miss Dean glanced at the clock, and then back at the chatty couple. "Fifteen minutes has elapsed, young people, and the extreme impropriety of this unsanctioned impromptu visit is striking." Miss Dean's face turned even paler. "Miss, what if your father comes and finds him here?"

Mark took the cue. He picked up Miss Southwood's hand as he rose. He bowed over it, as a wave of some minty, refreshing scent wafted up. He breathed deep and said his farewell. "Miss Southwood, the pleasure of meeting you again has put me in high alt, this time in good health. I never expected the honor of meeting you once more. You have my heartfelt gratitude for the care you gave me when I was injured. My felicitations are yours, and if I may ever be of service, please make use of this." He released her hand and stepped back, and deftly extracted a card from his vest pocket.

She stood, took his calling card, and gave a small

curtsy. "Farewell, Lord Russell. Thank you for stopping to say hello. It's been pleasant."

It was good-bye. The last thing he wanted to do was to leave her cheery and sweet presence. But he smiled his amiable best and bowed his way out of the room, no one else the wiser to his extended visit. As he exited the house, he marveled at the lightness of his steps and his heart.

~*~

Melissa held the card in her hand, studied it, and whispered, trying out the sound of his name on her lips.

Lord Russell.

The brief, unusual visit over, Miss Dean moved to a chair closer to Melissa's, and they both went back to their needlework.

"Miss Dean, it is good you were here. What would I have done? I shudder to think of the embarrassment of perhaps having to call a footman."

"Why did he say 'recuperating'?" The companion spoke barely above a whisper.

"He had an accident near the vicarage where I was staying on a visit to the country. My hosts and I tended him whilst he was in and out of consciousness."

"I see." The companion lapsed into silence.

"How agreeable Lord Russell seems, no?"

"Yes, an agreeable gentleman, if I do venture my opinion. Not that I presume to judge my betters." She pursed her lips. Miss Dean strived to keep to her place, even though Melissa treated her as an equal.

Melissa sighed. She wished she could tell the whole tale to Miss Dean, but it was probably better for her to forget about Lord Russell, else she'd forget about the man courting her.

The two women were subdued into silence. Melissa hummed a little melody reflecting her raised spirits. Would Papa relent and let her choose a suitor?

16

As with any young lady after a meeting with such a handsome, charming, and well-mannered man, Melissa found sleep elusive until the wee hours. But when she awoke the next day, it was with a new sense of resolve and purpose. She would meet with her father and hoped to convince him to be reasonable.

Melissa dressed with care. Her pink sprigged muslin with its scrumptious apple-green silk ribbon sash was a favorite. She tied on a pink ribbon to hold back her hair and donned pink velvet slippers. She selected pearl jewelry, hoping to appear more mature in her father's eyes. A pirouette in front of the mirror, and she was ready to face her father.

Anxious to make a humble appeal, she'd had to wait a week for him to find time. The agreed-upon two months of arranged courtship now drew near its close. Her heart, mind, and spirit told her not to decide yet in favor of marriage to Lord Peter Winstead. On top of the doubts, she'd met an intriguing possibility in Lord Russell. Why couldn't Papa have chosen him instead of Lord Winstead?

Papa's obsession with joining the upper class sprang from the days when he courted and married her mother, the daughter of a well-to-do squire, who belonged to the gentry. Papa, however, rose through the merchant class. Mama mingled some in the haute ton during her single years, but that ended with her marrying 'down.' Wealthy as the Southwood family was, the upper class snubbed them, and the coveted social whirl of the *haute ton* remained out of reach.

Melissa had no peace of mind concerning Lord Winstead, Papa's hand-picked selection. Arranged marriage sounded acceptable at first, but once on that path, she was less sure of her capacity to go forward. Winstead showed no fruit of sincere faith, causing her to lose confidence in Papa's choice. Part of her wanted it to work, if only to please and honor her father's wishes.

Since Lord Russell was in London, she became even less sure of Lord Winstead. Though Russell wasn't courting her, his very presence in town encouraged a delayed decision. He was real and gave valid substance to her reluctance.

She went over the facts. Lord Peter Winstead appeared acceptable. Handsome, polite, clean, lively, and intelligent, his low finances were not problematical because of her father's vast fortune. He possessed impeccable social standing, and his reputation was not sullied like many of the young gadabouts who came to London and pursued lives of rakish impropriety. Despite the list of positives, Lord Winstead's faith life did not make a good match for her own.

A maid appeared. "Miss, the master can see you now."

Melissa proceeded into the library where her father worked on the days he stayed home. As usual, she chose the comfortable armchair facing him across his desk.

"You wanted to speak with me, daughter?"

"Yes, Papa, it's about the arrangement with Lord Winstead." The words came out on a gust of courage.

Southwood grinned, sat straighter, and rubbed his hands together. "Are you ready to give your final consent and approval to my plan?"

"No. I decided to request an extension. Things are going along rather well, but I would like more time to decide." Revealing doubts about Winstead's faith would not help her cause. She twirled a wavy strand of hair around her finger.

"If you should reject Lord Winstead's suit, I will have to return to the drawing board, so to speak, and select another sprig of the nobility to present to you. I'll need to work that into my busy schedule." Mr. Southwood slumped in his chair and sighed. "How much longer do you need?"

"In one more month, I should be able to know."

"I'll see that Winstead is informed of the extension. My girl, if I have to begin again, I am afraid I won't be as patient." He shuffled some papers on his desk with a distracted air. This signal told her he'd already moved on to other thoughts and that the little meeting was about over.

The reprieve made her want to dance and skip. Before he could object, Melissa rushed around the desk, threw her arms around him, and kissed the top of his head. "I do appreciate this!"

Melissa scurried out of the room, and when she saw the hall was empty, she skipped to the stairway. A fizz of joyful hope bubbled up as she climbed the stairs. This delay was needed to decide what to do about Lord Peter Winstead. Thoughts of Lord Russell continued to intrude upon her peace, however, making it a chore to focus on Lord Winstead, her only sanctioned suitor.

17

Mark moved in a daze after the previous day's encounter with Miss Southwood. The normal male drive to obtain a goal warred within him. He had to quell urges numerous times to keep from taking rash action. *Lord, she's the desire of my heart. Please....* He trailed off in uncertainty. Unsure if his prayers were appropriate, he settled for an inward groan.

Southwood himself soundly rebuffed Mark's self-abasing and embarrassing advance. What to do? What tactic provided an approach now? Miss Southwood hadn't been seen at any social events.

Mark, alone in his private rooms at the club, wracked his brain for a plan. Southwood craved for his lineage to be connected to the aristocracy. Perhaps entrée to polite society and its frivolous round of balls, soirees, and routs would draw Mr. Southwood and his daughter out into the open giving Mark's chances to further the acquaintance. He'd seek an opportunity to be reconsidered as an approved suitor for Melissa. Was it possible Southwood might decide to allow more than one man to woo Melissa?

Mark grasped at straws. He kept his dim hopes alive by fantasizing scenarios in which he conquered as the hero. On their heels came imagined unbidden scenes of failure or the loss of his heroine. He took himself to bed, and to sleep—dreaming of his beautiful, golden-haired lady.

~*~

He woke to the sound of multiple church bells, leapt out of bed, and called for his valet, who shaved and dressed Mark. He ordered his carriage to be brought around. In no mood for breakfast, he dashed downstairs and into the shiny town carriage. He shouted directions to the coachman as he got in, and then rapped on the ceiling. Just enough time to get to his aunt's house.

"There you are." Aunt Lucy waited at the door, and Mark escorted her down to the waiting conveyance.

"The bouquet and note you sent were charming. Did you think I'd forget our plan to attend worship?" Her brow arched.

"No insult intended, Aunt Lucy. Merely following up. St. George's has a reputation for excellent music." He hoped the preacher was inspiring as well.

It was the first time he'd been in a London church since his conversion. He remembered attending church with his parents as a child. The services had been dry, unsatisfactory experiences, boring and meaningless to his young, unconverted mind. But now, the beautiful words of Old and New Testament scriptures rolled over him as he took in the passages being read by the minister. The service was the same, but his heart was new.

"… live a godly, righteous, and sober life …." He now owned these words as he said the Prayer of Confession. The liturgy suited him fine, and the worship refreshed and strengthened him.

The service ended, and he knelt one more time.

A Match for Melissa

Dear Lord, please smooth my path to find a wife—Melissa—if it be Your will. I need and desire a helpmeet, and I put all my plans and efforts in Your hands.

He got off his knees, straightened, and took Aunt Lucy's hand and patted it into place on his arm. They moved toward the door at the back of the church where the minister greeted each congregant and visitor. After they passed through that portal, they came out into the bright sun of the everyday world again. He wished the sunshine was a sign his bright hopes stood a chance.

Mark helped his aunt back into the carriage. They discussed the sermon as they rode home to her house for Sunday dinner.

~*~

In the drawing room at Aunt Lucy's townhouse, Mark set down his tea and turned to his aunt with a sigh of satisfaction. "Aunt, it's quite rewarding to feast on the products of your excellent kitchen."

"Now, nephew, don't stuff yourself on those seed cakes, because I've ordered a light Sunday dinner to be served not too long from now. My servants get each Sunday off, beginning at one o'clock. Many of them go off to their own families, and thus, we do dine a bit early."

The idea of enabling the Southwoods to enter society kept nagging at him. Having no better ideas of how to get in their good graces, he floated the plan to Aunt Lucy. "Do you think your superb staff would be able to cope if you hosted a ball?"

Aunt Lucy eyed him over the rim of her cup, brows elevated. "A ball?"

Maybe it was too much to ask. But he tried to respond with nonchalance. "Yes, a ball. You know, music, dancing, flowers, receiving line, and all."

She quirked her lips at his teasing explanation. "It's possible to have a ball here, but why?"

"Now I must confide in you. You indeed recall my initial visit here last week and our conversation about me wanting a wife?"

"I'd never forget such a scintillating talk." She toyed with the handle of her teacup.

He raised his eyebrows. "Do you also remember the rich merchant you mentioned? The one who seeks an aristocratic spouse for his daughter?"

Aunt Lucy nodded. "My memory is clear."

"Indeed. After I left here, I learned the most pertinent and remarkable facts about your snippet of information. The young lady in question, the daughter of the rich merchant, is Miss Southwood, the very young lady who was a guest at the vicarage in Russelton village when I was attacked."

Confusion danced across Aunt Lucy's visage. "What are you saying?"

Mark held out a calming hand. "Miss Southwood was the Cleavers' visitor at the time of my recuperation. She was the one who discovered me in the ditch after the robbery and went for help."

"Had you not been found…I shudder to think."

"Miss Southwood helped with nursing duties for two days after the attack—when I was in and out of consciousness—before she had to leave for London."

"She's in London now? I think I begin to understand." Aunt Lucy pursed her lips in concentration.

"I called on her father yesterday to inquire, and he

rejected me in no uncertain terms. Lord Winstead is courting Melissa with her father's approval. However, I encountered her on my way out of the house and talked with her."

"Was that proper?" Aunt Lucy sat and listened, with slight confusion on her face.

"Aunt, the important thing is that I am highly interested in Miss Southwood, and a ball given by you would provide me another chance to woo her away from Winstead."

"Why is that, young man?"

"Her father's goal is for his daughter to marry an aristocrat and join the haute ton. He'd surely covet an invitation to a ton ball. It's probable he has a yen to move in upper circles." Mark absently stroked his watch fob.

"Dear me, can't you approach the man once more and attempt to interject yourself into the running?"

"No. He is not an indecisive man, nor one easily influenced. Southwood thinks he's got a winner already and put me off in no uncertain terms. I've cudgeled my brainbox for a plan. I'd have at least a slim chance to establish a courtship if you were to invite them to your ball. It's the only idea I have and perhaps it will bring her father around to reconsider my suit."

"Do you think so? Balls *are* delightful." Aunt Lucy tipped her head to one side, considering, brows drawn together. "Are you sure it will benefit your suit?"

"It's a gamble. But since Winstead is up to his ears in debt, he can't host a tea party, much less a ball. A coveted invitation from you might cause Southwood to reconsider his rebuff of me."

"That man has a lot of brass to pass up a fine

suitor like you, Mark. He should think again."

"Even if not, Miss Southwood herself might become more resistant to accept Winstead if she has the opportunity to further her acquaintance with me."

"I hate how your hopes hang on such slim strands, but I am not opposed to your idea. It's been years since I've given a ball, and the idea has appeal. It might be fun."

She opened her arms for a hug and tilted her cheek to receive her nephew's kiss.

"You're a dear lady. It will be a lot of work for you."

"I relish the task."

"Send all the bills to me. You shan't spend a farthing on this."

After this agreeable exchange, Mark began to pace. Lucy sipped tea, started lists, and made notes.

The plan to host a ball would require Aunt Lucy to a hoped-for, but by-no-means assured, result. His mind swirled with scenarios. He'd love to sweep Melissa into his arms and carry her out of the ball, to his waiting coach, and head for Gretna.

Would the Southwoods even accept the invitation? He snapped out of his daydreams and reminded himself to take his worries to God. His plans were in God's hands. The Bible says a wife is a good thing. He hoped Miss Southwood was the one for him.

Urgency gripped him as he considered the numerous obstacles he must overcome to win her hand and her heart. He paced for a while.

"By the way, it was delightful to step down the aisle on your arm, nephew. But more than mere earthly delight the worship service brought me true renewed peace."

"I'm so glad for you, Aunt Lucy."

"I remember how much faith used to mean in my life. My spirit was refreshed this morning, and I am ready to serve the Lord again." Her cheeks were red and eyes bright. She patted the seat next to her with entreaty in her eyes.

"That's wonderful. I understand." He swept away the tails of his coat and sat next to his aunt, reaching for her hand.

"My attitude became sour in the sad years since my husband passed away. But now, I will do all I can to assist you, dear nephew."

"You are so loyal, Aunt Lucy." He patted her hand.

"I shall also cast about for some charity work to occupy my remaining years. Lord willing they'll be many. Mr. Banting wouldn't want me to languish away. I'm far too young for that."

"You aren't old at all."

She ignored his remark and went on. "Planning the ball can wait until after the Sabbath day. Tomorrow will be soon enough to choose the guest list, pick a date, write invitations, draft a menu, hire caterers and musicians, order flowers, and order the ballroom cleaned and prepared."

"You're absolutely sure?"

"The anticipation of wearing a new ball gown can commence as well, for I shall send out a summons to Madame Olivier too, requesting her to appear here as early as tomorrow afternoon."

18

Melissa stood at the glossy hall table in the family's mansion, shuffling through the mail five days later. A particular missive caught her attention. She turned over the luxurious envelope to find a return address indicating an invitation. *The Honorable Mrs. Lucy Banting*.

She tucked the interesting piece of mail under one arm and lifted the hem of her velvet-trimmed dress to accommodate her dash into her drawing room for a letter-opener with which to slit the envelope. Withdrawing the enclosed card, she read the engraved words within and sat down with a whoosh. A ball. What a surprise. Would Papa accept an invitation to a haute ton ball? They'd never received one before. Who was Mrs. Banting?

While she twirled a curl near her cheek, her mind flew to her wardrobe. How pleasurable it would be to wear the creamy white ball gown made by Madame Olivier. A ball would justify donning the luscious creation. The entrée into high society her father long desired appeared to be in his grasp.

He'd soon join her for tea. There'd be the invitation to discuss and distract him from his single-mindedness of late. He'd been rather impatient with her and prone to mention the courtship deadline every time they spoke.

Receiving an invitation to Mrs. Banting's ball was

an enigma, and solving that puzzle appeared to be a dead end at the moment. Her thoughts returned to her main trouble. Melissa wasn't necessarily averse to the thought of marrying into the aristocracy, but she wanted to make sure to marry another believer.

Lord Winstead's few expressions of faith amounted only to performing the appropriate responses during the Anglican worship service, and once saying grace before they lunched together at the Southwood home.

Did her suitor's actions present any evidence of a desire to serve the Lord? He'd been kind to her. Kindness counted for something. He treated her with no condescension, and he acted with politeness.

But there were incidents. A brusque response when they passed a beggar who held out a ragged hat. Even though Winstead's funds were short, he could have been gentler. Didn't some of his repartee veer over into inappropriateness? Had a few of his stories verged into the category of gossip? Maybe, but it was hard to say, and Melissa hated to criticize or condemn Lord Winstead. In fact, she felt sorry for him.

The man's attentions were dutiful, at least, never staying past the prescribed twenty minutes and alternating with drives every other day like clockwork. Reviewing their rote relationship flattened Melissa's mood and left her doubtful.

Males were almost a complete mystery to Melissa, making it even harder to evaluate one. Never spending time with any man except Papa created a significant deficit in her knowledge. Men were, in general, more rough-hewn around the edges than the ladies, and that alone may account for the questionable banter and tittle-tattle.

The door opened after a light tap, and Papa entered the room with his customary air of vibrant energy.

"Aren't you a picture, darling!" He bent over her and kissed her upturned cheek. "Stand up so I can see you better."

Exuding cheer, Mr. Southwood grasped Melissa's hands to help her rise from the chair and held them wide to admire her. "Your mama would be pleased at how you've blossomed into a real lady. You'll marry Lord Winstead, and you'll *be* one right and tight." Papa's compulsion to gain the social acceptance once close enough to grasp, drove him.

"Do let go, Papa." Melissa withdrew her hands from his and stepped away. "I've already ordered hot water for our tea, and the servant might return at any moment. Don't want them to think you undignified."

"Humph." He sat down.

"This came in this morning's post."

He accepted the envelope she handed across and began to peruse it. A footman entered, deposited a tray on the low table, and bowed his way out.

Melissa prepared the tea, acting the perfect lady. She placed a cup in front of her father, picked up her own, and took a sip.

Papa looked up, a gleam in his eye. "This is excellent!"

"The tea, Papa?" She presented an innocent smile, which soon gave way to a teasing grin.

"No, no, dear. The invitation. You've no idea how coveted Mrs. Banting's invitations are. It's said she hasn't given a ball for years, but the last one is still referred to as the ball of its decade."

"Are you certain? You wouldn't want to accept

just any ton invitation, would you?" Melissa couldn't resist bamming her father over this.

But he ignored her teasing with a wave of the hand. "We shall accept, of course. Now, Melissa, it would be most delightful for you to have a young, handsome escort. I will send a message off to Lord Winstead indicating he is to join our party."

"Is that how it's done? Not too forward, is it?" Deep down, she preferred to experience a ball on her own, unfettered by a suitor on a string.

"Darling daughter, put your fears to rest. I *do* know how to go about. I've made a study of such things for years. For me to include in our party an escort for you won't cause an eye to blink."

"As you say, Papa. What about you? Since I'll be escorted, will you forgo this chance to mingle with the upper crust?" Eyes averted to hide their amused gleam, she drank some more tea.

"Heavens, no. Decidedly not. Winstead shall act as your escort, but I will be in attendance and in the carriage on the way to and fro. One benefit of his presence is your assurance of at least one dance partner of your own vintage."

"Fine. You'll inform him he is to escort me? He's to call on me tomorrow morning, and you can get word to him at that time."

The tea time spent discussing the ball provided both father and daughter a diversion.

"You'll see, Missy, the ball will be the highlight of your life." Mr. Southwood rose to go.

"We shall see, indeed. I'm glad you are happy. I do love to dance." She threw him a bone, not really wanting to spoil his fun.

Melissa breathed a sigh of relief since the

invitation distracted him from the big question of whether or not Melissa would accept Lord Winstead.

19

Peter accepted the proffered invitation to accompany the Southwoods to the Banting ball. He continued courting Melissa, limited now to thrice-weekly morning calls. Peter's pockets were to let, and what little funds remained must keep body and soul together. Excess existed neither to provide more ices at Gunter's, nor purchase tickets to amusements, nor to hire carriages of any type.

The extra month of courtship Miss Southwood requested in which to decide did not favor his pockets. His anxiety grew, and he counted the days until Mr. Southwood would demand an answer from his daughter. Peter still enjoyed exclusive permission to court her, and if his suit succeeded, all money worries would be put to rights.

He didn't even accept many of the invitations to balls and banquets his title brought. He couldn't afford a new set of evening wear or to have his cleaned. Low finances brought the dismissal of his valet, making Winstead aware of the effort and expense it took to keep up a gentleman's wardrobe.

Considering all the care taken with his clothes, he briefly thought to beseech God about his future. He thought back to all the religious training he'd been given growing up but pushed such thoughts aside. Those beliefs wouldn't help him now, and he had no right to ask. Pride and a hard heart prevented him casting his cares upon the Lord.

Miss Southwood probed the matter of his spiritual condition—not something he'd outright lie about. She could only probe so far, however, and he'd deflected any pointed questions she'd posed. Her personality was not forceful and outspoken, and she didn't persist after he dodged her inquiries. He trusted her innate kindness, and she never pressed him too hard. If his suit came to naught, however, he'd be sunk.

~*~

Lucy Banting was ready for Madame Olivier's arrival on Monday morning to take measurements, select a style, and choose fabric for a ball gown. She was a longstanding patron of the popular modiste and sure of receiving the best service. Some other ladies of the *ton* rejected Madame Olivier services, saying she wasn't original enough for them. She suited Lucy well, however, because she herself abounded with originality to bring to the design process.

"My gown needs to be up-to-the-minute in style, Madame Olivier, but also unique enough to please my taste." Lucy loved attention-getting apparel. "The ball is two weeks away. It has to be completed promptly."

Madame Olivier unfurled one of her best French phrases. "*Que voulez-vous que je fasse?*"

Lucy's mastery of French allowed her to be patient with Madame Olivier's efforts. In fact, she'd used the gifted seamstress's services long enough Lucy believed she'd heard *all* of the woman's limited French expressions. "What should you do, Madame Olivier? I believe I'd like a new design. Yes, a gown with embroidery and pearls." She enjoyed selecting the design and what details to include.

Madame's head was down as she rummaged in her sewing box, and her voice was muffled. "Zat eez appropriate."

Surprised the modiste had lapsed into English so early in the appointment, Mrs. Banting smiled to herself, hoping the contrived French would now cease. She moved things along by verbalizing a decisive plan. "Fine. Let us proceed to the measuring, followed by drawing out my ideas. We'll select fabric and trim and have a ball gown planned by lunchtime."

"*Vous se lever*, Mrs. Banting."

Lucy did the seamstress's bidding and stood up. She sighed, renewing her patience with Madame's semi-mangled French, and shed the robe she wore. Now clad only in a thin chemise, Lucy turned this way and that while Madame Olivier recorded the pertinent measurements.

The seamstress's mouthful of pins didn't stop her stream of questionable French phrases. "*Beaute de forme!*"

"Enough nonsense, now. My form is adequate for someone of my age, nothing more. Please hurry so I can get into something warmer."

Measuring complete, Lucy donned her wrapper and sank down on a chaise to rest her feet. After much discussion and selecting, Lucy was satisfied, and Madame Olivier had put in writing their final decisions.

"Don't you agree the plum satin with the black spider gauze over-dress will be all the crack? So glad we chose a single scalloped-flounced hem. With black lace peeping out where the scallops rise, additional flounces would be too much."

"*Oui*, and the plum-colored embroidery of laurel-leaves will be *tres charmant*, as will the black bead fringe to adorn the dainty puffed sleeves." Madame chattered on.

Lucy let her mind wander while only half-listening to the seamstress's prattle. Lucy had been meditating on the proverb, 'She stretches out her hand to the poor, she reaches out her hands to the needy.' And that inspired her to prepare a surprise for Madame Olivier and the seamstresses at her workroom. "On your way out, make sure to take what my butler gives you. It's a sack of foodstuffs for you to distribute among your workers. I must rest now. Farewell to you, Madame. Please complete the dress in two weeks as promised."

"*Bonjour*, and *merci*, Madame Banting."

Lying back on the chaise with her eyes closed, Lucy planned a shopping trip to acquire a fillet of black jet for her hair. Slippers, gloves, and a fan would be a pleasure to shop for now that she'd completed the work of finalizing all the aspects of her gown. And no need for a new matching wrap or pelisse, because as the hostess of the ball, she would not leave her own doors. A little nap was now in order.

~*~

The responses to Lucy's invitations piled up on the mail table with every post. Almost all of the two hundred invitations sent out were accepted. Several distant relatives would be attending since Lucy had taken the step of reaching out to them. They would appreciate a chance to socialize, and perhaps she could renew and strengthen those family ties. Now that she spent time with Mark so often, she had a new interest in spending time with other members of her extended family.

The few invitees who sent regrets were either ailing or out of town. She took the swell of response as proof her invitations were still coveted after all these years. Though her townhouse did have a ballroom, the numbers would make it too small for true comfort. The fashion called for crowding guests in, and for one's ball to be called a "sad crush" was considered a compliment.

Her last ball was held eight years ago, and her husband passed away two years later. She hadn't the heart to host another until now. It had been a long while since she had the vigor necessary to do more entertaining than the occasional afternoon tea party for her lady friends. Lucy attributed her renewed zest for life to her nephew Mark turning up on her doorstep and accompanying her to church.

She mustn't forget the reason for this ball was to help Mark. The plans appeared to be progressing as the Southwoods accepted the invitation. Lord Winstead's name had been mentioned in the Southwood's acceptance note. That didn't offend propriety, and it suited her since it would allow her to get a good look at her nephew's competition.

Too bad Mark couldn't be even considered in the running by Mr. Southwood. Lucy enjoyed an excuse to have a ball, but she wasn't too optimistic about Mark's chances with Melissa Southwood. Her lack of optimism didn't take away from the excitement of playing a part in her nephew's pursuit of a match. Being his confidante added some much-needed spice to her quiet life.

She turned to her planning notebook, crossed out *order gown*, and perused the rest of her *to-do* lists, deciding whether she could do any more tasks related to the ball before she headed out to the shops.

Lucy's heart swelled with gratitude for the way her life had become richer since her nephew returned. She sought God's wisdom upon her efforts to make Mark's dreams come true. He needed all the prayers he could get.

20

Mark occupied himself meeting with the solicitors for the estate, visiting agricultural experts, and purchasing innovative implements for the home farms. Sporadic visits to various social events didn't relieve the tedium as he waited for the day of the ball to arrive. Aunt Lucy's ball would be his next chance to dance attendance upon the exquisite Miss Southwood. He held onto a faint thread of hope he'd somehow woo and win her away from Winstead.

The situation left him with a sensation almost as if he'd been punched in the stomach by an unscrupulous enemy. His mind stayed centered upon a young lady all but affianced to another. His heart gave a thump every time he recalled the encounter with Melissa at her home, and those few delightful minutes spent with her. To comfort himself in his desperation, he allowed his mind to replay their conversation and muse upon the beauty of her face.

Penning a letter to the Cleavers, Miss Cleaver and Jeremiah, he caught them up on events since he arrived in London:

... and I learned that the young lady who found me in the ditch and helped nurse me back to health, is a well-known subject of haute ton gossip as the one being courted by the impecunious Lord Peter Winstead. The news surprised me and seemed fortuitous, since I went to London for the very purpose of wife-hunting. I took myself off to the

Southwood mansion to meet with Mr. Southwood, the father of your lovely former charge.

This may sound bold to you, but it made sense to me that to pass over a young lady already known by me would be folly. Who's to say she wouldn't be the one the Lord has planned for me?

Having met Miss Southwood, my foreknowledge put me more at ease when appearing in front of the man, asking for his most prized possession.

Imagine my chagrin upon discovering myself to be too late. Winstead is the only sanctioned suitor, and my chances are dim. I will soon be seeing her socially, however, at a ball to which the Southwoods are invited. At least there, I will have access to Miss Southwood for a dance or maybe two.

Since I believe the Lord led me to meet her, I still hope her father may admit me into the running. With his desire to enter the ton, perhaps this ball will somehow whet his interest in allowing me a chance.

Sincerely in need of your prayers, Mark...

He signed with a flourish and leaned back in his chair to go over the possibilities. Beginning with the sublime, he wove a roseate dream of himself and Miss Southwood pledging their troth with rays of light creating a holy aura around their heads. His fingers found the edge of his cravat and pleated it.

Ridiculous, fanciful scenarios filled his head when he thought of the ball. Perchance Mark would sweep her off her feet, and they would float across the dance floor in music-induced bliss. Or perhaps Winstead was a terrible dancer, and she would take him in disgust.

Additional, more prosaic concerns rushed in soon enough. Suppose all did go well as possible? Would Southwood give him a chance? Would the ball be a sufficient wedge, opening the door to courting her with her father's approval? How would his hopes be realized?

His worries gave Mark an urgent desire to rise up and do something—anything. He rang for his valet, and upon the valet's breathless arrival in the room, delivered instructions.

"Thomas, get out my evening clothes. Inspect them with as careful an eye as ever you have. Anything with the tiniest flaw must be replaced. And make sure they are of the first stare of fashion. We ought to present our best front, or foot, or face, or whatever is the latest term. The get-up should all be right and tight by the Banting ball."

"Sir, the cravat you are wearing is, ah, damaged." The valet winced, disgust plain on his face.

"Fine. Bring another." Mark stared out the window where a flowerbed caught his attention. He turned back toward the servant. "Carry out an order of flowers. For Miss Southwood of Park Lane, a nosegay of the finest pale pink roses. For my aunt, Mrs. Banting, make it a large spray of camellias, and if those aren't in season, orchids will do."

Suffering the servant's ministrations, he called a halt as soon as the fresh cravat was tied. "There. I'm well satisfied. I'll pen a note to go with Miss Southwood's bouquet."

He sealed the missive, handed it to Thomas, and issued a final instruction on his way out the door. "Order my carriage. I am riding out this hour on business. That will be all, Thomas."

He descended to the main floor of the house, and as soon as his carriage arrived at the front door, Mark emerged and gave instructions to the coachman. He settled in the front-facing seat, thinking over the events of the day. The valet would ensure his evening clothes were of the first stare. With the flowers ordered, his mind turned to his other plans.

Since his conversion to Christ, he shouldered a new burden for those less fortunate. Today, a visit to a charity soup kitchen allowed confirmation as to whether his resources were put to good use in the Lord's name there.

He believed, as an agricultural landowner, it fitting to focus his charitable benevolence around feeding the hungry. For now, he provided funds. Later, he hoped to designate a portion of his annual yield to this work. Giving from his harvest would add extra savor and zest to the year-in, year-out pattern of planting, tending, and harvesting.

He planned to inspect the feeding program his London minister told him about before continuing his anonymous donations. He experienced a gladness and purpose missing in his pre-conversion days. It must be joy, he mused.

Nearing his destination, he banged with his walking stick the pre-arranged signal on the ceiling of the coach. As the coach pulled to the side of the heavily-traveled street, the sound of wood cracking preceded a shocking tilt of the coach. The vehicle slammed into the pavement, jolting Mark from his seat onto the floor. He landed well and lurched to his feet. Praise God he'd nothing but a few bruises as a result.

He pushed open the door, now above him, hoisted himself out, and then vaulted over onto the sidewalk. The coachman was unharmed but had his hands full calming the horses. Mark went forward to assist in loosening the traces. When they had the horses untangled, calm, and held by their bridles, Mark's mind flew to the oddness of the mishap.

"What caused the carriage to tip? I heard a crack." Mark used his free hand to pat the coachman on the shoulder, giving reassurance no blame was cast.

"Yon axle's clear broken, sir. 'Spect that's the cause."

Mark instructed the man to take the horses to the stable in the mews behind the club. The axle looked quite suspicious. He hired a group of urchins to move the damaged vehicle to the curbside and one to guard it until he made arrangements to remove it. Coins were handed out with liberality, and when he was assured all was taken care of for the time being, he calmly went on with what he came for.

The charity kitchen's dining room, though dimly lit, appeared to be efficient, neat, and well-attended by lines of scrawny men, women, and children. It gladdened him that he had not stinted with the amount he brought with him in the small, but heavy leather purse in his coat pocket.

The smells of stew and fresh bread were appetizing. He wanted good food to be given to the poor, not mere scraps.

As he looked around for the director of the feeding mission, he spied a youngish woman stationed behind the largest pot. Wrapped in a large apron, swathed in a kerchief, she was busy with her ladle. Nevertheless, something familiar in her demeanor caused him to move closer to investigate.

It couldn't be! *Miss Southwood, here?* Mark stood rooted to the spot, taking in the scene and immediately evaluating her safety. He spotted a brawny manservant in the Southwood livery in attendance. The man seemed alert, leaning against the wall about ten feet away from Melissa, acting as a bodyguard. The venue appeared orderly and safe, but Mark was relieved she had protection. There sat Miss Dean on a chair nearby, too. The faded older woman blended into her corner, but the motion of her knitting needles flashed in the dimness.

Mark stepped around the end of the serving table and began to pass bowls one at a time to Miss Southwood. She filled each bowl before handing it to the next in line. He chanced a peek at her and observed a flush to her cheeks missing earlier. So, perhaps she wasn't indifferent to him.

~*~

Melissa's face grew warm. A tremor of excitement sizzled within her, and her heart gave a leap upon sighting Lord Russell. The simple pleasure of seeing a friend brought joy, for she had few. But it was more than that, she'd admit, if only to herself.

"Good afternoon, Miss Southwood. What a pleasant surprise to see you in such un-illustrious but worthwhile surroundings."

The liveried servant pushed himself off the wall and appeared at Lord Russell's elbow, a pugnacious look on the man's face.

"Stephen, it's quite all right. This gentleman is known to both me and my father, so put down your hackles."

She turned back to Lord Russell.

"Good afternoon, to you, sir. I own I am also surprised. What brings you here today?"

"Oh, nothing. Investigating a local charity. Seems you've beaten me to the punch."

"La, no. I've not bested you. I simply happened to find this worthy work before you." She had to concentrate on the ladle and bowls so as not to spill. She enjoyed the attention from Lord Russell, but she didn't forget why she was there.

"This is a way I can give back out of the bounty He's given me. It is fine to provide money, but doing the serving does me as much benefit as the soup does them," she said.

~*~

The bag of gold coins Mark brought to donate burned a hole in his pocket. He looked around for an alms box or for a manager or matron. Spying an official-looking older man occupied with some type of checklist, he excused himself.

"Excuse me for a moment?" He smiled at Miss Southwood.

"Yes, certainly."

She took one more bowl from his hand, and he reluctantly left her side and approached the man.

"My good man, are you the head of this operation?" he queried.

"Aye, I be the one in charge. M'name's Reed." He made a modest bow.

Mr. Reed's expression turned to one of surprise as Mark stuffed a bag into the side pocket of the elder's old-fashioned frock coat. The man gave his coat a pat, heard the jingle of coins, and then came an even more respectful bow.

"One or two members of the quality have been here wantin' to give a donation. But never had a money bag stuffed into my pocket." He continued to pat his pocket. "Mustn't let the left hand know what the right is doing, if that be correct. Thank you, sir, in the name of the good Lord. Who might I be addressing?"

"As much as you'll allow, this gift is anonymous, not wanting my works to be seen before men." *Or young women*, Mark thought with another glance over at Miss Southwood. "Blessings upon your endeavors here at the kitchen," Mark added. "I'll be taking myself off in a moment or two."

"Must ye leave?"

"I shall contact your board of directors with a glowing report." He patted the man's shoulder and stepped back to the serving station, where he leaned toward Miss Southwood and spoke in a low voice. "Before I leave, may I ascertain one or two dances for the ball?"

Melissa stammered a bit. "Th—the ball?'

"Yes, the Banting ball. Your family accepted the invitation. Mrs. Banting is my aunt. I am anticipating it, and my joy would be full if you grace me with a dance or two."

Her cheeks flushed again, yet she responded with composure. "Indeed, I would be delighted. Please excuse me, Lord Russell, I must get back to my duties here."

"Farewell, Miss Southwood." Mark bowed over her hand and added in his mind, 'my dear.' Already smitten, he was now even more struck by the driving desire to make her his own.

21

The courtship period now extended by as much as another month, Peter scraped up some blunt to take his intended bride on another excursion to Gunter's tearoom in Berkeley Square. This popular destination provided the novelty of flavored ices, which were all the rage in London.

Miss Southwood's new companion, Miss Sarah Dean, accompanied them.

Peter tried to charm both ladies while he gathered the nerve to openly broach the subject of her response to his intentions. The carriage rides, excursions, and polite calls on Miss Southwood at approved hours, topped off by the visit to Honor's Point, were enough. "Miss Southwood, how do you like your lemon ice?"

"Very well, thank you. It is as good as the lime flavor I tried last time we were here. Miss Dean, what about you?"

"Delightful. I prefer it to the lime. Lord Winstead, do you care for your raspberry ice?" Miss Dean's sparse eyebrows shot up every time she asked a question. She was not too shy to enter into the frivolities.

"I'm partial to raspberries. They remind me of my grandmother."

The companion made to rise. "I want to examine those cups in that showcase across the room. I'll not be gone long."

Polite to a fault, Peter rose, assisted her with her chair, and sat again as soon as Miss Dean moved away from the table. He cleared his throat, gathered his courage, and spoke in a low voice. "I've wondered as of late, Miss Southwood, if perhaps you are anywhere near a decision in my favor? Since your father has given provisional approval, thus far I dispensed with doing the pretty and getting down on one knee, but if that's what it will take, my dear?" *Deuced awkward, courting a young lady for her fortune.*

She set down her spoon and pushed away her lemon ice. "Oh, la! I do not expect you to fall to your knees. I find nothing repulsive about your person, and you've shown me naught but the finest courtesies. Still, I wonder if we shall suit."

"What is the basis of your doubts, my dear?" Peter wanted to groan. *She sounds so prim and frosty. Why not fall for me like many frippery misses in the past?* Though he did not love her, it hurt his pride that she so readily fended him off. He wanted her to be more taken with him than the signs indicated.

"My expectation and desire to marry someone who is spiritually in tune with me is vital. Even though you and I attended church together every Sunday since we were introduced, we have yet to engage in a deep discussion of faith." She played with her spoon, eyes down.

"Don't dash my hopes because of that, Miss Southwood. I am a bit of a mutton-head when it's time to discuss profound spiritual matters with young ladies." This disarming remark came accompanied by his best, most dazzling smile meant to take the edge off the moment and distract her from the subject. He forged ahead. "My dear, are you saying a few faith discussions, and you will consent to be my bride?"

"I would love to discuss such matters with you, Lord Winstead, because you and I are friends, now, aren't we? I am simply not sure I'll be able to answer within the additional month my father granted to decide." Her brown eyes shone with sympathy.

He didn't want her pity, but it spoke well of her. She had every right to be nasty since he was courting her for her father's fortune.

Miss Dean returned and joined them at the table again amid the fluster of a slipped shawl.

For a moment, Winstead closed his eyes to gather his wits and to suppress the urge to slam something. Opening them, he acted as if he hadn't a care in the world other than dallying along, taking small bites of raspberry ice, and relishing those spiritual discussions in his future. He choked down his anxiety over the pressing creditors he'd been able to put off by making known his expectations to marry into the famous Southwood fortune. Dire circumstances sometimes required dire actions.

~*~

The day of the ball arrived, and although her plans had gone off without a hitch, Lucy Banting bustled around with a voluminous list. All stood in readiness. She still checked the list for the third time as she sat in her private dressing room off her bedroom.

Madame Olivier arrived with the gown at ten for a fitting. Last-minute alterations and adjustments complete, she gushed, with hands clenched in front of her bosom. "Delivering *zis* beautiful garment to my favorite customer is one of the greatest benefits of my calling as a successful seamstress and proprietress. *Magnifique, non?*"

"*Oui*, 'tis the loveliest ball gown I've ever owned. This is a creation to be remembered. It's put my spirits in high alt anticipating wearing this creation to the ball tonight." Lucy surveyed herself in the mirror, and her heart gave a lurch of happy anticipation of the evening ahead.

"Indeed. The dress reflects your femininity and unique vision. Zee plum-on-plum embroidery combined with touches of black accents lifts zee robe far above zee ordinary."

"Thank you. Now, Madame Olivier, I'd like to ask, if any other ladies will be wearing your designs tonight?"

"*Oui*. Perhaps Miss Southwood? Is she invited?"

Lucy nodded. "She's invited."

"She is *c'est belle*!"

"I agree she must be beautiful by all accounts, not having met her yet. Help me disrobe, and then you may take your leave. My butler has payment ready for you. See him on your way out. *Merci*, and *adieu*."

Madame having departed, and during a lull, alone in her private sitting room, Lucy mused over the night to come. She thought ahead to entertaining on a scale not ventured since before her husband passed away. The first years of grief were now over, and she did have Mark to take her mind off her loneliness.

A widow in her forties, she still enjoyed appearing at her best. Much time passed since she'd taken the trouble to order a gown made for a specific event, and doing so brought back some needed pleasure to her life.

Because of her nephew's interest in Miss

Southwood, it would also be fascinating to meet the wealthy Southwoods. Mark and Madame Olivier reported the young lady's beauty as something out of the common way. Her nephew's heart stood on the line, and Lucy wondered if Miss Southwood was a beautiful person on the inside as well. *Would the girl, or her father, give Mark a chance?*

Arrangements needed to be checked one last time for tonight's ball, but before she began the final round of checks, she'd catnap to hold her in good stead for the coming crush. She lay down and tried to put the to-do list out of her mind. Taking deep breaths, she soon slept.

~*~

Attending church, riding in the park, going for ices, and the like, gave only partial insight into Winstead's character. Not enough to satisfy Melissa. The calls he paid on her, mandated by propriety to be no more than twenty minutes in length, did not bring the level of acquaintance adequate for true discernment. He'd been quite guarded about any serious matters. Perhaps tonight would bring further wisdom.

Late in the day of the Banting ball, Melissa and her father entertained Lord Winstead, who had been invited to partake of dinner *en famille* prior to the dance. She sat silent, listening to the men chat before the meal.

When the time came to dine, she entered the dining room on her father's arm with Winstead following behind. Footmen stepped up and assisted them with their chairs and unfurled the snowy linen table napkins, placing them on laps in a seamless motion.

"Lord Winstead, would you favor us by saying the blessing?" She'd planned this request.

"Why, uh, yes indeed." Lord Winstead cleared his dry throat and stalled, taking a sip of water. Using a formal tone of voice, he spoke in low tones, "Ah, um, yes, Lord God of the universe, we humbly beseech Your grace and favor upon this household and upon this meal, Amen."

Lord Winstead sat back with an audible sigh of relief, and then smiled across at her. He reached for a glass of water. "My throat is so dry, excuse me."

Again, she found it difficult to take the measure of the man. His words lacked depth and vigor. Most people weren't used to praying aloud, though, so perhaps he was nervous.

As the meal progressed, superficial conversation reigned among the threesome allowing no further openings to probe into Winstead's character.

All courses complete, the men departed with due decorum for the traditional after-dinner brandy and cigars in the study. She, meanwhile, whisked herself up to her boudoir, and with the assistance of her lady's maid, put on the fabulous cream-colored ball gown, ordered on a whim, with nary a ball invitation in sight.

It would have been a sad loss for this dress to go unworn. She loved the way the creamy white complemented her coloring. The combination of satin and crepe fabrics accented by touches of gold embroidery, a square neckline, and small train gave the gown a regal, feminine character.

She checked the mirror to make sure her hair retained its style. She twirled the wavy golden strands near her face. A delicate heirloom tiara of gold, fashioned with laurel leaves and pearls, crowned her tresses.

As she thought ahead to the ball and how Lord Russell bade her to promise him dances, a flush of heat swept over her and breaths came a little bit faster than normal. *Why do I feel this way?* She was on the path to marriage with Lord Winstead, but when Lord Russell came to mind, Lord Winstead's courtship wafted away like a wisp of smoke on the wind.

Lord Winstead never took her to a ball in the few short months of her acquaintance with him. Perhaps he thought she'd be too uncomfortable in high society. Or maybe he was too low on funds to make the kind of splash many town bucks considered *de rigueur*.

She took a deep breath, one more glance into the mirror, and left the dressing room. Her first ton ball loomed ahead, and she was delighted to be going.

22

When Melissa descended the stairs, her father's gaze darted to the aristocrat who stood at his side.

She wondered whether he was belatedly considering Lord Winstead's worth. Was his mind flooded with doubts? Was his choice made too precipitously? Tonight's invitation came through Lord Russell, not Lord Winstead. She shoved those thoughts aside, determined to enjoy the evening.

She stood still as her father advanced toward her, took her hand, and lifted it to spin her around. "Yes, let's practice for dancing later." She laughed out these words, enjoying her father's lightheartedness.

He clasped his hands in front of his chest, resting them on his lavish white silk evening vest. "Dear darling girl, if only your mother were here."

"Yes, Papa, she'd love this gown and your evening suit, too." She leaned forward and kissed his cheek, before making a show of surveying him appreciatively. Dressed all in black, with a snowy white shirt and cravat, as deemed correct by the current arbiters of fashion, he'd make Beau Brummel proud.

Lord Winstead's appearance, however, would set all other female hearts aflutter. His dark blue, tight-fitting coat, which matched his eyes, was cut away at the waist, tapering into tails at the back. Black silk breeches hugged his thighs and clocked silk hose his calves. From the top of his gleaming, thick, near-black hair, to the toes of his shiny black dancing shoes, his whole appearance gleamed.

Eyes glittering, Lord Winstead stepped forward, took a velvet evening cape from a waiting servant, and with a proprietary air, put it around her shoulders. She shivered, and her teeth chattered involuntarily—due to nerves.

The party of three swept into the night air. A glossy black carriage stood ready. She and her father faced front, and under cover of a voluminous fold in her voluminous cape, held hands, giving an occasional squeeze. The invitation to the ball gave a common success to be pleased about, and their camaraderie ran high.

Shivering again, she clutched the front of the velvet cape more tightly closed. After a short ride, she was helped by a footman to alight at the stylish Banting mansion. All she must to do was put one foot in front of the other and proceed up the steps, which had been covered with carpet for the evening.

Once they passed through the portals, she hoped the ball would meet all Papa's expectations, because entering the hallowed halls of the ton had been one of his lifelong goals. Watching Papa gave her a needed distraction.

He glanced around, an air of nonchalance cloaking his demeanor. But she guessed at the awe within him as she observed how his gaze took in the glow of hundreds of candles, the scores of elegant aristocrats filling the entire hall, and the ornate gilded staircase rising to the ballroom.

Inching up the stairs, as everyone else was also doing, they reached the receiving line. She spied Lord Russell with a lady who must be Mrs. Banting ahead on the landing. She wore an exquisite plum and black ball gown. It appeared to be from Madame Olivier's salon since it bore her signature details and carried hints of Melissa's own dress. Amused, rather than jealous, as some would be, she looked forward to meeting the hostess.

Lord Russell stood with commanding posture at the hostess's side and wore subdued black evening attire with a diamond pin in his cravat. Different than Lord Winstead's handsome gleam, but equal in appeal. Melissa's eyes were caught by Lord Russell's gaze. His eyes radiated a mysterious message that coursed down her spine and made her tremble.

~*~

"The Southwood party." Mark leaned over to murmur this information to his aunt. Then he straightened and waited until each member of the group met his aunt first. He would soon have his turn.

Greetings and introductions made, the party of three began to move past Mrs. Banting and into Mark's sphere.

"Welcome, Mr. Southwood. I'm glad you could attend."

Shaking Mr. Southwood's hand, Mark moved the older man along, which allowed him to give his planned special greeting to Melissa. "The stars must be shining brighter tonight, Miss Southwood, trying to outdo you." Mark smiled right into her brown eyes, willing her to read his open interest. He forced himself to release her, and she walked toward the ballroom, trailing her delicious minty perfume.

"Winstead." Mark gave a brief shake to his rival's

hand and moved his attention to the next person in the receiving line.

During a break in the stream of arrivals, Mark turned to Aunt Lucy. "Do you understand now why I went to the extreme of suggesting this ball?"

"O my, yes. She is a diamond of the first water. Don't mind about the ball. I'm having the time of my life!" She made a happy flutter with her fan.

"You look beautiful tonight, Aunt Lucy. Entertaining agrees with you." More arriving guests soon interrupted their brief conference.

The opening dance provided their next opportunity to touch base. As Mark led his aunt out onto the floor for the first set, his eyes quickly located Miss Southwood's fair head. Her father and beau were nearby, in fact at each side of her. This did not stop a cluster of young men from jockeying for position as they vied for her attention and slots on her dance card. Soon, she moved through the crowd on Winstead's arm, and they joined the dancers already on the floor.

Waiting for the dancers to assemble and the music to start, Mark made a request. "At some point tonight, I'd like you to mingle with the Southwoods in order to strike up a friendship with Miss Southwood," he spoke quickly.

"Yes, my boy, as we planned. After the second dance, take me over to them, and I will do my best to befriend her."

"Good, that's when I'll obtain the first of the two dances she promised me the other day at the charity kitchen."

~*~

Swirling around the floor, Melissa sought out glimpses of Lord Russell. She wasn't sure, but she sensed he watched her, too. She considered him a friend of sorts, more than she could say about anyone else there. She told herself it was natural to watch for him; he served as a sort of anchor in the unfamiliar setting.

Acclimating to the dance steps, she wondered how a merchant's daughter would be accepted—invited guest notwithstanding. While whirling from one partner to another, she spotted a few acquaintances from her academy days. As yet, none of those young ladies made their way over to her. This didn't surprise her. She was used to their excluding ways, and thus unsure of their acceptance.

The first dance over, Lord Winstead promenaded her back toward where Papa stood by the edge of the floor. "My dear, may I take you for a drive tomorrow afternoon?"

"I see no reason why not." She fiddled with the fan dangling from her wrist.

"Excellent, I'll come by at three. Would you like some lemonade or ratafia?"

"Lemonade sounds nice."

He seated her and departed to get some lemonade. Papa stood at her side, and the cluster of young men closed in again, clamoring for her attention. She put her fan to work and fielded their attentions as best she could.

The small crowd of admirers made an opening for a dark-haired young lady to approach with two gloved hands extended. "Melissa Southwood! Could it be you?"

Melissa grasped the proffered hands. "Miss Cabot,

what a pleasant surprise." Here was her only real friend from the academy days. Melissa tried not to cling to Rosanna Cabot like a life-line. This extension of friendship rescued Melissa from potential social awkwardness.

All worries to that end evaporated with the rush of pleasure meeting a friend after a long dearth.

Rosanna began to chatter as if she'd parted from Melissa yesterday. "You must call on me. I own we can share some amusing insights about the marriage mart." Rosanna gave a cynical eyebrow lift along with a rueful smile.

"No doubt." She might have at least one or two stories to tell. Stories for which she didn't yet know the endings.

~*~

Mark deposited his aunt on a gilded chair before summoning a waiter to attend her. Not wanting her to be without at least a small crowd around her, he waited until several of her closest friends had moved into position near the popular hostess.

Spotting Lord Armbruster and Sir Walsh, he bowed to his aunt, promised to return, and sauntered over to the two men.

"Evening, gents. How are you enjoying my aunt's *soirée*?"

"I say, came here as a favor, but I'm glad I did!" Armbruster boomed his enthusiasm, held his glass up in the general direction of Miss Southwood, and gave a cagey grin. "A glimpse of that dazzler is worth all the trouble!"

"Here, here," Walsh added. "I concur. If I'd gotten to Miss Southwood before Winstead, stap me if I wouldn't have stolen a march on him. By the time I met with her father, it was too late."

"Indeed. As I recall, I first learned about their courtship from both of you at the club, did I not?"

"Sounds right. Can't rightly remember the exact details." Armbruster's drink sloshed over the rim with each broad gesture.

Leading the two sociable, harmless gentlemen into his benign clutches, Mark continued with a few chosen statements. He wanted to ensure Miss Southwood's popularity. The dear young woman deserved her moment in the sun.

"Either of you fellows secured a dance with the marvelous Miss Southwood yet? Her father aspiring to a title, it wouldn't hurt to be in line, so to speak, if Winstead doesn't go the distance." As he spoke this fustian, a stab of possessiveness flared, but hope spurred him on with his plotting.

Lord Armbruster eyes reflected a hectic glitter. "What? Is there some doubt he will step into parson's mousetrap? I thought I smelled April and May, and I have laid my wagers. Although I don't believe there's been any announcement."

Adjusting lavish cuffs, Sir Walsh chimed in next. "I shall sign her dance card and make every attempt to position myself favorably with her. Even if I have only a slim chance."

Armbruster, transfixed, stared at Melissa as she whirled by. "Hmm, she's a beauty for the ages. I shall write a poem about her."

Walsh tried to top his crony. "If I'd known of her exquisiteness, it wouldn't have taken any fortune for me to throw my hat in the ring. Now I'll write an epic ode to her beauty."

"Well, fellows, make Miss Southwood and her father welcome in society tonight, for I am sure that is her father's dearest wish. Can't hurt to be in his good graces."

"Russell, your benevolence is suspicious, but you were never a dull dog with the ladies."

"Benevolent or not, Sir Walsh, any single man with sense has got to be ruing the day he didn't beat Winstead to the punch." Speaking of his beloved to these two left him wanting to plug his nose, but he needed to assure her popularity with the ton. Otherwise, he wouldn't want them anywhere near her.

They were malleable, however, and might help his plan. If the Lord blessed him with success. If Mr. Southwood felt he had a place in the ton, he'd potentially drop his plot to marry his daughter off in order to jump the counter. Perhaps allow her a more natural course to wedded bliss.

After a few additional moments of desultory conversation with the two men, Mark moved on. Satisfied, he noted a small crowd around Melissa, and numerous men jockeying for position around the fringe.

Sweeping up to Aunt Lucy, he invited her to promenade with him. He maneuvered right over to the cluster of sprigs of the ton. The group parted ranks, creating a path for Mark and Lucy to approach Miss Southwood. Her father, who stood off to one side of his daughter, looked a bit overwhelmed.

Mark chatted with Mr. Southwood to help make him more comfortable at his first society ball while Lucy conversed with Miss Southwood. He could hear snippets of the ladies' talk.

"My dear, it appears our ball gowns are similar."

"Yes, Mrs. Banting. Do you perhaps use a certain 'French' seamstress as well?"

"I do. I knew it the minute I saw the beaded fringe and laurel leaf motif. How funny. Madam Olivier is very talented. However, I won't take her to task one bit. I only hope none of the tabbies here tonight notice our gowns' similarities and make tittle-tattle out of it."

"If they do, we will say 'Oh la' like we planned it."

Aunt Lucy gave an affable titter. "Yes, let's do."

Mr. Southwood droned on, and Mark nodded at the appropriate times, while he strained to hear Miss Southwood's soft voice talk on the topic of fashion with his aunt. A hint of fragrance floated his way. Mint. Such a unique scent Miss Southwood wore. He remembered it from their fleeting times together, which seemed so long ago yet nowhere near long enough to slake his thirst to make her his own.

The two ladies, though of disparate ages, struck up the kind of acquaintance that led to them planning to have tea two days hence. He could overhear only snippets of their happy chatter over the loud hum of the ball.

Satisfied his aunt had secured Miss Southwood's friendship, Mark stepped over in front of her, bowed from the waist, and then stood erect, extended his forearm in front of his chest, and requested the next dance.

~*~

As Lord Russell and Miss Southwood swirled out onto the floor, Peter's gut clenched with worry. Even though he wasn't heart-struck by her, he admired her. He acknowledged her loveliness as beyond that of any young lady he had ever come across, aristocrat or not. The idea of marrying for money, in reality, had turned out to be much less distasteful than he dreaded. *If I can gain her assent, I'll be in clover, in more ways than one.*

Something about the expression on her face while she danced with Lord Russell gave Peter a quiver of unease. Too dreamy for his liking. His creditors were pressing him. He'd promised them, based on his expectations, to take care of his debts soon. They were still hounding him, lest he forget his obligations.

When he took her on a drive tomorrow, he would press his suit and ask for a firm, assenting decision. If she didn't accept his proposal, he had another plan.

23

Melissa's eyes opened hours after her normal rising, when the maid raised the blinds and set a cup of hot chocolate by the bed.

How deep she must have dozed not to hear as her room transformed into a bower of bouquets. The custom for gentlemen to send a floral token to each dance partner of the night before made her suite resemble a flower shop.

A sip or two of cocoa brought her more fully awake. She folded back the covers, swung her feet over the edge, and stepped into her slippers. She went over to the nearest table to examine the cards attached to the bouquets. She moved from table to dresser to mantel where she at last found what she sought.

On a note attached to a tasteful cluster of yellow and white lilies, she read, "Russell, at your service," written on a dashing slant. Those four words caused a thrill of delight to rise from her toes and run through her whole body. The blooms were fresh and vibrant, the arrangement tasteful, and not overblown like so many others.

After shifting Lord Russell's bouquet over to her bedside table, she sat on the edge of the bed, sipped chocolate, and gazed at the lilies while thinking about last evening and the two men vying for her heart. A flicker of thought to the lack of even a posy from Lord Winstead didn't make her sad.

The ball began favorably enough, with many a young fellow asking to sign her card. Dancing with Lord Russell had been a treat. Two dances with Lord Winstead had been in the mix, too. Had he acted a bit anxious or irritable? She didn't want to care, and his moods had no bearing on her, but something was odd in his demeanor.

One of the side effects of Lord Winstead only courting her for her fortune was Melissa's dismissal of any responsibility for his moods or emotions. It might have been better if Papa had kept his machinations a secret. Nevertheless, as a Christian, she wouldn't hurt him on purpose, but she didn't owe him anything. Certainly not to coddle his sensibilities.

He had been pleasant enough, however, and not offensive in any way. Why did only apathy arise in her heart when she thought of marrying him? She'd given herself time to care for him. She hadn't purposely held back from loving him. She shouldn't feel guilty. *Oh, Papa—it's all your doing.*

She stifled a yawn, rose to her feet, and searched again through the array of bouquets until she found an offering from Lord Winstead. There, overwhelmed behind a lavish cluster of roses, stood one lone white carnation with a card stating his name.

Not inspiring at all. Oh, well, she'd feel worse if he'd spent more coins on her. Perhaps she'd bring up the courtship on their drive today, and she'd lay the groundwork for letting him down easy. Surely her father would support her. After all, Papa granted her the extra month. A month in which the engagement was not yet written in stone.

She bathed, and then with her maid's help, dressed in a blue carriage dress with matching spencer.

She dismissed the maid, deciding to do her own hair. While she brushed, coiled, and pinned, the longing for it to be Lord Russell courting her welled in her bosom. Why couldn't it be him who'd knock on the front door any minute now? Wouldn't it be fun if he took her on a drive today instead of Lord Winstead?

A housemaid entered to retrieve Melissa's cup. "Please take the bouquets to the drawing room. The scent is too much for a bedroom. Besides, my nose is starting to itch."

The maid put a few vases on the tray with her cup, and started to remove Lord Russell's flowers from the bedside table.

"Oh no, not those. Those I'll keep." Melissa went downstairs to wait for Lord Winstead and found Miss Dean seated in the morning room.

"Melissa, don't come near. I've got a sniffle." The woman's red nose and watery eyes revealed less than robust health.

"Oh dear, Miss Dean. You poor thing. Please take yourself off to bed. The weather's fine. Lord Winstead and I will travel in an open carriage to satisfy the proprieties."

Miss Dean gathered her knitting and shuffled away, sneezing.

Lunch arrived on a tray. Melissa nibbled sparingly, having little appetite, and occupied herself with needlework until the time came for her arranged ride with Lord Winstead.

As she waited, she practiced saying some phrases she could use to end the courtship. How about, "Lord Winstead, I believe I must decline your suit.' Or, 'Surely you'll find a true love someday."

She wondered how firm Winstead's determination

was to marry her. Would his reaction be gracious? Angry? Would he beg or cry? Shaking her head, she willed herself not to worry about Lord Winstead. After all, he was a man, and men were supposed to be strong, not given to excesses of emotions.

Soon, a summons came, and in the front hall, a maid waited with Melissa's light carriage cloak, gloves, bonnet, and reticule.

Lord Winstead rose from a side chair, and then held out his arm for her, never quite making eye contact. "Shall we?"

She murmured an assent and laid a hand on his sleeve to aid her descent of the steps toward the waiting carriage in which they would take their typical afternoon ride.

His distracted air set her nerves on edge and made her even more nervous about what she had in mind for him.

~*~

That same morning, Mr. Homer Southwood lay abed quite late. This infrequent happening stymied his valet. The man tiptoed into the room to see if the master was awake.

"Get me some coffee and a roll, or whatever is handy. You're not used to me being out on the town for all hours at society balls."

Homer sank back onto his plush pillows. Scenes from the night before passed before his closed lids, including dancing, meeting members of the ton, the welcome he got from Mrs. Lucy Banting, and the sublime dance he shared with her.

He chided himself for acting like a young fool with

his head turned. But a daydream of her returned within moments. Had her greeting held a hint of genuine warmth, or had her tone actually sounded perfunctory? He wasn't repulsive to women, after all. No. Several wealthy merchants' widows had set their caps at him, not to mention the numerous spinsters who cast out lures.

Chastising himself again for his silliness, he pondered the problem of Melissa and Lord Winstead. If only Melissa had taken a real shine to the poor but handsome fellow. Then Homer wouldn't bear as much guilt about pressuring her into matrimony. Too bad Lord Russell appeared too late in the process. Such a good chap and not snobbish at all. He'd have been an even better catch, but Homer was a man of his word, and he gave Lord Winstead permission to court Melissa.

Suppressing a niggle of remorse, he grabbed the bell pull. Where was that deuced valet? Coffee was what he needed now. He must talk to Melissa before the end of the week and push for a happy end to the courtship. If he brought pressure to bear, Melissa's resistance couldn't withstand his wishes.

24

Mark found St. George's sanctuary empty, common at four in the afternoon. He slipped into the third box pew to the right of the aisle. Flipping through the Book of Common Prayer, Mark turned to the back of the slim volume, scanning for an appropriate passage to read. He needed written prayers today, for his mind whirled.

A vague urgency rotated through his consciousness. Tension coiled in the region of his heart, but with no clear sense of its meaning or what action to take. So, he'd come to this beautiful church—to its solitude, solemnity, and musty air redolent of incense. The cool, quiet atmosphere began to soothe him. As his muscles relaxed and his breathing slowed, he pinpointed the source of his urgency.

Miss Southwood. How to obtain her for his own?

Slipping down onto a kneeler, he bowed his head over the open book and began to pray with some rephrasing of the words he read.

Almighty God, I entrust all who are dear to me, especially Miss Southwood, to Thy never-failing care and love, for this life and the life to come—knowing Thou art doing for her better things than I can desire or pray for.

Taking bits and pieces from some other pertinent passages in the book, Mark went on:

O Heavenly Father, I bring my perplexities to the light of Thy Wisdom. I humbly beseech Thee to bless her, now absent from me. Defend her from all dangers of soul and body—and grant that both she and I, drawing nearer to Thee, may be bound together by Thy love.

Continuing on in spontaneity, Mark groaned as he implored God for guidance.

Lord, I think I might love her. What should I do? Please, give me your peace.

He went on until the world slipped away, and he stayed in one position, half kneeling, half sitting, communing with God.

After a time in this posture, he became conscious of a shuffling noise behind him. Not wanting to be thought asleep, he straightened and glanced back over the high edge of the pew toward the rear of the sanctuary.

Moving across the aisle behind the last row of pews and disappearing into a side chapel were three people. Two men, and a smallish female. The dimness made it hard to make out detail, but it was clear one of the men impelled the woman forward while the other man looked over his shoulder as if to see if anyone followed.

In the quiet marble and wood-trimmed nave, Mark's nerves tingled as if in response to danger. Something about the group's movements were off-kilter. A trickle of sweat ran down his back, and his hands clenched the wooden rail in front of him.

Mark remained still and silent in the box pew while his misgivings grew. What was occurring? What if his sense of misgiving was inaccurate? He didn't want to cause a disturbance about a normal event.

He heard the distinct intonations of a priest. Some kind of ceremony went on, a sort of rite, ritual, or perhaps an unusual service.

He stared at the chapel entrance as he moved with stealth toward its carved marble doorframe. Within the dim chapel, the group stood facing a white marble altar lit by two guttering candles. Few details stood out in the smoky gloom.

A fourth person, a man garbed in the distinct dress of a Church of England priest, faced out, head bowed over a small, leather-covered book. Mark heard liturgical droning.

There was something odd about the woman. Not only were her hands behind her back, but they appeared to be bound by a silk scarf.

Though muffled and echoing, Mark recognized some of the words, "Do you take this man…?" He clenched the cold stone trim of the opening.

A stifled female voice made a croaking, angry, protesting sound. Not an 'I do' or even a 'yes'.

A silk scarf was knotted behind her head. He suddenly understood its position. It created a gag, front-to-back around the woman's head. The gag was probably across her mouth. Realization dawned. He'd become an inadvertent witness to a forced wedding.

He moved through the arched chapel doorway and approached the people. "What have we here, gentlemen?" He moved further toward the group.

The female turned around. With a shock, Mark recognized the captive 'bride' as Miss Southwood, and Lord Winstead stood near her. Mark's masculine reactions were on edge. Every muscle in his body coiled. He curled his hands into fists and fought the immediate urge to pound the man. He must be strategic—it was three against one. But Mark's drive to protect her propelled him forward.

Striding over, he faced Winstead and glared into

the blackguard's face. The balance of power changed. The priest sidled along the wall, shuffling toward the exit. The other man, clearly a hired henchman, complete with knobby low forehead, lurched toward Mark and grabbed his forearm, pivoting him away from Winstead.

Brushing off the underling's hand and unleashing his fury, Mark landed a quick punch to the man's nose and sent him staggering, bent over at the waist clutching at his face.

Mark commanded the bleeding man, "You there, make yourself scarce and forget what you saw here or not only will I give you more of a beating, but I will detain you for the magistrates."

The hireling nodded his head, tugged his forelock, and stumbled away from Mark, staggering toward the chapel door and out of the church door.

"Winstead, I should call you out for this. But since I am a Christian, I cannot murder."

"You may as well, for you've ruined me. Miss Southwood was promised to me, I'm sure you know."

Mark looked over at her, crouched, half hiding behind a chair. She shook her head and made a strangled sound. Her vigorous efforts to get loose told him she wasn't suffering too ill. He wanted nothing more than to cross the short distance to his love and release her silken bonds, but he had other matters to attend to first. He had an angry would-be groom yet to deal with.

Lord Winstead put up his fists, ready to vent his frustration. Before he made his move, Mark placed a left to Winstead's jaw, precipitating a grasping slide to the floor. The erstwhile groom, a now-crumpled figure, stretched out in a merciful blackout.

Merciful, because the righteous anger and protective urge motivating Mark itched to do more damage than a left to the jaw as recompense for Winstead's sins. Mark turned to Miss Southwood. She stopped struggling, but her breathing was ragged as she sagged to the floor.

25

Amid the aftermath of the violence and the shock of the event, Mark's fingers shook as he made quick work of untying Miss Southwood's wrists. With utmost tenderness, he removed the scarf tied around her mouth. "My dear, are you well?"

Her eyes fluttered open, she nodded, and tendrils of wavy hair swayed with her motion. "Yes, but quite upset by Lord Peter's actions. Thank God you were in this church."

"I agree, darling. It was the good Lord that caused me to be here when you needed me."

She clutched the edges of her cloak and spoke in a soft voice. "He took me out, with permission, on yet another drive in an open carriage and absconded with me. It seems, from what he said to the others, he hired the priest to ignore the irregularities."

"Irregular, indeed. I believe we are still alone in this place, and we must make a swift exit."

He checked Winstead, who appeared as if he would be out for a while yet but was breathing steadily. The cur could wake up, find a doctor, and make his own sorry way home.

Mark guided her just inside the main door. "Stay here one moment, my dear." He reveled in the pleasure of allowing the endearment to slip off his tongue. He stepped outside onto the front steps of the church and whistled for a hackney. A nearby cab immediately responded. Mark went back in to collect Miss Southwood.

He reassured her with a hushed voice and a gentle hand on her shoulder to encourage her. "Now, lower your veil to cover your face in order to prevent any suspicion should we be seen, and I shall carry you to the cab, keeping my head down to avoid being recognized. If we are seen, it will simply appear as if you fell ill. Young ladies drop like flies in stuffy sanctuaries."

"Whatever you think. I just want to leave this place." Her voice was weak, but he relished the trusting tone. Scooping her into his arms brought a wave of her refreshing minty scent up into his face. It reminded him to breathe.

Carrying her out was an excellent strategic touch, but holding her so close caused waves of sensation to crash over him. Having her in his arms ignited a deep longing, and being her hero pleased him to the core.

The subterfuge a success, they were soon inside the cab. Mark leaned out the window and instructed the driver. "There'll be a large tip for you if you go slowly. I'll give you our direction after a time. It'll be worth your while."

The unhurried pace wouldn't jostle her, but he also needed a few minutes to think. With nary a jerk, the cab moved off.

"Tell me about Winstead's remark. The part about you being promised to him?" Mark clenched his teeth, not wanting it to be true. He checked his pocket watch and held it loosely, cradled in his palm, touching it like a talisman.

"A grain of truth, I hate to say. I can only suppose you heard the tittle-tattle about how my father scoured the ton for a pockets-to-let aristocrat to marry me?" She averted her face and sniffled.

Poor little thing. "Ah, yes, I had heard something of the sort. You may not know this, but the day I met you at your home, I had come a-calling, throwing my hat into the ring."

She glanced, stricken, and lowered her gaze.

He hurried to explain. "I came, not because I need funds but with a sincere thought of you perhaps being the helpmeet I sought. The Cleavers told me such favorable things about you."

She spoke just above a whisper. "They are kind."

"And when I learned of your father's search for a titled man to wed you, I decided to apply for the position, so to speak. Your father sent me packing, since you were already being courted by Winstead." Heat crept up his neck—explaining this was deuced embarrassing.

She let out a held breath. "I understand. You were not seeking to repair your fortunes?"

"No, not at all. I assure you, dear, my motives are pure. I arrived in London and found out your father sought an aristocratic husband for you. Almost on impulse, I decided since I'd already met you and knew you were a believer, I would do the pretty and offer myself up to your father. In retrospect, it sounds a bit havey-cavey."

"Indeed."

"I sincerely thought it was the right thing to do at the time. Not my normal way of going about things. I don't need money, but the Lord led me." He realized he was babbling, repeating himself, and therefore, clamped his lips shut.

She swept the back of her hand across her pale

forehead and tucked a loose curl behind her ear. "I'm glad you told me."

Willing to beg, he pled, "Please believe me."

"I take your word, Lord Russell."

Satisfied with the air-clearing between them, Mark nevertheless needed to bring their talk back around to the current situation. He returned his watch to his pocket.

"Don't worry, but we do need to protect your reputation. If you return to your home with a different man, in a closed vehicle, it will provide scandal bait. The circumstances are too unusual and suspicious for us to be confident no word of the mischance will leak out." He ached to take her in his arms and comfort her. But that would be improper and taking advantage of the situation. "Servants do talk, and gossip leaks out."

"I agree that scandal is one wrong step away. My life as an unmarried young lady remains circumscribed by the dictates of society, and I fear too many rules have been broken today. I am sore afraid gossip will seep out, and Papa might blame me." She slumped against the unpadded side of the cab, the back of her hand laid on her forehead.

He took her free hand and patted it. "I would like to take you to my Aunt Lucy. She is a reputable lady, and you met her at the ball. From there, you'll send word home saying you encountered her while you were out and accepted an invitation to visit her overnight." Mark held her hand.

"Are her servants gossipy?" She withdrew her hand. He forbore to claim it again but noted the pleasurable tingle her touch left behind.

"Her staff is ancient and beyond the age of talebearing. I think you'll emerge from your visit there with no one the wiser." He itched to put a comforting arm around her but resisted, not wanting to press her after what she'd endured.

"But it's quite sudden. How will she like having an uninvited guest?"

"I am certain Aunt Lucy will love it." After giving Melissa one more smile, he leaned out the window, gave the address of their destination, and told the driver to pick up the pace. The events of the last hour were hard to believe. The traumatic ending to Winstead's suit meant a chance for Mark. Dare he hope?

26

"Miss Southwood. What a surprise. Do sit down," Mrs. Lucy Banting rattled off in a fluty voice. She patted the settee.

With relief, Melissa sank onto the offered seat, but she didn't take her eyes off Lord Russell. He was her lifeline to everything sane and good. Without his presence, she would collapse under the weight of the trauma.

Mrs. Banting rang a small bell, and a footman entered the room. "Forbes, I'll have tea in here today. Use the cart." She turned to Melissa and gushed, "This is wonderful. I love to have guests for tea."

"Aunt Lucy, I have a quick favor to ask before the tea tray comes." Mark stood, hands locked behind his back, the picture of leashed power.

Mrs. Banting cocked her head, and a flicker of concern crossed her face. "What is it?"

"Miss Southwood has fallen prey to a difficult circumstance. I am sure you will be quite sympathetic once she tells you. I must dash right now and make a few appearances to quell any curiosity about my activities. I may also tour some gossip spots on Bond Street to detect if there is nasty talk swirling around or not. If all goes well, the unhappy occurrence will not be public."

He bowed over Melissa's hand, locked eyes on hers for a moment, and then made his way out of the room and shut the door.

Bereft of his strong, reassuring presence, tears threatened Melissa's composure. She fluttered her fingers in front of her face. "Oh my." Her voice trembled as she tried to suppress shocked emotions.

"Now, now, don't cry." Mrs. Banting patted Melissa's hand. "With God's help, you'll get through whatever befell you."

The aged, myopic butler arrived with a tea trolley and put another log on the fire. When the door latched closed behind him, Mrs. Banting spoke. "You can confide in me."

Melissa, speech halting at first, told the tale with few adorning words. "You remember my suitor, Lord Winstead? He abducted me today and forced me to the brink of a spurious wedding."

"My dear, I am aghast at such sinful behavior. How dare Winstead." Outrage suffused Mrs. Banting's cheeks to a deep rose shade. "The cad. My dear, you poor thing." She pressed her fingers to her lips.

"Your nephew, in God's providence, rescued me and suggested I come here." Melissa's face heated with shame even though she'd done nothing improper. Head bowed, she stared down at her chafed wrists.

With a touch like a feather, Mrs. Banting patted Melissa's shoulder. "I can't help but notice your wrists, poor dear. I have just the ointment for your injuries. I'll get it soon. Do not be downcast. You did nothing to deserve what that young cur attempted to inflict upon you."

Melissa lifted her face, stricken. "I know that in my mind, but my heart is sore. My father encouraged Lord Winstead's suit even though I never wanted him. It hurts that my own father's scheme engendered today's events."

"Come now. Your father surely didn't realize he'd put you at risk. We must do a bit of plotting. I shall step over to my writing desk and pen a message to your father, explaining you are my guest."

Greetings, Mr. Southwood. Your dear daughter and I happened to cross paths today. I implored her to relieve the tedium of my days by spending an overnight visit at my home. Please have her maid pack a case for her, and my messenger will bring it back with your hoped-for assent. How pleasant to meet you at my ball the other night — perhaps we shall socialize again another day. Yours, Lucy Banting

"That should suffice." She signed with a flourish, sanded, and sealed the letter. "What's his address?"

Melissa gave the information, all the while marveling at the older woman's confidence and certainty. Would she ever be like her? So sure, so emphatic?

A footman arrived with the tea tray, and Mrs. Banting handed him the letter. "Deliver this right away and wait for a response."

Respite from worry washed over Melissa. She nibbled cucumber sandwiches and sipped hot black tea, so welcome after the shocking events of the day. She was amazed what a good time she was having, following so close on the morning's travesty. Mrs. Banting was amiable.

"I must compliment my cook. These are delicious." After tapping her lips with a delicately-embroidered tea napkin, Mrs. Banting went on with plotting. "Yes, tomorrow I shall take you home in my carriage, and to all appearances, everything will be above board. Guarding one's name is important."

"Mrs. Banting, it's kind of you to help me. A tattered reputation is not something I want."

"Indeed. I am proud of Mark for thinking to bring you here. Servants' gossip could proliferate if you'd arrived home with a different suitor than you left with."

"Your nephew's arrival saved me from a dire fate." She shuddered. "Forced marriage is distasteful."

"And disgraceful." Mrs. Banting graced her words with an emphatic nod. She probed for information. "How did it come about—you being courted by Lord Winstead?"

"My father is a successful merchant with a fortune not inherited. Earning his riches by trade excludes our family from the haute ton." Melissa paused to sip tea. She'd never voiced these truths before to anyone. But it seemed right to confide in this trustworthy lady.

She set down her cup and went on. "Entering the upper strata of British society has long been Papa's fondest dream, which led him to scour the ranks of the ton for a proper and willing match. Papa sought a nobleman in need of funds."

"Oh, I understand now. It's unfortunate he didn't find a man of good character to make a more appropriate match for you. You are pretty and ladylike."

"Thank you for the compliment. Father's fortune allowed me to be trained in the social arts. Though I was educated at an expensive academy, just like a lady, our family remained excluded from high society."

"Did this cause you to suffer?"

"Not really. I don't share my father's fascination with the *beau monde* but have been dragged along in the wake of his obsession."

A Match for Melissa

"It hurts me to think of a sweet young lady like you being snubbed and friendless."

Mrs. Banting's sympathetic tone warmed Melissa's heart. "I was fine. My family and my faith comforted me."

"Didn't you find any friends at the academy?"

"I made the acquaintance of many girls from noble families, and I did make one close friend there. Her name is Rosanna Cabot. In fact, I saw her at your ball."

"Oh yes, the Cabots—a fine gentry family."

"Rosanna is dear to me. When we spoke at the ball, we renewed our acquaintance and plan to call on each other soon. Even though we were friends, she wasn't able to afford me entrée into high society. Her mother also died, and it seems she didn't have things easy either. I suppose I will learn more when she and I visit."

Melissa enjoyed the sweet fellowship with Mrs. Banting, enjoying this interlude. Having a sympathetic ear was a balm.

"It isn't right for a charming Christian girl such as yourself to be excluded from social circles for which your training, beauty, and fortune suit you." Mrs. Banting lifted her chin, as if ready to do battle on Melissa's behalf.

Melissa found it a novelty for someone to champion her cause. "Nice of you to say, Mrs. Banting, but the lines between the classes are drawn very sharp. I accept this truth. To marry me off to an aristocrat, however, is a way for my father to achieve his goal. Some would call him a counter-jumping mushroom."

"This problem deserves additional thought. The ball provided a good beginning, but can more be done to help your social standing?" Mrs. Banting tapped her chin while thinking. "My nephew mentioned his own embarrassing attempt to 'get in the running' as your aristocratic suitor. Does your father remember?"

"I would imagine so. I believe Lord Russell joined the ranks of candidates never leaving the gate. You see, my father decided to select only one suitor, and he already chose Lord Winstead before Lord Russell arrived." Melissa hated to recall the whole circus. Her fingers flew to her forehead as a wave of chagrin swept over her.

Mrs. Banting spoke on in a lighthearted tone. "My nephew told me only the barest bones of the story of how he encountered you in London. I first learned of his interest when he asked me to host a ball for the express purpose of inviting you—and your father—of course."

"Oh! I wondered how the invitation happened to come our way. I saw him at my house on the day he asked to court me." It was a pleasure to remember their meeting—one of the best experiences of her life.

"How did that come about? You weren't present when he appealed to your father, were you?"

Mrs. Banting's pragmatic question brought Melissa crashing back to Earth. "No. Lord Russell left my father's study after being turned down. He noticed me as he passed the door of the first-floor sitting room. He came in to say hello."

"How deuced improper. But what a delicious set of circumstances!"

Melissa smiled. "Yes, but did he tell you we were not completely unacquainted at that time?"

"Yes, he told a very little about how he met you."

"You see, we conversed that day at my home, but I met him, so to speak, during my most recent visit to the country. To Russelton."

"Russelton's Mark's family seat." The woman nodded encouragement.

"My dear friend and former companion lives there. Her brother is the vicar, and she is now his housekeeper. A few days before I returned to London, I found Lord Russell near the road I used for my daily constitutional. He had been set upon and left for dead."

"He told me of the attack. He mentioned you helped nurse him. Such dire situations can foster intimate connections. And you departed for the city very soon after. Merciful heavens, what a story."

"It all has a fairytale quality, doesn't it?" Melissa hoped Mrs. Banting would not disapprove. Telling the story brought to mind how bereft her return to London left her—how much she'd missed Lord Russell.

"He shared with me the story of his subsequent conversion. I must say, he is a different young man now. He's even taking me to church every Lord's Day." Mrs. Banting smiled and squared her shoulders.

"I never had the chance or reason to tell my Papa about that adventure. He'd probably frown on it—even though I did the right thing. He has the idea that nothing out of the ordinary should ever happen to me."

"Does he need to be informed?" Mrs. Banting tossed her head.

"Since I hope to go to Russelton, to the vicarage, on a visit, it's not a topic I'll mention now. If he thinks the region is crime-ridden, he might forbid my trip. I am refusing my Papa's matchmaking schemes for now and the foreseeable future."

By the time their evening chat ended, the two were

bosom friends with excellent rapport. Melissa laid out her dilemma, and Mrs. Banting advised her wisely on some possible approaches to take with her father.

The brief cover-up visit blessed Melissa. She marveled at how pleasant an interlude it was, considering its cause. On her way home late the next morning, she reviewed her plans to set her father on his heels.

27

Melissa entered her father's study after a bath and change of clothes. Strengthened by Mrs. Banting's support, she resolved to have a heart-to-heart talk about her father's misguided plan to marry her off to a nobleman.

He was talking before she sat down across the desk from him.

"So my gel, what happy chance brought you under the roof of the admirable Mrs. Lucy Banting?" Papa rubbed his hands together, jovial and eager to learn about his daughter's impromptu social visit. "She is, in my opinion, a lady of quality and, therefore, a desirable contact in every way."

"Papa, it was far from an undilutedly happy event. Your hand-picked suitor has lost his patience, if not his mind. He abducted me, bound and gagged me, and dragged me into a chapel. There, your precious Lord Winstead attempted to force me to wed." She showed her father her profile, chin up.

"What?" he sputtered, half rising. "Forced? Were you harmed?"

"Only if you deem this harm." She held out her wrists, still red and chafed. "If Lord Russell hadn't happened to be in the church, I would now be married to that cad, Winstead. Lord Russell interrupted the proceedings and rescued me. Thanks to him I am not physically harmed. As to my name, if our subterfuge upon leaving the church is successful, my reputation will be unharmed as well."

"Harrumph. This is disturbing." He sat down and stroked his chin. He stuck his finger between his cravat and his neck, pulling the neckcloth out to ease its fashionable tight fit.

"I am quite shaken up, and I require two things from you. One, your agreement this husband hunt among the ton be set aside for at least the near future. Two, I need a restorative visit to the country." She held back the anger teetering on her lips and hoped she played her hand well enough—such a difficult man with which to negotiate.

He came around the desk, took her hand into his, and held it for several long moments. His palpable chagrin salved her pride and subdued her anger.

"Of *course* we can put it all on hold. Winstead is more than on hold—he is out of the running. He's gone beyond the pale."

"I agree, Papa." Melissa tried not to preen over her strategic victory.

"It's too bad his suit became somewhat public knowledge. We will need to let some time go by before we proceed with another candidate now."

She retrieved her hand from her father's. "How nice of you. However, I will not proceed with any more of your impoverished aristocrats, Papa. You must reconsider your approach altogether. Since you have such a talent at finding potential husbands, perhaps use a better set of criteria in the future." If only Papa placed more value on faith, this might never have happened.

"Now, daughter, I'll tolerate no disrespect. Through the years, I have learned a practical, businesslike approach to matters is indeed the best. When I deem enough time has elapsed to resume our mission, you and I shall meet again and review the strategy."

"Papa, remember this is your quest, not ours. Whether it ever resumes at all must be a matter for discussion. I've never been so mortified in my life. He bound and gagged me. Haven't you had enough of your schemes?"

"Well..." He sputtered to a halt.

"I am writing Miss Cleaver today and inviting myself on a visit there. Being abducted has cut up my peace." Melissa stood, scraped together her composure, and left the study.

28

Miss Cleaver hummed as she went about her duties at her brother's vicarage. Her presence as housekeeper contributed to the house running smoothly without many on staff. Betsy, the cook, Bert and Toby for the garden and stable, were supplemented by a kitchen maid and a housemaid who came in during the day.

A pile of mail lay on the hall table. Miss Cleaver always saved it to open when done with her morning round of chores—providing herself a small reward for her labors and an incentive to complete them in short order. She shuffled through the stack as she walked into the parlor. *Oh good, a letter from Melissa.*

She scrabbled in her reticule, which hung from the arm of her favorite rocking chair, for her eyeglasses. Convenience kept her from wearing them all the time—they so easily became smudged—since she only needed them for reading. Glasses on, she reached for the letter knife kept on the nearby table. Delaying gratification, she slit all the envelopes and perused all other pieces of mail first.

At last, she allowed herself the pleasure of reading the correspondence from her former charge.

Dear Priscilla, I hope this missive finds you well, and Mr. Cleaver in fine fettle, also. I've experienced a difficult turn of events in London of late and find myself in need of a time of seclusion, peace, and comfort. May I impose upon you for a visit at the Russelton vicarage? I promise I'll be no trouble.

The letter went on with proposed travel dates, and a smattering of other information, but it lacked clarity as far as she was concerned since there was no explanation of the difficulties. She bit her lip, worried about Melissa. London could be a treacherous place, and dear innocent Melissa may have fallen prey to scandal.

Miss Cleaver wanted very much for Melissa to come to stay. She went to the writing desk in the corner of the room and penned an immediate reply, imploring Melissa to visit without delay. Whatever events befell the poor, lonely young lady would wait. If she sent the letter today, Melissa could be here, telling her woes, in less than a week.

An insistent knock rattling the parlor door broke into her thoughts of her distant friend. "Yes? Come in."

Betsy, the cook, entered, hands clasped under her apron. "Miss Cleaver, a person came to the back door. I didn't know what to say, so I brought her to you."

That's when a dreary figure behind the cook, hovering in the recesses of the hall, came into focus. "Send her in. You did right, Betsy. You may go back to your kitchen."

Unknown visitors were a common occurrence at most vicarages. The long wars ravaged numerous families and sent the economy into a downward spiral, leaving many folks hungry. Where else better to seek aid than a vicarage?

"Don't be afraid. Come in." Miss Cleaver carefully removed her spectacles, set them down, and rose from her seat at the desk. With a coaxing tone and gesture, Miss Cleaver encouraged the bedraggled female to enter the parlor.

On halting steps, the woman moved forward. A pale, pinched face and pained dark eyes partly appeared, shadowed by a sad bonnet and lank tendrils of hair that couldn't decide to be brown or blond. Tidy enough clothing, but mussed and with the distinct look of having fallen on hard times—frayed cuffs, patched gloves, and a hem that needed the attentions of a needle.

"Are you not hungry? Why did the cook bring you to me?"

"I am hungry, ma'am." The woman, young but no longer in the first blush of youth, bobbed a curtsey, and then reached up and shoved the escaping hair back into the bonnet. This revealed a fine-boned face of singular sweetness. "But I asked for more than food. That's why the cook brought me forward."

"What is your request?"

"First, I'd like to properly introduce myself to you. My name is Miss Cassandra Chesney, and I am cast out into the world alone on my own devices. I need work. Oh, please…don't say no."

"I am Miss Cleaver, sister to the minister here. I normally don't hire people via the back door, nor when we have no opening." She laid her fingertips along her temples, stroking them in a rotating motion. "I shall ring for tea, and you can tell me how you came to this sad state of affairs." She lowered her hands and reached for the bell, giving it a shake.

"Oh, thank you, ma'am—so kind of you." Miss Chesney looked around for a seat but waited to be invited.

"Go on. Sit down. I, too, could use a cup of tea." Miss Cleaver herself sat in her rocking chair near the window.

Betsy appeared at the door, mobcap quivering with curiosity. "You rang, Miss Cleaver?"

"Indeed I did. Sorry to disrupt you, Betsy. Please send the day girl—if she's still here—with a tea tray. Add some cheese, meat, bread, and jam to the tray. That's all."

"Day girl's still here. She's helping me make cheese. I'll send her straight away, Miss." She bobbed a curtsy and departed.

"Now that's settled, why are you here?"

The woman sank onto a bench near the fireplace. "Miss Cleaver, I simply want to work—as a maid, even—scullery, kitchen, upstairs, downstairs—anything. I'm desperate."

"Back up and tell me where you're from and how you found yourself in such need."

She wrung her hands. "I hate to admit the truth in this instance."

Miss Cleaver's spine stiffened. "The truth's the only coin accepted here."

"No. I don't mean I'd lie. It's hard to reveal to anyone how far I've fallen."

"Fallen? I see. I'll be frank. Have you lost your virtue? Because there're homes for those unfortunates. I'm not sure this is the place for you."

"That's not how it is. My virtue is intact." She knocked a clutched hand against her chest. "I'm simply so ashamed to be destitute. They turned me out when the new people came. No room for me."

Determined to get to the bottom of it, Miss Cleaver pressed on. "And where was this?

"Two counties over. My father died and left me a penniless orphan with no relatives or other connections to take me in. I had no portion so never was able to marry. But that is the least of my problems now."

"So two counties over, you lost your home. And you came here?"

"Miss, my father often mentioned his colleague, Mr. Cleaver and what a kind, Christ-like man he was. In fact, my father admired him so very much. When I was put out, he was the only possible safe harbor I could think of. Grasping at straws, I know." A tinge of red crept onto the white cheeks.

Footsteps in the hall heralded the maid's arrival. "Here's the maid now. We'll speak no more at this time. Right over here." To the maid, Miss Cleaver indicated a round table near her chair. "That's fine. Thank you so much. I'll ring if we need you. Close the door on your way out."

Miss Cleaver leaned forward to serve. She poured cups of tea, and after adding a generous dollop of milk, passed a cup to Cassandra. "The tea will do you good. Now I'll fix a plate for you."

She handed the plateful to Cassandra who balanced it on her lap. The young woman sipped her tea in a polite fashion. Her manners were pleasingly refined.

"We'll talk more after you've eaten," Miss Cleaver said. She placed her own cup on the table, leaned back, and holding the arms of the chair, rocked steadily, staring straight ahead.

When the guest was done eating, she spoke. "Thank you. That was very good. I am grateful." Cassandra rose to return her plate and cup to the tray. Reseating herself, she looked at Miss Cleaver as if waiting for the questioning to go on.

"Your father was a colleague of Mr. Cleaver?"

"Yes. Apparently they had a collegial acquaintance through their mutual ministerial calling. Papa spoke exceedingly highly of him. I do apologize for coming here this way."

"You've come all the way here on a slim thread of hope?"

"Yes. My only strand of hope."

"I'll need to know your complete story."

"I will tell you all, but in utter confidentiality. I'd hate others to learn of my shame."

"Within reason, depending on your story; and if I have no cause to tell anyone, I shall be as silent as the grave. Now, why don't you slip off your bonnet and pelisse, and let's move over to the fire. The day is so damp." Miss Cleaver mixed firmness with kindness and hoped the woman understood the reason for her pressing inquiries. She could not take in a strange female with a shadowy past.

Shed of her bonnet and pelisse, Cassandra Chesney looked to be about thirty years of age. Thin and peaked-looking, Miss Chesney presented a frowsy appearance due to scarcity of food, Miss Cleaver surmised.

"Miss Cleaver, thank you for suspending your doubts enough to hear me out. I am the daughter of a minister in good standing. He never had money to put by for me or provide a portion for me. He gave much of his meager living to the poor of the parish, to his own health's detriment."

"And how did you end up cast out into the world?" Miss Cleaver thought she could guess the basic scenario. Poor dear—telling all might do her good.

29

"A new man came to take the parish. He and his wife and six children. There was no room for me, and they basically told me to leave. It sounds bad, but I really don't believe they meant for me to be homeless. They didn't realize I'd nowhere to go. My shame wouldn't allow me to bring myself to beg. Now, after two days on the road, sleeping one night in a barn, and one under a hedgerow, I have sunk that low. I implore you to have pity on me."

"My dear, you have my full sympathy. Pity I shall save for the man who cast you out. He'll have to answer for his uncaring action some day."

"All I ask is a corner of a room—the attic's fine. I'll work so hard, you'll forget how you did without me. I simply request that I be here anonymously. I'd like a private existence and for no one to know my story."

"You've done nothing to be ashamed of. But I see no reason to tell anyone."

"But it reflects poorly on others—on my father for not providing—and on the people who cast me out. I feel so worthless, and I'd rather be alone in my humiliation."

"Enough of that talk. I've noticed the stairs becoming more of a trial for me of late. I'm sure my brother will want to ease my duties, and he can well afford another maid. All we have now, besides the cook, and me as a housekeeper, are two day girls."

Miss Cleaver rose, and Cassandra followed suit. "My poor, dear lady," Miss Cleaver said, drawing Cassandra in with a hug around the shoulders, "you've been through the mill. Let's take you upstairs and get you situated."

~*~

"Come in, Priscilla." Mr. Cleaver called. *What now?* The door seemed to receive more traffic whenever he was writing a sermon.

"A surprising…shall we say…a visitor arrived at the back door today." She followed this odd preamble by placing her hands on her hips.

Decidedly martial. "What's got you up in arms?"

"Jeremiah, do you remember a colleague of yours by the name of Chesney? The man's orphaned daughter, Cassandra, appeared here today, looking quite worse for wear."

"An orphan? Here? What did you do with the child?"

"I gave her sustenance. Poor thing hadn't eaten for longer than I'd care to know."

"Well, good. Feeding the hungry's always a blessing. But an orphan? What can we do with a child?"

"Oh, no. Not a child—a young woman. Poor dear's asking for a maid's position. She's been humbled to the dust and will take any scrap or bone offered. Pathetic—about breaks your heart."

"How did she descend to this state?" He steeled himself for a depressing story. He was not disappointed.

"Her father, a minister, as you know, died, leaving Cassandra at the 'mercies' of the incumbent vicar. She was firmly ousted, as they had no room. I am outraged, but she says the new vicar didn't know she had nowhere or no one to go to, and she was too ashamed to tell. She remembered her father speaking so highly of you. So she came here. The poor dear is so worried about anyone learning her plight. It's heartbreaking."

"So, Priscilla, an adult orphan has arrived at our back door. May I ask what you intend to do with her?" He had his suspicions, since his sister took in any strays she could find.

"I want to keep her, of course. The question is, do you approve?"

"Keep her? I can't say 'no,' but please tell me your plans." He rocked back in his chair and inspected his pen point while he listened.

"She's an absolute love. Gentle-spoken, intelligent, and with a servant's heart. I'd like to hire her as my companion, with her doing some maid's duties in the house as needed."

"A companion, Priscilla?" He raised his brows, smiling inwardly.

Defending her request, she rounded on him. "As much as I like being your housekeeper, it gets lonely. A minister's daughter is the perfect match for me. I am sure she has refinements."

"Surely, she does, Priscilla. Of course."

"We have the room. You don't lack the funds to pay an additional servant—unless you've squandered your ample inheritance? And I'd dearly like some female companionship."

"You have my approval. You may hire whomever you deem appropriate."

"Thank you. I will." She smiled, stepped out of the door, and pulled it shut.

Back to his sermon preparation. Now, where was he? Matthew 20:28. 'Even as the Son of man came not to be ministered unto, but to minister, and to give his life a ransom for many.' One of the most sublime passages in Scripture.

~*~

Melissa received Miss Cleaver's letter of invitation and in swift order made preparations to leave London. Having been encouraged to come immediately for a visit and stay at least a month, she had a fair amount of packing to do, but before two days passed, she and Miss Dean bowled along in a carriage, headed for Russelton. They lodged at an inn for one night and were now within an hour of the vicarage.

Melissa's thoughts were full of Lord Russell. She traced the chain of events. Odd how the muddy victim she found in the ditch near the vicarage, turned out to be the returning heir. Hard to believe it happened over the last few days of her prior visit—only slightly over two months ago.

Unpleasant as it was to think about the courtship of the discredited Lord Winstead, she reviewed the debacle for the hundredth time. Handsome and not too objectionable in many respects, but she suspected all along any faith he claimed was merely a thin cultural veneer. His attempted abduction confirmed her doubts.

A strong faith remained her top criterion for a husband. She would have to make her father see reason. There existed no real reason to settle for less.

For now, she could set that problem aside and relish the peace and quiet of the country. Her last visit to Russelton proved quite pleasant and restorative, and she had no reason to predict less for this trip. The upset of the abduction still shook up her peace.

Visiting the vicarage would ground her, and help her recover. Miss Cleaver had been with her as nurse, governess, and then companion. She'd provided Melissa an excellent education. Miss Cleaver herself had been educated alongside her brother, thus obtaining superior learning. She passed on her academic knowledge to her charge, and spiritual training, Bible wisdom, and Christian doctrine provided unity and purpose to her studies. Miss Cleaver and Melissa used to pray and sing together every day as part of her education. Those were good days.

She pressed her face to the window as the carriage moved past the spot where she found Lord Russell after he'd been robbed. Reminiscing, her mind replayed the discovery and retrieval of the victim. Such a peaceful lane, it was hard to believe evil existed in the vicinity. Apprehension welled. *I wonder who the robbers were? Were they apprehended? Would they attack again?*

How lovely it would have been if she had heard from Lord Russell since he'd rescued her. To protect her reputation, he'd stayed away. Sadness tinged her mood. Sitting back, she thought about her clothes to distract her from missing him. The country visit didn't require many fancy gowns to be packed, but a clotheshorse nevertheless, her two large trunks were strapped to the roof of the carriage. She brought a gown for any possible event that might occur during

A Match for Melissa

her stay. It was vanity, but she did love a pretty dress.

Nearing the vicarage, she spied movement at a window. As the carriage drew to a stop, Miss Cleaver emerged onto the front steps, and as soon as the groom let down the steps, Melissa exited the carriage door and dashed up the walk.

An embrace reunited her with her closest friend. "It's such a wonderful thing to be here. How are you?"

"I am well, and my joy is complete now you've arrived." Toby, the handyman, came out and began the process of unloading the trunks. Melissa and Priscilla, followed by Miss Dean, entered the house.

Speaking to the day girl, Miss Cleaver gave instruction. "Show Miss Dean to her room, please. She'll want to settle in, and then unpack Miss Southwood's bags and boxes."

The cluster of females reshuffled in response.

Miss Cleaver gestured toward a nearby door. "Melissa, I'll be in the parlor. Travel is mightily wearying. Join me when you've refreshed yourself."

By the time she descended, Miss Cleaver was waiting with a steaming kettle. A tray holding teapot, cups, and scones rested on a lace-covered wooden table between the fireplace and a comfortable settee.

"Oh, my, that was a long sit." She arched her back. "Traveling is a necessary evil, but I am glad this trip is over. Do you mind if I stand for a while? I sat so long in the carriage."

"As you like, dear." Priscilla prepared the tea. It took both hands to lift the heavy pot.

Not wanting to wait any longer, Melissa broached the subject she longed to unburden herself of. "Priscilla, did you wonder at all why I invited myself to visit you? I haven't been in the habit of visits of this frequency, but I sorely needed a respite and some peaceful recovery time."

"What transpired, my dear? Your letter hinted at an unpleasant event." She handed Melissa a cup of tea.

She accepted the tea with a distracted air. "You'll soon understand why I didn't want to put pen to paper. I shall tell you plainly, now that we are together." Her cup began to rattle against the saucer, and she set it down, impatient to unburden herself.

"I mentioned in my letters that my Papa arranged a match for me with Lord Winstead? Do you recall that I demanded a two-month courtship and tentative right to refuse for a 'good' reason?"

"Yes, I remember your letters, explaining all the arrangements your father set into motion."

Melissa shivered and paused. "Well, two months were up a week ago or thereabouts, and I still wasn't sure."

"Here's your scone and butter, the way you like it, dear."

"Thank you." She accepted the plate, set it on the table, and forged ahead. "I will give Papa credit. He did allow me one more month to decide for sure. He clearly thought the delay a mere formality—sure of getting his own way."

"An extension—gracious and kind of your father, I must say. Many fathers show no such consideration at all when matters of matches arise."

"All proceeded somewhat well. I *was* sincerely trying to decide. Lord Winstead hadn't done anything truly objectionable.

"That's faint praise."

"Yes. But as I was saying, I wasn't at all ready to assent to marry the man. My spirit resisted—reason being, I wasn't able to discern a strong Christian faith in him, and that remains my first criterion for a husband."

"Marriage is a serious undertaking. I see why you had qualms."

"Thank you for understanding. I thought you would." Melissa lifted her cup and saucer again—no rattles this time—sipped, and put it back down. "I can only speculate the reason behind what occurred next. I believe Lord Winstead's pockets were to let."

"He was poor?"

"I am guessing he was at least at low tide. He took me out for a drive, one of our main courting activities, and asked for my answer right there. When I told him the truth—that I couldn't yet give him the 'yes' he desired—he pretended to accept it, but then he abducted me."

"Good gracious! Kidnapping's a hideous crime."

"Indeed." Melissa took a calming breath, reached for her plate, and then lifted the scone to her nose. "Ooh, lemon." She savored a bite of the tangy treat.

"Did he hold you for ransom?"

"No, he bound and gagged me and trundled me into a church. He had a special license in his pocket and a shabby minister hired to do the ceremony. I assume he planned to escort me there if I had agreed to marry him when he pressed me for an answer in the carriage, but being prepared for either answer. Obtaining that special license must have cost him his last coin."

Miss Cleaver hissed, vibrating with indignation. "What a merciless rogue."

"Yes, well. Unable to speak a word because of the gag, I did make the most negative sound I could when asked to say a vow, but if a rescuer hadn't arrived, they would have disregarded my protestations anyway." She took another nibble of the tart, buttery scone, and set it aside, too agitated to eat more.

Miss Cleaver clattered her cup into its saucer and swiveled to face Melissa. "Rescuer?"

"You will be most astonished at his identity. In God's providence, my hero was Lord Russell who was present in the same church."

Miss Cleaver clasped her hands to her bony chest. "Praise God." She breathed out the words.

"Yes, I am grateful. Lord Russell scattered my foes and spirited me off to his aunt's house, with society none the wiser. She is a sweet and attractive lady. You two would get along rather well, I declare."

"So Lord Russell saved the day. Oh my. What a tale. I must say, quite a shocking experience for you, my dear. We will lay low, dear, until you regain equilibrium. What an unsettling turn of events. Does Lord Russell know of your retreat to Russelton?"

"I have no idea. In his wisdom, he stayed away from my vicinity in order that not the least gossip would arise about me at this frightful time. He cared only to protect my reputation." She'd love to see him, but alas, she couldn't do anything about that. She could have her hopes, though. And he had her prayers.

30

Mr. Southwood had a rare day not chock full of business dealings. A few days after Melissa's departure, the only sound in his oak-lined study was the ticking clock. Comfortable in his upholstered and well-padded leather desk chair, he allowed his mind to drift back over his pleasant memories of the Banting ball not long past.

Ah, what an evening. Mingling with the nobility. Dancing with the aristocracy. Melissa fit right in. Too bad about Winstead. A dashed disappointment he turned out to be.

An idea formed. What prevented him from calling on the delightful hostess? Mrs. Lucy Banting didn't have a title, but she belonged to the ton, and the invitation to her ball showed she wasn't averse to his acquaintance.

He checked the time, and finding it within society's prescribed visiting hours, he rang for a servant to bring a carriage around to the front of the house. A few minutes later, he left to pay a morning call on Mrs. Banting.

~*~

Mrs. Lucy Banting had just rid herself of some pesky, gossipy callers. Relieved, she sat alone when the aged butler shuffled in to announce another guest.

"Mr. Homer Southwood is at the door. Are you at home?"

"Yes. Show him in." Mrs. Banting resituated herself and sat up straighter in anticipation of an interesting, if not necessarily pleasant, visit. She worried he'd blame her somehow. That would take nerve since it was entirely his doing. She wore a butter-yellow morning gown with a frothy fichu filling in the low, fashionable neckline. A feminine lace cap covered most of her hair, but soft wings of dark hair were visible at either temple.

The butler vanished into the shadows of the hall when Mr. Southwood entered the room. He bowed over Mrs. Banting's hand, and then sat on the nearest chair, first sweeping the tails of his coat out of the way.

He leaned forward with a confiding demeanor. "We—my daughter Melissa and I—had a wonderful time at your ball, Mrs. Banting. I thought you wouldn't take it amiss if I called on you to express my gratitude for the evening."

"You are quite welcome, Mr. Southwood. The bouquet of camellias you sent were exquisite, and their scent perfumed the air around me for days on end."

"My pleasure. Glad you liked them. Have you heard any on-dits about Melissa of late?"

"Why, Mr. Southwood, do you expect me to repeat such to her own father?" She batted her lashes a bit, believing it wouldn't hurt to distract the man.

"I'd like you to if you've heard any. You see, you are the only society lady with whom I am acquainted. I'll take the chance of trusting you. Something rather untoward occurred, and I'd like to know if it trickled out." He sat back and puffed out his chest.

"I'll admit I am thoroughly familiar with what

happened at St. George's that day. Rest assured, Mr. Southwood, word of your hand-selected suitor's malfeasance did not go beyond this room, thanks to my nephew's wise actions."

"Lord Russell is a fine young man and seems trustworthy."

"Your trust is not misplaced."

"You know all?" Homer's discomfiture was evident in the way he yanked at his collar.

"Melissa needed another female to pour her heart out to after her frightening experience. And to think the abduction came about because of what you put in motion."

Her chiding perhaps crossed the line of propriety, but Mrs. Banting didn't care if she made him sweat. She hoped his nose was out of joint from her chiding.

"Here, here. Don't rake me over the coals, ma'am. I've set aside my ambitions for Melissa for the nonce. Before you blame me for her abduction, you must understand the complete unpredictability of such an event. I had Winstead checked out in detail, and if he'd ever shown a hint of anything like this, he would never have been allowed through my door." Homer gave an emphatic gesture with his fist.

"Proving only more so, Mr. Southwood, that matters of the heart take a sensitive touch." Lucy tilted her head to one side. She fluttered her eyelashes at him.

His eyebrows rose a fraction. "Do tell. What makes you say so?"

"My own experience of courtship does, Mr. Southwood. Over twenty years ago, I married my dear departed husband, Henry. Like you, my parents also coveted a title, but when Henry Banting set his cap for me, and I for him, they gave me my way. They relinquished their ambitions. Mr. Banting and I had a fine marriage. I lived as happily as if he had been a marquis, an earl, or duke."

"I see. An interesting story. One which I shall take into consideration. Now, let's go back to discussing your ball and its splendor. Your musicians, your refreshments, the magical atmosphere. I could go on and on. They were all exceptionally pleasant. It was a privilege to have been a part of it." Homer Southwood sat forward eagerly and attempted to turn on the charm by pouring out the butter boat.

She saw through him but took this golden opportunity to laud her favorite nephew. "Think nothing of it. My nephew asked me, and I was pleased to include the family of such a pretty-behaved young lady as Melissa.

"'Twas my pleasure to be included, ma'am."

"My nephew, Lord Russell, the hero who rescued her from the heinous trap laid for her at the church," she raised her eyebrows and tilted her head, "happened to tell me he tried to enter into the courtship circus that you created."

"I recall something of the sort."

Lucy went on, making sure he recalled all the details. "Even though his efforts came to no avail with you, he still was kind enough to think of inviting you when he and I made up the guest list for the ball." There, a reminder of her gracious invitation.

"Very good of him. My daughter is off visiting her former companion. After her unfortunate upsetting experience, a country retreat serves as just the remedy. She'll return to London in one month. I did agree to postpone any match for at least that long." He leaned back, eyes distant for a moment.

"Wise of you, I'm sure." Lucy smiled, and widened her eyes as though she thought him imbued with the wisdom of Solomon. Let him think he's on top of it all. She knew better.

"Time will tell. She doesn't like the idea, but I am still going to try to match her with an aristocrat. With my fortune, it won't be a problem. I had many a lord come calling to request permission to court Melissa."

"You seem quite determined. Are you familiar with the region of the country in which your daughter is now visiting?"

"Not much. It's the village where her old companion landed when I dismissed her. I believe she is housekeeping for her brother, a minister." He vaguely waved his hand.

Mr. Southwood showed little interest in the exact arrangements of Melissa's trip to the country, and Lucy got the distinct impression he was not aware of the proximity of Mark's estate and the vicarage in the town of Russelton at which Melissa was guest. Mr. Southwood must not be aware of the propinquity involved. An idea formed in her mind, but she didn't speak a word of it.

"Mrs. Banting, would you care to take a drive in the park with me? Today? Or someday soon? I'd be honored."

"Driving out with you sounds like a fine treat, but I am afraid that I myself am going out of town soon. I don't have time to be riding about. I've got to prepare my household for travel, so I must bid you adieu for now. I've enjoyed your visit, and I shall send my card when I can take you up on your kind offer of a drive in the park." She raised her hand, and he sprang up to bow over it, kissing the air one inch above the back of her fingers.

As soon as Mr. Homer Southwood bowed his way out, she scribbled a note. She rang for the butler and arranged for the missive to be delivered.

31

Mark put down the morning paper when the butler brought in an envelope on a silver tray. He opened it and read:

Dear Nephew, today Mr. S. paid me a call. I'll tell you the details later, but I got the distinct impression he doesn't realize your estate is in the same town as the friends Miss S. is visiting. She is visiting the C's and I propose you and I take a visit to Russell Manor.

I think you would be able to further your acquaintance with Miss S. there, without her father's interfering machinations. I'd as soon spend some time there, and I can be a convenient chaperone if needed. Fondly, LB.

Since no gossip about Miss Southwood had flared up, nothing required his presence in London for damage control nor for anything else. Aunt Lucy's excellent idea lit his heart with hope. He threw the note in the fireplace, lit it with a match, and watched it burn. He wanted no risk of a nosy servant poking into the master's plans. The future was taking shape, and a favorable outcome was in sight.

The only reason he came to London in the first place was to secure a wife—a helpmeet. Since his heart was set on Melissa, he wanted to go to her. He had every right to return to his estate and to take Aunt Lucy with him—if that also brought him into contact with Melissa, so be it.

~*~

Traveling together in his family coach gave Mark ample opportunity, over the two-day journey, to discuss with Aunt Lucy, his chances to further his acquaintance with Melissa.

He chafed at the enforced inactivity but enjoyed discussing the object of his affections. "At some point, I will need to approach her father again."

"But, surely you aren't required to tell him you're in your own village," Aunt Lucy suggested.

"Agreed. As a neighbor, however, I am well within the bounds of propriety if I choose to invite the Cleavers to Russell Manor for dinner. If their houseguest happens to be included in the invitation and chooses to accept, we are not to blame, are we?"

"No, no, Mark. You've stated an excellent approach to the matter. And if you and I pay calls to some of your more prominent neighbors, such as the minister, no one could fault you." She clasped her hands in front of her bodice.

"I hope this isn't dishonest of me."

"Mark, how is it deceitful to go to your own manor? Or to visit neighbors?"

"It's not actively deception, but I still intend to keep strict limits on myself. I won't spend time with her alone. Nor will I allow 'happenstance' to find us together unchaperoned."

"That sounds quite reasonable to me," Aunt Lucy replied.

"Can you think of anything else I should do, or not do, to keep my unofficial courtship of Miss Southwood within appropriate boundaries?"

"Aah, 'courtship.' I love the sound of that word. I

love words ending in 'ship.' They're all splendid: worship, friendship, courtship. What were you asking?"

"Aunt, you do have a love for words. But be serious. Have I overlooked anything?" He wanted to give her every chance to express doubts.

"I'm a bit rusty on the subject of courtship, but it seems to me you may proceed as you've stated. Your plans seem to be appropriate to the circumstances. I own that I'm anxious for a refreshing time in the country. Your campaign will add the right amount of spice to life."

~*~

The servants were all lined up in the hall to greet the returning Lord Russell as was customary. He and Aunt Lucy went down the line, giving a kind word here, a smile there.

Tradition satisfied, the butler stepped forward, gave a bow, and made a request. "If it be your pleasure, sir, may I have a moment?" Mr. Crabtree said.

"Let us step into the library this minute, Crabtree. Mrs. Good," Mark turned to the housekeeper with his index finger raised. "Please show Mrs. Banting to her rooms, direct a substantial tea to be laid in the front parlor in one hour, and bring hot water to both of our suites. Travel proved dusty."

"Yes, Lord Russell, I shall have all in order." Mrs. Good curtsied, and then shooed the other servants. "Get back to your duties."

32

Delivering his information with an air of some self-importance, Crabtree intoned, "Lord Russell, the magistrate has called here once a week, wanting to give an account of the search for the scoundrels who robbed you."

"Is there anything to report?"

"There've been no results of the searches. He asked me to inform you without delay that he remains on high alert."

"Very good. Anything else?"

"Thought we should talk in here. I've been trying to keep it all somewhat quiet. No need to remind everyone of what happened to you and have the staff scared of their own shadows." The man's chest puffed out.

"You did right, Crabtree. I had things to do in London, but now that I am back, I aim to bring those malefactors to justice if it's within my power. Can't allow our blissful surroundings to be marred by the lurking presence of ill-doing reprobates."

"Thank you, Lord Russell. I have kept my own eyes sharp but haven't seen hide nor hair of strangers hereabouts. Any further instructions, sir?"

"Only tell Mrs. Good to expect to consult with my aunt in regards to some entertaining she and I plan to do. She will be acting as hostess for me during her visit. It seems I will be busy with the estate—and other things."

Mark went to his rooms, where his valet assisted him out of his traveling clothes. A hot bath sat ready, and with gratitude, he sank into its sudsy depths. As he relaxed, his mind wandered. *Lord, I put my courtship of Miss Southwood into Your hands. Let it be successful if it be Your will.* She was his top priority.

What to do about the thieves suspected to be prowling the district? Other than stumbling across a thieves' den, he didn't truly expect to be the one to solve the case. But he'd meet with the magistrate and develop a plan from there. This would be a good chance to show leadership. To show himself to be a conscientious landowner. The burden of filling his brother's shoes hung ever-present over his head.

He wanted to apply his new firmness of character to the local situation. He didn't intend to sit careless or idle, simply enjoying riches. He had some ground to recover. The desire to do right by the inheritance surprised him with its strength. His goal was to be an excellent landowner and a good steward of his inheritance. Owning property brought responsibility.

Because of his status as Lord Russell, he held the power to do good through his position in the community. He would look around and seek out avenues to help others.

An hour later, he found Aunt Lucy already in the drawing room, enjoying the shade-dappled late afternoon sunshine streaming in the south-facing windows of the pleasant room. Sumptuous upholstery, blue walls, white-painted satiny wood trim, and striped damask drapes combined to give an atmosphere of comfort.

"Mark, dear, shall we call on the vicarage right

away tomorrow morning?"

"Yes, that's the first thing I want to do. Afterwards, I'll locate the magistrate and set up a meeting to plan the capture of the robbers who struck me down—if they are in the vicinity, of course."

Aunt Lucy held up the teapot and arched her brow. "Tea?"

"Yes, please. The cook here is excellent. Her biscuits are superb."

"I suppose you'll be busy with the estate for the duration of our stay?"

"I have a strong desire to fulfill my duties. Not to be served, but to serve. Do you understand what I mean, Aunt Lucy?"

"Oh, my yes, I, too, itch to get at something like that. What do you think about knitting?"

"Knitting? I never think about it. Why do you ask?"

"I had the thought that it would be good to teach the serving girls to knit. Having another skill is always of benefit. It's a simple handicraft, but 'hands to work, hearts to God,' after all."

"Not taking them away from their duties too much?"

"No, I'll be careful about that."

"Fine. That's the sort of improving work you should lead. It's also suitable for Russell Manor. I approve. You may have free rein, Aunt. You will be a responsible and kind teacher to them."

"I'll speak to Mrs. Good and get her cooperation first. Then I will know how many students to buy yarn and needles for while we're in town to see Miss Southwood. And the Cleavers."

33

"How is the new companion settling in?" Jeremiah Cleaver lowered his newspaper.

"She's a dear—so willing to help and enjoyable to have around. We've gained a gem in Cassandra."

"I heard the piano yesterday. No offense, but the playing sounded more advanced than yours, Prissy." He wiggled his eyebrows to make sure she knew he meant no insult.

"That was Cassandra. She's an accomplished pianist. Well-read, too, with several foreign languages to her credit. It's a joy to discover a new friend and learn of her gifts."

"I am glad for you. As you said, you'd been lonely, and now you have a like-minded companion. I hear a carriage outside." He rose and looked out. "It's Lord Russell and an older lady." *No, not that old, and actually quite attractive.*

"Must be here to pay a call." Miss Cleaver smoothed her hair.

Cassandra, having answered the door, entered the room to announce the callers.

"By all means, bring them in, please." Mr. Cleaver couldn't wait to see Lord Russell again—and hear how he'd been faring since going up to London.

Cassandra slipped away as the arrivals entered.

Lord Russell spoke first. "Mr. Cleaver, Miss Cleaver, I'd like to introduce my aunt, Mrs. Banting."

Jeremiah bowed over her hand first. Then her blue eyes caught his attention as he straightened. "Welcome, Mrs. Banting."

She smiled, and her eyes seemed to sparkle just for him. He turned to Lord Russell and clasped his hand in a firm shake. "So good to have you back in the neighborhood."

Miss Cleaver patted the settee next to her, and Mrs. Banting joined her there. Soon the ladies were chatting like old friends and were settled in for a visit in the homey parlor.

Not much time at all went by when tea was carried in by Cassandra, again acting in her role as maid.

~*~

Mark noticed the new maid was thin and pale, and she kept glancing at the minister as if to make sure he had all he needed.

"Thank you, Cassandra. Inform Miss Southwood we've guests and we'd like her to join us for tea? And bring more hot water in about fifteen minutes, please." Mr. Cleaver's tone exuded kindness.

The meek maid left the room, eyes down.

Mr. Cleaver rushed to explain. "Miss Cleaver convinced me to hire a new live-in servant. She acts as maid when needed and as a companion for Miss Cleaver. I think we have made an excellent choice in Cassandra."

Mark battled to keep his eyes from straying to the door. "That's nice."

"Lord Russell, how have you been faring since we last saw you?" Mr. Cleaver queried in a jovial voice.

"I've been in fine health and spirits. Subsequent to my recovering here, my life has been much more peaceful than in the past." A wide unbidden smile crept onto his face as he remembered the days spent at the vicarage.

"Glad to hear it. Oh, here's Miss Southwood." The two men rose, and Mr. Cleaver stepped over and took her arm as she entered, drawing her into the circle. "Look who's visiting, Miss Southwood!" He gestured toward Mark and Lucy. His booming voice resounded in the small room.

"Oh. How nice to see you, Lord Russell, and you, too, Mrs. Banting." Melissa bent to sit, averting her face to adjust her shawl.

~*~

Her face must be red. It felt warm. Such a surprise to find Lord Russell in the parlor—she tried to calm her erratic heartbeat. Melissa had no idea he was back in the district. After her shocking abduction, suitors were far from her mind. Well, to be honest, she had been troubled by thoughts of missing Lord Russell at times—every night, to be truthful, as she went to sleep. To be honest—he visited her dreams.

She forced herself to attention. Miss Cleaver spoke social niceties to the guests. "Mrs. Banting, do try one of these tarts. Our cook calls them her specialty, and I shall hate to explain to her if no one partakes."

"Oh, don't mind if I do." Mrs. Banting lifted a tart onto a plate, and then inhaled its scent. "Lemon. My favorite." She took a bite. "I declare these are the flakiest, most tender, most delicious lemon tarts it has ever been my pleasure to experience."

Melissa helped herself to a tart, too. It gave her hands something to do besides fidget. Before she bit into it, she sneaked a glance at Lord Russell. What caused his return to Russell Manor at this time? Whatever his reasons, Melissa thrilled to the sight of him—warm effervescent shivers of delight rippled up and down her body. Even though her experience with men was limited, he was decidedly special. His masculine vigor combined with simple human compassion, and his pleasant and humble demeanor made him a breath of fresh air. She adjusted her position on the serviceable horsehair settee. What to say? What a relief when her host spoke.

"Mrs. Banting, have you been in the district often?"

"Yes, I grew up here. Lord Russell's father was my brother." Mrs. Banting sipped her tea and reminisced. "Those were wonderful days. Since my marriage twenty-some years ago, I've visited only on the rare occasion and not at all from the time when I was widowed."

"I see—you are a widow. So sad."

He didn't sound sad, Melissa noted.

The minister went on, "How was your journey?"

"Travel was without any disruptions." Mrs. Banting sniffed. "Thank the Lord we experienced no repeat of the disastrous attack on my nephew."

"Indeed. The robbery of Lord Russell appears to be a singular event. Almost like he was targeted, as hard as that is to believe."

"I've wondered about that myself." Mrs. Banting raised her eyebrows and tapped Mr. Cleaver's arm with her fan.

Melissa, observing all this interplay and able to

hear every word, began to wonder at Mr. Cleaver's attentiveness. He showed all the signs of being smitten by Mrs. Banting.

"Have you any plans for your time in the area?" The minister went on with his queries of the lady and there were no more conversational gaps. The outgoing and talkative siblings Mr. Cleaver and Miss Cleaver overflowed with fine cheer as usual.

Melissa had forgotten the full extent of Lord Russell's amazing good looks. His handsomeness made it hard to contribute to the chatter with this virile man sitting not even five feet away from her.

She lowered her eyes, scolding herself for staring so much at Lord Russell. She recalled how once he appeared at her home in London, and how he came on the scene too late to be chosen as her sanctioned suitor. Then she encountered him at the feeding mission. Quite a fascinating discovery to find out he cared for the poor and hungry, supporting the same charity work she did. His work for the Lord indicated him to be a sincere believer.

Outwardly relaxed upon the settee, with conversation flowing around her, her mind wandered on to the other encounters they had. No one would notice her silence, with all the chatty folk gathered at the vicarage today. She remembered him at the ball. How considerate he was of his aunt. That was, indeed, a good sign. He was an excellent dancer, too.

This brought Melissa's reminiscences up to the abduction and the way God sent Lord Russell to rescue her. Since that day, she'd wondered if he would seek her out, but she hadn't seen him until today.

~*~

Mark watched Miss Southwood as she sat silent. He caught her eye to share a smile but achieved limited success. Was she avoiding him for a reason? Had she taken him in dislike? Perhaps the sordid affair in the church mortified her to the degree she hated to be reminded by his presence. He dearly hoped not.

She appeared to be daydreaming but looked adorably fresh and demure in her muslin dress. She had a quirk—she'd twirl a curl near her cheek around her finger, and then release it, whereupon it would coil back into a natural ringlet. She didn't glance his way again, so he turned to Mr. Cleaver and tried to give him full attention. This did not stop Mark from being acutely aware of the loveliness embodied by Miss Southwood. Seeing her afresh, he was newly astounded by her beauty.

Cassandra returned. The maid handled the hot water and heavy teapot with practiced composure. Mark wondered at a servant with such a fanciful name from Greek mythology. The woman did seem to be competent and took special care of the minister's tea cup. She curtseyed before departing, angling her bob toward Mr. Cleaver. He must be a good employer—surely all his workers admired him and wanted to do their best for him.

Though distracted for a moment by his observations of the special deference of the maid to the minister, Mark's eyes had a will of their own, still trying to catch Miss Southwood's glance. Not succeeding, he satisfied himself with watching her every few minutes. He'd seen many a beautiful woman in his life. What was exceptional about her? It wasn't simply her smooth skin, her shiny golden hair, or her classic face. Her beauty set her apart from many of the other young women he'd come across—but it was more.

"Mr. Cleaver, would you and your sister and guest honor my home with your presence for dinner tomorrow evening?"

"We'd be delighted, wouldn't we, Priscilla? Miss Southwood?"

"Delightful. We will be glad to accept your kind invitation." Miss Cleaver looked at Miss Southwood, and smiled with brows raised, clearly confident this would be acceptable to her. Melissa nodded and murmured her assent.

"I've been telling my aunt about your charming gardens. Before we depart, may we all take a turn in the vicarage garden?" Mark caught Miss Southwood's gaze at last and received a tentative, yet sweet smile.

"Excellent. Just the thing." Miss Cleaver beamed, and the men rose first.

Mr. Cleaver held out his arm. Aunt Lucy laid her hand on it, and they led the way out. Mark bent both arms and escorted Miss Southwood and Miss Cleaver.

Once out in the garden and on the smooth looping paths, Miss Southwood let go of his arm and moved off a ways. Bereft, he comforted himself that at least she was near. The gardens lay arranged around a fountain and bordered by boxwood hedges. Even though he wanted to, Mark didn't make his attentions too pressing. Without permission to court her, he must avoid any efforts to attach her affections. This limit became a battleground because every bit of him wanted nothing more than to pursue her. He even went so far as to discuss various flora with Miss Cleaver while he forced down the desire to get close to

Miss Southwood.

The garden was small, however, and thus he, independently deciding to peruse a sumptuous rose bush laden with pale pink blooms, soon found himself in proximity to the object of his affections.

Miss Cleaver turned away with no little alacrity and took Aunt Lucy by the arm, steering her to the opposite side of the garden. "I want to show you my favorite arbor."

Miss Southwood smiled up at him from under her lashes, and a connection simmered like an invisible thread. Mark reached out and touched a rose, stroking its velvety petals. "This rose is beautiful. God provides such splendor in nature."

"Yes, He is a loving, creative God." Her pensive tone touched his heart.

"The way He has ordered creation is a marvel too vast to comprehend, but we can observe His glory everywhere." Mark arced his arm in an encompassing gesture, but his words held a double meaning as he drank in the sight of her feminine beauty.

She gazed right at him. "These flowers remind me of the bouquet of lilies you sent in London. It was very pretty. I never thanked you."

Thrilled that she was giving him eye contact, he almost forgot to respond. "You are welcome. I am delighted you'll be over for dinner tomorrow evening. I look forward to it."

She agreed. "I expect it will be a night to remember."

Memorable because she'd be with him, he hoped. The two ambled on through the small garden in plain sight of the others on the circular paths.

A Match for Melissa

~*~

Concentrating on writing a sermon didn't come easy after the distraction of a visit by an exceedingly pleasant set of guests—Lord Russell and his aunt. Who knew Lord Russell had such an attractive aunt? Quite interesting, too—so lighthearted and amusing, in a modest way. Jeremiah stared off into the far corner of the room, not seeing. Was this love coming to him late in life? He exhaled a breath he didn't realize he held and it came out a sigh.

"Sir? May I pick up the tea tray, now?"

"Oh, Cassandra. Certainly. I was gathering my thoughts for Sunday's sermon."

"So impressive, the way preachers can illuminate the Bible for those in the pews. Father used to practice his sermons and often I acted as a trial congregation, giving him my reaction."

"Now that would be helpful. He must have appreciated you. I remember him as a very godly man. You surely miss him very much."

"Yes, sir. He and I were close. He was my tutor and shared with me as much knowledge as I could absorb. I do miss him."

"Mr. Chesney possessed a fine education. I recall him having a fondness for languages—Greek, Latin, and Hebrew. Is that correct?"

"Oh, yes. Father was a scholar." Her hand shot up to cover her mouth, and she dropped her head, scooped the tea tray, and scurried toward the door. "I must go now."

"Perhaps you'll be able to help me with a tricky translation some other day." He stopped speaking since she slipped through the door and was gone.

Thoughtful, he dipped his pen in ink and began again to concentrate on the sermon—but distracted by thoughts of a little blue-eyed orphaned maid.

34

At Russell Manor later that afternoon, Aunt Lucy planned the menu, closeted with Mrs. Good. With attention to detail, Aunt Lucy would be working off a list, choosing flowers, china, and plate. The dinner party would keep her busy. Confident in his aunt's hostess abilities, Mark put his mind to other matters. Determined to hold his own as master of the estate, he met with the local magistrate, Mr. Billington.

"I've taken out a search party weekly. I personally searched the neighborhood several times—every free hour, Lord Russell. Can't find a shred of evidence pointing to the presence of any outsiders. We being located remote-like, most criminals would have to wait around a while for a coach or traveler to rob." He clutched his hat in this hand, rolling the brim.

"You've checked for gypsies or for reports of highwaymen in surrounding counties? It should be easy for the folks hereabouts to spot interlopers slipping across county lines." Mark tapped his fingertips on the desktop.

Billington's face fell into creases. "I've inquired of my colleagues. No rash of highway robbery, no gypsy encampments—nothing. Not a clue's shown up as yet. I will remind the locals to be alert. The roads have to be kept safe. It is such a shame and a scandal for the new lord of the manor to be struck down in broad daylight—"

"Enough." Mark held up his hand to halt the flow of regrets. He didn't care for how his attack was made out to be more important because of his status. Anyone left for dead should get the same level of concern.

"Yes, sir, of course. I just meant—"

Mark cut off the man's words again. "I came out of it fine. But, of course, I don't want anyone else to suffer a similar or worse fate. I'll be patrolling the boundaries of my lands several times a week. Perhaps I'll spot someone or something out of place." The lack of criminal activities or clues made him wonder if the attack targeted him specifically. An agent of doom, lying in wait for him alone. But why? He was aware of no enemies.

After dismissing Billington, Mark went out to walk off his frustration. He stalked along the paths, eyes staring straight ahead, hands clasped behind his back. The mantle of victimhood did not sit well with him. Various plans and schemes to capture an amorphous enemy traipsed through his mind, never amounting to a workable plan.

Thoughts of Miss Southwood soon overtook sordid thoughts of crime. He'd much rather think of her than of footpads knocking him over the head. Conjuring her in his mind's eye brought a smile to his heart.

When the path took him by the edge of a cool, deep pond, he scooped water up and splashed his face. This cleared his head further and reminded him of the portion of Scripture he read that morning. *Thou wilt keep him in perfect peace, whose mind is stayed on thee: because he trusteth in thee.*

Without intending it, he walked on, arriving at a stile marking a shortcut to the vicarage. Up and over, down the path. His legs had a mind of their own. He soon knocked at the vicarage door.

The new maid answered the door. "Good morning, sir."

Her well-modulated voice surprised him. Perhaps she was a penniless gentlewoman fallen on hard times. The Cleavers were so kind, they probably couldn't turn anyone away. "Good morning. You're new here, aren't you?"

She bobbed a curtsey. "I'm Cassandra." Composed, the small woman stood her ground.

He realized she was waiting for him to say what he wanted. "Lord Russell, here to visit the minister."

"I'll see if he's receiving." She turned away, swift to do her job.

Mark busied himself with shedding his hat and gloves but wasn't left to wait long.

"Follow me, sir." Spine straight, Cassandra led him to the correct door. "He's in here."

"Hello. Come right in," Mr. Cleaver's loud voice boomed, and he waved Mark into his cramped study. "Pleased to see you again so soon. This will give us a chance to talk without the ladies." He gestured, indicating two matching armchairs in front of the desk.

Mark settled into a chair, and Mr. Cleaver came around the desk to sit in the other. He crossed his legs and angled toward Mark. "Is Mrs. Banting enjoying her visit?"

"Aunt Lucy is happy here. She'll soon be occupied teaching our serving girls to knit. Being of service to others is a new focus of hers. You see, in London, after she learned of my conversion, she had a renewal of her own faith. We began observing the Sabbath together." Mark tented his fingers under his chin.

Mr. Cleaver's face lit up at this news. "She's a fine lady. And what of you, Mark? Tell me why you're back in Russelton this time?"

A tap sounded on the door.

"I'll answer that question in a moment."

Cassandra entered, balancing a heavy tray. After taking special care of Mr. Cleaver's plate, napkin, cup, and milk, she curtsied her way out, and the men helped themselves to biscuits.

"That reminds me. Your new maid seems quite refined for a simple housemaid. And that name, Cassandra. So fancy? How old is she?" Mark picked up his cup.

"Poor thing. Looks about thirty. She appeared at the back door on her last legs. My sister and I determined we needed more help, and there you have it. She also considers the young woman to be a companion for herself. Priscilla deserves some company instead of being alone with just me all the time. I'm happy she likes the maid that well. A mystery exists about how Cassandra, a minister's daughter, came to be cast out on the world. My sister has the details, but she didn't repeat them. Whatever the troubles, honest work is hard to find—certainly for a young woman with no relatives nor any place to go. That much I can surmise."

From a distant room, came the sound of a piano. A talented pianist was playing an arrangement of a hymn. "Who's the pianist?"

"Not my sister. She's never gotten this advanced. It's the maid, Cassandra. She's very accomplished in her education, being a minister's daughter and only child. She asked to use the piano, but I had no idea she could play this well."

"She's quite a musician." Mark leaned back and enjoyed the distant melody.

"Indeed, she is. So, you've returned to the country after your time in London. Your note said you were going there for personal business. Did that go well?"

"Yes and no. Since I trust you not to gossip, I'll explain all."

"Strict confidentiality, my boy."

"I decided to dip my toe into the marriage mart in search of a helpmeet. A wife is a good thing, the Bible says."

"But it didn't go as planned? I've certainly heard nothing of a betrothal, nor have I seen an engagement announcement in the *Times*. And you indicated in your letter that your eye had been taken by a certain young lady." Cleaver waggled his brows.

"My initial plans failed, but I haven't given up. You asked me what brought me back to Russelton? That's an easy one. Miss Southwood. I don't need a reason other than I consider this to be my home, and I find it pleasant. I only left for London when I did to perhaps secure a suitable wife on the marriage market. If it hadn't been for that motive, I'd have burrowed myself away at Russell Manor for the rest of my days. You read my letter? Yes, well, I seem to be in a bit of a hard spot."

"Your letter. Quite a dilemma you placed before me. How goes it?" Cleaver uncrossed his legs and leaned forward, one elbow on the arm of the chair.

"My dilemma is one of honor opposed to desire. I purposely 'followed' Miss Southwood back to this neighborhood. I believe it is acceptable for us to be in the same vicinity, yet I don't believe it would be honorable for me to openly court her without her father's permission."

I won't let her go—nor let her slip through my fingers again. If I don't win her, it won't be because of a missed opportunity.

"So you are planning to further your acquaintance via proximity, but not outright pursuit?"

"You've stated exactly what I'm thinking. That is my hope. Do I at least have your approval to some degree?"

"I can't say I'm knowledgeable about winning a young lady's heart, but if you are able to spend time furthering the acquaintance while in company, I don't see harm." He stroked his upper lip with the side of his forefinger.

"Your good opinion means a lot to me. And since I value and respect your opinion, Mr. Cleaver, I promise to keep you apprised. Thank you for the tea and the visit. I'll let myself out now."

After a handshake, Mark moved out into the hall. The maid, Cassandra, handed him his hat and cane somewhat hurriedly. Then she turned and slipped into the study.

Mark reached for the handle of the front door. It opened, and Miss Southwood moved through the door, bent over, fussing with the hem of her dress, caught on a rough spot on the doorframe. She looked up after getting it loose. "Oh my!" Her hand flew to her throat.

They smiled at each other. Mark stepped to one side, only to find she'd moved in the same direction. A blush touched her cheeks, and he chuckled.

After three attempts, Mark swept his arm out to the side, bowed, and then backed up to the wall. "Allow me to step aside."

"Thank you, sir." A smile added to Melissa's lighthearted tone.

"Quite welcome, Miss Southwood. It's wonderful to see you, but alas, I must go. Farewell until the dinner party tomorrow."

He caught a flash of disappointment in her eyes before she lowered her gaze. His pulse leaped.

She gave a muted "Farewell" in response. He went out the door and closed it behind him. It took all he had not to skip down the path on his way home.

35

He left in such a hurry. She thought he would try to further the relationship now. After all, he wanted to court her in London.

Since they were both in the same neighborhood, with Winstead out of the picture, Melissa expected an active pursuit by Lord Russell. He acted so warm and friendly in the vicarage garden this very morning. But now, he left when he might have lingered in the hall with her. She didn't understand.

She hastened up the stairs and entered her pleasant guest bedroom, light and airy on fair days, cozy and warm on the gloomy ones. Miss Cleaver selected modest new furniture and décor when she took over the vicarage housekeeping. Her tasteful choices lent to the charming comfort of the armchair, bed, and padded window seat.

Wrenching off her shawl and bonnet, Melissa dropped them on a chest at the foot of the bed and dashed to the window seat. She sat and swung her legs up, and then wrapped both arms around her knees, eyes following Lord Russell's retreating form until he disappeared from view. Resting her cheek on her knees, she noticed her heart throbbing but attributed it to climbing the stairs, not to seeing Lord Russell.

She rose from the window seat and walked over to the open wardrobe. Hanging there were at least a dozen dresses. She scanned them, moving from right to left. Deciding what to wear to the dinner party at Russell Manor tomorrow night distracted her from wondering why he hadn't stayed on in the hall for even a brief conversation.

Blue. Men liked blue, didn't they? She held the cornflower silk gown with a white lace overskirt and intricate stitching across the bodice in front of herself and looked in the mirror. A possibility, but perhaps too fancy for a country dinner party?

She turned back to the wardrobe. Fashion was a hobby to her. She'd spent hours on it for lack of anything else to keep occupied. Lonely, and not allowed much freedom, she took pleasure in the colors, fabrics, and sketching styles. It was all vanity—she understood that. Other people painted, collected books, or wrote poetry that never saw the light of day. Melissa liked clothes. That didn't make her a bad person, but rather a well-dressed one.

White was the mode for people her age. Setting the blue dress aside, she pulled out a white satin gown figured all over with pink embroidered flowers. She loved the femininity of embroidery, but when held up to the mirror, it washed out her complexion. No, definitely not the white gown with pink embroidery. Perhaps another time. Maybe the blue, after all.

Melissa admitted to wanting Lord Russell's attention. She'd always been quite unself-conscious, but now his potential reaction informed her selection.

She chose the blue. Even touching the luscious fabric gave her delight. The soft silk sent her into a reverie of imagining the gleam in his eyes when she walked in. Her breathing became a bit faster. Waiting until tomorrow night to see him would be painful—strong yearning for his presence swept over her.

Shaking her head to banish the unwelcome sensation, she glanced again at the other dresses. They also were beautiful, but the blue gown best complemented her coloring. She liked the high-waisted dress's fit and its understated lace overskirt. The bodice's filmy silk fichu filled in the neckline, bringing it up to a modest position.

Tomorrow's dinner gown decided upon, Melissa picked up her Bible from the armchair, intending to have a quiet moment with God. She read for a time, and then took her cares to the Lord.

...and forgive me for wanting to run ahead of Your plan for me. Please help me to be patient about finding a husband who shares my faith in You. I put it all in Your hands, Lord Jesus, Amen.

~*~

Mr. Cleaver stuck his head in the door of the small music room. He cleared his throat to alert Cassandra to his presence. "Seems you have quite the touch with that hymn. What one was that?" He stepped into the room.

"I hope it didn't disturb you. Miss Cleaver said I could play when my morning tasks were done." She raised her brows, beseeching.

Her frightened, questioning eyes smote Mr. Cleaver's heart. Why, the little thing was afraid. "Cassandra, by all means, use the piano. I trust Miss Cleaver's judgment, and I certainly liked what I heard. What was that again? I recognize it, but can't put my finger on the words."

"It's an English melody for Psalm 64. *A Little That the Righteous Hold.*"

"Of course...'better than the wealth untold of many wicked men.'"

Cassandra completed the verse. "'Destroyed shall be their arm of pride, but they who in the Lord confide shall be upholden then.'"

She looked embarrassed. He wondered why. Nothing like a good Psalm to straighten out one's heart.

"It appears that my colleague, your father, provided you with musical training. Many would give their eyeteeth to play so well."

"Thank you, Mr. Cleaver. If only he'd provided me with a portion...and a home."

"You had no dowry? No home?"

"He consistently gave his money to the poor. I don't begrudge them a farthing, but he inadvertently left me poor. At least if I'd married, I'd have a home to call my own." With a rueful face and an impatient motion, she shoved her hair behind her ears.

"I shall leave you to your music. And thank you—it's a delight to hear." He backed out of the room and gently closed the door.

~*~

Back in London, on a typical, foggy, wet day, Mr. Southwood sat in his study and opened a letter from his daughter. He settled back into the chair behind his desk to enjoy it.

The missive read as follows:

Dear Papa,

You'll be glad to learn we arrived safely. We are enjoying good weather and the quiet environs of the vicarage. We're invited to a dinner party tomorrow night.

The Cleavers are accepted into local society due to his position as vicar. I, too, am included in the invitation to the local manor house. Country society is perhaps more welcoming than London's.

It has been a peaceful few days, and my wounds are beginning to heal. Some of the old contentment taken away by my shocking experience of a few weeks ago is returning, as is my normal equilibrium.

When I am ready to return to London, I shall communicate again—probably in a month or so. God be with you, Papa.

Love, Melissa

One eyebrow elevated, he slapped down the sheet of paper, grabbed up the envelope, and re-read it, paying special attention to the return address. Rising, he plucked a well-thumbed copy of Debrett's Peerage off a bookshelf and went back to his chair. He searched Debrett's until he reached the "R's." Running his thumb over each page, he sat up straight when he found the entry he sought.

Scanning the entry, he murmured *"...family seat: Russell Manor, Russelton."* He cast his mind over their conversation. Melissa had told him her destination was the vicarage, but he hadn't realized the Cleavers lived in the same town named after Lord Russell's forebears. Anger and suspicion mounted within him. Melissa wouldn't set a foot wrong, therefore, he turned his spite on Lord Russell. There must be a secret intent in the fact he hadn't been told this little detail. Casting his mind back to his visit with Mrs. Banting, he couldn't remember her mentioning the proximity of the Cleaver's vicarage and Lord Russell's ancestral home, either.

He labored over a message. How to hit the right

chord of insouciance yet incite an informative reaction? The resulting note read,

Dear Mrs. Banting,

Thank you for the visit the other day. Any word from your nephew lately? Any repercussions from the 'incident'? My daughter is out of town, rusticating.

Yours, Mr. Southwood

Homer sent a messenger boy over to Mrs. Banting's townhouse with the note and instructions to ferret out information.

The boy returned and reported. "The old butler let slip about Mrs. Banting being out of town. He wouldn't say more, but I went 'round to the kitchen entrance and loitered a bit. Got to chattin' with a scullery maid. She bragged at how her mistress was off in the country with Lord Russell, wot's her nephew."

"This report shall earn you a reward." Mr. Southwood reached into the desk. "Hold out your hand." He placed a few coins in the boy's palm. "You may go."

"Cor! Thankee." The young servant yanked on his forelock, bowed, and backed out of the room.

Homer wanted to spit, he was so mad. Too bad there was no spittoon in this refined home. How could he have been deceived? He would need to show them he was not to be trifled with.

Mr. Southwood yanked a piece of paper out of a drawer and smacked it down on the desk. He pulled a pen and ink bottle forward. He wrote a lengthy list of instructions. He rang for the housekeeper, apprising her of his departure. His valet was commanded to pack, and the butler gave orders for a coach to be readied. To the secretary lurking in the dark corner of the study, he said, "Step up here. I need you to take the reins of the enterprise while I am in the country for a few days. Here are your instructions."

If he left immediately, he could arrive in Russelton by afternoon the next day. He didn't relish the danger and discomfort of traveling around the clock but didn't want to delay arrival on the scene. If he stopped to sleep at an inn to break up the trip into two reasonable daytime stretches of travel, he would grievously suffer from the enforced inactivity of biding at an inn twiddling his thumbs.

No, the sooner he arrived at the manor, the sooner he could find out what the intentions of Lord Russell were toward his daughter. Anger fueled him, and he rehearsed stern speeches to deliver when he got there. Even though Russell held a title and the Southwoods did not, that did not give Lord Russell the right to pursue some havey-cavey romance without a father's permission.

It took an hour to go over the list of instructions with the secretary, and by then the coach was prepared and his bags packed. Mr. Southwood's air of restrained energy was even more intense than usual and he vaulted into the coach and shouted to the coachman, "Be off!" as soon as the door clicked shut.

36

Only two hours remained before guests would begin to arrive for the dinner party. A loud pounding arose at the front door.

Lucy Banting registered the racket but ignored it, busy upstairs in her boudoir with her lady's maid, preparing for the evening. A tap sounded upon the bedroom door.

"Enter. Yes?" Lucy gave only half of her attention to the housemaid who entered.

"Beg your pardon, ma'am, but there's an angry gent, Mr. Southwood, he sez, downstairs. Butler's put him into an anteroom to cool his heels. Sez he's got to see the master. Master's not here right now, ma'am." The drab little housemaid looked frightened half out of her wits.

This caught Lucy's full attention. She glanced at the clock on her mantel before responding. "Don't worry. His bark is worse than his bite, I'm guessing. This is quite an inopportune moment, but I shall do what I can."

She rose from her seat at her dressing table, ready to defend and aid her nephew's cause. As appealing as Mr. Southwood was in some ways, his insensitivity to the young people rankled. She would not let him get the upper hand by allowing him to throw his anger around. Grabbing up a rose pink watered silk dressing gown, she handed it to her lady's maid, who held it out for Lucy to put her arms through the voluminous sleeves. While tying the sash with vigor, she marveled at the man's temerity.

Squaring her petite shoulders, she descended the stairs with as much dignity as possible while wearing one's dressing robe. The frightened housemaid slunk behind. Lucy held her head high while curiosity and necessity gathered within and drove her to greater speed than normal down the curved, oaken staircase. Even under the foreboding shadow of an unpleasant confrontation, she stayed calm. Whatever the meaning of this intrusion, there was no time to dilly-dally. She had a dinner party to host tonight.

They reached the hall, and Crabtree stepped forward. "Ma'am, he's in there. He says his name's Southwood, and he's got to see the master. Shall I bring him to the parlor?"

"Yes. I shall see him there. Give me a moment." She turned to her right and entered a small sitting room off the main hall.

She didn't have long to wait. Mere seconds later, the butler ushered in Homer Southwood, whose bluster carried him into the room on a cloud of aggrieved self-importance. Chest out, hands clenched, a stern expression adorned the man's flushed face. He reminded her of a bottle with a cork in it, and his demeanor revealed to her an imminent outpouring of anger.

"Why, Mr. Southwood, what an unexpected pleasure." Lucy's words fluted, pouring out like the sweetest honey. She batted her eyelashes and gazed up at him.

He stood stymied. Good. She widened her smile. She laughed inside as he visibly subsided. Placating an angry Mr. Southwood was surely an honorable use of her feminine wiles. She held out her hand, and he moved forward with great alacrity to bow over it and bestow a kiss upon it.

She withdrew her hand when he straightened. "You've arrived at such a fortuitous time!" Tilting her head flirtatiously, she took the moral high ground and pasted a good face on his untoward intrusion. "Please join us for dinner this evening, won't you? We are having a small party."

Strong suspicions told her his appearance at Russell Manor stemmed from an attempt to control the situation involving his daughter Melissa and her nephew Mark. It had crossed her mind to wonder how long it would take him to put two and two together about the location of Russell Manor. Now the answer stood before her. He showed all the marks of a man unused to events getting away from him.

"Yes, well, I, um…Dinner? I hoped to have speech with Lord Russell…"

She heard the stammer and seized the upper hand. "He's out for the moment. You must stay here tonight. There won't be time for any more serious talks this day. I shall instruct the staff to carry in your bags." She raised her brows and coyly touched her cheek to her shoulder. "You do have bags?"

He nodded, again at a loss for words.

"I'll order a room prepared, and your baggage taken up. You can go up and refresh yourself in no time." Tonight's dinner party would be even more diverting than expected. For all his bluster, he appealed to her.

~*~

Mr. Southwood followed a servant upstairs, where he was ensconced in a lavish and comfortable guest suite. He bowed to the inevitable with a grudging inward admission of satisfaction. Accepting the assistance of a temporarily-assigned valet, he rid himself of travel dirt and dressed in evening clothes.

Suddenly caught up in the bosom of the *ton*, he experienced less anger and a sense of well-being unequaled since before his wife's death. His heart floated lighter than it had for many months. He wouldn't relinquish his mission to investigate the intentions of Lord Russell. However, that didn't mean he couldn't relish the moment. Wasn't this the sort of invitation he long coveted? An invitation received in an unorthodox manner, but his fondest dreams were within reach. It almost seemed as though Mrs. Banting was flirting, too. Was that even possible?

37

Mark entered the drawing room to wait for the dinner guests to gather and found his aunt already there, arrayed upon a settee near the fireplace.

After bowing over her hand, he spoke. "Aunt Lucy, you're younger every time I see you these days."

Mark threw back the tails of his formal dinner coat and sat down next to her. He studied her. Her flattering, cocoa-brown silk dress had coral-pink velvet ribbon accents at the high waist and on the puffy sleeves. A simple coral cameo adorned her neck, hanging from a delicate gold chain. Her paisley cashmere shawl in shades of brown and coral completed the ensemble.

On closer inspection, he noticed a worried wrinkle creasing her brow. Assuming she was anxious about the party, and setting out to reassure her, he launched into a review of the seating arrangements.

"This promises to be an agreeable dinner. The five of us, correct? You, me, the Cleavers, and Miss Southwood? Even though the numbers are uneven, Aunt," he went on, "you'll sit at the foot, the Cleavers to your left, Miss Southwood to your right, and me at the head. Are you satisfied?"

"That arrangement would have been fine. We received an unexpected guest. Miss Southwood's father arrived at Russell Manor while you were out. He was in high dudgeon."

"What? What is he doing here?" Mark's stomach dived to his shoes and he shot to his feet.

"Calm down. I smoothed his ruffled feathers by inviting him to be our guest. Now, listen, before he gets down here. He's asking—no, demanding—to 'have speech' with you." She rested her hand on Mark's forearm.

"This is a disturbing turn of events. I thought to have an interlude in which to spend time with Miss Southwood." Disgruntled, and a shade disheartened, his mind went to work to predict what her father's arrival meant to his plan and how to maneuver around this new development. "I am exceedingly thankful my heart and mind rest in Christ now, not in my earthly strategy. He will guide me through this." Without faith, this would possibly crush his hopes or stir him to anger. But, with faith in God, this occurrence wasn't a defeat.

"Nothing makes me happier than to hear you say that. Oh, here he is." She clasped her hands in front of her waist.

Mark stiffened as he turned toward Mr. Southwood, who entered the room and approached. The man's eyes held an uncertain, hunted look. He went straight to Aunt Lucy instead of to Mark. That was good—at least Mr. Southwood didn't come and punch Mark in the jaw. He'd have no right, but enraged fathers were something of a wild card.

Mr. Southwood bowed and scraped before Aunt Lucy. "Mrs. Banting. You are ravishing."

With surprise, Mark sensed Southwood's distinct air of a suitor pursuing a lady. Perhaps Mark should inquire of Southwood's intentions, not the other way around.

"Too kind, sir. Please do be seated." Aunt Lucy indicated the place next to her on the settee by tapping it with her fan. She cocked her head, looking up at Southwood through her eyelashes, and astonished Mark with the coquettish mannerisms she produced.

With no force, her flirtatious demeanor clearly brought the interloper under her sway. Her ability to subdue such a vigorous man impressed Mark.

The doorknocker banging against the solid front door disrupted the scene.

Revealing her nervousness, Aunt Lucy fluted an obvious remark. "The other guests have arrived." Mark intercepted a nervous glance from her before she turned a charming smile toward Southwood again.

The footman opened the drawing room door, stepped back, and the butler entered with a sweep of his hand. "The Cleavers. Miss Southwood." Thus announced, the group entered.

Aunt Lucy approached Miss Southwood instead of waiting for her to draw nigh. Aunt Lucy clasped both of the younger lady's hands in her own to greet her and leaned in. Mark, having joined them, heard his aunt whisper, "Your father arrived here less than two hours ago."

Then turning to the Cleavers, Aunt Lucy and Mark gave them a gracious, warm greeting. The group moved over to the fireplace to where Mr. Southwood stood. Mark sensed indecision wafting from the man. He deserved to be ill at ease, having shown up uninvited, but Mark tried to be compassionate.

"Papa?" Melissa approached her father with a stiff, quizzical smile on her lips and reached up to place a light kiss on this cheek. "What a surprise to find you here."

"Yes, well, Mrs. Banting invited me to be a guest at Russell Manor."

This vague response served to change the subject from the oddness of his presence. Mark marveled at the audacity of the man.

Southwood held out his hand to the man of the cloth. "You must be Miss Cleaver's brother?"

"Mr. Southwood, it's my pleasure to introduce you to Mr. Cleaver," Mark interjected. "He is the local vicar and a leading citizen of this fair community. Is it correct Miss Cleaver worked for your family for years?" The Cleavers' presence should help smooth the path of this uncomfortable turn of events.

"Yes, yes. She, shall we say, retired less than a year ago. How does Russelton compare to London? Is it to your liking, Miss Cleaver?"

"Since leaving your esteemed employ, though I miss my young lady, I am very content living here. Many ways to serve the Lord exist right here in this little burg. How have you been?" Ever polite, Miss Cleaver did her part to smooth things over.

While this exchange went on, Mr. Cleaver took Aunt Lucy's arm and moved off to another part of the room. He was smiling, nodding, and listening intently to whatever she said. The interchange didn't appear to regard a problem, rather a congenial meeting of the minds, thus Mark turned his attention back to Miss Southwood.

For a moment, Mark allowed himself to believe all would smooth over. Then she spied him looking at her. She first blanched with surprised shock, and now her cheeks changed to embarrassed red. The poor, sweet young lady. She was so refined, and her father so overbearing. Did she understand the meaning of her father's presence here?

She appeared thoroughly chagrined. Mark sent encouraging glances her way, trying to reassure her of his support. Even he admitted, however, the appearance of her father on the scene unsettled him as well. But she had suffered more. Her father had already hurt her with his disastrous scheme, in which he selected a cad for a suitor.

38

If one followed the dictates of etiquette, the persons of highest rank went in to the dining room first. Mark broke with tradition and held out his elbow to Miss Cleaver. She took his arm, beginning the procession across the hall to dine. This suited his hastily-cobbled agenda to deflect suspicion. He didn't want to give Mr. Southwood's suspicions any credence, and perhaps he'd step up and partner Aunt Lucy.

Mark glanced over his shoulder. *Oh good.* Mr. Cleaver held out his arm to escort Miss Southwood. She could avoid her father for the moment. Aunt Lucy and Mr. Southwood brought up the rear. He beamed as he escorted the attractive widow into the dining room. She'd turn the lion into a lamb.

Seating arrangements perfected, even with the addition of the last-minute guest, Aunt Lucy glowed, presiding at one end of the table, appropriate for the hostess, and Mark sat at the other end.

A delectable meal was guaranteed—although Mr. Southwood's presence did Mark's appetite no favors. He'd told Aunt Lucy three courses were ample. In London society, three wouldn't be adequate, but as each course comprised many dishes, tonight's dinner would still be sumptuous. All the better to impress Melissa's father.

Mr. Southwood looked about to burst the buttons

on his waistcoat once seated to Aunt Lucy's right in a place of honor. Mr. Cleaver sat to her left. Mark held forth at the head of the table with Miss Southwood to his right and Miss Cleaver to his left. Pleased at the outcome, he noted propriety would be fully served as well by this arrangement.

Miss Southwood so close at hand proved a distraction. Near enough to touch. Any remaining appetite fled. Delectable dishes came and went. Her nearness dazzled his senses, and delicate waves of her delicious minty perfume infused his head. *Was this love?*

By the second course, the group was comfortably settled. Conversation flowed well, considering the tense undertone caused by the presence of Mr. Southwood. Aunt Lucy kept him occupied, facilitating Mark's ability to speak freely with Miss Southwood, who sat next to him at his end of the table.

"I hated leaving you yesterday morning when we ran into each other at the vicarage. But I denied myself to linger with you as was my wont."

"You have a pattern of self-denial?" Her hand went to her throat.

"If it gains me my ultimate goal, yes. You see, until I have your father's approval, I shall not strive to engage your affections."

"Are you sure such striving is in order?"

The little minx, she was baiting him. Delightful.

"I will be meeting with your father very soon. Tomorrow, Lord willing."

"That sounds interesting. A clash may be on your horizon."

"Miss Southwood, a different sort of battle is shaping up." Amused, with a subtle tilt of his head, he indicated Aunt Lucy's attention being drawn first by Mr. Southwood, and then by Mr. Cleaver. Her coral earrings jiggled each time she turned. No sooner would one man receive a response from her to a conversational gambit and the other gent would chime in, attempting to secure her favor and interest.

"I'm glad I don't have to compete to speak with you." Mark gave Miss Southwood the sweetest smile he could muster, poignantly raised from deep within his heart. The desire to touch her, even her hand, welled strong.

The table happened to fall silent the exact moment Aunt Lucy asked a question. "Mr. Southwood, where do you attend divine services in London?"

"I attend at...I don't attend—anymore," Southwood sputtered, turning red and staring down at his plate.

"Once upon a time, you did? What happened?"

"My wife's unexpected death took me away from my normal churchgoing."

Mark smiled behind his napkin when, with a quietly sympathetic tone, Mr. Cleaver used the opportunity to exhort, "Most believers find great comfort in the hope of eternal life at such a time. I understand, however, others can spiral into a spiritual morass of confusion when a dear one passes on. I'd be happy to lend a listening ear and perhaps offer some hope."

Mark knew more than anyone how good a counselor and listener Mr. Cleaver was.

"Oh! How kind of you." Aunt Lucy interjected, bestowing a gratified smile on the minister.

Mr. Cleaver cleared his throat and lifted his hand, palm out. "Don't dwell on giving me credit. I live to guide the flock, comfort the bereft, and so forth. Come call on me at the vicarage some day during your visit."

"I'll try to find the time," answered Southwood. "As how Mrs. Banting has been so kind as to extend an invitation for me to be a guest at Russell Manor, I would like to rusticate a bit and tour the countryside whilst I am here. It's been years since I've been out of the city."

Miss Cleaver entered the conversation, offering a change of topic. "I miss some of the amenities of London, but not the noise or the stench." She raised fingertips to her blushing cheeks and subsided, leaning back against her chair, eyes closed.

While the two older men took turns grappling for Aunt Lucy's attentions, Mark conversed with Miss Southwood, finding it easy to talk to her.

"I enjoyed seeing you at the ball. I'm so glad you attended." Amusement tickled him to say this since the entire ball being concocted to bring her into his orbit.

"It was a lovely evening. I had a wonderful time."

"Your gown was beautiful. Am I mistaken or did my aunt say you and she share a modiste?"

"Too true. Much to our mutual delight." She glanced toward Mrs. Banting, and then back at him, smiling.

"You are a delightful dancer." Mark loved the way Miss Southwood's cheeks turned a delicate pink at the words of flattery.

Miss Cleaver leaned forward again and caught Mark's eye. "Miss Southwood's dancing flourished during our later years together. A dancing master was brought in to train her."

"Oh, Prissy, 'tis a miracle I even remembered the steps, never having a chance to use them until Mrs.

Banting's ball. You do boast of me."

Mark recaptured Miss Southwood's attention. "Quite a surprise your father showed up here. And on the night of our dinner party. Grateful he agreed to stay."

"Your aunt kindly invited him. I hope you don't mind?" Melissa's delicate eyebrows lifted as she asked.

She clearly wasn't so embarrassed at her father's machinations that it prevented her ability to relax and enjoy the evening—showing remarkable poise. Mark spoke, intent on preventing her any anguish over her father's actions. "I certainly don't mind, and Aunt Lucy loves having guests. Why, look, she's happy as can be with an attentive man on each side."

He infused his words with lighthearted empathy and understanding, wanting Miss Southwood to be comfortable enough with him that she might someday turn to him as a confidant. He'd never bring up the rescue in the chapel at St. George's—interrupting a disastrous abduction.

He decided to include Miss Cleaver, who'd sat silent for too long. "Ladies, I'm starting to notice that my life has been accident-ridden of late. If you can call being robbed an accident." Mark made a rueful face.

"Shocking experience," Miss Cleaver said with a lift of her chin.

"God's grace worked it for good because I received the gift of faith during my recovery."

"So glad you speak so freely of your newfound faith. Praise God." Miss Southwood tapped his forearm with her fan and tilted her head toward him with an air of sisterly concern.

Miss Cleaver chimed in, "Lord Russell, I agree wholeheartedly that faith is a gift, and it's amazing, too, that God planned your salvation from the beginning of time." She spoke with assurance.

"Such a blessing he dragged me unto himself—dead in sin as I was. Thank you for reminding me of that." Mark glanced down, humbled. "On the other hand, the purpose of my carriage accident in London isn't clear yet. But since I don't believe in luck, good or bad, there must be a reason for these trials."

"You had a mishap in London as well?" Miss Cleaver pursed her lips and raised her brows.

"I shall tell you about it another time." Mark arranged his face in reassuring lines and glanced toward Miss Southwood, tantalizingly close to his right. He felt the world fall away as his eyes met hers.

"I hope my father will be reasonable about our friendship. He can't keep me prisoner." She sighed.

Mark allowed his hand to cover hers for a mere moment, and their eyes locked again. Friendship was not the word for what surged through his blood.

He withdrew his touch as footmen circulated with the final course, a dessert called strawberry fool. He wanted to respond to her last remark but couldn't because the room had suddenly fallen silent as the guests delighted themselves with the luscious fruit-laden confection. He'd wait a while longer to further his suit. Perhaps tomorrow held an opportunity to spend a few precious moments with her.

39

Homer Southwood appeared in the dining room the next morning, and after bowing, his gaze landed on Lucy. She offered him a welcoming smile. "Blessed day, isn't it?" Lucy sipped her breakfast coffee and glanced out the window.

"Lovely day." He moved toward the buffet, made his selections, and with his full plate, seated himself close to her. "Your dress is such a pretty color. What do you call the hue?"

"Jonquil." She fluttered her lashes in his direction.

"May I escort you on a circuit of the garden later this morning, ma'am?"

The man surely seems smitten. How sweet. "A walk in the garden would be most pleasant. Please do have some breakfast."

She sent Mr. Southwood an invitation to the ball. And when he arrived on the doorstep yesterday, she'd invited him to be a houseguest at Russell Manor. Her only motivation the desire to help her nephew's suit with Melissa. But now flutters and unbidden stirrings of affection for the man rose within—despite the inauspicious beginnings of their acquaintance. Had he been brought into her life for another reason? She enjoyed his company.

"Tell me, how are you faring as a widower, Mr. Southwood?" Lucy sat back and waited for his answer.

He stiffened, coughed, but after a moment he

gazed into her face. "It's been a painful year. How long have you been a widow?"

"It has been six lonely years."

"An excellent woman like you? I find that hard to believe."

"It's true. If not for my nephew—such a fine young man—I think I'd still be pining away, alone, in my London house. Ever since Mark inherited the title and became a believer, he's been a different person, and very kind to me." A good word never hurt. She dabbed the corners of her mouth and wiped her fingertips with a napkin.

"Since you brought up the topic of your nephew, let me ask you a few questions. What can you tell me about his character? He's quite different from the usual pink of the ton." Homer bit into his toast and leaned forward to listen to her answer.

"Now that's a topic I am very familiar with." She poured herself some more tea from a pot on the table before speaking again. "Mark lived as a typical care-for-naught until brought low."

His brows snapped together. "What do you mean by low?" His brows snapped together.

"Don't you know? He was set upon and robbed on the way home to Russelton."

"There are robbers in the vicinity? My Melissa—has she been in danger?"

"No, it appears to be a one-time occurrence. Not a violent crime since."

"Tell me about Lord Russell. How bad was he hurt?"

"He was beaten severely, but his injuries were not permanent. While he recuperated at home here, and took up his responsibilities to the estate, he was converted."

"Converted?"

"Yes. The Lord worked faith in his heart."

"Ah, yes. Fascinating. Allow me to ask you something more personal, Mrs. Banting, if I might. How have you dealt with the Lord since you were widowed? Have you accepted his taking your husband—and you still in the prime of life?" Southwood lowered his fork and tossed his napkin on the table next to his plate.

"I had to." This conversational direction took her by surprise, but she didn't care. To talk about her loss didn't hurt anymore. She made to rise, and a footman shot forward to pull her chair out. Before he could retreat to his position against the wall, Lucy spoke to him. "Nip out to the entry hall and get my parasol and gloves, please."

Southwood, having risen as well, extended his elbow. She laid her hand on his sleeve. "We'll go out here." She gestured toward the French doors and referred to his earlier question. "Let's move outside into the sunshine, and I will tell you more. Such topics need the light of day." The footman opened the doors, and she walked through, hand on her guest's arm.

Stepping across the terrace and gaining the lawn, she resumed the conversation. "You asked me about my reaction to the loss of my husband." As she spoke, Lucy tugged at her gloves and smoothed them over her hands."

"Yes, I did ask, but since it's nice out here, maybe we can talk about your widowhood another day. I probably shouldn't have asked." His cheeks tinged red.

"I'm not bothered by talking about it, as it's been a long time." She opened her parasol and twirled it over

A Match for Melissa

her shoulder.

He persisted with his backpedalling. "I'd never dream of making you uncomfortable. I simply wanted to hear from someone who has gone through the loss of a spouse, too."

Lucy's heart went out to him. Men were seldom able to share their deep emotions with others.

"Let's sit here." She indicated a stone bench near a fountain, and after Southwood brushed off the seat with a large handkerchief, she sat.

He looked down and studied the toes of his boots. "I've had no one to talk to about my loss."

Refreshed by his frank honesty and prompted by his inquisitiveness about her widowed state, Lucy forged ahead. "It's quite all right. These things need to be brought out into the light—the light of the love of the Son." She watched his face as he processed her words.

"If you're sure." He yanked down the edges of his vest.

"Won't you sit down?" She patted the bench. "It's taken time, but I've learned to accept the loss of my husband."

"But how?"

"It helps to remind myself he is now with the Lord. I, too, shall someday pass into eternity. I am sad to have lost him, but he has gained heaven, and I also have hope in the resurrection."

"That's quite theological."

"Yes, but theology is a good thing. For example, we must number our days because man is like the grass which withers. I've had to learn to love life again."

Southwood leaned back, stroked his chin, and let

out a sigh. Lucy sensed his struggle as emotions flickered across his face.

"You've gotten right to the core of my problem, Mrs. Banting. I have been so angry at God for taking my wife I've overlooked the blessings of the living. I will admit to cutting myself off from God—after a long life of believing and serving Him."

"I am happy to hear your testimony of faith." She ceased talking and opened her fan, giving a few desultory waves. Maybe if she stayed quiet, he'd say more.

"It's time I accept my wife's death. I can't punish God or truly cut faith out of my life. God's Word expresses it well. 'Where can I go from Your Spirit?'" He hid his face in his hands.

"Oh, yes, His love is bigger than our grief." She patted his shoulder with the lightest of touches.

He lifted his face. "Mrs. Banting?"

"Yes? Please call me Lucy."

He rose and turned to face her. "I need to make amends with my daughter. I must go think. Time with you is special, Lucy." He bent over her extended hand.

"You are welcome, Homer. Farewell." She watched him hasten toward the stables.

40

Mark had an early breakfast and went out to ride the bounds of the estate. When he returned, he bathed and changed clothes to rid himself of the odor of the stable. Before long, he descended to his desk to study some maps of his lands. He racked his brain for inspiration of how to find clues to the identity of the rogues who attacked him. Responsibility for the continuity of his family property and the welfare of his tenants caused a constant niggle of unease to set up residence in the back of his mind. The safety of the entire locality burdened him, and criminals on the loose cut up his peace.

Voices sounded from the breakfast room across the hall. A door opened and shut. Then silence. Aunt Lucy and Mr. Southwood. They probably went out the French doors to the gardens. Aunt Lucy loved to show guests the flowers. It dawned on Mark as a chance too good to pass up. She might keep Southwood occupied for the greater part of the morning.

He wouldn't be questioned or observed. The day shone too bright to be sacrificed to studying maps, especially when the presence of a special young lady beckoned his heart. Butler not in sight, Mark grabbed his gloves, hat, and cane from the hall table, let himself out, and set out on foot at a brisk pace. In less than ten minutes, he reached the front door of the vicarage.

Miss Southwood opened the door as he raised his

fist to knock. She must have seen him coming. Time stood still as he drank in the charming picture she made—rosy cheeks, lace cap, and tendrils of blond hair peeking out around her face.

"Lord Russell! Good morning. Won't you come in?" She stepped back to make way for him to enter.

"I'll stay out here. Indeed, it is an excellent morning—too nice to be indoors." He spoke from the doorstep, having no wish to compromise her by entering the house without anyone else present. "It's good to see you, Miss Southwood. Would you care to take a stroll on the vicarage grounds?"

"That sounds delightful. I'll get my things." She turned away toward the hall and emerged after a minute or two—wearing a bonnet, gloves, and shawl, and with Miss Dean following a step behind.

He paused on the front stoop and smiled down at her. He extended his arm to the side, bent at the elbow, and she placed her gloved hand upon the sleeve of his coat. They stepped down onto the stone-covered front walk and followed it to where it turned, leading to the gardens in the back of the house.

From a few steps behind, Miss Dean said. "Don't worry, I shall be nearby but not so close as to intrude. Enjoy your stroll." He paused to allow the companion to pass, and she wandered ahead to examine a sundial on the other side of the clearing.

He smiled down at Miss Southwood, and she squeezed his arm. Though much smaller than the gardens of Russell Manor, he thought the vicarage garden was charming—especially with Miss Southwood in it. An orchard abutted the gardens. He guided her toward an alluring bench beneath an apple tree on the edge of the orchard. His pretty walking partner gave no resistance. With a gloved hand, he swept the stone seat clear of fallen petals.

As if to echo his courtly gesture, Miss Southwood made a small curtsey before seating herself in the dappled shade of the tree. Maintaining a proper distance from her on the stone bench went against his natural inclination, but he willingly refrained from getting cozy. He smiled at her. She reciprocated, and the mutual gaze lasted for a lengthy moment before he broke the happy silence.

"Miss Southwood, I hope my words do not cause you discomfort, but I need to ascertain whether you are amenable to me renewing my suit at this time. I must obtain your father's permission, but before approaching him, I want to make sure you would consider me."

"Please call me Melissa—at least when no sticklers are in earshot. I'd love to consider you if father approves. After all, you did save me from a cruel fate, and for that alone I hold you in high regard."

"Only due to that? And here I was beginning to think you liked me."

"We do have much in common, not the least of which is our faith, not to mention our interest in the same type of charity work. But are you certain now is the moment...Mark?"

"In my humble opinion, yes. Now is the time, I am sure."

"I see. I, too, have enjoyed our various interactions, but I'll need to mull it over."

His heart plummeted to the soles of his shiny black-tasseled boots. After all his patient waiting, it wasn't easy to understand why she needed time to think. He worked to keep the smile on his face. She did say she enjoyed their interactions and had a lot in common. That was something.

"Mull?" He stalled, thinking furiously. He didn't want to manipulate her, and his intentions were good. Surely, God would forgive him—he merely wanted her to love him enough to marry him. Still, seeing an opportune moment for his suit to prosper, he marshaled his wits and began to talk.

"I'd like to explain myself." He glanced at Miss Dean, relieved to see her still occupied with studying the sundial a good thirty feet away. "My dear, you must remember the day we first encountered each other in London? How we met at your home, the day my suit was rejected by your father?"

"I clearly recall that meeting."

"Yes? My heart was engaged the moment I laid eyes on you there. My desire to court you has not diminished over the intervening months."

"Oh! But you'd seen me here at the vicarage. Did I not win your admiration then?" She twirled the tassel on her shawl.

"Ah yes, you may not realize that I was half out of my head. I even got confused and asked if you were an angel. You called on me at the manor. Then you were gone, and I had to not only recuperate but also to adjust to the estate's management duties."

He read her expression as dazzled and confused but forged ahead. "Don't think I forgot you. I just didn't know you the way I do now. I walked over here this morning to have this chance to speak with you."

"I am enjoying your choice of topic."

Her harmless flirting amused him. She was charming. "Wonderful. Your father is out strolling with my aunt this morning, so while he's busy, I thought it a good moment to slip away to see you. I plan to meet with him as soon as possible to request formal permission to court you. Please—I want to be able to tell him you are ready to be courted again."

She looked down and fingered the edge of her shawl before responding. "I, too, have enjoyed our acquaintance. When you came to the house, and me already being courted by…that other man…it was a surprising turn of events for me. My gratitude to you for rescuing me exceeds all bounds. The Lord knew I would need help, and surely he caused you to enter the nave of St. George's church when you did."

"I believe so, too. Please say you agree to my suit?" He wanted to wrap her in his arms and reassure her of his love. The urge was strong, but this was not the time.

"I'll admit I am favorable to you, but the timing…and my father." Her face paled. "I fear he will give you the right about."

"Why? He wants a nobleman to marry you." It made logical sense.

"He's the type of man to say no perhaps out of caprice or a desire to be in control, regardless of the fact he is a guest in your house. He prefers everything to be his idea."

"Are you afraid of him?"

"No, but I can't say I've ever witnessed anyone get the victory over him when his mind is made up. Knowing him as I do makes it hard for me to answer. I don't wish my father's wrath on your head." She gazed off into the distance

Clearly, she was stalling for time…time to heal. Touching her chin with his fingertips, he gently turned her face toward his. She met his eyes. "Don't worry. I am not afraid. I intend to win his permission. When I court you, it will be with full parental approval and only when you are ready." Determination blossomed in his heart, and the warm depths of her gaze spurred him on. The drive to make her his own grew stronger every moment he spent with her.

He bent over, about to kiss her hand, when something whizzed by his ear.

"My lord! What was that?" Miss Southwood asked.

"To the best of my knowledge, it was a bullet. We must get to the safety of the vicarage." His arm around Melissa's shoulder, he called out to Miss Dean. "There was a stray shot. Follow us." He shepherded the women into the house.

Cassandra met them in the hall, eyebrows raised. "I heard the crack. Sounded like a gunshot. Are there poachers in the vicinity?"

"Hard to know. Seems odd that someone would be shooting around the vicarage." Mark kept his tone calm.

Melissa's fingers fluttered to her forehead, and she paled. "You could have been killed. Gun accidents are not an everyday matter. Something must be done."

"Cassandra, please have tea brought to the sitting room," Miss Dean said, and then took Melissa's arm and guided her to a comfortable chair.

Mark followed and stood by Melissa's chair, about to speak, but a knock came on the outer door. A maid soon ushered in Mr. Southwood.

"Melissa. I'd like to speak with you." He looked at Mark, affronted. "Surprised to find you here."

Realizing it would be inappropriate to remain longer, Mark hoped that by leaving by the front of the house, he'd be out of sight of the shooter. "That's all right. I was just leaving. Farewell, Miss Southwood, Mr. Southwood." Mark departed.

Melissa half-rose as if to protest, biting her lip. How he hated to worry her.

~*~

Melissa said a quick prayer for Mark's safe return home. She took a deep breath to calm herself. "Papa, to what do I owe this impromptu visit?" Melissa sensed her father had something on his mind. Playing for time, she lifted a nearby bud vase and inhaled the calming scents of lavender and roses.

He sank down into the chair across from hers. "Can't a father visit his daughter without an excuse?"

"Of course. It's just that, knowing you, I expected there to be an agenda." Turning, she spoke to Miss Dean. "You may be excused, Miss Dean. Now would be a good time to mend that torn hem we noticed earlier." Miss Dean nodded and left the room just as Cassandra brought in a tray.

"Here you are, miss." Cassandra set the tray down without the slightest clatter and departed.

Melissa took her time preparing two cups of tea and gestured to her father to partake before raising her own cup to her lips. A restorative was certainly in order...what with the shot and the coming confrontation.

After a moment in which Mr. Southwood wore the look of someone measuring his words, he picked up the thread of conversation. "My dear, the only agenda is for me to ask your forgiveness." He wiped his forehead with a linen square.

"I'd certainly be happy to grant that, but I must know what it is I am forgiving," she spoke evenly, surprising herself with her composure. A pleasant breeze moved the dimity curtains at the nearby window. She sat across from him and waited.

"Where do I start? I feel so guilty for the way I behaved during the last year—dismissing Miss Cleaver, raging about your mother's death, refusing to attend church. Those are for starters. Then my poor choice of a suitor for you, almost causing your ruin. I'm heartily sorry, and I humbly beg your forgiveness."

"Papa, it's yours. Thank you for such a full expression of your remorse. We need say no more for now. I am very pleased you are on an even keel again."

He picked up his cup and saucer, probably tepid now. "We miss your mother, don't we? But we have the hope of seeing her again in glory. She's gone where I cannot follow until it's my time to go. I can accept that now."

Holding back tears, Melissa leaned forward and patted her father's knee. "I miss Mama, too. It would have been wonderful to enjoy her with us longer."

"I wonder what she'd think of Mrs. Banting, er, and her nephew?"

41

Pondering her remarkable visit with Mr. Southwood, Lucy sat alone under her parasol. She heard someone approaching, singing.

"Since with my God with perfect heart…" Abruptly, Mr. Cleaver ceased his song as he came into the clearing and lifted his hat. "Good morning, Mrs. Banting."

My, he was tall. "Good morning. Was that a Psalm?"

"Yes, a versification of Psalm eighteen."

"Ah. I too love the Psalms. Reverend, do tell me what brings you to Russell Manor this fine day."

"Certainly, but first, please call me Mr. Cleaver. I don't use the title Reverend. Or better yet, call me Jeremiah, if you'd like."

Warning bells went off. First name basis? Only if she wanted to encourage him—and none too sure about that, she nattered on, not addressing his implications. "Aren't you busy with parish matters? Perhaps calling on the sick?" She twirled her bamboo-handled parasol.

"Merely on my daily walk, and I spied you among the blossoms. Wanted to pay my regards and thank you for the delightful dinner party last night. No doubt I'll be home well before I'm needed to resume pastoral duties. In fact, would you like to take a stroll?"

"Delighted." She placed one hand on his extended

arm to rise and held the parasol in her other hand. She left her hand on his arm as they moved down the garden path.

"How are the knitting classes going?"

How thoughtful he was. "Oh, thank you for asking. Quite well. I am surprised how easily the women are taking to it."

"I heard about it from Cassandra. The new maid we hired at the vicarage."

"That Cassandra. She's an ideal student—since she knows how to knit already." Lucy chuckled. "Not a dropped stitch or a tangle. She can help the other women, too. Such a blessing."

"She is terribly talented. Each day seems to bring a new revelation of her gifts. Languages, music, needlework—it has no end. Little did we know what a paragon had landed at our kitchen door."

"A perfect fit as a companion for Miss Cleaver, too?"

"They get along famously. Back to your class, though. How many women attend?"

"Sixteen. Some from both the manor and the village. So you see why I need Cassandra's help. Oh, and she leads prayers at the beginning and end of each session."

"A marvel."

"She has a beautiful voice and can start us off on the right note, too. Singing while we knit—who'd have known how fun it would be."

"What are you knitting?"

"The whole class can knit scarves now. We shall be moving on to caps, next. We hope to learn stockings before the end of the year."

Lucy couldn't recall when she'd been this

comfortable with a minister. She hazarded a few imaginative guesses as to why he'd never married. Maybe he never experienced the urge toward pairing off with a female. Some men eschewed marriage when they entered the church. Or perhaps he had a tragic love story. Perhaps, with his unofficial confirmed bachelor status, the women of the vicinity had given up on him. *I'm just curious, nothing more.*

She wondered if he harbored a tendre for her, stumbling upon her so conveniently, such as he had, though it could have been happenstance. For certain he acted comfortable with her. Maybe it's because they were of the same vintage. "Mr. Cleaver, what do you think of the flowers?"

"Pardon me? My apologies, Mrs. Banting. I must have gotten caught up in a daydream—one of my besetting faults."

"Give it nary a thought. A place like this induces musings. I merely asked your esteemed opinion on the flowers."

"The flowers, you ask? Russell Manor's exemplary gardens provide a feast of fragrance and beauty. The grounds here are some of the most agreeable I've had the pleasure of experiencing."

While he waxed on about the flowers, she decided she may have been mistaken about his intentions. He wasn't trying to fix her interest. Perhaps her suspicion of him cherishing tender feelings was absurd. He was a good friend, a pleasant neighbor, a fine minister.

Maybe she should interrupt his talk about flowers and attempt to ascertain his intentions. "Do you have many widows in your parish?" There. That got his attention.

"Many? I wouldn't say many. The ones we have

are quite old. You are by far the youngest widow I am aware of."

Awareness. That's a clue. "Do you believe widows should remain unwed?"

"No, I don't. A woman does well to remarry—many benefits adhere to the wedded state, and for no reason should most widows forego marriage."

"I've heard tales of heirs being against remarriage so as to keep control of their mother's fortunes."

"But you have no children, correct?"

Hmm, now he was venturing onto personal territory. "Alas, I don't. Mark is my heir, but he has such a grand fortune of his own, he doesn't care a farthing to add mine to his. He's never breathed a word of opposition."

"Such a fine young man, your nephew. I had no idea he had such a beautiful aunt." He laid his free hand on hers.

That remark cleared up any doubts. The dear man called her beautiful. She withdrew her hand and grasped the parasol with two hands. No sense encouraging him unless she was sure she wanted to draw him unto herself. To decide that would take some time. Much to think about with two swains.

The interesting interlude came to an end when a footman appeared around the end of a nearby hedge. He bowed and said, "Mrs. Banting, two gentlemen, Sir Walsh and Lord Armbruster, have arrived. They say they are distant relatives."

"That's a surprise. Tell them I'll be in soon to greet them. Place them in the morning room and get them tea."

Turning toward Mr. Cleaver, she touched his arm with her fingertips and said, "I've so enjoyed our chat.

I feel ever so uplifted by your visit. Please walk back to the house with me. I hope we can do this again. These two relatives that arrived are somewhat of a trial—so pray for me."

"That I shall." After that, he fell silent. Reaching the house, Mr. Cleaver bowed over her hand. "Farewell, ma'am."

"Adieu—until we meet again." Mrs. Banting let him go with a sigh.

Uninvited guests were often a bother, but these two were in a class by themselves. Their presence was sure to be a chore. She'd never liked the custom which decreed propertied nobles must accommodate drop-in visits from any aristocrat, related or not, who happened to be traveling in the vicinity of a country estate. With society so rule-bound, why did this egregious liberty prevail?

Slipping in through the French doors, she came upon the guests, heads together, engaged in agitated whispering.

A ladylike throat-clearing caught their attention. "Good morning. To what do we owe the pleasure of a visit?" Pasting a social smile on her face, she moved toward them but halted out of reach. She wanted to afford no opportunities for hand mauling from these two. The few times she'd ever met them, at large family gatherings, their off-putting personalities were unforgettable.

Lord Armbruster, the larger of the two, rose and performed a flourishing bow. "Mrs. Banting, charmed." His deep voice held a false note of sycophancy. He flopped back into his chair.

Sir Walsh now did the pretty, creaking over at the waist for a bow before raising a quizzing glass to look her over—aping the affectations of a London fop. "We are delighted to see you, Mrs. Banting. It's been too long."

Not long enough for her. Steeling her spine, she engaged them in social conversation. "What brings you our way?"

"Passing through. Never want to neglect family ties." Armbruster crossed his arms over his chest after this remark.

"And you, Sir Walsh, do you travel much?"

"Tra-la. Much travel. Trot trot."

Oh my. The man's a lunatic. "I see. How is the tea? Hot?" She indicated their cups with a tilt of her head and a lift of her brows.

"Superior tea. Perhaps some biscuits would be nice. It's been a long morning since we were ousted—I mean rousted—from bed."

She turned to a lurking footman and requested a plate of baked goods. While waiting, she interacted more, but the men never clearly indicated why they appeared at Russell Manor other than 'passing through' and 'dropping by.' She could only assume they were perhaps low on funds, traveling from one victim to another, each too polite to refuse them hospitality, by which means they avoided paying room and board by freeloading.

Sir Walsh wheedled, "You'll put us up?"

"I'll meet with the housekeeper. She'll have a couple of guest rooms aired within the hour. A servant will come for you when the rooms are ready. You may relax here 'til then. I've ordered a plate of biscuits, which should be here soon."

"Tra la, biscuits." Sir Walsh rubbed his hands together.

"Lunch is served at one o'clock. You'll be in your rooms by then, so listen for the gong." She pointed to the clock and sailed out without a backward glance.

After making arrangements for Russell Manor's two uninvited guests and requesting a pot of tea brought to her rooms, Lucy went to her bedroom. She put her feet up and laid her head on the back of the chair. It was time for a respite. Being squired about by two men on the same morning, and then for two relatives to arrive to stay proved tiring. She'd met them in the past, but as to why they chose to appear here in the country during the season didn't make sense. From all she could recollect of them, Sir Walsh and Lord Armbruster were social animals and loath to be apart from London's doings. Why were they here?

The maid came with tea, and after she'd had a cup, Lucy climbed into her four-poster bed to snuggle under a downy throw. Eyes closed, she pondered the morning's events. Could it be Homer developed a tendre for her? All signs said yes.

Mr. Cleaver acted like a suitor as well. Could it be that he, too, thought of love? Toward her? How droll—a smile stole over her face before she nodded off for a late morning nap.

~*~

It was time for lunch, and Mr. Southwood's hunger could not be denied. Informed by a footman that a cold collation was arrayed on the sideboard in the dining room, he paused outside the threshold of the door. He heard snatches of a baffling conversation.

"...he's got nine lives, he does," the first voice said.

"Don't give up. You're next in line. This means everything to you," said a second, deeper voice. "You deserve the inheritance. He's been undeserving all these years. What about your expectations?"

Catching himself eavesdropping, he decided to enter the room and try to make sense of the overheard words later. He tucked away the odd snippet of conversation in his prodigious memory. He made his entrance, and the owners of the two voices looked up, startled. They both began to rise.

"Please, don't bother rising on my account. I shall join you instead." With a disarming and purposely silly smile on his face, Homer filled his plate, and then moved over to the table. He pulled out a chair and placed his plate in front of him.

"Gents, my moniker is Southwood, Mr. Homer Southwood of London. Guest of the family—invited by Mrs. Banting. Who might I be lunching with?"

"I am Sir Giles Walsh." This introduction belonged to the first voice he'd overheard. Short and corpulent, Sir Walsh wore an unbecoming suit of clothing all in shades of brown and violet.

Then the deeper-voiced man spoke. "I'm Lord Armbruster. How do you do? We, too, are guests of the family. In fact, we are family. Arrived on an impromptu visit." Much taller than Sir Walsh, Lord Armbruster wore a garish green and yellow striped vest with numerous fobs.

Socially ambitious, Homer would normally be delighted to be on speaking terms with two members of the aristocracy, as these two obviously were. Their titles and elaborate apparel spoke of that. But he couldn't enjoy the meeting as a benevolent happenstance due to what he heard while eavesdropping. The accidentally-ingested words lay locked firmly in his memory and left a bad taste in his mouth. Raising one finger, Homer spoke to the footman. "Coffee, please." Addressing himself to his food, Homer lapsed into silence. The gentlemen across the table did the same.

The two guests excused themselves and rose. Reluctant to let them leave without gleaning any information, Homer seized the opportunity. "How long shall ye be here?"

"Not sure. Not sure." Amrbruster waved around a vague hand as he answered.

"Ye say you're related to Lord Russell?" Homer held his breath and hoped they'd engage in some idle, revealing chatter.

"Yes, we are relatives." A snobbish tone overlaid the words as if they hadn't the time for such a commoner as Homer. They left the dining room without adding any clues.

Caring little about being snubbed by two such unpleasant noblemen, Homer had a final cup of coffee. He must tell Mrs. Banting how excellent the brew tasted. She'd like hearing how it was better than any in London. He decided to take a short stroll outside on the terrace and maybe venture out on the lawns beyond. Perhaps, he'd go see Melissa again at the vicarage.

Emerging from the house, he took a left turn onto the terrace. He paced for a time, unsettled by the encounter with the two gentlemen. He needed more strenuous walking to help him think through the portion of the conversation he had overheard. So, spying an appealing path diverging from the far side of the terrace, he accessed it and found himself on a footpath encircling the large house.

What had they said?

"…he's got nine lives. Don't give up. You're next in line. This means everything to you. You deserve the inheritance. He's been undeserving all these years. What about your expectations?"

Nine lives, inherit, undeserving.

Homer once again heard the distinctive deep voice and stopped in his tracks. This time the voice came out of an open second-floor bedroom window above his head. Riveted to the spot, he was torn whether to listen or leave.

"Jenks, I don't need you plotting on my behalf. You don't seem to know your place."

A quieter, whiny, uncultured voice responded. Homer couldn't catch the words.

But the deep, easily recognizable voice of Lord Armbruster spoke again. "You'll get yours when my plans come to fulfillment, not before. If I can make it look like an accident, well then, all's the better. I will let you know when and if I need your help. You've tried, but for now, keep your eyes and ears open around the manor, and don't forget you are my valet. Also, watch that Sir Walsh makes no silly mistakes. The man is losing his mind. See you have this jacket brushed and pressed. You may go."

Jarred out of his eavesdropping, Homer scuttled away down the path, puzzling over even more suspicious words of which to try to make sense. They were certainly plotting no good, and Homer feared for the target of the nefarious plot he'd overheard. But he squashed the thought of Lord Russell being in danger. That was too farfetched.

42

The gong sounded for lunch long ago. But after his intense interlude with Melissa ended with a gunshot, Mark had no appetite and sat behind his desk, feet up, staring at the ceiling. Thoughts swirled: *Why was someone using a gun in the vicinity of the vicarage? No hunting grounds lay nearby—no reason for anyone to be shooting.* With no reasonable conclusion, he trusted the Lord to protect him from all harm. In fact, in His providence, the bullet missed him.

Another serious mishap. Life threatening. The attack on the road in early spring, the carriage accident in London, this morning's stray gunshot. Intuition pointed toward something, but he couldn't make logical sense of it.

He rose and stood at the window, immediately spying Mr. Southwood coming around the corner of the house, head down. Mark pushed the French doors open and stepped out. "Sir! Mr. Southwood!"

Melissa's father looked up and strode toward Mark.

Here's my chance. Please let him be receptive. Mark kept his manner solicitous. "Say, I seem to remember you wanted to speak with me. Would you join me in my study?"

Mr. Southwood looked over his shoulder. "Yes, let's get inside."

Why the furtiveness? Mark stepped back through

the doors, and Southwood followed close at his heels into the study.

Homer sank into one of the dark brown leather chairs in front of the fireplace, deep in thought.

Mark decided to be bold. He sat in the matching chair, leaned forward, rested his forearms on his upper legs, and cleared his throat. Then he spoke. "Sir, I'd like to renew my suit with your daughter. Your first candidate is disqualified, and after enough time passes for Miss Southwood to get over her shocking experience, she'll be ready to be courted again. By me. You are aware that I am a marquis?"

Southwood slapped the arm of the chair for emphasis. "Certainly—very aware. Courting would be acceptable. But don't presume to think she's available for the taking. I've always coveted a title for her, but I've learned my lesson. She's going to have the final say. I'll hold you accountable for her happiness."

"Thank you. I'll make no presumptions. No presumptions at all." Mark smiled to himself. He had no need to presume. Such swift capitulation was a pleasant surprise. The man was less difficult than he'd feared. Mark's gaze drifted to the diamond-paned window, allowing himself a brief fantasy in which he strolled in the formal gardens with Melissa.

Snapping back to attention, he continued, "Now Mr. Southwood, you realize of course, I do have a title and a tidy fortune. I am not at all entering into this courtship with any designs on a lavish marriage settlement."

"Yes, yes. I understand. I am not concerned."

Mark rose and extended his hand for a deal-sealing shake, but Southwood gestured for Mark to sit down. "Be seated, young man. I need to go over another more urgent matter with you."

Mark dropped his hand and sank into the comfortable leather chair. At this point, he could afford to be patient even though he wanted to get up and dance a jig. This man would become his father-in-law if his pursuit of Melissa went well. It didn't matter what Southwood wanted to talk about. "An urgent matter?"

Homer leaned forward, eyes narrowed. "Two additional guests arrived here this morning."

"Guests? Well, who are they?" Mark sought to get down to the point of this delay. He wanted to plan his next outing with Melissa. As much as he needed a good relationship with the man he hoped would be his future father-in-law, there were other things he'd rather be doing at this time.

"Distant relatives, according to your aunt." A smile crept over Southwood's face. "Lovely lady—Mrs. Banting."

"Some of my relatives arrived here? How unusual. I've issued no invitations." As these words came out, Mark wanted to bite his tongue since the man before him also arrived without being invited. But Mr. Southwood didn't seem to notice the gaffe.

"Yes, right. Two gents. One is tall and deep-voiced. His name's Armbruster. The other one is average in size, wearing a terrible brown and plum-colored get up and named Walsh. Are they cousins of yours?"

"Maybe. Not *first* cousins certainly. I've known them all my life. See them around and about London mostly. They don't figure largely in my family picture, shall we say. I'd have to spend some time to put my finger on the exact relationship. Akin to third cousins once removed or the like."

"My advice is to keep your eyes on them. Something is not altogether right."

Mark could tell Southwood held back. Perhaps uneasy he would offend Mark by criticizing his relatives.

"Please elaborate. Whatever you say will not go any farther, and I will not take offense." Mark leaned back against the chair, intent on listening, his fingers steepled.

A tap sounded on the door. Both men jumped, startled by the interruption.

"Come in," Mark called. A maid pushed in a trolley bearing a pot of tea, two cups, and two plates holding an assortment of ham, cheese, and fruit left from the lunch served earlier in the dining room. The two men sat impatient and silent while she poured each of them a cup, bobbed a curtsey, and left the room.

"I chanced to overhear some disturbing and confounding remarks." First, he repeated what he'd heard from outside the dining room. "I heard the tall one, who has a deeper voice, say, 'He's got nine lives. Don't give up. You're next in line. This means everything to you. You deserve the inheritance. He's been undeserving all these years. What about your expectations?'"

"That's odd." Intrigued, Mark steepled his fingers near his upper lip. "You must have a prodigious memory to rattle off such a detailed word-for-word report."

"Some say I have a memory like a steel trap." Southwood went on, "There's more. The loud one, Lord Armbruster? I went outside to walk about, and I heard his voice coming from an upper window, saying to his valet, 'You'll get yours when my plans come to fulfillment, not before. If I can make it look like an accident, well then, all's the better.'"

"I find this hard to take in. Those words sound like...well, what does it sound like to you?" Dismay settling in his chest, Mark rubbed his forehead and raked a hand through his hair.

Southwood took a deep breath and let it out again before speaking. "I hate to even voice this, but it sounds to me, putting together what I heard, like the two relatives are plotting against someone, and Armbruster and his valet have someone else in their sights as well."

"Sounded like plotting, but against who and why? Not me, I hope. What would be the motive?"

"Now, this may be farfetched, but who is your heir?"

"My heir? Can't say I know who it is. It must sound strange to you, but I've been in such turmoil since my brother's death. Inheriting and shortly thereafter getting robbed, beaten, and left for dead. In my grief, if I was told the identity of the heir, it may have gone in one ear and out the other, and the beating may have knocked any such knowledge out of my head. I'll have to look into that matter."

"Robbed and beaten? Left for dead? I'd forgotten about that. Shameful business." Southwood's brows shaped a furrow, and he scowled.

"On the way home to take up my place as new master of this estate. I inherited the title after my older brother's sudden death. I was overtaken on the road and robbed. I can't remember any details of the crime, but I landed in a ditch, close to dead. My memory of the event is unclear."

"The situation seems quite havey-cavey. You must get an immediate message to your family solicitors. I am suspicious of these two distant relatives. I heard the words 'undeserving' and 'inherit,' and wouldn't they fit my hypothesis? It does seem too farfetched to be true, but how else to explain the words 'you'll get yours when I get mine,' and the snippet I overheard between Armbruster and his valet about getting one, and then the other?"

"You have a hypothesis? What is it?" Mark asked, heart sinking with a glimmer of the truth.

"These two bounders are probably in line to inherit. They are trying to kill you. Is that a clear enough hypothesis statement?"

"With all respect, Mr. Southwood, I don't want to believe this. In fact, it sounds straight out of a nightmare. But since I've experienced two other suspicious accidents since the robbery, I'll grant you the possibility. I'll pen a letter this hour and have it couriered to my solicitors in London. We may have our answer as to the name of the heir within three days' time."

Mark's anxiety level heightened. Now that he was in love, he wanted to live more than ever before. He must live to marry Melissa, have a family with her, and grow old together. Nothing must happen to prevent that.

He told Southwood the whole story of the life-threatening incidents. "I can't remember the attack, but my horse ran off and was found on the village green, my saddlebags were rifled, and I was dragged into a flooded ditch."

"That could have gone poorly for you, young man. Glad you pulled through."

"Then there was a carriage accident in London. The vehicle had been tampered with. I wasn't hurt, but I could have easily been killed if God hadn't preserved me again."

"I suppose if someone's behind these 'accidents,' they are getting desperate and are likely to try anything."

"This morning, a bullet whizzed by my head." He avoided mentioning Melissa's presence when the shot zipped by them. He had permission now and didn't want to muddy the waters. It was an innocent walk in the garden of the vicarage, after all. "I wonder where the two relatives or the valet were at that exact time."

"Perhaps I can find out. But even on the existing evidence of their words and my justifiable hypotheses, they deserve watching. I will stick close to Armbruster and Walsh, no matter if I have to force myself on their company. They can't possibly make another attempt with me right there." Southwood's voice conveyed resolve.

Mark said, "God knows what they'll try next if our guesses are accurate. Thank God you came to me with your suspicions. And, even more, thank you for permission to court Melissa." He again tried to rise and shake hands, but the older man interrupted.

"Russell, sit down. Your mention of courting reminds me of something. I, too, want to do things right, and you probably should know of my honorable intentions toward your aunt."

"I see. Do you think she'll favor your suit?"

"I'll do my da—I mean best, to win her. Can you tell me if she has any other suitors? Anyone poised to come crawling out of the woodwork?"

"Not to my knowledge. I can't promise you a clear

field. It's up to you to vanquish all others on your own, without a father's approval. I'm only a nephew and have no authority over Aunt Lucy."

"But are ye against me? I'd be your uncle if all goes as I'd like."

"How could I oppose such a reasonable plan? Besides, you'll be my father-in-law, too, Lord willing," Mark said, suppressing a snicker.

"I think I'll go find her now if she's not resting." Homer extended his hand, and Mark took it. Worried though he was about the mysterious words, he wanted to dance at the thought of having full approval for pursuing Melissa.

~*~

Homer meandered around the main floor of the house looking into rooms, hoping one of the doors would open onto the sight of Mrs. Banting. He wanted to waste no time. No reason to delay wooing. Not often did such an opportunity present itself—sequestered at a lovely, isolated estate, and he the only invited guest. The two relatives, even if up to no good as he suspected, at least presented no competition for the fair lady's hand.

He rounded a corner and caught a whiff of a pleasant floral perfume. He'd noticed his intended ladylove wearing it. She must be nearby. Ah, another door to try, this one's open. He could just peek in with no one the wiser if she was not there.

Lucy glanced up from the desk where she sat, pen poised above paper.

Oh, good—she's smiling.

"Hello. Are you searching for someone?"

"Good afternoon. I was looking for you. May I come in a moment?"

"I suppose. It's such a small room, but I like it here. I've claimed this nook as my study, and I write my letters here where I can refresh my eyes viewing the outdoors every so often."

Homer needed only a few steps to cross the diminutive room. He faced the window. "Very pretty. Such gardens Russell Manor boasts—magnificent." His back to the room, he faltered. *How to proceed? Test the waters or jump right in?*

Lucy interrupted his deliberations. "Do you have a garden in London?"

He turned to answer. "Only a pocket garden. The grounds are pleasant, but necessarily small. We do have an apple tree. It had just finished blooming when I left London."

"How sweet. I love apple blossoms." She propped a finger under her chin, clearly waiting to see what he wanted.

He threw himself into a chair—the one nearest her—took a calming breath, and spoke. "Have you ever thought of marrying again?" *There. He dove in. No going back now.*

"In general?" She tilted her head, quizzical, and then capped the ink bottle before turning her full attention on Homer.

"In general, yes, but in particular as well." Homer yanked on his vest, pulling it down to cover a bit of shirt which emerged when he flopped down. His thumbs went into the vest pockets.

"I must say, I'm surprised by your query, but I'll try to answer." She paused, tapping her cheek a few times. "I've thought of it here and there, fleetingly, but never dwelt on it in particular because the question hasn't arisen until now."

"Well then, I am particularly interested in pursuing getting to know you better. I lo—like you very much and would be very happy if you said we could spend time together, doing the things courting couples do. I know we're not that young anymore, but it would be pleasant and appropriate to go on drives, picnics, walks, and the like. Do you agree?

"That it would be appropriate? Yes. And I would very much like to explore our friendship in the manner you've laid out. Now, since we are close to becoming an *on-dit*, you must leave before scandal brews. We can't be alone together like this. We are no longer simply hostess and guest. We are partaking of the marriage mart, and we must follow the rules." She smiled and held out her hand. Homer clasped it, trying to rein in the silly smile on his own face. But it couldn't be helped—not when a new chapter in one's life was about to begin.

43

With satisfaction, Mark spotted a mounted groom emerging from the stable at a fast clip mid-afternoon. The task of acting as a courier to London thrilled the young worker. To anyone else observing him, a servant on a horse appeared as a common sight, and if noticed at all, the activity would be surmised to be a trip to exercise one horse or another. Only Mark and Mr. Southwood were aware of the rider's important errand.

Life at Russell Manor must continue with routine activities, though Mark's awareness remained heightened because of the mysterious words spoken by the distant relatives. A strained atmosphere floated around the dining room that evening. The tension easily attributable to the two unappealing, unexpected guests arriving and topped by Homer's suspicions, a miasma of unease hovered in the air.

"Mr. Southwood, I understand you deal in shipping interests. Can you tell us any fascinating tales of voyages?" Aunt Lucy said.

"I've never experienced the drama of a ship sunk, thank the Lord, but have had a ship embargoed. In order not to take a complete loss on the cargo, the captain slipped out of a guarded harbor during a moonless, cloudy night. He waited until the deepest dark of night, caught the tide, and away he went. Would have loved to be there. But most of my work finds me in my London offices."

"I can picture that. A ship gliding silently—ooh, gives me chills." She tapped Southwood's arm with her fan and flashed her dimples.

Mark admired how Aunt Lucy did her best as hostess to make the meal a success, but he could see it was tough going. He interjected a remark to provide direction. "I'm sure Lord Armbruster and Sir Walsh have had a long day. As have I. What say we forgo cards tonight and make it an earlier evening?" The suggestion met with approval, and relief swept over Mark as the others agreed to retire early after the meal.

"Excellent. That's a fine idea." Aunt Lucy hid a delicate yawn behind her fingers and made to rise. A footman appeared to assist with her chair, and all the men leapt to their feet and bowed as she rose, and then sailed out of the room, silk gown's train flowing behind her like the frothy wake of a boat.

"Russell, won't you partake of brandy and cigars?" Lord Armbruster, forward as ever, boomed in an insistent tone.

"Only if Sir Walsh and Mr. Southwood care to."

"No cigars for me." Southwood puffed out his chest and smacked it with his fist. "Got to keep my lungs clear. I've many good years ahead, I hope."

"Gents, what say I pass out some of my Jamaican cigars and you two can blow a cloud out on the terrace?" Mark addressed the relatives.

"Excellent idea. Giles, let's take Russell up on this offer. I can't abide missing my smoke after a fine dinner."

"I'll be right back." Mark left the room, shoulders relaxing as he traversed the hall, relieved they didn't insist on following him.

A Match for Melissa

Upon return, Mark handed each man a cigar. "After you." He herded them out the door of the drawing room, which led directly to the terrace. He chuckled at their looks of surprise when he swung the door shut from the inside. He turned away with a sigh and went through the room to the hall where he bumped into Southwood.

"You're back. Good. I was disturbed that you were going outside for a smoke. Not with those two. Russell, I'll be seeking you out tomorrow to talk. Good night." With that, he turned and marched up the stairs.

~*~

The next day dawned and promised to be another one of those rare days of English late spring: light breezes, sunny, but not too hot. Mark stretched his arms above his head and relished the moment. A brand new day with appropriate weather for a drive with one's intended. *Tonight's another dinner party—I'll see Melissa twice today.*

He got out of bed with eagerness and ate breakfast before any of the other inhabitants of the house stirred, and then went to the study. The peaceful room soothed, and he passed by a book-lined wall trailing his fingers along the spines, past his desk and over to a sparkling diamond-paned leaded glass bow window. He put a hand on either side of the frame and leaned forward to stare out, not really seeing the pretty grounds before him but instead lifting his cares to God.

Lord, please allow my pursuit of Melissa to be successful. Please help me to be honorable and righteous.

After meditating a few moments, he sat at his desk. He attended to some estate matters, wrote a couple of letters, and then grabbed his hat. A morning drive should provide the perfect opportunity to carry the courtship forward. The grooms would be happy to pull a carriage out—a break in their daily tedium of mucking stalls and brushing horses.

He helped the grooms hitch a horse to the small open carriage. He swung up onto the seat, slapped the reins, and tooled along, inhaling the fresh air, redolent of the surrounding woods. Happy thoughts flew ahead to guessing Melissa's reaction when she learned he'd obtained her father's permission to proceed toward possible matrimony. His face ached from smiling. Would she be receptive or hold herself aloof out of fear?

He didn't really blame her for being a bit skittish after the contretemps with Winstead. Shuddering with disgust as he recalled Winstead's shocking abduction attempt, he thanked the Lord that Melissa retained the air of innocent purity which held great appeal to a once-jaded former libertine such as himself.

Mark pulled the carriage to a stop in front of the vicarage. He sat a moment before alighting as an idea coalesced. Perhaps a number of casual, innocent outings would be best to help Melissa be comfortable. Maybe he should pace his quest in a more gradual fashion.

But he had to know. He could reassure her of his love their whole life long. High hopes animated every vigorous move as he jumped down, tied the horses, and covered the ground to the entry. He used the brass knocker on the gray door, schooling his features to calmness while waiting.

~*~

A Match for Melissa

Melissa looked up from her book at the sound of banging on the front door.

"Who do you suppose is knocking?" Miss Dean said, looking up from her knitting, brows raised.

"We shall see." Melissa yearned. *Mark, let it be Mark.* Oh, it was nice to allow her thoughts to drift to him. They'd agreed to use each other's first names, and the simple notion of him possibly being the one knocking at the front door of the vicarage gave her a charge of pleasure unlike any she'd experienced when Lord Winstead courted her. Winstead's arranged courtship had been a prosaic duty compared to this bubbly joy.

The maid's footsteps sounded in the entry hall. The door creaked open, and a deep male voice sounded. The maid gave a soft rap on the sitting room door before stepping in.

She spoke, just above a whisper, "Miss, Lord Russell is calling. Are you home?"

"Yes, have him step in here."

Soon he stood before her, his large frame crowding the cozy sitting room. Very masculine, yet she sensed no threat from this man. She enjoyed his presence. The two shared a smile, and he spoke at the same time she did.

"Miss Southwood?"

"Lord Russell?"

Flustered, she lowered her eyes and said, "No, you first. What were you saying?" Composing herself enough to look up, she found she experienced a compelling sensation when she looked into his dark sea blue eyes. Her hands yearned to reach for his.

"I'm calling with the purpose of inviting you for a

morning drive. I spoke with your father and want to tell you about it. Are you able to accept, or do you have plans?"

"There's nothing I'd like better." She stood and glanced out the window. With relief, she saw he'd brought an open vehicle. "Miss Dean, I'm going on a drive, and I won't need you to go along."

"Have a splendid time." Miss Dean didn't miss a stitch.

I love you, Miss Dean. You're the perfect companion. "I'll get my wrap from the hall tree. If they ask, tell Reverend and Miss Cleaver I've gone out for a drive."

"That's right, Miss Dean. I'll have her back well before noon, and I'll look after her as if she were my own," Mark stated.

Miss Dean answered with a light titter, keeping her eyes on her handwork.

In the hall, he retrieved his hat, and Melissa draped a blue cashmere shawl over her arm and selected a bonnet from several hanging on the hall tree. The chip straw decorated with silk daisies complemented her white muslin dress and blue sash.

He held the door 'til she passed through and gave her his arm. The pleasant sensation of being protected by this man swirled through her. He assisted her onto the padded seat before climbing up beside her. Contentment swept over her. This could go on forever.

"Are you comfortable?" he asked as he arranged the shawl around her shoulders.

"Yes, very much so." She patted the seat, indicating the plush leather cover.

He snapped the reins, spoke to the horse, and they were off. Another strong wave of well-being swept over her as the beauty of the day sank in. The less-confined life she experienced on these visits made her not ever want to go back to London. There, every move was put under scrutiny and restricted by rules and societal expectations.

A fizzy bubble of hope rose in her breast. This is what courting should be. Happy and exciting, not tense and pressured.

44

Melissa settled in to enjoy the outing. Compared to the bustle of the streets of London, where she took drives with Lord Winstead, this country drive suited her taste better. The scents of spring delighted her—from the simple smell of wet soil to the lush perfume of flowering trees. Bowling along in the open carriage, nature surrounded her senses. Her hand developed a mind of its own, as it yearned to reach across the seat to touch Mark.

She liked this new sensation of romance. She'd had little enough affection in her life since her mother's death and father's subsequent descent into bitterness. She longed for the day she'd have her own husband and family to love.

Comfortable silence together. Wasn't that a sign of compatibility? Her dream of a husband of like faith was materializing and within her grasp. Mark had a strong faith. She had plenty of evidence. And would God allow her to have this strong attraction toward Mark if he wasn't the one? She didn't think so.

He glanced at her every few minutes and before long, turned into the beginnings of a field road and stopped the carriage. He hopped down, tied the horse to a fence post, and moved around to her side.

"There's a scenic overlook at the hilltop. It's not to be missed," he said as he reached up to assist Melissa.

He gently grasped her around the waist and

swung her down, letting go after she had her footing.

Thank you, Mark."

"I thought you'd enjoy the exercise. As I recall, you take a daily constitutional, so this won't be too hard for you?"

She drew in a happy breath, realizing he remembered those little things about her. Lord Winstead never had. She smiled up at him and hooked her arm through his. "An excellent idea. And I'd love to climb the hill. Hills are among my favorite things."

Touching his arm gave delight. Reveling in it for only a moment, she reined in her wayward imagination, deciding to bring the conversation to a higher-minded level. A little probing wouldn't be amiss.

"I've noticed you attended services on Sunday. Do you like the preaching?" she asked. He shouldn't be reluctant to discuss church matters.

"Yes, it's quite satisfying to my soul. I daresay Mr. Cleaver rivals the best I've heard—so erudite, yet sensitive. So logical, yet soul-stirring. I found his sermon from the Book of Philippians extremely edifying and inspiring."

"Any verses in particular?" She extended this conversational thread while rebellious romantic thoughts kept slipping off to the handsomeness of her escort.

"Yes, the 'whatsoevers.' Do you remember it? 'Whatsoever things are pure, whatsoever things are lovely…'?" Mark placed his free hand over hers.

"I do love that passage. Honor, truth, justice, virtue—to think God gave us His precious word to inspire us on our paths in life leaves me awestruck. What are the other two whatsoevers? I know there are more."

Mark took a moment. "I've got it. Praise and good report, which means good reputation."

Reputation. A small niggle of worry crept in. Though they traveled in an open carriage, this secluded spot provided something of a risk of temptation. As soon as the thought entered, she put the fear away, knowing unless she or Mark revealed it, no one would ever learn of this idyll. Their reputations would not be harmed. She trusted him with her honor.

Hoping he hadn't noticed her lagging response, she said, "Oh, good, Mark, you thought of the rest. It would have nagged at me otherwise."

They reached the top of the hill, and she let go of his arm to drink in with awe the charming vista before them. As she admired the prospect, a flash of insight filled her imagination, showing her that life lay before her—for the taking. What a wonderful time to be alive and in love.

She let out a small gasp of exasperation at her own wayward thoughts. She must stop this fantasizing. Trying to anchor herself in the present, she looked down at the clover and violets interspersed with the grass covering the ground. She breathed in the languorous sweet scents perfuming the warm air, and her unruly mind raced ahead again to a fantasy of Mark's arms around her.

"Shall we sit down?" He shrugged out of his well-fitted blue coat and laid it on the grass at the brink of the hill. Sweeping his arm in a charming courtly way, he smiled at her with a question in his deep blue eyes.

Her heart beating at an excited pace, she stepped forward and sat, with as much poise as possible, on the coat. She wondered if it offered enough sitting space for both of them. Gladness bloomed when he dropped to the ground as well. They sat next to each other, her legs bent and out to the side, and his out in front and crossed at the ankle.

She kept her eyes forward, admiring the vista before her. A patchwork of fields and roads, hedgerows and fences created a feast for the eyes. She plucked a stem of clover and twirled it between two fingers.

She turned toward him, about to comment on the scenery, when he cleared his throat. "I spoke to your father, my dear. He gave approval, but of course, you hold the final say."

He maneuvered onto one knee in front of her, blocking the view, and all she could focus on were his dark sea-blue eyes. He picked up her hands, lacing her fingers through his. It surprised her how warm his hands were. A proposal? She wanted a proposal, but was she ready? "Mark, you've amazed me."

45

He reached out and lightly touched her shoulder, and then brushed a strand of rose-golden hair off her cheek. "Melissa, my love, the impediments are cleared. Can I hope for the day we will belong to each other? All that I am and all that I have will be yours. Will you be my bride?"

Melissa's head and heart reeled with happiness. She hadn't expected him to declare himself so soon. Her loving heart wanted to reach out and accept the love being offered, but her cautious mind checked her response. As much as she would like to say 'yes,' a knot of inner turmoil held her back.

"Mark, I need more time. This is sudden. When did you speak to my father?" Even to her, this babbling sounded like a coy tactic, but she couldn't just rush in and agree to everything this compelling man proposed. He released her hands, and she drew them back into her lap.

"I spoke to him yesterday morning. The choice is yours, but it's clear I'm rushing my fences."

The realization bore down on her that she hadn't yet recovered from the shock of Lord Winstead's sickening betrayal. It affected her ability to trust. But Mark lived a different sort of life, and a man of honor such as he would respect her and treat her well. Her heart still hurt, though, and only time would heal it. She didn't want to go into a pure and holy marriage before dealing with the traumatic aftermath of betrayal and abduction.

Mark got up from his knees, and reaching out, pulled her to her feet before he spoke again.

"Melissa, my love, please tell me how much time you need before you can be sure. I, for one, have never been surer of anything in my life. You see, I love you."

She wasn't ready to exchange the words 'I love you.' "Can't we go on with our courting for a few weeks more? I very much want to accept, but something is holding me back. Please be tolerant with me. I must overcome my fears."

Hurt flashed in his eyes, and her own heart ached at the sight. He blinked and lowered his lids for a moment, as if in pain. When he spoke, it was with composure. "Yes, my love. We can court all spring and summer, fall and winter, if that's what it takes to win you. I'll be patient with you as long as you need. I hope you grow to trust me with your heart, and together we will conquer any fears. With God's help."

His kind and patient response humbled her. He'd proved his love. Her own affections were engaged as well. But the dreadful aftereffects of the abduction still hung over her like a dark cloud, and she couldn't accept his offer. Not yet. She still needed to heal from the harrowing experience.

They wended their way down the hill to the carriage, and Mark returned her to the vicarage.

"I shall count the hours until the dinner party tonight. And I promise to call on you again and take you on another drive very soon, perhaps tomorrow. I know of other beautiful scenery in the vicinity." He bowed over her hand, and his lips brushed her fingertips.

~*~

"Here's lunch." Miss Dean backed into Melissa's bedroom at the vicarage, holding a tray and turned to push the door shut with her foot.

Melissa unfolded from her perch on the window seat, stood, and came over to examine the tray's contents. "Thank you. Would you like to join me? There appears to be plenty. I'd like the company. Ooh, lemon cookies. My favorite."

"Don't mind if I do. I can use this bread plate." The companion bustled about, arranging two armchairs near a low table.

Toward the end of the meal, Melissa offered Miss Dean a tidbit of the day's news. "Lord Russell and I had a pleasant drive."

Three taps and the door opened to admit Miss Cleaver. "Hope I'm not intruding. How was your drive with Lord Russell?" She approached the table, eyes shining with interest.

"I was just going to tell about that. So glad you came in time to hear." Melissa pulled another chair up to the table, and Miss Cleaver joined them.

"It was a lovely day for driving. Where did you go?" Miss Cleaver's eyes peered across at Melissa.

"We climbed a hill. But the *where* wasn't as important as the *what*, ladies."

"The what?" Two voices spoke and two pairs of gray brows flew up.

"He proposed." She dropped the remainder of her crisp cookie onto her plate and brushed her fingers over the tray.

"A proposal? Oh, my." Setting down her cup and

pushing back her chair, Miss Dean swept up her knitting bag and resituated her project.

Miss Cleaver clasped excited hands under her chin, and her eyes sparkled.

"It came sooner than I expected. But not unwelcome." A cold wave of regret washed over Melissa. She couldn't just enjoy young love because Winstead's folly besmirched her heart's peace.

"Well, what was your answer?" Miss Dean's eyes, lowered to her needles and yarn, gave nothing away.

"I said no for now." Melissa's head hung down, and she rubbed her eyes, wiping away an errant tear. She sniffled. "I did give him hope, though."

"Hope is a good thing." Miss Cleaver chimed in with wise words and reached to pat Melissa's arm.

"True. It's simply too soon after Lord Winstead courted me, and you are familiar with that debacle. Such a shock."

"You did right, dear. Lord Russell will need to wait. A heart heals at its own pace." Miss Dean spoke as if experienced with a broken heart once upon a time.

"You are both excellent listeners. I hoped you'd understand." Amazing how talking it over helped. Melissa's spirits rose, and she picked up the cookie again. An appetite was a good sign. "And I'll spend time with him tonight at the dinner party at Russell Manor. I'll wear my blue silk. The new one."

After lunch, she spent a few hours assisting Miss Cleaver with the mending, and then making calf's foot jelly. These domestic activities soothed her anxiety.

Neither Miss Cleaver nor Miss Dean had any personal experience in matters of romance that Melissa knew of. But what a blessing she had two older women to confide in. How would she have born this alone without their support?

The last jar of jelly sealed, she departed the kitchen and sought solitude in her room where she had time before the party to pray, think, and read the Bible.

She was able to nap and slept dreamlessly. She awoke to the sound of knocking—Miss Dean, ready to help her dress.

~*~

Mark spent some time alone in his study after the drive with Melissa. While staring at a blank sheet of paper, he daydreamed about the day she would become his bride. Even though she'd said no, he believed she was to be his.

She'd been shaken to the core by her harrowing experience at the hands of that bounder, Peter Winstead. Mark himself witnessed the denouement of that heinous scheme. Her caution made sense, and he didn't want to rush her to a decision.

Reviewing the morning's interactions, he doubted his own timing. He hadn't intended to propose yet. He'd gotten carried away by the moment on the hilltop. He was grateful she hadn't recoiled from his importunities, but he kicked himself for rushing his fences.

Nothing, however, would keep him from his goal. She was the one woman for him, and of that he was certain. He's never cared anywhere near this much about any of the young misses who crossed his path in the past. The drive to love, protect, and provide for Melissa coursed through his being like the blood in his veins.

He ordered lunch to be brought in on a tray.

Without much appetite, he ate merely out of habit. After a few quick bites of food, he shoved back the plate, pushed his papers and books into the semblance of a pile, and got up. He stretched his arms above his head, and then put on his jacket to go in search of his aunt.

46

"There you are, Aunt Lucy. Are you alone?" Mark entered the sitting room at Russell Manor after lunch, his mind searching for the right words.

"Yes, for now. The cousins are napping, and Homer—I mean, Mr. Southwood—is visiting his daughter. This is perfect timing for a coze." Lucy patted the seat of the high-backed settee. "Sit by me. That way we can both enjoy the gardens."

"A view of the gardens is always a pleasure." He sat and leaned his chin on his fist.

"I am partial, but I still think Russell Manor is an exceptionally beautiful estate. I believe it to be one of the finest in this part of the country."

"I'm glad. I hoped to bring momentous news for you today, but the young lady involved answered otherwise." He kept his voice light, but his heart gave a twinge.

"Mark, don't say you proposed to Melissa and were rebuffed."

"Yes, I did. And she turned me down." He held up his hands, palms out, to forestall further expressions of sympathy or consternation. "She asked for more time."

Exhaling a ladylike, yet flustered sigh, Lucy sat, temporarily wordless. Surely, she'd have some wisdom for him.

While waiting for her answer, he inserted a plea. "Don't allow disappointment on my behalf to lead you to withdraw your approval of Melissa. Your support means a lot to me."

"My dear nephew, never fear on that count. I cherish that darling girl. You have every reason to hope, don't you?"

"I'd like to think so."

"She seems favorable towards you. What I see when you two are together tells me that much. I've even begun to mull over a few preliminary wedding plans."

"All signs do point to a positive outcome, Lord willing."

"I imagine you are in a bit of a quandary. Your urge is to press on to your chosen goal, but you must restrain your strong inclinations."

"So true. I have never experienced such a strong tendency toward a young lady."

"Restraining one's penchant when in love can be a trial." Lucy uttered her agreement in a soothing, reassuring tone and reached out to touch his hand.

"I must strike a balance."

"A balance between showing encouraging love to Melissa and not putting on undue pressure?"

"Exactly, Aunt Lucy."

"I certainly advise you to put no pressure on the poor girl. Remember, the Lord doesn't tempt us more than we can bear. Therefore, you must be patient and trust providence with the outcome."

Mark stood, paced the room several times, and then stopped to brace his hands against the mantel, leaning forward, head down.

"You are correct, of course, Aunt Lucy." A faint moan escaped his lips.

"It is a strong belief of mine there should be no

manipulation or compulsion in the procession to the altar. Too many friends and acquaintances of mine have born the results of marrying under familial duress. I have an absolute loathing for the like." She smacked her palms together for emphasis.

He lifted his head, swung away from the fireplace, and came back to join her on the settee. "Her father gave me permission to court Melissa."

"That's a blessing."

"He also permitted her the final say as to the outcome of the courtship."

"So excellent to hear. I am sure you are thankful for the gift of faith which sees one through earthly love's tumultuous circumstances." She patted his knee. "I will keep the matter in my prayers."

"That's what I need." He crossed his legs and leaned back.

"Things are smiling upon your suit, though." She ticked off a list on her fingers, touching each digit as she made her points. "No one else is courting her, her father has approved, you are an excellent catch, and didn't you say she insists on marrying another believer, which you are?"

"Yes, I agree, Aunt Lucy, the outlook's optimistic."

"Waiting for love is a trial. It's against your nature to be passive." She took up her knitting, fumbling the needles into position. "My dear boy, I have a very good premonition about this all. Don't fret."

He absently watched stitches form as she knitted. Then she sighed, and he glanced up at her face, wondering what caused the sigh.

Aunt Lucy's eyes took on a faraway appearance for a moment. "My perspective sees something beyond the momentary trials you face. I have a letter to write, my good nephew. Please open the writing desk for me on your way out." She returned the knitting project to her workbasket.

He got to his feet and assisted his aunt to rise. He opened the desk, pulled out the chair, and helped her get situated.

She patted his hand. "I promise. It will be fine. You'll see."

"You're right. The Lord already knows the outcome, and that's a comfort to me."

She chewed the end of her pen and gave the last word. "So true. He knows our needs. Summon a footman for me, please. I'll need a message delivered."

47

Lucy leaned forward to allow the maid to fasten the necklace. Jewelry provided the finishing touch as she readied herself for the dinner party.

She stood, smoothed the purple taffeta skirt of her gown, and then touched the high-waisted black velvet sash, making sure of its position. Tilting her head this way and that, she noticed a pleasing sparkle glinting off the jet jewelry. Wearing deeper, darker colors was one consolation for getting old. By contrast, she'd wager Melissa would appear in white or pastels—not that the dear girl wouldn't look lovely as can be.

She flicked at the black lace trim on her sleeves. "That will be all. Thank you, and don't worry, the party will not last until all hours." She hated for the maid to wait late to help her undress, but it couldn't be avoided.

Filled with happy expectancy, she journeyed to the drawing room where she'd receive the guests. A simple country dinner party seasoned with the prospect of an evening with her admirers. Acting as hostess came naturally, but having two swains circling heightened her nerves to a pleasant level of anticipation.

"Mrs. Banting?" Crabtree intercepted her.

"Yes, what is it?"

"One of yer guests is here already. The minister."

"I see." She straightened her shoulders, lifted her

chin, and moved through the doorway, deciding to stop a few steps in. It had been a long time since she'd made a dramatic entrance, and it was fun.

Mr. Cleaver shot to his feet. In several long strides, he reached her and swept up her hands, bowing over them, murmuring fervently words she couldn't make out.

She yanked her hands away, and then to cover her abrupt withdrawal, inquired after the others. "You've arrived without the rest of the group from the vicarage?" Not to mention early.

"The ladies are coming in a carriage which seats only four. I enjoy a good walk, however, and came on ahead, hoping for a chance to be alone with you."

"Alone with me?" *What is the man thinking?* Only recently had she even realized his interest, and he was openly stating his hopes of finding her alone.

"How else shall we know if we suit?"

He did have a point. Though she'd not given serious attention to evaluating his suitability.

Ignoring the remark, she indicated a settee and proceeded to sit. He seated himself next to her, and wasn't it a hair too close?

He angled toward her, his knees almost touching hers. "I enjoyed our visit in the garden. Would you have time to go on a walk there with me tomorrow?"

"Tomorrow?" *He continued to rush on, didn't he?* "Perhaps. I must see how I feel after teaching my knitting class. Amazing how much energy that takes. Shall I send a note once I decide? For I couldn't say yes or no just now. My mind is full of tonight's party, of course."

"That would be fine. I will await a message from you. So good of you to teach knitting to the women of the district."

"I hope the skill becomes a form of provision for the families. Scarves, socks and the like come in quite useful." She was blathering, but it couldn't be helped.

"Lately, I find several women of the congregation knitting at their homes when I visit. No idle hands." His right hand sneaked along the back of the settee, and his left hand crept inexorably toward hers. What to do?

The answer was taken out of her control when footsteps alerted them to the presence of another person entering the room. Mr. Cleaver pulled back his hands and smoothed his cuffs while a blush slunk up his cheeks.

"Mrs. Banting, good evening." Mr. Southwood, looking elegant in severe evening garb that would make Brummel proud, passed by the hand extended in his direction by the now-standing minister.

Instead, he bowed over Lucy's hand, kissed the air above her knuckles, and then gave her a speaking glance—the eye-contact holding a promise she'd need to think about later.

With an air of impatience, he turned to Mr. Cleaver. "Cleaver. I'm surprised to find you here so early." He jutted out his hand, gave a shake, and turned back to Lucy. "If tonight's dinner has half the panache of your ball, I am in for a rare treat."

"The ball? You enjoyed that, didn't you?" She looked up at him, reminiscence bringing a warm flush of pleasure at his compliment.

Turning again toward the minister, Mr. Southwood spoke to him once more, tone laced with irritation. "Where's my daughter and the rest of the group from the vicarage? You didn't escort them?"

"I came on ahead. They are properly attended by a coachman and groom."

"Somewhat surprised, what with the robbers who beat Lord Russell still not apprehended, that you'd not stay with them."

Nonplussed, Mr. Cleaver fumbled for words. "I thought—I believed—it's never been a problem." He ended weakly.

Lucy cringed at this awkward interchange, at a loss for how to smooth things over. She, being the cause of the friction, wanted to solve it. Lack of any ideas of what to do, however, caught her in a limbo of inaction. Each man had an aggressive gleam in his eye, chest puffed out, and hands clenched. Deliverance came with the announcement of another arrival.

"Lord Russell." intoned Crabtree.

Thank the Lord. Her jaw unclenched as she flew to her feet and sedately scurried to Mark's side. "Help, these two are daggers drawn. I'll explain later," she whispered these words out of the corner of her mouth.

Mark didn't let her down. He welcomed both men, putting them on equal footing, and launched a rousing discussion of horse breeds, distracting them with his equine knowledge.

She laughed inwardly, marveling at Mark's excellent choice of topic. The older men's faces took on the gloss of boredom. When each one glanced her way, she smiled, fluttering her lashes. That would give them solace and perhaps cool their anger at finding themselves not alone in their attraction to her.

"Miss Southwood, Miss Cleaver, Miss Dean, Miss Chesney." Crabtree held the door and disappeared when all four women gained the room.

Much calmer now, Lucy stepped over to the

cluster of ladies and greeted each one. "Melissa, Priscilla, how good it is to see you." She patted their hands. "Miss Chesney, I am so delighted to entertain you here for the first time. And you too, Miss Dean. So kind of you both to help a befuddled hostess make up her numbers. When our distant relatives arrived, it threw the seating completely out of order." Lucy laid her fingers over her bosom in mock discomfiture. She meant her words sincerely but overlaid them with a jesting tone to lighten the moment for all. And she wanted the two dowdy companions not to feel any awkwardness in their position.

The pair of cousins entered unannounced, either ignoring the aged butler's attempts to announce them, or perhaps Crabtree had his fill of the pair.

"Oh, here they are now. Lord Armbruster and Sir Walsh are cousins of ours. Do come over and pay your respects to the ladies who've just arrived."

As the two men complied and introductions were made, Lucy winced at the mustard yellow breeches worn by Armbruster, which clashed horridly with his orange and plum-striped waistcoat. His black evening coat may have been a nod to fashion, and she was thankful it toned down the putrid colors paired with it. Walsh sported satin knee breeches and a frock coat of emerald green, stylish twenty years ago, as well as frothy jabot and cuffs, the lace worse for wear. He preened as though all present were blessed by his appearance.

"Now that we are here, let us proceed into the dining room." As hostess, she decided to put a period to the pre-prandial social time. She glanced around, looking for the bell with which to call the butler. "Where is that bell?"

A Match for Melissa

"Here it is. Why you!" Mr. Southwood wrested the bell away from Mr. Cleaver.

"Me? I simply tried to give Mrs. Banting the bell she asked for, you…" The minister's face turned white, and then red, and he clapped a hand over his own mouth.

Mr. Southwood elbowed past the mortified man, and with a gloat, presented the bell to Lucy.

"Thank you," she said in a repressive tone. She took the bell, rang it, and gave it back to Homer with a quiet hiss. "I'd be more pleased if my guests were in accord." Her fan went into action, hiding the lower half of her face and fanning away the sudden heat in her cheeks.

"Aunt Lucy?" Mark drew her attention. "May I claim the honor of escorting you to dinner this evening?" He held out his forearm and dipped his chin in a gesture meant to brook no indecision.

Since Mark held the highest title in the room and she was the hostess, it was more than appropriate to lay her gloved hand on his arm, smile, and sail forward, trusting the others to sort themselves. Her two putative swains could shift for themselves among the assortment of females available. That would teach them to battle for dominance in the drawing room. The choice of whether and who she would court fell to her and her alone. They could bicker all they wanted, but that wouldn't make her choose one over the other.

Mark brought her to one end of the lavish table, and he departed to the other end, too far away to help her now. Not predicting their mutual antipathy, she wished she'd known. Now stuck with Mr. Southwood on her right and Mr. Cleaver to her left, she'd be trapped between two sets of daggers drawn if she couldn't smooth things over.

Nervous though she was, it pleased her to see Mark aiding Melissa into her seat and begin to charm his way further into her heart by the look of their smiles at the far end of the table. Melissa's father, preoccupied with vying for Lucy's favor, allowed Mark clear sailing as he wooed Melissa. Such a handsome youthful couple, radiating the joy of young love.

"Ahem, Mrs. Banting, I beg your pardon for my behavior a few minutes ago. Inexcusable." Mr. Southwood humbled himself readily, surprising Lucy with the speed of his remorse. "And Mr. Cleaver, please forgive my handling of the bell situation. So sorry."

"Quite so. Pleased to forget it happened." Mr. Cleaver didn't linger on the embarrassing topic and turned away, finding Cassandra Chesney seated to his left.

"Miss Chesney, how have you been since arriving at the vicarage?" Cleaver asked.

Lucy murmured inconsequentials to Mr. Southwood, giving him only half her attention, saving at least one eye and ear for the interaction between the minister and Cassandra. The young woman was passably attractive, looked around thirty, and held herself well. An appealing blush rose to Cassandra's cheeks and long lashes bedecked her sparkling eyes.

Inveterate matchmaker that she was, her thoughts rushed ahead to clarity. Wasn't Miss Chesney a minister's daughter? *Such a more appropriate match for Mr. Cleaver.* Lucy needed to repress any further tenders of interest from him. She liked him fine, but her heart must not be divided. The poor man couldn't see how green his own grass was. Southwood may be impetuous and aggressive, but something about him touched her heart.

~*~

"You look lovely tonight, my dear." Mark murmured so only Melissa could hear. "What do you call that shade of blue?"

"Azure, I believe." She glowed under the attentions of her dinner partner. So this was love. The constant warmth, excitement, and floating on a cloud of delicious imaginings of the future together. Could he perceive her affections via their emotional bond?

She addressed a few remarks to the guest on her left side, Sir Walsh. "Have you enjoyed your visit to Russell Manor?" She hoped this was a suitable topic. Her doubts were soon over as this innocuous question elicited a veritable outpouring of words.

"The room I was given is tolerable, but the view is not to my liking. I hate trees, and I'm staring out the window into a tree. Trees in full leaf, outside my window, blocking sight of anything else is far less than I am used to. Sharing a valet with Lord Armbruster leaves so little time for my needs to be addressed. The horse I was given to ride is not as good as I'd like. But…"

"Oh, I'm glad your stay is adequate. Surely such an invitation is prized?"

"Invitation? No, none of that. We simply decided to visit. That's what we do." The man's lace cuff trailed into his soup as he turned a querulous gaze onto Melissa as if seeing her for the first time.

She glanced over his bent shoulders to lock

amused eyes with Miss Dean, whose merry expression told Melissa her companion heard the whole interchange. She carefully turned her attention away, a degree at a time, to survey the assemblage. Straight across the table sat Priscilla, dutifully keeping Lord Armbruster, who sat to her right, in conversation.

Grateful this wasn't a party for which she was responsible, she exhaled and looked again at Mark as to a touchstone of delight, if not peace.

"Ah, Melissa. Are you enjoying the dinner? The fare this evening was selected to use as many local products as possible, my aunt tells me. Do you recognize the radishes? They are from the village market." His eyes twinkled, and she suppressed a happy laugh—appreciating his touch of silliness to lighten the atmosphere.

"It was lovely of your aunt to arrange this dinner so that you and I could have social time together. I am enjoying myself. This room, the table, sitting next to you. It's all special."

His voice took on a hush. "My dear, to me it is exquisite to have you by my side and to hope for that joy to become a daily event. You and I supping together—for decades, Lord willing."

She wanted the same thing but needed more time. She loved his words, but the more love he poured out in her direction, the more pressure she felt. "You mustn't say such things." She tapped his forearm with her fan.

So hard, this time of waiting for wholeness. Sometimes she wondered if the soreness, the pain caused by the abduction would ever leave her. It even intruded on an evening of delight, like this one.

48

Mark's thoughts tumbled. *She's such a darling. Little does she know how patient I can be.* If it took months—no, years—he wouldn't abandon his hopes. Melissa was the woman for him, but he must contain his desires. Even his little words of love and of hope unsettled her. *When will I learn? She needs me to be constant, yet hold back my feelings and be better about restraining myself.* Such a trial but with a delightful goal at the end.

The evening flew by and ended with handing Melissa into the vicarage carriage. He latched the door and stood waving until the vehicle went out of sight before turning back toward the house, toward where Aunt Lucy waited alone at the top of the steps. Mr. Cleaver had departed with the women, this time riding up on the driver's bench with the coachman, eschewing a long, solitary walk home in the moonlight. The houseguests were inside, probably lingering on in the drawing room, hoping for a hand or two of cards, waiting for Mark to make the fourth.

He bounded up the steps and put an arm around his aunt's shoulders. "Isn't it a bit cool out here?"

"Yes, but I needed some fresh air. Did you pick up on all that commotion before we went into dinner?"

"How could I miss it? That's why I summarily decided to whisk you out of the room on my arm. That way if they came to blows, you wouldn't be a party to it."

"Oh, bosh. They weren't near to violence."

"So you say. I disagree based on the look on Mr. Southwood's face. The man appears besotted with you."

"I must decide what to do about that." Aunt Lucy disengaged herself from Mark's arm, clutched her train, and slipped through the front door.

Hesitating to follow, he scuffed his feet on the top step and shoved his fingers into his vest pockets. Because playing cards wouldn't satisfy his need for action, he jumped off the step and walked off down the gravel driveway, intending to stargaze and think about the object of his affections. Clear nights upon which one could see the countless stars above had a way of putting problems into proper perspective. He spotted the constellation he used to call "Angel's Necklace" when he was a child. Thoughts of an angel wearing jewelry made of stars caused visions of Melissa to supersede the sight of the twinkling stars, and he barely registered the rustling in the hedges lining the drive before a stout blow caught him across the back of his head.

Waking to a still-starlit sky, he groaned, rolled to his hands and knees, wincing at the pain from the blow, and stiff from lying on the damp ground. Whoever attacked him did not stay around to finish the job, and for that he was grateful.

Staggering up the drive, marveling at how close to the house the brazen attacker dared approach, he let himself in through the French doors of his study. Careful to lock the door, he decided whether to rouse the house. Decision made, he'd not tell anyone besides Mr. Southwood at first. Consulting his probable future father-in-law came naturally to Mark., but it could wait for the morning. He stretched out gingerly on the sofa in one of the book-lined alcoves and flung an arm up over his eyes.

Waking sore again, but at a daylight hour, Mark made it to his bedroom undetected and stripped off his disheveled evening clothes. Let the servants wonder—there's no help for that. He put on a dressing gown to wait. His manservant usually appeared at eight o'clock—only a few minutes away. A bath and coffee would set him right.

While he waited, his heart swelled in thanksgiving for the gift of continued life in which to pursue and obtain Melissa as his bride. Ideas of ways to see her this week formed. He grabbed a pencil and paper and scratched out a list of things to set in motion.

After a hot bath and donning fresh clothes, famished for a hearty breakfast, Mark entered the dining room, selecting bacon, eggs, coffee, and toast. He seated himself in a shaft of sunlight, hoping it would ward off the damp. The bath hadn't banished his aches and had left him with a chill. Spying a footman up against the wall, he set the first of his plans in motion.

"Grayson, is that you?" He peered into the dimness where the man stood next to the thick, plush drapes.

"Yes, sir, 'tis I, Grayson, at yer service." Heels clicked, and his old childhood playmate Grayson White emerged from the shadows.

"Grayson, I'd like some flowers from the succession house. Can you, when you have a moment, check and see what's blooming? There's a young lady, you see…"

"Yes sir. I can go right now, if you please."

"Now would be excellent. Report back."

He returned to sipping coffee and reading the *Times*—news a few days old but still fresh to him.

Peace ended when Mr. Southwood walked in. "Morning, Russell. How do ye fare this fine morning?" Melissa's father gave him a cursory glance before loading his own plate.

"Sit down, and I'll tell you." Mark waited for him to sit, actually eager to spill the tale of his misadventure. Here was his strongest ally.

"Tell me what? How you fare? A formality—simply asking how-de-do. Not more, not less." Homer showed himself to be a bit of a grump the morning after a party.

"You'll be quite interested. I was attacked while on a moonlit stroll last night."

"What?" Homer gagged on his toast, and a coughing bout followed.

"Shh. I haven't told anyone else. I wanted to consult with you first. I wasn't far from the house, but far enough to be along some hedgerows. Someone rushed out of the bushes and slammed something heavy onto my skull. It stunned me, but I came to and took myself home while it was still darkest night."

"Praise God they didn't stay to finish you off. I have to admit your two nasty relatives couldn't have done it. I heard their snores all night long. Who could have hit you?"

"I don't know. You did hear that valet of theirs scheming with one of the cousins, correct? What about him?"

"I will covertly confront that weasel after breakfast. In business, I've become very adept at ferreting out liars. Can see it in their eyes, their movements, and so forth."

Grayson entered the room. Quietly, he came to stand near Mark's right shoulder.

"Yes, Grayson?"

"Sir, the succession house's got many flowers in bloom, including lilacs, tulips, and some more what I can't pronounce—as well as what's outside in the garden beds—that's straight from the gardener, sir."

"Very good. Please step out to the hall and get Crabtree in here for me." The footman departed. "Mr. Southwood, do you think I should arrange a bodyguard? Or is that too much?"

"No, that's not too much. That's exactly what you should do."

Crabtree entered with Grayson at his heels. "Ye called for me, sir?"

"Crabtree, I have instructions. Ready?" Mark wanted to give the elderly man time to organize his mind. "I want the gardener to pick an extra-special bouquet's worth of flowers every day—starting with today. They are to be taken to Mrs. Good for arranging. Have a footman deliver the bouquets each day to Miss Southwood at the vicarage in Russelton."

"Yes, sir." Crabtree's face lit up with glee, and his eyes twinkled.

Mr. Southwood grinned. "She does love flowers. You'll do yourself no harm with that."

"That's all for now, Crabtree." Mark dismissed the butler.

"I will organize it. Don't ye worry. We'll all do our part." He bowed his way out, looking about to burst with importance.

Mark was amused by the butler's noticeably proprietary pleasure in aiding him in his suit.

"Enough talk of flowers," Southwood barked. "Back to your idea of a guard. Do you have anyone suitable?"

A cough came from the vicinity of the drapes where Grayson had receded.

"Grayson here would be suitable." Mark waved the footman forward. "He grew up on the estate. His loyalty is without question. He's a prime one with his fives and can keep his mouth shut and eyes open. What say, Grayson, care to give up the footman's life for a time? Be my bodyguard?"

"Yes, sir. Glad to."

"Go tell Crabtree, and change out of that getup, and then report to my study."

"Be careful, Russell. Don't let go of vigilance just because you have a guard now."

"I won't. Rest assured." Mark finished his breakfast, and then went off humming. He had invited Melissa out for a drive, and the new bodyguard could ride along, sitting with Miss Dean. It seemed best to take a chaperone, even though he'd take an open carriage. Less temptation to press his suit. More comfort for Melissa to relax, enjoy, and get over her trauma.

Conversation over the next week wasn't exactly stilted, but Mark didn't speak his heart. On the drives, dutifully accompanied by Miss Dean and Grayson White, they talked about topics such as botany, books, and parish news.

"Those hawthorns must be fifty years old, based on their size."

"Indeed, and did I tell you I ordered the new book by Sir Walter Scott? It's said to be excellent and selling well."

"No, you didn't mention that. Widow Cranston's chimney caved in. Her cottage is quite covered with soot. Miss Cleaver and the rest of us plan to go help her clean it."

Talk went on in this vain. Mark didn't resent it. He kept his mind on his goal and patiently took Melissa out on drives each day, always accompanied. She seemed to blossom under his relaxed attentions, and the pinched look around her eyes showed up less and less often.

Midweek, he and Grayson, his new shadow, walked to the vicarage at tea time. The bodyguard insisted on carrying a stout club, and strode along, eyes darting to and fro, vigilant for the least bit of movement, ready for an attack. Mr. Southwood's interview of the guests' valet hadn't produced anything definitive, but an eye was being kept on him.

Mark hid a small pistol ready in his boot, but his thoughts wandered. How long would it be before he could try again to secure Melissa's hand in marriage? When would she be ready? Doubts surged on and on.

Sitting down for tea, he found himself alone with her for the first time in over a week. Grayson stood guard at the front door, taking tea from a mug, brought by the day girl, who visibly simpered as she passed Mark's line of vision.

"Seems my guard has an admirer."

"How do you like having a bodyguard?" Melissa's voice carried worry.

"He's a childhood friend, so we rub along well. My chances will be better with the two of us if I am attacked again."

"Hard to believe I was bowling along home after the dinner party, and at the same time, you were being beaten down. I hate to think it."

"Thank you for caring so deeply, my lo—, my dear." Mark's eyes caressed her face, looking for any sign of further encouragement. A look of desire for him lay deep in her eyes, he was sure, but nearer the surface, fear still laid claim upon her. "Don't be afraid. We will stop the next attack if it comes. I shall see you tomorrow in church. Thank you for the tea. I must go." Mark bowed over her hand and kissed the air above it.

~*~

"It will be nice to see him at the worship service," Miss Dean piped up from the corner where she worked with her needles. "He cuts a fine figure and sings very well."

Melissa recalled those comments when Mark entered the pew across the aisle the next morning and bowed his head to pray. Hard put to keep her mind on her own prayers, she wrenched herself back to them. *Lord, please heal my fears so that I can love Mark with my whole heart the way he deserves.*

49

Throughout the next week, Mark took solace from the admiration he sensed from Melissa each time he was with her. The simple pleasures of a country courtship—rides, picnics, walks—made her glow with delight. She increasingly relaxed with him as he gave her ample opportunity to observe his steadfast disposition and his kind manner to all. She must be nearing a decision in his favor, he concluded.

He worked out his latest idea with Aunt Lucy over breakfast. "Can you help me organize an afternoon party to feature lawn games? Perhaps for tomorrow afternoon? I have a short guest list and getting invitations out won't be too difficult."

She put down her fork. "Lawn games? Such as what?"

"To begin with, battledore and shuttlecock. It's easy to learn as well as to play."

"I agree. Sounds like fun. The rackets are light, so we ladies can participate. I may even practice today so I can compete. It would be so humorous to best Mr. Southwood." She gave a short burst of jolly laughter.

"We have five from the estate—us and the guests—and there are five from the vicarage. That's enough." Mark toyed with his cup's handle while envisioning Melissa at the gathering.

"I can take care of inviting and refreshments. Lemonade and shortbread come to mind. Perhaps some berries." Lucy's eyes sparkled. "Simple fun, yet so engaging. Can't wait to see the men battle it out. You're all so competitive."

"Right now, I am only concerned with competing against Melissa's fears." He drank the last of his coffee, and then stared into the bottom of the cup as if the answer to his woes lay written there.

"Rest assured, she will come about, and all these days of waiting will become a bittersweet, distant memory.

~*~

Melissa donned a sprigged round gown for the lawn party. Miss Dean helped her with the fastenings and dressed her hair.

"Miss Dean, you are a wonder. I love this style, and it will fit so well under my bonnet." Melissa lifted her favorite chip straw bonnet, carefully placed it upon her hair, and tied it under her chin. "I'm ready. Is Mr. Cleaver driving us?"

"Yes. I just looked out the window, and he's waiting with the carriage." Miss Dean positioned her own bonnet on her gray curls and picked up two parasols, two reticules, and two shawls.

"Thank you for thinking of everything. I'm so excited I can't remember my own name." With Miss Dean following close behind, Melissa descended to the carriage. Bubbles of anticipation raised her mood.

She greeted Miss Cleaver and her companion Cassandra, already ensconced in the carriage, saying, "Remember ladies, regardless of how ridiculous my attempts at sport, you must not laugh." The carriage took off with a jolt and gales of merriment rang out.

"I assure you, I will be too mortified by my own efforts to think of yours." Miss Cleaver chuckled, smiling, and went on, "Being as the last time I played battledore and shuttlecock was a good twenty years ago, I know what to expect."

"We will only hope the men are as rusty. I wonder if we'll play as teams or individually." Miss Chesney joined the conversation. "I'd like to be on a team, so my deficiencies can perhaps be hidden."

The south lawn of the manor lay to the left of the drive. As the carriage slowed, Melissa spotted Mark immediately and her heart leapt. Gratitude welled up that her beau was so patient. She sensed he'd wait forever, but she didn't want that. She wanted to move on. The tender place was a bit less sore and would soon be gone.

Mr. Cleaver stopped the vehicle, handed the reins to a groom, and stood by to help the ladies down. A footman appeared with a set of portable steps. Melissa had to hold back from rushing out to Mark and forced herself to a demure pace, arm hooked with Miss Dean's. How nice that Cassandra and Miss Cleaver got along so well. They followed, meandering along, also arm in arm.

"Welcome, ladies. Feel free to be seated under the pavilion." Mark gestured toward an open-sided tent a few yards away and approached Melissa. "May I escort you?"

He smiled down at her, and her heart melted a little bit more. He treated her so politely, so patiently. She'd love a lifetime of his kindness. "Yes, of course." She laid her hand on his arm, and they meandered to shelter.

"How have you been, Melissa?"

"Do you mean since yesterday?" She smiled up at him. "I've been excellent, and with such beautiful flower bouquets arriving on a daily basis, there's no fear that I'll go into a decline."

"So glad they've had a good effect on you." He cast a gentle, teasing look at her and his eyes roamed her face. Melissa's cheeks grew warm.

"Aunt Lucy had the cook bake some of my favorite shortbread. We have chocolate and lemon. Would you like some? With lemonade?"

"I'd love some." A swift jolt of bereftness landed on her as he moved away. *My, one got used to a loving presence, didn't one?* Should she be steadier, not needing him close? These warring thoughts played havoc with her serenity until he returned, and worries receded at the sight of him advancing with a cup and plate for her. Footmen served the others.

She took the proffered refreshments and sampled them. "These are delicious—lemon cookies and lemonade. There's no such thing as too much lemon."

"Sweet and tangy. Just perfect." Mark smiled down at her as if his words had a double meaning.

"Can you sit with me for a time? Or do you have host duties?"

"No duties. Everything's ready for the games." He sat next to her, surely too big for the delicate folding chair. She hoped it didn't collapse under him—such chairs were meant for ladies—wallflowers, perhaps.

As she nibbled the crisp, thick, buttery cookies and sipped the tart, fresh beverage, Melissa surveyed the other guests. There were the two cousins, off to the side of the temporary court. They each had a racket, also called a battledore, and were whacking them against their palms and making aggressive practice swings. It looked as if they were bickering as well.

"Mark, those two scare me. I hope I don't have to compete against them. They'll defeat any efforts I make, by the looks of them."

"Ha ha. Those two will probably give up after a few volleys. They're all show."

There stood Papa, weaving a story, she was sure, for Lucy Banting's enjoyment. Whether his tale was a true one or not, Lucy appeared highly amused and chortled softly. Up walked Mr. Cleaver, an uncertain, but determined look on his face.

"Your father looks none too pleased at the presence of the minister," Mark commented.

"No, I wouldn't suppose so. Papa's got his heart set on your aunt, I'm sure."

Mrs. Banting stood silent while the two men interacted, and all laughing ceased. Miss Chesney sidled up to the group and tapped Mr. Cleaver on the arm, spoke, and gestured toward a hedge. He followed her, and using his great height and long arms, proceeded to rescue a kitten she pointed out. After freeing the mewing, crying animal, he handed it over to Cassandra, who wore a worshipful expression and couldn't take her eyes off the man. He stood straighter, threw back his shoulders, and a considering look came over him.

"I'd like to know what he's thinking." Melissa thought she knew but wasn't sure enough to speak of it.

"I more wonder about you, my dear. How blessed I am, and I marvel at how my life is so full of hope now. There's room in it for you, whenever you are ready." Mark folded his hands in his lap, and his posture was one of humility and defenselessness.

Melissa knew the answer he wanted but wasn't quite prepared to give it. Not yet. And it appeared the games were about to begin. Mark laid out the rules. Then he and Grayson played a sample volley as a demonstration. When that ended, Mark explained more. "Since we have ten players, we'll play three games, best two out of three with mixed teams. Then we'll break the teams up into the ladies against the men."

Some murmurs arose, but Mark tamped them down. "One of the excellencies of battledore and shuttlecock is that ladies can excel as well as the men. It's not a game of strength, but one of agility, and sometimes even delicacy."

Melissa rose, and Miss Cleaver and Miss Dean, who were also in the pavilion, clustered near. They moved out to be divided into teams. Mr. Cleaver, Miss Chesney, Lord Armbruster, Miss Dean, and Sir Walsh made up a team. Melissa, Mark, Priscilla, Lucy, and Mr. Southwood the other. A mix of heights, ages, and gender on each side.

Melissa enjoyed being on the same team as Mark. She got off a few handy returns and acquitted herself fairly well, not embarrassing herself like she dreaded earlier. A refreshment break after the first game, and then back at it.

"We won, but we mustn't let down our guard." Mark coached his team as they stepped into formation on the other side of the line for game two.

So busy watching the shuttlecock, yet Melissa had time to catch glimpses of interplay between the players on the other side. Mr. Cleaver stinted not at all with praise for dainty Miss Chesney, who revealed acute hand-eye coordination and emerged as the best player on that team.

"Miss Chesney, surely you are not an athlete, too—along with all your other talents?" He jested, just loudly enough that Melissa, close to the net, could hear him.

Cassandra responded, shy pleasure audible in her voice. "You're too kind. I simply played this for hours on end back home, entertaining the parish children."

Expert opponent or not, because Melissa's team won the first two bouts, the round in which the ladies competed against the men began.

"Miss Chesney, with you on our side, we have a chance." Melissa cheered her team of ladies on. "We can do it." They clasped hands a moment, and then got into position.

The men looked embarrassed to be playing against ladies, but they went ahead and defeated the ladies' team roundly in the first game. Chivalry didn't preclude the looks of satisfied glee some of them tried to hide. Armbruster and Walsh strutted and preened as if their efforts had made the win.

The ladies took the men by surprise the second game, winning by one point.

"Let's have a break before the last game." Mark herded everyone to the pavilion. "Gents, it appears we may have been overconfident. We took a beating."

The two cousins glanced at each other. Melissa looked away. Odd—those two had the distinct taint of guilt on their faces. What were they up to?

Scattered around the perimeter of the tent, a few couples seemed to form naturally. Melissa and Mark, and her father and Mrs. Banting being the most obvious. But to Melissa's keen eye, another couple, recently formed, was Mr. Cleaver and Miss Chesney.

She was a nice-looking lady of about thirty-some years, good posture, and more than passable manners. It was no accident that Mr. Cleaver carried a cup and plate over to Miss Chesney and proceeded to sit on the vacant chair, not one foot away from her.

She'd be a perfect minister's wife. And wouldn't that make sense, since it was clear that Mrs. Banting and Papa were well down the garden path to love. And sensible because Miss Chesney was a minister's daughter and would know all about how best to be a help to a husband who was a minister. Besides, the thought of the elegant Mrs. Banting burrowed away in a country vicarage made her laugh softly.

Mark spoke up from his place at her side. "Is something funny? I could use a laugh."

"Just thinking about your aunt. She's so amusing. I treasure a hope that she'll become a member of my own family soon."

~*~

Mark swallowed the comment that sprung to mind. Marrying him would achieve that same goal. In a more pleasant way, in his opinion.

The final game fell to the men. He wouldn't have minded losing the round to please Melissa, but some of the men would have taken that amiss, no doubt. As he walked her to the carriage for her trip home, he reflected that the lawn party was a success. Everyone was chatting and having a wonderful time, win or lose.

He chafed with impatience, but since she enjoyed the status quo, he refrained from hurrying on to formal engagement and all the corresponding public attention. This idyllic interlude of life was too special to be cut

A Match for Melissa

short. *It isn't as if I need to be concerned about another man winning her heart first. She's to be mine.*

Handing Melissa into the carriage, he gave her hand one last gentle squeeze. "Until tomorrow." After gazing deep into her eyes, he turned away and went to stand under an oak tree, watching the carriage 'til it went out of sight.

~*~

The day after the stunningly successful lawn party dawned cloudy and breezy. Windy weather precluded taking out an open carriage. Mark penned a note:

Dear Melissa, as it is too windy, we must forego our drive this day. My thoughts, prayers, and heart are with you. May I look forward to a drive—perhaps a picnic—tomorrow? Yours, Mark

With a flourish, he signed it, sealed it, and set it in a basket with other outgoing missives. The servants would know to trot over to the vicarage with this one. In fact, they could deliver it with the bouquet. The plan of a daily floral offering was going on like clockwork, the staff getting a big kick out of be a part of the master's romance.

Windy, cloudy days can have silver linings. Perhaps a day without seeing him would allow Melissa the needed spur to decide.

When would he receive word from the solicitor? The unknown hung like a cloud over his head. He pushed away from his desk and heard a tap on the door. "Enter," Mark responded. His relatives—Sir Giles Walsh, all in puce and Lord Anthony Armbruster, in glaring yellow—sidled into the room. These two—what brought their suspicious arrival at

Russell Manor without an invitation? Because they were rarely known to leave London, so it was odd for them to be traveling in the area.

"Morning, Russell." Bushy eyebrows raised, Lord Armbruster intoned with his deep voice, "Splendid party yesterday. Yes, a very entertaining diversion. Wondering if you'd take us about on a bit of a tour? We've been here quite a while, and we've not yet seen the full extent of your fine estate. We are sure you want to do your hospitable duty by us. I insist on a tour before we depart for London."

Mark didn't relish giving them a tour, but the intimation they would depart soon motivated him. If a tour was required to get them to leave, he would oblige. He had neither a fondness nor particular antipathy toward them. But because of their odd remarks, overheard by Homer, their mere presence proved awkward and unpleasant. Perhaps the courier would return from London soon with the information reporting the identity of his heir.

"Right-o! I was about to ride out myself. I'll order three horses brought around to the front door in one half hour. With this wind, we must take a sheltered route, but you should still be able to view most of the highlights of the property." He rounded the corner of the desk and herded them out the study door. The two would-be dandies went upstairs to change into riding clothes.

Grayson came forward from where he'd been standing by. "Should I mount up as well?"

"Yes, that's an excellent idea. Make arrangements for four mounts. We're riding out in one half hour." Grayson withdrew.

Mark began scheming to rid the house of the

cousins. Perhaps mention a boxing match or a racing meet scheduled soon and somewhere on the road to London. Tell them about the Red Lion Inn, about five hours away, which had one of the best chefs in the region. Maybe have a farewell lunch, send them on their way, and they could be at the inn by supper.

Would it be too rude to take more direct measures? No, they'd been here long enough. Mark resolved to see their backs. Deciding to give some discreet departure assistance to the two cousins, he gave instructions to Crabtree. "Have their trunks and bags brought down and placed in their rooms. Tell that valet to pack up their things." When they got back from the tour, they'd see the luggage and get the message.

Thinking about them ending their visit put an extra spring in his step, and in one half hour, he and Grayson sat astride their horses waiting for the other men to emerge from the house. Mark relished the breezy, cool weather. Two other mounts stood at the ready, held by a couple of grooms. *Where are they?* The guests were taking a long time to prepare for a simple ride over the estate.

50

Lucy sat reading her Bible in her private sitting room when the footman tapped on the door. He stuck his head in and informed her, "Mr. Cleaver and Miss Cleaver have arrived to pay you a call. They've got Miss Chesney with them, as well."

"Thank you. I'll come out to greet them." She closed the book and set it aside. At a good stopping point, she was in the mood for visitors.

She stepped out into the hall to find the ladies having just handed bonnets and shawls to Crabtree when Armbruster and Walsh brushed past to leave the house.

Their abrupt demeanor brooked no delays. "Morning. We're going to tour the estate with Lord Russell. Sorry to miss visiting with you." Armbruster styled himself a ladies's man and took time to ogle Miss Cleaver on his way out the door. He made awkward attempts to be ingratiating toward whatever women crossed his path.

Mr. Cleaver, Priscilla, and Cassandra followed Lucy into the morning room. The *clip-clop* of hooves could be heard through the open window. The sound faded away as the riders left on their tour, heading down the sheltered, tree-lined drive. Reverend Cleaver spoke as he stood watching out the window. His voice held mild curiosity. "So you still have your guests? We saw Lord Russell outside waiting. How is the visit faring?"

"It's going tolerably well, but I still don't understand why they are here. Arriving unannounced for an unprecedented visit and staying for such a long time is unusual. But it is my nephew's home and not for me to say who comes or stays. And how is your houseguest enjoying her stay?"

"Melissa's blooming here. The country does wonders for one's state of mind." Mr. Cleaver didn't elaborate, veering toward discretion whenever discussing a parishioner, houseguest or not.

"I'm sure you are aware my nephew has his heart set on winning her hand. I have enjoyed getting to know her. What an exceptional girl she is. Interesting how the Lord brought them into each other's lives, no?" Lucy smiled.

"We also approve of Lord Russell. You are no doubt aware that Miss Southwood found him left for dead and that he was brought to the vicarage. We had the privilege of being used by God as a small part of the conversion he experienced. Providence is seen clear in such a circumstance as this."

A loud banging on the door, followed by the sound of excited voices reached their ears. The butler opened the door without warning, "Ma'am, please, there is a 'person' clamoring to see you immediately."

Lucy raised her eyebrows. "Show them in, please."

Madame Olivier rushed into the room. She tucked a letter back into her reticule. After an aggrieved glance at the butler, she spoke. "I had to prove you sent for me. This man didn't seem to know I was invited."

"I'm sorry, I had no idea you'd arrive this soon." Lucy tried to soothe the modiste whom she had summoned mere days ago, forgetting to mention it to anyone else.

"Mrs. Banting, it's terrible, it is. Seen a man struggling with two other men before being dragged into zee woods. Just off zee road, right before we turned into zee drive to zis *chateau*." Madame Oliver's agitation mounted as she related what she witnessed.

Lucy noticed Madame's grammar and her French accent were both slipping due to her rising level of alarm over what she had seen. "Calm down, Madame Olivier. Start over, slower this time."

Before she began to tell her story again, Mr. Southwood rushed into the room. "I beg your forgiveness for this intrusion, ma'am. Lord Russell and I sent a man to London with a message. We wrote to Lord Russell's solicitor inquiring about the identity of his heir. We had suspicions over a series of life-threatening accidents which continued to befall him. I'll grant I am the more suspicious one. But I digress. The response from the solicitor just arrived, and I took the liberty of opening the letter. It contained some disturbing news. Those two misfit relatives visiting? They are numbers one and two in the line of succession. Where are they now? Where is Lord Russell?"

"He took them on a tour of the estate."

A shriek tore the air. "*Sacre Bleu!* The fight I saw. It so happened that I look out the window of zee coach when the gates come into view. At zees exact moment I looked out, I see zis upsetting sight."

Mr. Cleaver and Mr. Southwood rushed out the door. This left Lucy, Priscilla, Cassandra and Madame Olivier to wring their hands and pray.

~*~

"There's a shortcut," Crabtree held the front door open, pointing left to an opening in the woods. Homer ran ahead, and Mr. Cleaver jogged after them.

"Come on!" Homer shouted over his shoulder to Mr. Cleaver.

Homer entered the woods to the left of the driveway and ran. He stopped short and held his arms out to each side. "There's a commotion in a small clearing up ahead. I hear rustling and voices."

Mr. Cleaver caught up, breathing hard.

"Let's go," Homer hissed and barged forward into the clearing, slamming his heft into Armbruster, knocking him flat. Homer placed his knee on the man's back, at the same time wrenching off his neckcloth, and then handily tying the man's wrists.

"Don't hurt me." Walsh's voice quavered, taken by surprise as Mr. Cleaver secured the man in a chokehold. Both men sported bruises indicating Mark had put up a fight before being subdued.

The butler arrived in the clearing. From his position on Armbruster's back, Homer shouted, "Crabtree, check on Lord Russell and Grayson, too. Make sure they're alive."

The butler hustled over to where two prone figures lay sprawled. He felt for Lord Russell's heartbeat, and then Grayson's before pronouncing their state. "Both be alive, but milord's much worse for wear."

Grayson rolled over and sat up, shaking his head.

Homer got to his feet, dusted off his hands, and addressed the bodyguard. "You can tell us what happened on the way back. Are you well enough to help Crabtree carry Lord Russell back to the manor?"

"What about these two coves?" Grayson demanded, blinking and shoving back his disheveled hair.

"I'll personally escort this shady character, and Cleaver's got t'other handled right and tight." Homer nudged Armbruster with his foot. "To your feet, cur."

Armbruster staggered to his feet, eyes wild. "I hope I've killed him. He never deserved to inherit—nor did his brother."

"Shut yer bone-box, or ye'll be sorry. A taste of me fives would quiet ye." Homer's veneer of refinement slipped, but he didn't care.

The odd procession moved through the trees traversing the shortcut again, much slower this time—encumbered as they were, leading captives and carrying a victim.

~*~

Lucy rose to her feet, hand at her throat. "I hear someone." She went to the door.

Homer's commanding voice rang out from the hall. "Lock them in the cellar!" He assigned the job of impounding Walsh and Armbruster to the butler and footmen. "Time enough to decide what to do about them later. Cleaver, Grayson, help me with Russell." The men came through the door of the sitting room. "Good job. We'll set him on the divan."

"Oh, Homer! I mean, Mr. Southwood. Oh, I'm elated you found Mark. What happened? Is he all right?"

Unoffended when Homer held out his hand, she slipped her hand into his. How natural to turn to him in a crisis.

A Match for Melissa

"It appears his two visiting relatives tried to kill him," Homer answered with characteristic bluntness.

Mr. Cleaver's eyes fixed on her hand in Homer's. He looked nonplussed, but simply moved to Mark's side to look him over.

Homer patted Lucy's hand, speaking soothing words. "Ma'am, don't worry, now. Those two miscreants didn't have time to deal him a death blow, and Lord Russell looks to have put up a fight."

Mr. Cleaver addressed the group. "Yes, don't worry, ladies. Dr. Swithins has been sent for. Lord Russell's heartbeats are adequate, but he is insensible and should be kept warm. Is there a blanket handy?"

"Here, use my shawl for now. I'll ring a maid to fetch a blanket and a cool cloth to help bring him around." Freeing her hand from Homer's warm clasp, Lucy moved to ring the bell and gave it a jingle before moving to Mark's side. "There. Let me think, what else can we do for him before the doctor gets here?"

"Zee young lady. Mademoiselle Southwood. Is she not visiting zis area? I think she should be *avec beaux amor*."

Lucy's hands flew to her cheeks. "Of course! How could I have forgotten? Yes, by all means send for Miss Southwood. Thank you, Madam Olivier. I am certain she'll want to know of this turn of events."

51

Melissa entered the room. "Papa! Where is he? Where's Mark? Oh, my dear Mark! What have they done to you?" She approached the divan, sank to her knees, and put both arms around his neck. A maid appeared with a blanket, and Melissa stopped hugging him only long enough to tenderly place the woolen cover over him.

"I must sit down," said Miss Dean, who'd followed Melissa into the room. She collapsed into chair at the foot of the divan. Visibly shaken and stunned, the quiet woman fumbled in her large reticule for her knitting and wiped her eyes with the half-knitted stocking on her needles.

Shattered, and with her heart in her throat, Melissa crooned and murmured. *Lord, don't let him die! Please spare him. He is to be my husband. All my doubts and fears are swept away. Please.* Her tears soaked through Mark's shirt in the few moments before Dr. Swithins entered the room.

He touched Melissa's shoulder. "Now, Miss. Enough saltwater. Let me examine Lord Russell—I've done this before."

Her father appeared at her side and helped her to her feet. He wrapped his arm around her shoulders.

"Missy, your young man is strong. Mr. Cleaver did a preliminary exam. He's no medical doctor, of course, but he thinks all will be well in time. Hush now, while we wait for the doctor's findings." Homer patted Melissa on the back with one hand and used the other to extract a snowy handkerchief from his pocket. He blotted her face a bit before guiding her over to a comfortable brocade armchair.

Dr. Swithins straightened, turned back to face the occupants of the room, and snapped shut his black bag with a flourish. "This patient will be fine. In fact, other than some bandaging of scrapes, all he'll need is rest. His eyelids are fluttering which leads me to believe he's about to come around."

Melissa, who'd been holding her breath, let out a sigh of relief, and then murmured, "Thank You, God. Thank You."

After the others echoed her thanksgiving, the doctor gave instructions, and then Mrs. Banting invited everyone to stay for some sustenance. She bustled out of the room, all vapors over, to make arrangements for servants to carry Mark up to his room, and for a cold collation to be set in the dining room.

Madame Olivier moved toward the door as well. "I must see to my bags. In ze excitement, I jumped out of the coach, forgetting everyzing else."

~*~

Melissa went back to Mark, whose remarkable sea-blue eyes were open. His large form draped on the rose-colored damask upholstery of the delicate divan now struck her as incongruous, especially the sight of his booted feet hanging off the end. Happiness and relief made her want to laugh. Smiling down at him, she tried to compose her thoughts into the right words. The other people in the large room drew away to give the young couple privacy.

"Mark, when I heard you'd been injured again, my heart was struck to the core."

"Melissa." His voice was weak and exhausted, "When they attacked me, I fought so hard for fear...I'd not see you again." A tear rolled out of the corner of his eye.

"Darling, let me speak. You must rest." She dropped to her knees and placed her hands on his blanket-covered arm. "Now *I* am on my knees, dearest. I have had my mind marvelously cleared by this occurrence. Do you remember what you asked me at the hilltop?"

"Yes." His words a hoarse whisper. "I remember."

"I can't go on without you, Mark. At least I don't want to. At all. If I cast my mind to a future without you in it, I see a bleak and empty picture. You were patient with me, but now I am ready to answer. I'd be honored to be your wife."

His eyes closed and a smile spread across his face. His lips were moving, and she leaned forward, a futile effort to hear his words. She squeezed his hand and closed her eyes. *Lord, thank You for sparing the man who is to be my husband. I know You brought him into my life. Let me be an excellent wife to Mark.*

The servants arrived in the room with a stretcher on which to carry Lord Russell to his rooms. She stepped back. The others gathered around.

"Not to worry, Miss. He's in good hands." The doctor waggled his brows at her.

"And I've sent for the magistrate," Mr. Cleaver reassured. "Something the men said lead me to believe they were behind the death of Mark's brother as well."

The men all left the room in the wake of the

stretcher, leaving Melissa to the tender mercies of Priscilla, Miss Chesney, and Miss Dean.

"My dear girl, such a sickening state of affairs boggles my mind. To think those two cousins may have been behind all of these misfortunate incidents in Lord Russell's life." Miss Cleaver clasped her hands under her chin.

"I agree—shocking." Melissa put a hand over her heart. "How thankful I am, though, for how it has turned out. If I hadn't found Russell in the ditch, and if he hadn't learned of my existence and followed that by coming to try to court me in London—ooh, it's terrible to think about it all."

"Melissa, you mustn't forget this outcome is not made up of 'ifs'. It's God's hand sustaining you through His good providence." Miss Cleaver easily slipped back into her role of teacher. "But you know that, don't you, dear?" She patted Melissa's hand. Miss Dean sat by, needles clicking as she stitched another row on the socks she'd cried into moments before.

"Yes, I do. What a comfort to know this whole circumstance has been in God's hand all along. It just seemed iffy."

She fell silent for a moment, heart welling with gratitude.

"Let's all join the others in the dining room, shall we? All this commotion has given me an appetite."

Madam Olivier emerged from the green service door as the group of women crossed the hall. When she saw Melissa, she became animated. "There you are. You are *c'est tres jolie*."

Melissa's hand shot up to hide her smile and her amusement that the modiste was no more French than she was. "Madam Olivier, what brings you here? Did

Lord Russell's aunt, Mrs. Banting, require your services?" She spoke in a low voice.

"*Non, mon infant,* I was called out to Russelton for you." Madame Olivier whispered back. "She thought you would be in need of zee wedding clothes?"

"I see. How very thoughtful of her. Let the three of us meet tomorrow."

~*~

Madame Olivier went below to eat with the housekeeper. Melissa, Priscilla, Cassandra, and Miss Dean joined the convivial group already gathered in the elegant dining room. Oil lamps and beeswax candles shed their light and dispelled the gloom of the cloudy, dark day. Mr. Cleaver sat at the west end of the table, nearest the window. He had a heaping plate of food and was deep in conversation with Dr. Swithins. Papa and Mrs. Banting were ensconced at the opposite end, sitting side by side, smiling at each other, clearly having forgotten all about the food on their plates.

Moving over to the buffet, Melissa picked up a plate. Slivers of ham, a small wedge of cheese, and five fat strawberries from the succession house was plenty. She went to the table and sat beside her father. Out of the corner of her eye, she watched as Cassandra slipped into the chair next to Mr. Cleaver, who promptly ceased talking medicine and turned his entire concentration toward the lady.

Melissa tapped her father's arm to get his attention. She spoke in hushed tones for only Mrs. Banting and Papa. "Papa, I have decided to accept Lord Russell's offer. You'll get your heart's desire." It pained her the way his ambitions for a title had ruled him for such a long time, but with the good outcome now in hand, Papa's ambition didn't hold the sting they once did.

"My darling girl, what wonderful news." His eyes glistened and he patted her hand. "You and your Lord Russell have my absolute approval. I will meet with you two tomorrow morning. I have some news for you as well."

News. She wondered if she could guess—but no, she'd wait to hear it. "Fine, Papa. We'll meet you in the drawing room at ten if Mark's up and about." She hoped her father hadn't come up with another condition to obstruct her wishes, but she suspected it was something else.

"Very good. If he's still on bed rest, we'll go to his rooms together." He turned back to Lucy.

~*~

Melissa entered the sunny drawing room the next morning. Ensconced on a divan, with his legs propped on an ottoman, Mark looked less peaked. When she approached, he swung his feet to the floor, shoved the ottoman aside, and sat up straight. He patted the divan, indicating she should sit next to him, a wish she was happy to grant. He immediately captured her hand in his.

"I wasn't dreaming it, was I, my love? You agreed to be my wife?"

Her face flamed, and she lowered her eyes, the intensity of her emotions too much to reveal. "Yes." She spoke just above a whisper, remembering her forwardness.

"No, darling, don't be shy. This is the happiest day

of my life." His fingers found her chin and he tipped her face toward his. Her heart tripped at the nearness of his lips to hers. When his mouth descended upon hers, it sent trills rippling over her, as if she'd landed in a cool river and a warm blanket at the same time.

She let herself wilt into his arms as they went around her and she leaned against his chest. The pure feeling of love, combined with the warmth of his kiss, brought such pleasure that she felt weak. After what seemed a long time, he left her lips bereft but recaptured her hand, holding it like a delicate treasure.

"You've made me the happiest of men. I'll live my life proving my love."

The clocks struck ten, and Melissa's father and Mrs. Banting walked in. When the timepieces stopped their cacophony, Mark spoke. "I must reduce the number of clocks in this room. Three different chimes going off at once are too much for even a healthy man to endure."

"Indeed." Melissa's father smiled at Mrs. Banting.

Melissa couldn't help notice that the older pair were also holding hands. "Papa, I'm anxious to hear your news. Let me guess." Melissa's eyes twinkled. "You are going to buy a home in Russelton?" She wanted to make her father squirm.

Papa's mood was jovial, and his jesting good-natured. "How many guesses do you need?"

"Oh, I know, you finally talked Lord Russell into selling you that horse you want? Mrs. Banting has consented to introduce you to some nobles?" She decided to end the teasing before he got too embarrassed.

His face red, her father harrumphed and cleared his throat. "Let's stop all the guesswork now, my girl.

I'll tell you flat out. Lucy here has consented to do much more for me. More than I had ever thought of when I met the dear lady."

At this, Melissa squirmed. When would he get to the point?

"I am the happiest of men. Lucy and I...well, she said she'd be my wife before the year is out. Prior to any congratulations, however, I must give all the credit to God. He brought us together and gave me all the many blessings I do have."

Touched and thrilled by her father's words, Melissa clasped her hands in front of her heart. Her mouth opened to speak, but words weren't sufficient. She arose and threw her arms around his neck. His beefy arms encircled her slim back and she laid her head on his shoulder. "It's all right now, and Lord Russell will regain his health, you'll see. There, there, Missy." He used her childhood name as he patted her back.

After a few moments of hugging, Melissa extracted herself and wiped her eyes. She joined Mark on the divan, and he again secured her hand in his.

Congratulations in order, Melissa enthused, "How perfect. I'm very happy for you both. Now Madam Olivier will have a gown to make. Aunt Lucy...may I call you that? You will have the modiste all to yourself."

"But what about you, Melissa? I don't want to steal your dressmaker." Mrs. Banting spread a hand over her chest.

"The ivory gown I wore to your ball will serve as my wedding gown." Melissa turned to smile at Mark, and her lips trembled. "He was much in my mind and heart when I had the gown made—never knowing if

I'd see him again."

He cleared his throat. "Mr. Southwood, you recall giving me formal permission to court Melissa? She tells me you know my suit has prospered. I hope we can count on your final approval?"

"Yes, I heartily approve of this match. It's a match arranged in Heaven—as is ours." Melissa's father put his arm around Mrs. Banting, and they moved off to the French doors.

"We've made a match of it, haven't we, dear Melissa?" Mark squeezed her fingers.

Melissa's heart swelled with bubbling joy. A blast of happiness like a warm wind swept through her, and she had a brief vision of many blessed years ahead with this man. "You, Mark, are my hero, friend, and perfect match."

About the Author

Susan Karsten lives in a small Wisconsin town, is the wife of a real estate broker, and mother of a son, daughter-in-law, and two daughters, and two grandsons. Her hobbies include fitness, quilting, and reading.

Her love for writing developed while in college where she earned a BS degree in Home Economics.

Child-rearing days having drawn to an end, Susan now invests time in fiction writing. With three Regency historical romances and a humorous middle-grade fiction book complete, she is in the process of writing another book. Her personal blog can be found at Graciouswoman.wordpress.com.

Thank you

We appreciate you reading this Prism title. For other Christian fiction and clean-and-wholesome stories, please visit our on-line bookstore at www.prismbookgroup.com.

For questions or more information, contact us at customer@pelicanbookgroup.com.

Prism is an imprint of
Pelican Book Group
www.PelicanBookGroup.com

Connect with Us
www.facebook.com/Pelicanbookgroup
www.twitter.com/pelicanbookgrp

To receive news and specials, subscribe to our bulletin
http://pelink.us/bulletin

May God's glory shine through
this inspirational work of fiction.

AMDG

You Can Help!

At Pelican Book Group it is our mission to entertain readers with fiction that uplifts the Gospel. It is our privilege to spend time with you awhile as you read our stories.

We believe you can help us to bring Christ into the lives of people across the globe. And you don't have to open your wallet or even leave your house!

Here are 3 simple things you can do to help us bring illuminating fiction™ to people everywhere.

1) If you enjoyed this book, write a positive review. Post it at online retailers and websites where readers gather. And share your review with us at reviews@pelicanbookgroup.com (this does give us permission to reprint your review in whole or in part.)

2) If you enjoyed this book, recommend it to a friend in person, at a book club or on social media.

3) If you have suggestions on how we can improve or expand our selection, let us know. We value your opinion. Use the contact form on our web site or e-mail us at customer@pelicanbookgroup.com

God Can Help!

Are you in need? The Almighty can do great things for you. Holy is His Name! He has mercy in every generation. He can lift up the lowly and accomplish all things. Reach out today.

Do not fear: I am with you; do not be anxious: I am your God. I will strengthen you, I will help you, I will uphold you with my victorious right hand.
~Isaiah 41:10 (NAB)

We pray daily, and we especially pray for everyone connected to Pelican Book Group—that includes you! If you have a specific need, we welcome the opportunity to pray for you. Share your needs or praise reports at http://pelink.us/pray4us

Free Book Offer

We're looking for booklovers like you to partner with us! Join our team of influencers today and periodically receive free eBooks.

For more information
Visit http://pelicanbookgroup.com/booklovers